Praise for *LALA*

Winner of the Paszport Polityki Award
Longlisted for the EBRD Literature Prize 2019

'*Lala* is a wonderful mosaic of stories…outrageous and humorous…spell-binding and captivating.'
Foreword Reviews

'Jacek Dehnel paints prewar Poland – "laced with gilt and stucco in the cities, and heavy with the smell of cow pats and fruit lying in the grass in the countryside" – in the vibrant hues of a fairy tale. A multigenerational epic that spans a century and most of Eastern Europe, *Lala* is an astounding achievement, particularly considering Dehnel wrote it between the ages of 20 and 22…magical.'
Chicago Tribune

'Lush… Tender and droll, rueful and rousing, [Lala's] stories trace one Polish family's journey from the 1860s to the present day… [Jacek Dehnel] chronicles her decline with delicate but unabashed realism, as well as great humour, and Lloyd-Jones captures these qualities perfectly.'
The Quarterly Conversation

'Dehnel uses his grandmother's life and reminiscences as a springboard for a sweep through Poland's turbulent 20th century, mingled with musings on the nature of storytelling…[there are] some exceptionally beautiful passages…poignantly alive with loss and love.'
Kirkus

'*Lala* is unique – no author displays such maturity of style, knowledge of form and literary erudition at the age of twenty, because nobody is ever as well read or intellectual at that age. Dehnel – who wrote this book aged twenty to twenty-two – is the exception that proves the rule.'
Gazeta Wyborcza

'Lyrical passages, some endearingly eccentric characters, a flyby through twentieth-century history, and a convincing voice for Lala.'
Booklist

'A declaration of love for literature and a tribute to an extraordinary woman.'
Berliner Zeitung

'A masterfully constructed novel…mature and highly entertaining.'
a

'Dehnel is gifted with superb lite
et

Jacek Dehnel is an award-winning poet and novelist. He has published seven volumes of poetry and eight works of fiction, and his work has been translated into several European languages. He is also a translator from English into Polish of poets including Philip Larkin and novelists including F. Scott Fitzgerald. *Lala* was his first novel. A bestseller in Poland, it has been translated into more than a dozen languages. His second novel, *Saturn*, based on the life of the painter Goya, was published in English in 2012. Born in Gdańsk, he now lives in Warsaw.

Antonia Lloyd-Jones is an award-winning translator of Polish literature, including fiction, literary non-fiction, children's books, poetry and essays. She is a mentor for the WCN Emerging Translators Programme, often contributes to public events to do with literature in translation, and is a former co-chair of the UK Translators Association. She lives in London.

LALA

Jacek Dehnel

Translated from the Polish
by Antonia Lloyd-Jones

ONEWORLD

A Oneworld Book

First published in Great Britain, North America and Australia
by Oneworld Publications, 2018

Originally published in Polish as *Lala* by Grupa Wydawnicza Foksal, 2006

This mass market paperback edition published 2019

ISBN 978-1-78607-498-0
eBook ISBN 978-1-78607-359-4

This book has been published with the support of the
©POLAND Translation Program

Typeset by Divaddict Publishing Solutions Ltd.
Printed and bound in Great Britain by Clays Ltd, Elcograf S.p.A

Oneworld Publications
10 Bloomsbury Street
London WC1B 3SR
England

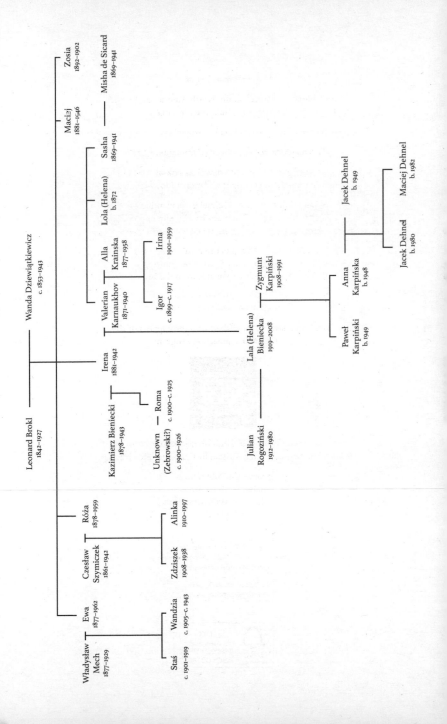

A Note from the Translator

Famous historical or fictional people, places and events and other useful facts are marked by asterisks within the text, which refer to the endnotes at the back of this book.

I

The house in Oliwa* already looks different now. And when Granny dies – which will be soon, and I can write that with a tranquil mind, firstly because we've long since come to terms with the idea, and secondly she's never going to read this anyway because she doesn't read any more – the whole place will change out of all recognition. Things will be inherited, and will have to find other shelves and cupboards for themselves in other homes. The edition of Stendhal with Julek's dedication, which for the last thirty years has stood spine to spine with Flaubert's *Three Tales*, will stand between other books. And what will happen to the glassware collection, to the three or four hundred vases, goblets, jugs and vials, red, sapphire, lime green, with bubbles and without, opalescent, cracked or frosted?

As she sits there like an old Chinese empress, oblivious to power or duty, muffled in rugs and baggy knitted waistcoats, so very thin, small and light, it's hard to connect her with our memory, where there's no room for the nose wiping, the nappies and the constant silence. Except that she's smiling – so we can comfort ourselves that in her own way she's happy, but that's like talking about the feelings of a sea anemone or a coral reef.

So this is how my story ends. But where does it begin?

In Lisów* perhaps? In small, shabby Lisów, the place that smelled of fallen apples, and that was such a disappointment when I made a journey to the promised land, to Canaan, whose geography I knew to the last detail purely from her accounts – I knew the location of the garden gate, which the horse used to

open with his head, I knew where the drawing room was, and
where Aunt Róża's bedroom was; I knew where the busts of
Napoleon and Lenin stood, and the large table, on the corner
of which the thieves had piled the silver; and finally I knew
where the desk had been, off which my ninety-year-old great-
great-grandmother Wanda had shooed the German officer. But
what did I find? The grandest remaining part of the manor
house was the chimney, with the remnants of some stone walls
around it. They drew a vague rectangle on the ground, half a
metre high in places, and a whole metre in others, but this
shape was definitely far smaller than the old manor had been,
because the field margin had been redrawn through the middle
of several rooms, and where the grand piano had once stood,
potatoes or buckwheat were now growing.

No, maybe my story starts in the town house on such-and-
such Prospect, a fairly good address in Kiev* and home to three
families – the Bienieckis, the Karnaukhovs and the Korytkos –
where the Fates wove a tangled web around their apartments?

Or perhaps in that strange space that I cannot begin to
imagine, because I'm not a young-Polish-rebel-writer-trav-
elling-east, in that strange space called 'the Ukraine', where
plants grew that were different from ours, and people lived
who were different from ours, speaking in deep but melodious
voices, those peasants going about in coarse linen shirts, who
chased my great-great-grandfather Leonard's automobile with
wooden stakes and pitchforks?

I don't know where to start this story, because I've started
it so many times before; not just now, but ten years ago, when
with the bombast typical of a fourteen-year-old author I
thought up the title *Polish Ghazals*, because a ghazal is a
'poem like a string of pearls', thus splendidly suited to the
stand-alone-yet-connected themes of Granny's narrative; and
finally so many other times, when I haven't written a thing,

but have simply related it to my friends, cousins, lovers and passengers on the express train that runs from Gdańsk to Warsaw and back again.

Because the truth lies somewhere else. In actual fact the story begins, as usual, in pieces, now here, now there, in all sorts of different places and bodies, most of which ceased to exist long ago, but until now its steward and guardian has always been Granny. A granny of solid, reliable stuff who, following some minor repairs and some more serious renovation a couple of years ago, still preserved so much sparkle and wit that when friends came to see me from faraway countries I always took them to visit her, because, of all the antiquities to be seen in my northern Polish city, she was the most fascinating.

🌸

Among Granny's charms – in the days when she still spoke – were the beginnings of her stories. In fact, it was (and is) always one and the same story, convoluted and blackened out of recognition under various layers of varnish and soot, starting in multiple places and generally never ending, at best interrupted by the end of the visit or by nightfall. Let us add that at Granny's house in Oliwa nightfall, meaning the end of the conversation and the start of the going-to-bed ritual, occurs at around midnight at the earliest, and is not always definitive, because any great story has a tendency to grow rhizomes, to billow and expand at the peripheries and at the least expected moments, and so it does the job of reining us in, rather than vice versa.

The beginning usually coils, like a cross between the tendril of a plant and an animal's prehensile tail; it wraps itself around an object, a person, a smell or an anecdote, and then goes mad, putting out shoots and proliferating into whole thickets of words and punchlines; unrestrained, it multiplies at random, makes the tea go cold, overcooks the pasta, and startles things that matter out of the memory. There we have it.

It might be something like this: 'When I paid a visit to Count Krasiński and his wife and I knocked the araucaria off the guéridon...' or else: 'When Grandpapa Leonard was facing the tsarist firing squad...' or maybe: 'When a thief stole all the cabbages from the orphan's field at Lisów...' – in short, you never know where a listener might be found, peeping into the world through a suddenly exposed lens. That is, a chance listener; as for us, we already know the whole story – chopped into separate chapters, but we always know – in minute detail.

'One time, just imagine, Grandmama Wanda – and she was over ninety by then – quite simply vanished from Lisów at around noon. It was the middle of the war, there were Germans everywhere. We seek her here, we seek her there, there's no gig and no coachman. We run about, we start to fret... why are you making those faces?'

'We know the story.'

'You do?' asks Granny in disbelief, but she's not in the least put out, not a jot. 'So how does it end?'

'She'd gone to the hairdresser's...'

'All right, you do know it,' says Granny, briefly downcast, but quick as blinking she regains her composure. 'But no harm's done. One day, just imagine, Grandmama, and she was ninety by then... well, so she came home – with a permanent wave. "I am over ninety years old," she said, "and it would be silly to die without ever having had a permanent wave."'

❧

Margot is walking about my room with cup in hand, looking for something new. Whenever I visit her, I do the same. 'Where

did you get this?' I ask. 'And what is this?' Her world is beautiful
and harmonious, which means that every bit of it is equally
fascinating. Margot is called Małgorzata, or Margherita, or
Pearl, and she really is as pearly as a pearl. Now she's approaching the cupboard and picking up a photograph.

'Did you buy this at the flea market?'

'No, it's from home. I begged it off Granny because there
were two like it.'

I have hardly any photographs from her childhood. I don't
know what Grandmama Wanda, Grandpapa Leonard, Uncle
Maciej, Aunt Ewa, Aunt Sasha, Milewski or Apollo-with-the-
braces looked like, I don't even know what Lisów was like.
During their offensive the Russians – the Soviets, says Granny,
they were the Russians before the revolution, and then there
was the Soviet rabble – lit the fire with the photographs that lay
in a large wooden chest in the hall. They burned the photograph of Romusia, standing over the five-dozen eggs she had to
drink raw each day, egg after egg, which even so did nothing to
stop her galloping consumption; they burned the photograph
of Grandpapa Leonard in a white pinstriped suit, leaning
against the shining body of the first automobile in the Ukraine;
they burned the photographs of her father in his invariable hat
on his invariably bald head; they burned the photographs of
her mother in flowing dresses; they burned the postcards from
faraway cities with fancy-sounding names and the sepia repro-
ductions of sculptures and paintings from the spacious rooms
in distant museums.

There are no faces. There are no hands. There are no door
frames, tables, prints, piles of magazines or books with gilded
edges. Just a couple, literally just two, sepia shots'... at least
we have these. My great-grandmother, straight as a ramrod,
wasp-waisted, leaning on a black umbrella; in the background

the light is sifted through the leaves of foreign trees, plane trees perhaps, and in the corner there's a white caption: 'Abbazia'.

Good Lord... Abbazia...

'Mama was so beautifully proportioned,' I hear Granny's voice behind me. 'So beautiful... she looks tall, but she was tiny – she came up to here on me, to my shoulder, when I was young, now she'd probably have come up to my cheek, one gets so much shorter... but anyway, look, she had the proportions of a tall woman, and she was tiny around the waist too. She always moved at a run, a dainty little trot; I can't remember her ever walking normally. When she was ill she'd shuffle her feet slowly, just like on the last day, the day she died, sitting in this armchair... but walk in an ordinary way? Oh no. She always ran.'

❧

When the world was still very young, laced with gilt and stucco in the cities, and heavy with the smell of cow pats and fruit lying in the grass in the countryside, people were smaller. Maybe they had no reason to climb, and stood on tiptoes less often than today, maybe they ate without following the wise rules of healthy nutrition, and grew in a different direction, or maybe they simply weren't bothered about being taller, because they could find everything they needed close to the ground.

Grandpapa Leonard was a fraction over one-and-a-half metres tall, with raven-black hair – until he changed into a white raven – a swarthy complexion and sky-blue eyes.

'According to Wandeczka,'' he wrote in the diary that Granny and Julek found in the drawer of his inlaid desk after he died, 'I am not plain Mr Brokl, but a count, de Broglie in a distorted form, because I have such southern looks. But as far as I know we came here from Germany out of dire poverty on dogcarts and settled here. We've been Brokls for generations, at most Brockls...'

On that cold January day the Soviets burned all the photographs of Granny's grandfather, so the fragile structure of soft tissues covering his skeleton formally ceased to exist for future generations. I have often tried to imagine this good-natured, well-mannered old gent (who seems to have been an old gent his entire life, because that was how his granddaughter remembered him), a lover and collector of art, a bibliophile and erudite, a chemist by profession and a landowner by fate, though neither one of them went very well for him.

'After High Mass on Sundays,' said hunched old Mr Tarapatka when I made my trip to Canaan, 'the old gentleman used to buy a bag of sweets, and we children would run after him all the way to the manor, because he handed them all out... the old gentleman was your granny's grandpa, the Squire.'

The Squire wasn't born a country squire at all, but a townie, and a penniless one at that. His was probably the first generation in the family to speak Polish, and I can't state for certain that he wasn't born in Germany. But as he acquired Polish, he also acquired the trappings of the Polish nobility – some Slavonic blood began to throb in his veins, and with the daring typical of an eighteen-year-old he decided to fight in the January Uprising of 1863,* and then was sent to Siberia as a true Polish patriot.

In ill-recorded circumstances Grandpapa Leonard Brokl took a degree in chemistry, came back from Siberia, settled in Kiev, gained thorough knowledge of the most arcane mysteries of the sugar industry, attained the title of professor and married Grandmama Wanda, who was a very wise, but none too intellectual woman, then he fathered four children and became a millionaire.

At this point it would be an error to mistake the penniless Leonard Brokl for a carefully disguised financial shark. Grandpapa Leonard knew nothing at all about percentage points, dividends and currency rates; he lived the life of a drunken child in the fog. But as chance would have it, someone advised him to buy a large packet of shares in a particular firm. By the same or another stroke of luck, in just a few days the shares gained greatly in value, because the empire happened to be going through an economic boom at the time. Evidently finding this pastime amusing, Grandfather mobilised his savings and bought up a few more packets of shares. And as they went up in value again, within a month he became one of the wealthiest men in Kiev.

This is how all such stories should end.

But unfortunately, they usually continue.

Grandpapa Leonard bought himself a sugar factory, an automobile and a large house. He travelled around the world, buying paintings, lacquered screens, sculptures and furniture, and corresponded with learned sugar manufacturers in Berlin and Paris.

'Hence the shirts at Lisów,' said Granny, folding the laundry removed from the washing line once it had dried in the midday breeze. 'Grandpapa travelled about Europe and constantly complained about the laundries there, saying they did the job badly, putting their stamps anywhere and everywhere... in fact I was assured of that myself, because when Julek sent his shirts to the laundry in Brussels they stamped them on the chest, and then they were surprised when he made a fuss. Grandpapa never made a fuss – he would simply buy as many shirts and collars as he needed, and come back to Kiev, to Mnin, or to Morawica* with trunks full of linen. Many years later the peasants* used to carry off whole basketfuls of those shirts from Lisów. They'd be drying on washing lines, the peasants would sneak up, and half the shirts would be gone. Or at night, when the shirts were in baskets under the window, they'd slip in ever so quietly and in the morning there'd be no trace of them. But even so the wardrobes were full.'

Grandmama Wanda, née Dziewiątkiewicz, was a tiny, petite woman with an intellect appropriate to her size. She lived to the venerable age of ninety – maybe because her small body only used up small portions of time, and significant events spared her by giving her a wide berth. Her parents died when she was still a very young child, and she was sent to live in a convent, a large grey building with thick stone walls and long corridors, down which the hushed echo of the nuns' and their charges' small footsteps resounded all day long, making them conscious at every second of how insignificant they were compared with the power of the Lord and the problem of a dowry. And it was from there, from this reliquary of wood and stone planted somewhere in the eastern wildernesses, amid lairs swarming with vampires and lakes where many had drowned, that Leonard Brokl took young Wanda away, on returning from exile and deciding to don the shackles of matrimony. Unlike her legendary namesake, the princess who refused to marry a German, Wanda wanted hers, and for better or worse, he wedded her before the Lord, unaware of the fact that in time he would become a millionaire. Wanda was even more unaware of this fact than Leonard, who was at least a man, and therefore had some personal plans and ambitions slowly hatching in the coils of his scientific brain; but as for her – what were her chances? If one is an orphan from a convent, with almost no dowry, does one expect to marry a millionaire?

And just like in a moral tale, the virtues of modesty and resignation were rewarded with wealth, luxury and the pleasures of this world – though the logic of moral tales is generally suspect – and little Wanda found herself among the great and the good of this world, the world of Kiev in 1875, sparkling with candles burning in tall candelabras, glittering with ball-gowns from Paris and tailcoats from London, flowing with rivers of champagne and streams of pearls.

'It seems they were deeply in love; Grandmama Wanda used to tell me, oh yes, that Grandpapa would kiss her all over, every little bit, from top to toes, not a single tiny scrap of her body was left without a kiss,' says Granny, and sniggers; her grand-mother probably sniggered in just the same way as she told her granddaughter this story. 'I don't know what he saw in her, because she was neither a great beauty nor a great intellect... she lived in Kiev for twenty-five or thirty years without ever learning Russian – she could only speak halting French, as much as one gains in a convent. She went everywhere, to Paris and Rome, Brussels and Vienna... except for London, New York and Japan, because the one time they tried to sail across the English Channel she had such an attack of seasickness that they had to turn the ship around... the doctor said she wouldn't survive to the opposite shore... and from then on, as Julek so meanly used to say, the old boy only ever travelled overseas... but that's not my point. She'd done a great deal of travelling, you see, but if I asked her what the Dresden Gallery was like, or the Museum of Antiquities in Berlin, she'd say that in Dresden the shops were awful, and from Berlin she'd brought back beautiful silk, but she couldn't remember the gallery; Grandpapa would dash about the place, always getting excited about something, and buying works of art, but it bored her. But she did have plenty of gump-tion, thanks to which she saved Leonard Brokl's life a good many times – he may not have been tall, but he went about with his head in the clouds all day, and was as gullible and helpless as a child.'

Granny always has a story to tell whenever she has to deal with complicated machinery. For instance, it's enough for the

Grandpapa Leonard on the beach at Kolberg, c. 1905.

toast to jump out of the toaster with a loud ping at breakfast – as for those incredible Oliwa breakfasts, they deserve a paragraph of their own – it's enough for my parents to have brought her an electric kettle ('Well I never! I thought I'd burn it dry in an instant because it doesn't whistle, and without the whistle I'll forget it's on, but what do you know, it switches itself off! Though actually it's too quick, because I used to have time to put on the water, slice the bread, spread the butter, make sand-wiches, slice the cucumbers and tomatoes, and only then did the kettle squeak. Then I'd pour the boiling water on the tea in the pot and put it next to the kettle to stop it from going cold… but now it boils in an instant. Though the new kettle is nice and flat on top, so I put the pot on top of it…'), it's enough for someone to have mended the cooker or the washing machine for Granny to say: 'Well, well, what a fancy washing machine (toaster / radio / torch) – what a lot of screws there are in it, what a lot of metal parts and bulbs and dials. Do you know how Grandpapa Brokl drove across the Ukraine?'

'I have no idea,' I say, but Granny either can't hear, or refuses to hear the irony in my tone of voice.

'Grandpapa had an automobile, the first one in the Ukraine. Of course he had a chauffeur to go with it, but he often drove it himself, for the mere pleasure. There were photographs of him standing by the car with his driving goggles up on his forehead, wearing special gloves and a dustcoat thrown over his pinstriped suit… so smart and spruce from head to foot, as if they'd manufactured him and his entire outfit along with the car, just for that photograph. But if he was travelling with Grandmama, they took the chauffeur and sailed across the Ukrainian wilderness, across boundless fields and forests, along inhospitable roads, under an infinite sky. Miles of bent grass and all that, you see. And one day, under this infinite Ukrainian sky, they had to make a sudden stop in the middle of the highway, because a pack of hairy Ukrainian peasants had surrounded them, half furious and half terrified, shaking their scythes, axes and stakes, and yelling that here was the devil himself. Grandpapa had already told the chauffeur to force his way through the crowd, but Grandmama took matters into her own tiny but heroic hands – she had him open the door for her, she stepped out into the road, raised her veil and asked – in Polish, of course, because she couldn't speak Ukrainian – what did they mean, the devil? Then they roared,

Grandpapa Leonard (in the back, with hand raised) and some unidentified people in his car, c. 1910.

but more quietly now, that here came the devil, it was the devil's own carriage because it had no horses, and yet it was moving. So Grandmama said: "Have you ever seen a steamship?" They hadn't. "Are you familiar with a chaff-cutter?" They weren't. Finally she came round to a threshing machine or something of the kind, and they knew it. "But a threshing machine has an engine!" the crafty fellows argued. "This has one too," replied Grandmama, and called out the chauffeur, who already had a tight grip on the crank handle, useful in case of a fight, and told him to open the bonnet flap and show the peasants the engine, the radiator and whatever else. And they stepped aside. They even sent news to the next few villages ahead to say it wasn't the devil, but it had an engine – and from then on they weren't accosted any more.'

II

At this point I should do a bit of housekeeping. As I've already said, Granny's story has no frame or confines – it's blurry, branching off every which way, without bounds. What's more, I've already told everything that I'm writing down here many times before, and of course a large part of what Granny has told us was told to her by others in the past. The repetition of wise and beautiful things is wise and beautiful in itself, and is the same sort of virtuous act as feeding the hungry, caring for animals, watering plants or donating to charity. But a story takes place within a time, and doubly so – firstly because it describes a time that's past, bygone, elapsed, organised into a provable chronology and order of events, and secondly because it also describes that time within another time – during a conversation. And so a multitude of characters are going to appear here who will seem at first sight non-essential: acquaintances, chance passers-by, closer and more distant relatives, and above all some of my friends, male and female – not as protagonists but as listeners. But how different these stories are for each of them! How much plainer they are when stripped of charm, nothing but illustrations of events, like a digest from the *Herald* to meet the needs of Madzia-who-brings-the-milk or the lady at the market – but how they sparkle with wit when Granny pulls out the stops… Only a few years ago, when most of the former regulars at her name-day and birthday parties had already passed on, Granny would make herself into the sacred queen of the drawing room, and always did for my friends, hence their presence in this story. In any case, if they're in my life, they're also in Granny's, just like Jadzia Kontrymówna or the Japanese spy, all those people who are strangers, and yet are part of my life too.

So they're going to appear, and in a completely unruly manner. Don't be surprised if a story starts in one person's presence, and ends in someone else's. This is in the mysterious nature of storytelling: the same start can also mean different endings, and different starts can lead to the same finale. It's all subordinate to the greater narrative, which starts somewhere in Kiev, at a good address, in a large residential house with caryatids... and that's the only thing organising the episodic, though in fact necessary characters to whom it is told. And so past time will come to form time that is passing.

There are also the sort of stories that we only pass on to very few people. Not because no one else would understand their moral or laugh at their punchline, and not because we'd rather keep them for special occasions, but just because some stories race headlong towards some people, they soar, fly and plummet at breakneck speed, jumping about like dogs who've been pining for their masters. I usually tell Margot stories about ghosts, about the loving affection of the dead, and about beautiful places and images, such as the white cornettes of Beguines reading their breviaries, floating above the narcissi in the convent courtyard in Bruges. The stories I tell Basia are about malevolent aunts, sudden escapes, unexpected plot twists and bizarre connections. Scandalous incidents also give her a thrill. Radek likes to hear about himself, so he doesn't belong in this book, but he does belong in others. And so on, and so forth

– each story has its favourite listener, and each listener has his or her favourite story. Sometimes we also find a place that's ideal for listening, or a time that's just waiting for one particular story to be told.

I told Basia the story of Grandpapa Leonard, Grandmama Wanda and their children in Pelplin.*

If you've never been to Pelplin, do go there. You'll find yourself at a small station, where the trains arrive empty and depart full in the morning, and vice versa in the evening; a little further on you walk past a crumbling factory where something or other is made, sugar perhaps, then a small square, a handful of houses, and once you've lost hope of finding anything, you come upon a vast medieval cathedral, which, like a red-brick jewellery box with very fine vaulted ceilings, houses some unimaginable Gothic and baroque, Cupids and cardinals, skulls piled in reliquaries, a dancing Christ and many other spectacular things.

It was there that I said to Basia: 'Look at that – the light from the stained-glass windows shining on the choir stalls would make a superb photograph.'

But Basia frowned.

'It can't be done. It won't work,' she said.

'For a professional photographer it would,' I said in a patronising way. And of course she took the picture, and it worked, and now she's going about proud as Punch.

A lot happened that day. There was the girl we saw in the cathedral doorway… writing about it here makes no sense at all, because I should be writing about Wanda and Leonard, and about Ewa, and Róża, and so on, but where else am I going to write about that girl? So she's here too.

We were waiting in the vestibule. One leaf of the wide gates was set ajar, and through a grille we could see the

honey-coloured interior of the cathedral – the gilded beaten
egg-whites of baroque altars, the angelic tribe and the dark
choir stalls.

Basia tugged at my sleeve. I turned, and there was the girl. I
had seen her earlier, but I'd come in here telling a story, very
happy that Basia was dazzled, and that she was going to be even
more dazzled – and here was this girl, who had popped up from
nowhere, stick-thin, pallid, with a bluish complexion. She
looked about fourteen years old. She was standing on the stone
threshold, between the door and the grille, almost entirely
hidden behind the mighty doors and their ironwork, overshadowed, so that all I could see was a protruding knee, some long
fingers, one cheek and a grey-ringed, lustreless eye under a
narrow lid. Perfect for a picture.

Basia drew me to one side, as if to show me a notice.

'Do you think she'd agree to pose for me?'

'I think you could ask.'

For a while I felt like a summer vacationer from the year
1923 – the eastern borderlands, impoverished children, seek-
ers after local colour in plus fours and tweed jackets. I moved
a little further off and jotted something down in my notebook, while Basia conducted the negotiations, and then took
the pictures – but by now the magic had gone. And again I
saw this vision – the Hutsul region* in 1923, and me saying:
'But no, my dear Klementyna, there may indeed be a certain
noble roughness to it, a certain tough quality as in the Italian
primitives, but the young lady's grace was so much greater
when she was quite unaware that you wished to immortalise
her... by the by, how about indulging in some of the whole-
some local fare?'

Finally we were let inside. As usual, we were shown around
by a seminarian; a gauche young thing, he was (as Granny

would have said). He talked about a Rubens that hangs in the Old Pinacolada in Munich. I told him that piña colada is very nice too, though not necessarily old, but what they have in Munich is the Pinacotheca. Or there may even be two.

'I'm so sorry, I got it wrong. But I've been here since ten this morning,' he replied with a disarming smile, 'and that's not the first nonsense I've spouted today.'

Basia vanished, but a little later we ran into each other again – I was with a small group of tourists, obediently hearing for the nth time that 'the man who made the Gothic choir stalls portrayed himself close to the ground as if out of humility, but in fact out of conceit, because everyone has to bow down to see him, ladies and gentlemen'; and Basia was scurrying along from the entrance, out of breath, loaded with all her bags, cameras, lenses and apertures. 'She's called Liliana Liliańska.'

'Who is?'

'The girl. I promised to send her the picture. And I took a second one, from inside. It probably won't work.'

We did a tour of all the nooks and alcoves; once again I saw King Jan Sobieski* portrayed as a rich man feasting, the Christians being torn to pieces by wild animals, and the bricks polished by monks sharpening their knives against them on their way to the refectory. Now and then Basia tugged at my sleeve. Or I at hers. By the dancing Christ on top of the organ ('Noo, it won't work. But I'll try if you like.'), by the coloured spots of light sifted through the stained glass onto the tracery topping the choir stalls ('Noo, it won't work,' 'It would for a professional,' 'Maybe so, but not for me. Though it won't hurt to give it a try.').

'What about the reliquaries? Would you please show them to us, Father?' I asked.

'Er… I'm not a Father yet,' said the seminarian.

'Sorry.'

'No matter. It's not usually done…' – oh yeah? I thought, it's almost always done – 'but as an exception…'

And once again I stood before the small wooden doors hidden in the altar, behind which several rows of skulls were neatly stacked, wrapped in red or blue velvet. And wearing crowns embroidered with pearls that shone festively, like a sort of tarnished chronology of monarchs, scanned in hexameters.

'Look at that,' I whispered to Basia, 'the epitome of eternity – some nice little skulls in velvet, some incense and some gilded bits of rotten wood.'

But enough about the girl called Liliana Liliańska, a name we liked very much, enough about the seminarian, enough about the museum where they have the Gutenberg Bible and umpteen Gothic sculptures and altars, and where we came upon dreadful mayhem caused by a local restorer who coats the Gothic altars with metallic paint in primary colours, which hurts the eyes, but wounds the spiritual organs worst of all.

I don't know how we fitted it all in that day, but Basia also told me about Loleczek, and I told her about the aunts, which were highly appropriate stories in highly appropriate places, including a little village graveyard, a pizzeria and the station. But it started innocently enough.

'Tell me,' said Basia, walking at a brisk pace, as she sometimes does, 'that auntie your granny was talking about at breakfast, what sort of an auntie was she? And why did she hate your great-grandmother so much?'

'Aunt Ewa, the loony.'

'The one who married a general?'

'No, not that one.'

The Brokl family on holiday. From the left, General Szymiczek, Aunt
Róża, Grandmama Wanda, in front Grandpapa Leonard and
Uncle Maciej, c. 1905.

'The one who married a violinist?'

'No, that was Aunt Sasha.'

'So please clarify. One by one.'

'All right. There was Leonard Brokl, my granny's grandfather, and her grandmother, Wanda, née Dziewiątkiewicz.'

'Yes, yes, I know about them. Go on.'

'So you mean later on, because there isn't much of what
came earlier. All I know is that there was a paternal uncle's wife
who was a Scipio del Campo, and that's a remarkable, grand
family, and various others hanging around in the genealogy,
such as Prince-General Zajączek. Grandpapa Leonard Brokl...'

'What about Zajączek?'

'He's nothing, just your typical prince-cum-general – boring. But we're related to him through his wife, a Frenchwoman. And she's an interesting character,' – note the artistry of the storyteller, as with a clean conscience I sacrifice an Uprising general for a scandalous general's wife, who will certainly please Basia – 'just imagine, Zajączek's wife was a woman of great beauty, and she continued to be one to a very great age. Even when she was eighty she had lovers among the cadets.'

'Was it a career move for them?'

'I wouldn't rule it out, but that's another matter. She was very well preserved, you see. She used to cover herself in fresh meat…'

'The cadets?'

'No, fresher than that, just slaughtered. Slices of good meat. And she slept in a bed with large blocks of ice underneath it all year long. And she rouged her heels, knees and ear lobes. And so on. Thanks to which she retained her freshness and vigour. But we're not descended from her, because the general died without issue. Though we are descended from a sister of hers, or a sister-in-law, perhaps a cousin, also none too virtuous, who in her turn regularly slept with Grand Duke Konstantin Pavlovich, after which her husband acknowledged all their children, nothing but daughters, as far as I know, as his own. That gave him permanent access to honours and riches.'

'How did anyone know they were the Grand Duke's children?'

'By their noses. He had such an insanely ugly nose, sunken as well as snub, you know the kind. And all the daughters were the same. Hence my turned-up nose. In any case, be that as it may, that makes me a descendant of the Empress Catherine the Great.'

'But you were going to tell me about the aunts.'

'And I shall. And the uncle, because there was an uncle too.

Altogether there were five of them, but one died in childhood...
a little girl, I think, yes, it was a girl. Oh yes – Zosia, pretty and
clever, the bane of the naughty children, straight out of a
governess's sermon. She wrote poems in French, played the
piano beautifully and had a heart as big as the Palace of Culture.
Or rather the Winter Palace. But at the age of ten she had an
attack of appendicitis; the doctor thought it was plain indiges-
tion, so he gave her castor oil as a purgative. A terrible death,
fitting for the heroine of a moral tale for children. The others
were Ewa, Róża, Maciej and Irena, my great-grandmother.
They all grew up in a large, affluent home, because their father,
as you know, happened to have made a great fortune on the
stock market...'

'But which was the one who married a violinist?'

'Aunt Sasha, but she was my great-grandfather's sister, not
my great-grandmother's. Don't interfere, I'll tell you about
Sasha too. In any case they were all very wealthy and happy,
Grandmama Wanda had lovely dresses and lots of servants, the
children played with toys from the most splendid shops in
Vienna and St Petersburg, they had china dolls, whole armies
of little tin soldiers, and so on. And they were sent to school, to
very good schools, the best in Kiev. And then Grandpapa
Leonard went bankrupt.'

At this point there's a digression. It was typical of Grandpapa
Leonard to go bankrupt from time to time. Then he'd buy
something, sell something, lose the rest of his gold roubles on
something, until suddenly, quite out of the blue, the goddess
Fortuna, who was particularly kind to Grandpapa Leonard, for
no obvious reason would shower him in golden rain, and
Grandpapa could buy himself an automobile, for instance. Or
a sugar factory. In his delicate hands, made for stroking
lacquered screens and holding *Vieux Saxe* cups, the landed
estates would mysteriously evaporate – it was as if they still

Leonard Brokl (in white hat) on a pleasure boat in
Abbazia (now Opatija, Croatia), 1907.

existed, comprising such-and-such a number of acres and buildings, while the state continued to demand taxes from them,
and yet someone else had been managing them for years,
someone else had been picking the apples in the orchard,
someone else received the peasants in gloomy drawing rooms,
and other women entirely waded through the clumps of phlox
and rose bushes. Under the influence of Grandpapa Leonard's
imprudent activities bookkeeping, bills of exchange, credits
and debits changed into real beasts, living their own, unbridled
life, and leaving their patron far behind.

As I've said, after a golden period of prosperity on the Kiev
stock market, Lala's grandfather went bankrupt for the first
time. Brought up in a solemn belief in steam and electricity, the
natural sequence of events and the logic of cause and effect, he
must have felt cheated. And how – he'd been buying shares, just

as before, and selling shares, just as before, but instead of gaining money, he lost it. Unfortunately, the cast-iron consistency of chemistry, the precision of elements combining to form compounds and the exact proportions of bromine and chlorine molecules had no *raison d'être* among the voracious sharks of Little Russian high finance. Once bought, shares could either rocket in value, or drop, and no amount of potassium could possibly help or hinder them in this process.

Yet Grandpapa Leonard Brokl was brought up not just in a belief in steam and electricity, but also some extraordinary ideas about a businessman's honour, which even the Buddenbrooks would have found perplexing, because he turned out to have talked several of his close friends into buying shares (after all, if it's such a splendid way to acquire manna of gold...). So not only did he lose his own capital, he also felt obliged to reimburse everyone who had lost money as a result of his advice.

'And then,' as his wife Wanda told Lala, 'my husband, who was your grandfather, went bankrupt. We locked and bolted the house, stopped receiving guests and dismissed all the servants, so only the butler and the housemaid remained.'

As my monologue had gone on for too long, at this point Basia took my photograph, partly because it was a nice shot, and partly to draw attention to herself.

'Thanks. Aha... and so Lala's grandfather went bankrupt. Somehow he and his wife could cope with the fact that only the butler and the housemaid remained, but they could no longer afford to pay the fees for their three daughters' boarding school. Their son Maciej was at the polytechnic in Germany, which was costly, but he was a boy. Whereas the young ladies... would just have to stay at home, play the piano, paint and embroider in the expectation of making a reasonable match. And then Irena's friends from school clubbed together for her – Lala's future mother and my future great-grandmother. They were all so fond of her that for two or three years they jointly paid her school fees. Her sister Róża wasn't all that upset, because she had never liked school, whereas the third sister, Ewa, who was very intelligent, went wild with rage, because her friends didn't club together for her. Apparently she had great artistic talents, embroidered and painted beautifully, but chose rather psychedelic themes for it.'

'Psychedelic embroidery?'

'Well, maybe not the embroidery. Although there was a cushion decorated with rapacious sundews... I meant the paintings. On the Japanese lacquered cabinet... as Granny would say, "you know, that hideous object, my grandfather brought it back from Japan, but it's such a piece of junk". I'd give a fortune for a Japanese cabinet, but never mind. Ewa painted a manor house on its doors, quite like Lisów, their country place, but not Lisów, with a flowerbed in front of it, on which there was a huge toad, bigger than the house. Ewa hated her sister Irena, partly because she was jealous of her education, and partly because she was simply a nasty person, who probably had a screw loose too.'

'I'm not surprised Ewa hated her...'

'Her hatred grew, because by the time their father recovered financially, it was too late for Ewa, but Irena went on to college. First to the conservatory, then to study astronomy. On top of that she knew five languages – English, German, French, Russian and Polish. As you know, in those days such a well-educated woman was a rarity.'

'I'm not surprised Ewa felt like that...'

'Well, quite. To cap it all, now that their father had money again, a car and a sugar factory, he was corresponding with chemists all over the world, collecting works of art and cruising around Europe, and he always took Irena with him on his travels, because she was his favourite, cleverest, most beautiful daughter.'

'I'm not at all surprised Ewa was upset.'

'Nor am I. But that's nothing. Ewa had a fiancé. He was called Mech. Too bad. But as the name implies, Mech – meaning moss – was soft and nice. He was also charming and intelligent, as the name does not particularly imply. But meanwhile, out of boredom and the need for some intellectual occupation, Ewa had been going to meetings of the young anarchists and regarded herself as a liberated woman, emancipated and modern. She'd stuffed her head with all sorts of theories, which found fertile ground in the unweeded garden of her mind, to put it rather grandly, and now she wanted to dazzle Mech with her erudition and anarchic ideas. But who should spring up in her path?'

'Irena?'

'Irena! And she "was a woman ahead of her time…" '

'Not amused by "flirts who flatter"?'

'No, but by intelligent young men, absolutely. Eventually the poet Bolesław Leśmian* fell in love with her, whom she always spoke of as "Bolek Lesman". She used to play the grand piano while he stood leaning against that varnished whale, gazing into her eyes. He probably dedicated something to her. It was the same for Mech – officially he came to see Ewa, but he always knocked at her hated sister's door first, and spent a long time discussing things with her, either books, or music, or philosophy – while Ewa waited.'

'Do you know what?'

'What?'

'I'm surprised Ewa didn't do her any harm.'

'You may have a point there. Either way, in the end she got her Mr Mech. He was her official fiancé, and he became her official husband. It was worse for the other sister, Róża. She too had various admirers, some of whom were regarded as excellent matches, but she refused each one in turn. Until finally, when she already counted as an old maid because she was over thirty, General Szymiczek appeared. He courted her, and asked her parents for their daughter's hand in marriage, to which they said: "My dear sir, we'd be delighted to have you as our son-in-law, but unfortunately the final word belongs to Róża, and she usually refuses proposals." They went to Róża and said: "Róża, you won't marry the General, will you?" And Róża said: "Weeeell, I think I might." And she did. She became Mrs Szymiczkowa,* the general's wife. And every time some-one said: "Szymiczek? Is your husband a Czech?" Aunt Róża went purple with indignation and cried: "Not a Czech, not a Czech. He's Austrian!" Or she said of him: "My husband, General Szymiczek. He's Austrian." '

'What about your great-grandmother?' asked Basia.

'Irena? Irena fell in love with Dr Bieniecki, a murderously handsome man, an army doctor who specialised in, would you believe it – gynaecology. And he fell for her too, they got married, and had a daughter, Romusia.' And then I revealed the story of the house in Kiev, which I must have told her at least three times more since then. But I know, I know – I must make an abrupt shift from Pelplin to Gdańsk, to tell it the way Granny told it to me.

It all starts with the word 'Kiev', which I heard over and over in my childhood. 'Kiev?' What could Kiev mean to me, that strange name, which to my Polish ear sounded like a piece of wood tapping or dry twigs snapping, a name that cast glints of Byzantium on bulging cupolas? I knew that on one of the most elegant boulevards – which Granny called 'prospects' – carpet sellers who came to the city from the east used to spread out their wares.

'Even in the worst mud, in rain and slush the carpets lay out on the cobbles, on the pavements,' said Granny. 'Your great-grandmother told me she didn't want to step on them to avoid dirtying them, though they were already covered in mud, but the carpet sellers, with their glittering eyes and dark complexions, beards and eyebrows so black they looked dark blue, would come out of their tents and invite people to tread on their rugs, because they were new, and no one but the nouveaux riches would buy a new carpet. So people walked about on them, muddied and soiled them, even drove droshkies over them, until they were patinaed enough to be cleaned at last and spread out inside the tents. They came out and asked.'

So in the recesses of my childhood Kiev took on this picturesque image of a city whose streets were covered from end to end in patterned Persian carpets, touted by clamorous salesmen with beards and eyebrows so black they shone dark blue.

There, in a large residential house on such-and-such Prospect, lived three families – the Bienieckis, the Karnaukhovs and the Korytkos. Their fates were closely observed, not just by the nosy neighbours, but also the Secession gargoyles with protruding lips and the busty caryatids holding up the balconies on their frail shoulders and on bouquets of lilies; however well acquainted with knots of art-nouveau tendrils, they could not cease to wonder at the tangle of human emotions they witnessed, and were always raising their eyebrows in speechless amazement until the plaster began to crumble on their foreheads.

On the first floor lived the solicitor Valerian Karnaukhov – a Russian – his wife Alla, their two children, a nanny and a maid.

'Let's go, let's go,' said Granny, pinning a mother-of-pearl brooch at her throat, 'we're always late everywhere we go. Do you know,' she added, once we were on the stairs, 'I inherited it from my mother? Mama was always late too.' There was a hint of pride in her voice. 'Whenever she and my father were

off to the theatre or a concert, at the very last minute she'd
remember some fact – that she'd forgotten to tell the maid
something, that her dress wasn't right, or her hat was a little
too light or a little too dark... And if they finally did manage
to get going on time, because my father had started the exodus
ceremony far enough in advance, Mama would stop on the
doorstep, cast an eye around the drawing room or the dining
room, and suddenly be seized by the temptation to move a
chest of drawers, shift a table or, worst of all, turn a carpet to
the diagonal, which required lifting up all the furniture; my
father would pant and groan as he uprooted first an armchair,
then a sofa, while Mama commanded him with the tip of her
umbrella. They always came in at the beginning of Act Two or
the second half of a concert. And once, I've forgotten when it
was, it may have been a recital by Hofmann* – no, I went to the
Hofmann recital on my own, by some miracle I managed to
get a ticket from some friends, just imagine, what an experience! Hofmann played so incredibly well, he made some of
the notes within a single chord sound a tiny touch louder than
others, I sat there riveted to my seat...' (Meanwhile we were
crossing the evening city by taxi; the driver was a bit lost,
because he found himself in the middle of a dynamic narrative, but had to be content with a curt: 'To the Philharmonic',
because Granny wasn't going to interrupt her flow) '...and I
listened to all those wonderful chords, until suddenly after the
interval a man in black came onto the stage and said in a sepulchral voice that the pope had died. And just at that point in the
programme there was a sonata with a funeral march. Amazing,
isn't it?' and she turns to face me abruptly, as if expecting me
to react to this revelation with an 'Oooh!' or a bit of dumb
show, just as if I had never heard the whole story before.
Nothing doing. Granny goes back to her earlier theme, and
the driver makes some progress in getting lost.

'Anyway, they were going out somewhere, to a concert or the opera. And once again, Mama was tugging at a kilim, demanding a hammer and some nails. Papa stopped and gazed at her with boundless love as he said goodbye to Act One of *La Traviata* or *Norma*, took me aside and whispered: "I remember I was once on my way out to a party with Alla. She was wearing a lovely dress made of cherry-coloured silk, with four flounces at the bottom. And as chance would have it, one of them got caught on a chair leg and the seam gave way. I said I would wait for her to change, but she just said it was a waste of time… and riiiiip! She tore off the cherry-coloured flounce, flung it onto the chair and we were off." '

Apart from ripping off her flounce in one sharp go, Valerian's first wife, Alla, had lots of special merits. She was educated and well read, extremely intelligent and progressive, she believed in the idea of improving humanity and in liberation from oppression, she read and had things to say.

'What about the children?' I asked.

'The children? Well, what about them?' Granny looked at me with a patent lack of understanding. 'Irinka was looked after by the nanny and Igor was taken care of by the tutor.'

One day, amid all her pressing affairs, Alla saw the light. The entire house had already seen this particular light earlier, from cellar to attic, because everyone, including the caryatids, gargoyles and little children, knew that the neighbour, Mr Korytko, was an alcoholic. Alla, however, had to have a revelation to discover this fact. Quite simply Mr Korytko, a man as handsome as he was drunken, appeared to her one day on the stairs leading up from the ground floor in the full glory of his beauty and drunkenness.

'Valerian,' said Alla to her husband after a brief conversation with the rather flushed Apollo, 'I shall be frank with you. Mr Korytko is a man of great virtues, but since his wife's betrayal

Alla Karnaukhova, c. 1905.

he has sunk into a terrible addiction, which is destroying all his sound and noble instincts. He needs a strong woman. We both know that's the sort of woman I am. I must take care of him and rouse his dormant seam of strength and decency. I'm leaving you. Forgive me,' she said, stroking his cheek, 'you will manage without me, Valerian, you will manage in life. You are a person of action, just like me. Anyway, you have Marfa and Olga to help you. I will visit you and the children.'

And she moved in with Mr Korytko.

Meanwhile we were driving up to the Philharmonic – just in time for the second half of the concert. 'So what happened after that?' I asked politely an hour later as we emerged into the fresh air.

'After what? Do up your top button.'

'No, it's all right as it is. What happened to Mr Korytko, Alla and Valerian?'

'Ah, yes. As chance would have it, Valerian saw the light as well. In the throng of his daily duties as legal adviser to South-Western Railways, halfway through the afternoon, between conducting a case for the South-Western Railways versus Andrei Porfirych Ketterl and his evening violin lesson, one frosty January day he had a revelation too. Do up your top button. The entire house, from cellar to attic, including...'

'... including the caryatids, gargoyles, little children and servants...'

'... and servants knew that at number six lived the beautiful but sad Mrs Bieniecka, with her husband and their teenage daughter. Dr Bieniecki had been cheating on her left and right for ages, he had incredible charm – I met him when I was still a student in Warsaw, I happened to be with a girlfriend from school, I introduced them to each other, and she went completely red... he was well over sixty by then, and she was about twenty. As long as there were lots of these girls around,

Kazimierz Bieniecki, c. 1900.

Mrs Bieniecka didn't get too upset, but when he made do with just one, and a neighbour to boot, a certain Mrs Korytko, ooooh... then she realised it wasn't for the best. She tried thwarting their plans and mixing up their pre-arranged signals by moving flowerpots, lighting or extinguishing candles on the windowsill. And grew sadder and sadder. Which everyone could see, except Valerian, who needed a revelation. One day he bumped into her in the entrance hall. "Allow me, Madam," he said, offering her his arm before they went outside, "it's very slippery today." And beautiful Mrs Bieniecka looked up at him, with sapphire-blue fires burning in her sad eyes, and from a proud height of one-and-a-half metres she retorted: "A Russki? I cannot take the arm of a Russki." And of course, as she was always running about and falling over, she was soon lying on the ice, with Valerian looking at her despondently. "Well?" she cried. "If you're such a gentleman, aren't you going to offer me your arm?" "But I am a Russki! Surely you can't take the arm of a Russki?" As he said this, he leaned over and gently picked her up.'

And two months later when Alla came home repentant, painfully admitting that she had failed to rouse Mr Korytko's dormant seam of strength and decency, Valerian said that of course she could come and live at number five on the first floor again, but meanwhile he was caring for beautiful, sad Mrs Bieniecka at number six, whose husband, an army doctor specialising in gynaecology, was most conspicuously cheating on her with Mrs Korytko.

And so, as Julek used to say, one word led to another, and Lala was born.

III

But before Lala is born, we should mention Aunt Sasha and Misha de Sicard.

Valerian had two sisters, Lola and Sasha. Sasha was boring and ugly, so of course he was stuck with her for half his life. Lola was the same sort of crazy scallywag as he was – she was his favourite sister and best friend, so of course for half their lives they never had the chance to see each other. They grew up in a beautiful, secluded spot on one of the big Russian rivers – the Volga, the Dnieper or the like. Their father died when they were little, and their mother had to deal with running the entire estate. And it's only thanks to divine providence that the children didn't drown in that great big river, because they were brought up by the housemaids, who thought the best way to be rid of Lola and Valerian was to send them off on all-day boating trips. They were given food for the whole day, a pot of buckwheat and dripping, apples, pears and goodness knows what, and they'd pack it into the boat and cruise about on the great big river until late at night, when they'd come home with bruised knees, grubby faces and empty stomachs, by which time the docile Sasha, who spent the livelong day practising scales and reading, would have been sleeping the sleep of the just for hours.

As Lola and Valerian hadn't drowned, their future had to be secured. Valerian took a law degree, and all I know about Lola is that she stayed by the great big river, while Sasha went to the conservatory. And this is where Misha de Sicard appears.

'Poor, handsome Misha de Sicard! Have I ever told you about him?' asks Granny, and I nod indifferently; indifferently because I could just as well deny it – resistance is quite irrational in the

face of her non-stop narrative. 'Misha studied with Papa's
sister, Aunt Sasha, at the conservatory. He was a beautiful boy,
tall, with black eyes and black hair, dark and well built... an
Apollo. And an excellent match, because the de Sicards had a
chain of banks throughout imperial Russia, from St Petersburg
to Kamchatka. Not surprisingly, half the conservatory made
eyes at him and sighed with love sickness. But Aunt Sasha...
well, she was small, with little blue eyes, chubby cheeks and a
small, round nose, just a squashed button really, nothing to
look at. She had a nice laugh. And she had lovely hair right into
her old age, but once I went into the bedroom and there was
Aunt Sasha's lovely hair hanging on a special wooden sphere,
while my aunt had just a few white strands tied in a little top
knot. But in her youth she must have had real hair. And just
imagine, one day the handsome Misha went down on one knee
before her and asked her to marry him. Aunt Sasha! Small,
chubby Aunt Sasha with a nose like this' – Granny flattens her
nose with the tip of her index finger – 'all squashed. And what
do you think she said to him?'

' "Why me?" '

'How do you know? Have I told you? Yes, that's just what she
asked: "Why me?" And then he said: "Because you're the only
one who hasn't been chasing after me." And they were married.
From then on she travelled the world with Misha de Sicard,
who really was a first-rate violinist, and frequented the drawing
rooms of the top aristocracy and the wealthiest bourgeoisie.
Paris, London, New York, Vienna – they went everywhere, and
with them went Fyokla and Anyuta. Because Fyokla and
Anyuta, Misha's former nannies, were the only ones who had
any patience for his constant hysterics. That the water in the
bath was two degrees too hot or too cold. That he didn't like
the accompanist. That the viola player had a squint. That he
had a migraine. That he didn't want to play, no, no, no, he

would not and that was final. And Fyokla and Anyuta ran after him with violins, first an Amati, later a Stradivarius, with rosin, and with an album of family photographs. "Look, my little angel, there's Mummy, Mummy and Grandma, look, my golden boy, there's Daddy, now now, enough of your sulking." But time after time Misha tore up a contract or refused to play a concert because he didn't like the hall, the weather was bad, or he simply wasn't in the mood. Aware of this, the impresarios included astronomical penalty fees in his contracts, so he tore them up and paid the forfeit. His brothers, with whom he had jointly inherited the chain of banks, sent him an enormous monthly stipend, as long as he kept well away from the business, so he had money pouring in anyway. Aunt Sasha told us that one time in Brussels he dropped a cigarette butt on the ground. A policeman came up and issued him with a fine. Misha paid it, bowed, and a hundred metres further on he dropped something else. And paid up again. That's what he was like – rich, handsome and spoiled rotten...'

And here comes the moral. It may not be an exception in Granny's stories, but it certainly isn't the rule, because life in general is not terribly moral-producing, and Granny's stories are taken from life. Granny builds up to the moral in an almost invisible way, totally imperceptible to the unconscious observer and listener. Only a seasoned connoisseur of her narrative will catch the latent haste in her tone, offset at the climax by a masterfully dispensed deceleration; drawing out the syllables, and then the sudden punchline... what virtuosity in an eighty-one-year-old! ('But what's eighty-one years for a young woman?' Granny would say sententiously.)

'And, you see, at this point that American woman appeared' – the demonstrative pronoun 'that' is obvious here: it's about 'that' particular woman, that vixen who took Misha away from Aunt Sasha – 'and went after him from city to city, from capital to capital, from one concert hall to another, she always sat in the best seats, wrapped in the most expensive, though not the most tasteful stole, sent baskets of roses to the dressing room and swooned with rapture. And Misha ran off with her, and sailed away to the States, leaving Aunt Sasha with nothing to live on. But fond as she was of the handsome violinist, the American woman was not going to tolerate his tantrums. She dismissed Fyokla and Anyuta, and when the first hysterical scene occurred she called for the maid, said: "Would you please fetch the gentleman a glass of cold water – he seems to be having convulsions", and left the room.'

'I know. And then she threw him out, so poor Misha – he really was poor by now, because the revolution had occurred, the chain of banks had been nationalised, and the de Sicards had got the chop – ended up playing his fiddle in the bars of New York or Chicago in exchange for a bite to eat. I wonder if he sold the Stradivarius first, and then played in the bars, or might he have played the Stradivarius in them?'

But Granny had already opened her book, fallen asleep in her armchair or passed on to another story. Anyway, not even she knew the answer to that question.

❧

And so, one word led to another, and Lala was born.

But plenty more happened before that. Several royal cousins, sitting on various European thrones, had themselves the most spectacular family quarrel they could possibly afford; or in fact that they could not afford, because in the process they lost not just numerous territories, palaces, wives and children – not to mention subjects and ammunition – but also several thrones.

Beautiful Mrs Bieniecka, who still had the surname

Irena Bieniecka née Broklówna,
Abbazia (now Opatija, Croatia), c. 1905.

Bieniecka, for somehow they hadn't yet got around to all the divorces and weddings, left Kiev in a panic for her parents' estate somewhere in so-called Vistula Land*, the Russian partition of Poland.

Aunt Sasha blushed when presented to her former acquaintances as governess to the children of Mr and Mrs M. or B., or von K. in Royal-Imperial Vienna, gradually setting in a fiery red-and-gold glow of burning buildings. Grandpapa Leonard still corresponded with all the more notable sugar-making experts, guided not by ethnicity, but purely by scientific reasoning. And as he lived in the Russian Empire, where the relevant organs always had perfect knowledge of who was guided by what sort of views, quick as a flash he was arrested, without undue ceremony branded as a German spy and sentenced to be shot. And at this point Grandmama Wanda, who remembered nothing of Dresden but the silk shops, and nothing of Paris but the hats, once again demonstrated remarkable fortitude.

But here we must bring on stage Madzia-who-brings-the-milk. Unfortunately.

'Madzia has a canny mind,' says Granny, 'because she comes from the Kielce area. My part of the world. All the peasants there were so intelligent. Naturally, they hadn't been to school, they lived in abject poverty, but they were incredibly smart, because there was a tsarist prison in the vicinity, Holy Cross...'

The story of Holy Cross and how it affected the peasants' intelligence will be told elsewhere, but for now let's return to the colourful character of Madzia. In the communist era, when alcohol was not sold until one in the afternoon, Madzia was a real potentate, a five-star bootlegger on a par with Ford or Rockefeller (or considering the branch of industry, Al Capone), though of course on the modest scale of Oliwa's Liczmański Street and the immediate area. Remaining from that era was her common-law husband, Oktawian, a former customer of whom she'd been particularly fond; applying her skilful management of resources, Madzia keeps him on a short rein, allocating him an appropriate measure of vodka per Sunday and per public holiday, never letting him go on the razzle with his mates and consistently rejecting his intermittently repeated proposal of marriage, because she knows perfectly well that as his actual wife she would have far less influence on Oktawian than she has as his common-law one.

Ever since the twenty-four-hour shops arrived in the 1990s and cut off the branch of professional bootlegging, Madzia has withdrawn from the trade – though out of habit, and for sentimental reasons, she always keeps a few bottles in the sideboard for a rainy day, but she regards it as a retirement hobby and as a hook for Oktawian, rather than genuine business. Instead she has devoted herself to her other passion, and being a perfectionist, she now plays the role of William Randolph Hearst on the same modest scale, producing and transmitting gossip about everything and everyone within the radius of a kilometre. And so she sits down at our breakfast table and hurries to tell the news. 'Mrs Karpińska, it's enough to make your hair turn white, as the saying goes. Oktawian's leg was hurting again and he ended up in hospital, where he got jaundice, because nowadays if you end up in the hospital you catch it immediately, and so I...'

'Enough to make your hair turn white?' Granny interrupts her in a tone that brooks no opposition, heralding a digression. 'It's perfectly possible for your hair to turn white.'

'Well yes,' Madzia timidly ventures, 'that's what I'm saying...'

But all of us, I as I write this, and you as you read it, are laughing at this clumsy attempt to stem the tide of Granny's narrative. All the more so, seeing that we left Leonard Brokl, the chemistry professor, in a carefully ironed shirt, facing a firing squad.

'Just imagine if you please, my grandfather's hair went white in a single day. Because you see, my grandfather, Leonard Brokl, was a chemist, an expert on manufacturing sugar. Ever since he'd made a fortune on the stock market, he did his scientific work for pleasure rather than anything else, but even so he corresponded with scientists all over Europe, in England, France, Russia, Germany and Austria-Hungary. And as chance would have it, the First World War broke out...'

'Yes indeed, so it did...'

'And war is unfavourable for sugar-making, just as it is

unfavourable for growing orchids, making Italian ice cream or weaving on mechanical looms... oh yes, Grandpapa Leonard' – Madzia has lost all hope of butting in, and glumly sips her coffee, clinking her horse's teeth against her glass – 'naturally, Grandpapa Leonard did not break off his scientific correspondence, until one day they came to place him under arrest, saying he had betrayed state secrets to the enemy, that he was a spy, and of course there would be a court martial. Anyway, perhaps in his naivety he had betrayed some secrets, such as the location of sugar-beet fields in the Ukraine – who knows? And then my grandmother Wanda, who was altogether a woman of fairly limited intellect, but very wise about life, appealed to her dear friend, Mrs Hołojewska, who had a post-chaise and relay horses... You know what I mean, Madzia, relay horses – every few dozen kilometres a fresh pair would be waiting at a coaching inn, and the tired ones were replaced by the well-rested ones, so the whole journey could be made at a gallop. And so my grandmother travelled to Kiev, where she dragged some high-up official out of bed in the middle of the night, and he in turn dragged out another one, until she had obtained a very important document that acquitted Grandpapa Leonard, and then back she went, using the relay horses again, to the fortress where he was being held in the death cell. They were due to execute him that morning. And my grandmother arrived as dawn was breaking, just as he was being led out in front of the firing squad, showed the documents and saved her husband's life. They were given an apology and allowed to go. And then, once they were out of the gate, my grandmother noticed that my grandfather's hair was as white as snow. It had changed colour in a single night.'

'That's what I'm saying...' says Madzia, trying to get a word in. 'It can happen the other way round as well. Just imagine... would you like a tomato?' says Granny.

'I've had my breakfast and I've been to the market already – I ran into that Mrs Orłowska from number three, and she says to me...'

'So just imagine, when the war broke out and the Germans invaded, on the third or fourth of September Mama said: "I say, Lala, when did you last wash your hair? It's quite dark with dirt." So I looked, and indeed it was. But even though I washed and dried it carefully, it was still dark. My hair had darkened because of all the upset.'

'Well I never!' says Madzia, capitulating.

And now we can go back to our revolution.

We've left Sasha in Vienna, and de Sicard in poverty, and (thanks to Mrs Hołojewska's relay horses and Grandmama Wanda's presence of mind) we've rescued Grandpapa Leonard, so now we can deal with his son, Uncle Maciej.

Uncle Maciej – engineer, syphilitic and madman, he studied in Munich, whence the syphilis... you know... the student fraternities, Schubert, Leverkühn, the light white wines... he came back to Kiev with spirochetes and a diploma. He worked at a factory in the Ukraine, and was caught in the machine of history: when red trade unions were founded at the factory, he founded white ones. And on top of all that, as if there weren't enough colours, along came the Black Hundreds* – the violent ultranationalists – and wiped out both red and white unions, because all they cared about was slaughter, burning up documents, ripping apart safes and smashing machines. Uncle Maciej was working in his office, and when he heard the shooting and screams of the wounded, he jumped out of the window. There was a stack of timber underneath it, arranged in a square – two beams lengthways and two crossways. And he jumped straight into this stack, because his office was on the first floor, or maybe the raised ground floor. There he sat, as quietly as he could, watching through the chinks between the stripped tree trunks as bayonets severed aortas and softly pierced bodies, as typewriters were thrown out of the windows and came flying down onto the cobblestones, where they shattered, sending a spray of long metal type-bars in all directions; he saw a forty-year-old man cut off the head of the thirteen-year-old office boy – slowly, carefully, just as one cuts a head of cabbage from its stem. He saw them. And they saw him. Unhurriedly, they came up to the stack with bayonets bared, and stabbed away at random, through chinks that were two fingers wide. Then they decided that Uncle Maciej was dead meat and went off into their Black-Hundred world, leaving him to the mercy of scavengers. Meanwhile Uncle Maciej had only suffered a few grazes, but for that quarter of an hour, while the blades were slicing the air right by his eyes, lips, temples and nether regions, Uncle Maciej went mad. Of course, there were also clandestine whispers at home that it was the syphilis that had deprived him of his wits, brought home from the bawdy houses of Munich during his tempestuous youth as a student at the German polytechnics, but that did nothing to alter the fact that Uncle Maciej was insane. He'd spend all day long observing insects, having bright conversations and making little boats out of bark, string and bits of canvas, and so it would continue for months, until suddenly he would attack a member of the family with a knife, try to drown them in the pond or strangle them with his bare hands. Afterwards he'd apologise, and return to his boats and centipedes.

And then there was Uncle Eugeniusz, a mythical figure from God knows what branch of the family. He featured in the regular set of dinner-time stories, and it was easy to summon him out of the forest of Granny's memory by adamantly refusing to eat pasta or mashed potato for long enough.

'You'll end up like Uncle Eugeniusz,' she'd boom in a sepulchral tone, until the opalescent vases and sapphire-blue wine glasses in the drawing room went a shade darker. Then there would be a pause, and soon after the topic would be resumed.

'When the revolution broke out' – it's impossible to write the word 'revolution' the way Granny utters it; it's something akin to 'unmentionables'; it may well exist, but it's not to be talked about at table – 'Uncle Eugeniusz, who lived in a large house on one of Kiev's main prospects, announced a formal strike. He dismissed most of the servants, heedless of the fact that in doing so he would impose duties on his wife, rather than on himself, shut himself in his study and stopped accepting meals. He resolutely insisted that he would not eat the muck they were serving him – because the poverty was atrocious, a virtual famine, and his wife spent all day long running about the markets, to bring home nothing but some buckwheat and frostbitten potatoes – and, as befitted a gentleman, he kept his word. And died of starvation.'

So much for the adults. And what about the children?

'Roma, Irena's daughter by Bieniecki, survived the siege of Kalisz – the devil knows how she ended up in Kalisz, but end up there she did, because during a war people can suddenly find themselves in all sorts of odd places. At one time it was a famous siege – famine, filth, shells, but later on there were lots of other famous sieges. In any case, that was when Roma contracted tuberculosis. What about Alla and Valerian Karnaukhov's children? Igor, who had bad luck – and bad luck would seem to have been the major affliction of those times – fell in love with the wife of his commander from cadet school. There was a dreadful scandal' – Granny smiles knowingly – 'and whether to endear himself to the officer's wife, or out of sheer despair, I have no idea, he set out to drive the reds away from a position that had long since been regarded as lost; apparently the Bolsheviks had an almost one-hundredfold advantage, and when they withdrew and moved on, they

left behind bodies so badly mutilated by sabres that they
couldn't be identified. Anyway, only Aunt Sasha knew about
it, and from her so did Mama. His father never found out how
Igor perished. Or maybe he did? In any case, it was shrouded
in secrecy. Whereas Igor's sister, Irinka, survived the revolution, then the purges of the 1930s too, and also the siege of
Leningrad... it's hard to say which of those was the hardest to
endure. First she corresponded with my father and aunt, later
with my mother, and finally with me. She wrote a few books,
published some Russian fables and a collection of short
stories, or a novel about the siege in fact... I think it was called
Friendship. It should be on the shelf somewhere over there –
oh, there it is. And then the letters stopped coming, and that
was that. In the 1950s or '60s, when delegations of our Soviet
comrades used to come here, or if someone from the radio
went to the USSR on a friendship visit, I always inquired
about Irinka, or asked them to inquire on the spot. And it was
always the same: "Oh look, a bird", "We see that your accent
is improving, Comrade", "Comrade, have you ever been to
Nizhny Novgorod?" or something of the kind. Until finally
someone drew me aside and asked if I was determined to land
them and myself in hot water, and that Irina had been
deported. I never inquired again.'

But there was still one of Valerian Karnaukhov's children
left, a female, born in the almost equally newborn Polish
Republic, in Kielce, in 1919. The child bore the surname of a
Polish army officer, that first-class gynaecologist and lady-
killer, Mr Kazimierz Bieniecki, who, acceding to the request of
his – in principle already ex – wife, adopted her.

'Oh dear, various acquaintances, especially the white
Russians, frightened Mama into thinking that if I was called
Karnaukhov the Poles would beat me up, spit at me and
insult me for every imaginable deportation, uprising, for the

Valerian and Alla's son, Igor Karnaukhov, in uniform, c. 1916.

partitions that wiped Poland from the map, for every Russian general and statesman who crushed the Polish insurgents. And officially I was my real father's step-daughter... I wanted to change that of course, as soon as I came of age, but I married Julek and it was all over bar the shouting.'

All right then. So the child had Mr Bieniecki's surname. What about her first name? Well, she didn't actually have one. Somehow or other they ended up postponing the christening

Valerian and Alla's daughter, Irina Karnaukhova,
at boarding school, c. 1915.

until Valerian arrived, but he couldn't get out of Soviet Russia
very easily, so Granny was called 'Lala', because she was like a
lovely little doll, and in Polish *'lala'* means a doll. Grandmama
Wanda, Grandpapa Leonard, her mother, the maids and the
village women always called her 'Lala', 'Lalka' or 'Lalunia'.
And only when she was about four years old, when she was
presented to a large, bald man with a beard and told 'This is

Lala.

your papa', did they start looking for a name to match these
diminutives. From among all the Luisas, Halinas, Lenas and
Karolinas the name Helena was chosen. Admittedly, even the
simplest version of ancient history didn't exactly present it as
the ideal name, but as we all know, from time to time history
likes to repeat itself.

As I've already said, Granny's narrative twists and coils like a pea plant, putting out endless unexpected shoots that grab hold. Here I owe the reader yet another long, green – or rather in this case sepia – tendril of a digression, because I feel I must rescue from oblivion at least some of the adventures that fell to the lot of my great-grandfather Valerian Karnaukhov, former legal adviser to the South-Western Railways, before he came to reside at Mrs Wolgemut's and made his cocoa in a separate little saucepan.

'Papa was a smooth talker, as a lawyer should be, and somehow he managed to win over the Bolsheviks so successfully that although he was obviously a bourgeois of the first order, they not only didn't shoot him on the spot, but liked and trusted him so much that they assigned him the role of block warden. And so they'd come along, ask him questions and chat away, until one day my father says: "Hmm, you people are always talking about honesty and principles, but if you'll forgive me for saying so, you're just spouting nonsense, because you've stolen my beaver-fur hat." So they look at one another, and at him, and at one another again. "Beaver-fur?" they ask. "Beaver-fur, Citizen Valerian Ivanovich Karnaukhov? Then we'll search for it." And they sought, and they found, and they beat to a pulp the man who'd stolen it, and brought a side of pork as a peace offering. Can you imagine your scrupulously honest grandfather Zygmunt in a situation like that? He'd say there was really no need, all he cared about was the hat because it's so warm and cosy, ideal for the frosty weather. And they'd have been furious and shot him on the spot. Not so my father. He roasted the pork, invited them all, including the thief, to dinner, poured them glasses of vodka, and they ate and drank to make peace. And then, slightly under the influence, they told him that as he was such a great friend of theirs, perhaps he would help them, because some counter-revolutionary bastard

was going about at night, cutting their communication wires
– every night it was the same, and communication, pardon the
expression, is no bloody joke, it's an important thing at war.
And my father agreed. He went about the district with them
and beyond, pushing his way down lanes and wading through
streams from sunset to sunrise. But there was no one. Just once
he told his Bolshevik comrades that he'd seen the saboteur: a
small, red-headed shrimp of a fellow. A small, red-headed
shrimp, because he himself was bald and the size of a wardrobe, and of course it was he who went about at night cutting
those wires, in revenge for Igor.'

But soon the revolution led to the birth pangs of the state.
The blood of Their Royal Highnesses, the heir to the throne,
the princesses, Dr Botkin* and the servants spattered the walls
of the cellar in Yekaterinburg; Felix Edmundovich* worked
unstintingly day and night, thanks to which many years later
the dissidents painted his hands red on all the statues; and life
in general became increasingly dangerous, so that knowing a
few Bolsheviks wasn't enough for a quiet life any more – obviously, a doctor is useful, we could also say a painter is useful,
but a lawyer? A lawyer is the worst type of bourgeois, the worst
bloodsucker on earth, living off human injustice.

Not to mention the fact that he was missing beautiful Mrs
Bieniecka and their child – he didn't even know if it was a boy
or a girl. So he sold the furniture, the flat, the cutlery and the
pictures, and instead bought diamonds, rubies, emeralds and
gold, which was always in plentiful supply in Russia, sewed all
these valuables into the lining of his coat, took a small travelling bag and headed into the unknown, with nothing to guide
him but a slip of paper, on which the name of an estate near
Kielce was written, 'Morawica', in the former Piotrków
Governorate in former Vistula Land.

At the station in Warsaw, hardly had he pushed his way

through the crowd before he noticed that his coat had been slashed with a razor and gutted in the most authentic Warsaw cutpurse style. Half an hour later on Marszałkowska Avenue, or maybe on Nowy Świat Street, he heard: 'Eee, I don't believe it! Eee, Mr Karnaukhov the lawyer, eee, may lightning strike me down if my eyes are deceiving me!' He looked up and saw before him Mr, let's call him Rosenzweig, timber and paper, wholesale and retail, for whom he had handled some small matters in Kiev. 'Why so glum, my good man?' he heard after the initial greetings. 'However it used to be, it used to be somehow. It never happened yet that it was no-how. Well I never, are you really here, in Warsaw, at the station? Oh yes, that's what we call bad luck, that's what we call a decree of fate!' And after a pause he added: 'How much do you need?' 'But I won't have anything to pay you back with...' But at that Rosenzweig squinted and said: 'I will, I won't... If you will, then pay it back, if you won't, then don't pay it back. The sky is not going to fall on our heads as a result.' That was how Mr Rosenzweig lent Mr Karnaukhov however many marks or zlotys of the day, who on earth still remembers? And then he recommended the guest rooms of Mrs Wolgemut, a very respectable widow, who wouldn't fleece him like a racketeer, and was altogether a thoroughly honest woman.

And so Valerian and his travelling bag found temporary lodgings in Mrs Wolgemut's guest rooms, where he spent his days fathoming the nuances of Polish grammar and the commercial code, preparing for the exam to have his legal qualifications recognised in Poland. At the same time he tried to find Irena Bieniecka, daughter of Wanda and Leonard Brokl, owners of the Morawica estate, which in any case was in totally different hands by now.

As luck would have it, by asking enough people, Valerian ended up at Lisów, where he found them all – in the first place

Irena and Lala, and only further down the line his future parents-in-law. Grandmama Wanda took one look at him, clenched her lips and merely hissed: 'A Russki, I ask you!' And that was her only comment on the whole situation. What's more, for many years to come, whenever she heard anyone praising her son-in-law, she would repeat those final words on the matter – 'A Russki, I ask you!' – regardless of whether they were admiring his cooking, his musical taste or his ability to cure migraine headaches by the laying-on of hands. Only towards the end of her life did she start to call him 'my dearest darling defender'.

Either way, Irena and Valerian had found each other again, and in the process her future husband's accommodation was thoroughly searched by his future wife, and that is how there floats to the surface of this narrative the notorious saucepan, in which Valerian made cocoa. And as he only ever made cocoa in it and nothing else, he never washed it, for whatever might happen, cocoa is cocoa. And just as my great-grandmother had shown Granny, so Granny would show us on any small saucepan the two-centimetre layer of legendary cocoa deposit.

And as soon as they were done with the saucepan and the necessary formalities, they contracted – admittedly with some delay – a legitimate marriage in a Calvinist chapel, because they couldn't have either a Catholic or an Orthodox wedding. To this end one of them had to convert to Calvinism. 'Ooh, I can convert,' said Valerian, 'and the child can be Catholic.' And afterwards the Catholic child stirred waves of outrage when she boasted in the company of her little friends from Mrs Możdżeńska's kindergarten of how she had attended her parents' wedding, wearing her best white frock, embroidered with tiny roses.

IV

Lisów. What can the name 'Lisów' mean to someone on the other side of this book? I might just as well write Jędrzejów, Kurozwęki, or Staszów. But for me, who spent so many evenings before bed, smelling of soap and smelling of water as only children can, listening to hundreds of tales of that place, Lisów was a mythical land, Narnia, or Canaan, separated from me and from all of us by the great curtain of war, a war just as remote and incredible as the Roman Empire's fight against the Marcomanni and the Chronicles of Flavius.

So Lisów was beyond a great ocean, beyond an impenetrable wall, in the bizarre world that we agree to call the past, and that we cleverly put behind us – just as once upon a time paradise and the Lotus Eaters were located on the most distant islands of the East or West, under the ground or above the clouds; for me Lisów was like Eden, Jerusalem, Sodom, Paris and Venice…

One would need to open one's eyes in Lisów, just as Granny opened hers there, and many years later, so did I, guided by her stories into the corners of the rooms, among black ostrich-feather fans and plaster gargoyles, among apple trees and pear trees, violins and mirrors; one would need to open one's eyes just as one opens them in a dream, as one steps into the bright circles of non-existent vistas.

❧

But Lisów, that magical, ethereal land, didn't just come out of nowhere, out of some atmospheric plinking and choirs of angels, but resulted from Grandpapa Leonard's roubles, or in

The house at Lisów, c. 1942.

fact from Mnin and Morawica – in other words, here comes a digression.

It was before the revolution that, in one of his periods of accidental prosperity, Grandpapa Leonard Brokl had come into possession of the chauffeur-driven car, the paintings, the lacquered screens and the sugar factory in the Ukraine, but he only had this last item until the revolution, when his workers went feral, thanks to which a man called Ostrovsky wrote a book called *How the Steel Was Tempered*, but that's another story. In any case, before the workers went feral, Grandpapa Leonard decided to become a landowner. I don't know which I prefer in this story – silver roubles or rainbow-coloured banknotes straight out of Dostoyevsky – but in any case, Grandpapa Leonard exchanged a large number of one or the other for land, and as he was an Austrian subject and wasn't legally able to own land within the Russian Empire, his dearest, cleverest daughter Irena was named as the official owner in all the relevant documents. First she was the proprietor of Mnin, a sizeable estate, apparently more than a thousand hectares, but it died a natural death before the Great War, and all its hectares, or perhaps voloks, vershki, or however it was measured, remained as nothing but long rows of shapely numbers on foolscap paper, because someone else was managing the land. There was some sort of cunning fraud involved, because in the 1930s, being a solicitor, Valerian Karnaukhov had a lot of explaining to do for not having paid the land tax on this immense estate inherited from his father-in-law, but which he had never actually set eyes on.

After the loss of Mnin, with the rest of the money left from his Kiev days Grandpapa Leonard bought Morawica, outside Kielce, an estate that may have been smaller, but was quite opulent, with an eclectic manor house, an orchard and an orangery.

'At Morawica,' Grandmama Wanda always used to say, 'we had melons in the orangery, but when I treated President Mościcki˙ to them he didn't like the taste.'

But then came the Great War, and army units kept marching through Morawica, until so many had been there that Grandmama Wanda lost patience and had a hysterical fit: 'The Germans came through and looted. The Russkies came through, and looted even more. But when the Austrians came through, they didn't even leave the door frames – they just hacked down to the bare walls.'

After which she refused to live in a manor house deprived of door frames. As a result, Grandpapa Leonard leased out Morawica, and to live out the rest of his days in comfort, bought nearby Lisów, the rump of an estate, which though small, had been run in exemplary fashion by Squire Eysmontt, a great lover of noble varieties of fruit tree. He had planted the Lisów orchard, which in terms of abundance of species had no equal in the vicinity. Apart from a sizeable piece of land, the orchard and the garden, there was also a small, six room manor house with an accommodation block for the farm workers, a coach house, a stable and a barn, and also a stone ice house – let's not forget the ice house, full of blocks of ice sprinkled with sawdust – you could stand on top of it in the evening and look towards Chęciny, and if the castle towers were visible, it meant that tomorrow was going to be a fine day.

The Lisów of my childhood was the Lisów that Granny drew for me one evening on one of the reams of white paper she had bought to write a novel about her life; she'd even chosen the title: *My Birth Sign is the Maple Leaf*, because she'd always loved maples, but then she found out that in some Gaelic or Welsh calendar the maple really was ascribed to her. She was going to write it in her retirement, gather and rework all her radio broadcasts, supplement them a little and publish it; but just at that point I was born. And along with me came all sorts of jobs that this house had not seen for years: nappy changing, lulling to sleep, dandling and shaking a rattle with your fingertip. And very quickly the printed book changed into a spoken book.

Either way, one evening (and this was in the days when rattles had long since ceased to interest me), Granny was telling me a story that was particularly complicated in terms of topography, in which the layout of the doors or windows was important, and so she mapped out the manor house for me on a sheet of paper, including the stable and a small cowshed, the coach house, the farm workers' accommodation block, the rainwater barrel, the outhouse and so on. There was also a long lawn with phloxes growing by it (tall on one side, small on the other, because the ground there was so uneven – every half-metre the fertile soil changed into the poorest sand, as if some-one had cut it up with a knife and moved it around), and rings of darker grass in the orchard.

On the next sheet was the village: a road with houses on either side, and two hills – the manor house on one, and a church on the other.

'The church,' said Granny, 'was exquisite, baroque and very much like home, because all the rugs and lace-trimmed table-cloths were donated by Grandmama Wanda. In one of the chapels, fenced off by a beautiful wrought-iron grille, were the tombs of the Krasińskis or Krasickis. The ceiling was painted... I remember St Nicholas, with his mitre and crozier, and three little girls to whom he was giving a dowry; they all had rather gypsy looks: dark eyes, black hair and olive skin.'

Next to the church was the presbytery, where the parish priest officiated; all I know about him is that he was a hand-some man who improved the local stock.

'The peasants didn't hide the fact at all. One man used to show me his children and say: "These be mine, and them two be the priest's". And another, himself a son of the priest, would say: "The priest'd run in to see my mother like a dog into a butcher's shop: he'd come in, do his business and leave." But the priest was an excellent preacher, you have to give him that. A real maestro. I don't know how he did it, but whatever the theme of the gospel, he always came around to the fact that the peasants had been stealing the apples from his orchard again. The reading could be about the feeding of the five thousand, the raising of Lazarus or the baptism in the River Jordan, but he always managed to bring it round to those apples.'

On a third sheet of paper there was a map of the manor house: the vestibule, the kitchen, the pantry, Grandpapa's

Lisów, with the church and the road in the background; on the right, part of the farm workers' block, c. 1942.

study, where Grandmama Wanda showed the Germans the documents from Archduke Ferdinand, Aunt Ewa's large bedroom (where plaster casts of gargoyles from Notre Dame hung on the walls and a Satanist-anarchist odour lingered in the air), Uncle Maciej's room, Granny's little room and the large drawing room, where Grandpapa Leonard's pictures hung on the walls – all those Bouchers, Potters[*] and minor Flemish masters; as well as that there was the bust of Napoleon, and on the other side of the room a bust of Lenin, brought from Russia by Valerian, who had in fact been a cadet, in other words a constitutional democrat, an opponent of the revolution, and who had after all severed those communication wires, despite which he respected Lenin and regarded him as a great man.

So that was what Lisów was for me at the time – a few pieces

of furniture standing in a house, and some maps roughly
sketched on loose sheets of paper.

❧

But with age the past was bound to catch up with me, just as it
was catching up with all of us: Basia, Gosia and Mateusz; it
chased us not just with the stories of grannies, granddads and
aunts, but also with the patriotic rhyme every Polish school-
child learns, 'Who are you? A little Pole', pictures, films, the
battles of Grunwald and Berezina, paintings by Matejko and
Brandt, the Winged Hussars,* and the photographs on the
chest of drawers. Gradually I became aware that Lisów had
existed in real time, that it had a genuine, tangible dimension:
the apples in the orchard weren't black and white and could be
eaten, the sun shone, and the trees were stirred by the wind,
real wind that you could feel on your face and under your
unbuttoned shirt. And the same was true of Lisów, Kiev, the
battles of Cedynia, La Rochelle and Saratoga. The existence of
history, meaning the recurrent nature of beings and events
that at the same time were constantly changing – what a
discovery!

History was filtered through objects. At first hesitantly and
rather mysteriously, then faster and faster, broader and deeper,
in waves, as boundless as the sea. But I think it all started with
the signet ring.

I remember it like a chapter cut out of a bigger book: in the
light, in that warm light of the big room in the house in Oliwa,
before the old lampshades made of raffia baskets turned
bottom to the ceiling were replaced with Japanese crêpe-paper
lanterns, in that warm, capricious light that laid itself on the
furniture and books in a thick layer of speckled gold, my

grandfather let me into a secret whose nature would remain a mystery to me for many years to come.

From an old cardboard Twinings tea box my underground-resistance-fighter, partisan-in-the-forest grandfather first tipped out some buttons, then removed a ball of cotton wool, and finally, after reverently unrolling it on the table, he extricated a large signet ring.

And how am I to describe the complex, hazy emotions that in those spots of speckled light suddenly swirled in my childish soul, which – they were shyly hinting – was actually the soul of a young nobleman?

'Here,' said my grandfather, clearing his throat again and again, as if it were the secretly repeated refrain of a banned song, 'the family crest of the Karpińskis, the Korab coat of arms, you see that? A boat with a tower and two lion heads, one on the prow...'

And there it was – a boat, with one lion head on the prow, the other on the stern, but it was a tiny boat, with another even smaller one above it.

'And on the right there's the family crest of my mother, your great-grandmother,' – how typical of his generation to specify 'my mother, your great-grandmother'; all the family photographs have captions: so and so, our paternal uncle, so and so, our great-grandfather – 'Julia née Modzelewska. The Bończa coat of arms.'

Seeing the amazed look on my face, he said it again.

'The Bończa coat of arms. A white unicorn on a blue field.'

But the signet was carved in a dark, slightly translucent stone the colour of red wine (that drink which even we, the children, had had the chance to try once in a blue moon, just a drop with dinner, served in special wine glasses, and which we didn't like one bit... but apparently there were sweet wines, which we were never given, to avoid – as Granny would say – spoiling our taste and to teach us to drink the dry ones; what a fate!).

My grandfather took the signet in two fingers, raised it to the warm glow of the lamp and silently showed me how the light shone through the dark-red stone. Whereas the stone evidently had no intention of betraying its true shades to me – the gold of the ship and the white of the unicorn; but I solemnly believed in my grandfather's words, for they were like the fragments of a beautiful epic poem, scattered long ago, that suddenly I longed to learn.

From a second box of buttons my grandfather reverently removed a dark, glossy little stick of sealing wax, said 'Sealing wax', let me touch and sniff it, and finally, after turning it over the lighted stub of a candle, dripped a few seething drops onto a small piece of card that came from a box of German chocolates and then crushed them with the signet.

We both watched in awe, as from the remote past – which, I later realised, was the past of only two generations – the regular, beautifully imprinted, double shape of the twin cartouches appeared, in a whirl of mantling and peacock feathers.

I looked at my grandfather. In a halo of feudal gold, forlornly he wrapped the signet in its ball of cotton wool, put it back in the Twinings tea box, sprinkled some buttons on top and put it away in the drawer. But the gold had slipped out, spilling slivers onto the floor.

🌺

From then on I kept coming across scraps of former splendour. Part of an amethyst necklace... 'Grandmama Wanda always spoke of amethysts with disdain. She kept them in the drawers of her escritoire, mixed with moonstones, rock crystals, malachites, garnets and all the jumble that we gradually sold during the war just to get by. And this one... this one was from a complete set of amethysts, Grandmama got it before a ball during Grandpapa's first bankruptcy, when he couldn't afford anything better...' Large volumes of nineteenth-century musical scores, signed on the first page in elegant Cyrillic 'M. de Sicard, Kiev', salt cellars, teaspoons and fans.

And finally my great-great-grandmother's sunken dinner service.

The stifling atmosphere of the start of a name-day party was whirring around us. Granny was bustling about in the kitchen, setting out bowls of turkey in Malaga wine with one hand, and pinning a cameo brooch at her throat with the other, while at the same time issuing orders with truly Napoleonic mastery: 'And you, darling, get on the stool, but take the cushion off it first or you'll slip and go flying, that's right, set it beside the cupboard and reach up to the top storage space. That's it. Open the bolt. And fetch me out a large platter, please.'

Before my eyes appeared a scene of waters receding after a flood. Lying one on another in the dark depths of the top shelf were the bloated white bodies of plates, vases and sauce boats, with the varicoloured veins of cracks and patterns drawn on their pale skin.

'What's this? It's part of Grandmama's dinner service. English. For twenty-four people, nineteenth-century faience. Hand-painted. Somehow the NKVD man didn't take it, but lots of it got broken – oh, you see, here's a sauce boat with no handle, and this is chipped...' – reverently I touched the blue, plaited convolvulus winding around the plates and on the belly of a vase – 'and that's Ćmielów porcelain, oh, pass that one down, the ham will look good on it.'

There in the darkness of the top cupboard lay the torpid hulks of vessels rotting away in solitude, coated in the barnacles of chipped designs and the algae of twisted cutlery. If objects have a posthumous life, their souls had most definitely gone to some other world, where, *da capo al fine*, they had never stopped living the years of their Kiev, Morawica and Lisów past.

I handed her the Ćmielów platter, and once I had stroked the stems of the convolvulus again, gone blue from being forgotten, I locked and bolted the top cupboard, stepped down from the stool, replaced the cushion and set about carefully laying slices of ham on the painted bouquets of roses.

V

After Kiev, after Mnin, which fell apart in the Brokls' hands, after Morawica, abandoned because of Grandmama Wanda's hysteria, the Brokls settled at Lisów, which – why hide the fact? – was a godforsaken hole. But Wanda, who in her heart of hearts thought of her husband as the Duke de Broglie, was determined to resurrect the splendours of old at Lisów, and took it upon herself as a point of honour to organise a party on a ducal scale.

She walked about the entire manor house – not that there was much walking to do – with a sense of mission in her eyes, overseeing the cleaning of the silver and the polishing of the wine glasses, supervising the girls who were peeling almonds and slicing figs; she stirred the pots, tried the dishes, racked her brains over the seating plan for the guests, arranged the flowers. She did the work of two or three, while Grandpapa Leonard, in his typical way, went out into the garden and took deep breaths as he inspected the blossoming trees and the dark rings of tall grass.

'... because I don't know if you know, but our horse, Kubuś, was an extremely methodical horse, I suspect he was sold off from a circus, because he loved to walk in circles and do tricks, at any rate he even left his droppings in rings, or rather spirals; he'd start somewhere in the middle of the lawn, and then, leaving one bit beside another, gradually turn wider and wider circles, until finally he'd think it was just right, and start in a new spot, while the grass that grew over the old one was taller and darker than the rest... anyway, the horse came into the garden whenever he liked, to my grandmother's consternation;

the gate would be locked, but Kubuś could manage it: first he would steal up behind Grandpapa, then gently nudge him aside with his muzzle and be on his way. Then he mastered a method of opening the bolt with his teeth, or was it his lips? ... No matter. Grandpapa would be out in the garden, taking in the air, feeding the horse sugar lumps and cheerfully agreeing to the demands of his wife, who would keep running up to complain about the lack of basic items, such as a gong for calling the guests in from the garden or a suitable number of monogrammed napkin holders.'

Finally the great day came. The guests drove down from near and far, in coaches and britzkas, bowed and greeted each other, praised the artistry of the lady of the house, admired the flowers, heard the stories about the orangery at Morawica and how President Mościcki hadn't liked the taste of the melons, and so on and so forth. They walked about the garden, exchanged compliments, admired the rose bushes and the phloxes... The air was close and sultry, there was a storm gathering, the gentlemen were perspiring under their summer suits, their shirt collars were digging into their necks, the ladies were fanning themselves with their handkerchiefs and shielding themselves from the blazing sun with parasols, or sitting about in the shade on chairs courteously fetched by their husbands. Finally, a maid appeared in the window, who had been instructed to bang on the gong three times and invite the company in to supper. She appeared, banged the gong three times and screamed: 'Hey, you lot, come 'n' eat, they're servin' up.'

Grandmama Wanda stiffened, but seconds later, melting into smiles as if nothing were wrong, she had escorted the guests along the jasmine walk and stepped with them through the double door into the tidied, dusted, swept, waxed, polished and flower-bedecked manor. There was a flash of lightning and a clap of thunder, as if a higher force were absolving the bungled banging on the gong, and the ladies and gentlemen poured inside all the quicker, then followed the corridor to the drawing room, where the table was standing. From the threshold the table – or at least so it seemed to Wanda – was already glittering with glints of silver and sparks of light on the rims of the wine glasses, it was fragrant with lilac and lilies, it was groaning with dishes – even those not yet brought in – in short, it was an absolute masterpiece.

And when everyone had sat down to this masterpiece, when everyone had enthused about it, when they'd fallen silent for that short pause before each would pick up his knife and fork and set about tasting the first dish, there was a flash in the room – and through the window, left open by the servants, fell a ball of globe lightning, a sphere of electricity the size of a lamb's head. It raced around the table, jumping from one piece of cutlery to the next, from knife rest to knife rest, and then flew out via the chimney just as abruptly as it had flown in, leaving behind it the dumbstruck guests, twisted forks and spoons, scorched wine glasses, and a long black streak burned into the table and the tablecloth.

❧

In the Oliwa wardrobes, which moved house from Lisów to Siedlce, from Siedlce to Białystok,* and from Białystok to Oliwa, there are still the remains of lightning-twisted knives and forks lying about at random, stamped with the interwoven letters WLB. Since that sultry evening heralding a storm, so many balls of lightning have blasted through Mitteleuropa that nothing is left of that day but a few bits of metal and the lasting belief that the party was a failure, whose guests had gone off home sooner than expected.

Sometimes, as I've been gazing at my cold, northern city from the top of one of its hills, which start just beyond Granny's garden, I've had the impression that it is charred at the edges too, that from under the layers of Polish plaster and paint it smells of burning too. And I'm always reminded of the innocence of lightning.

I come from a family in which the women are proud, stubborn and strong – and Grandmama Wanda doesn't come out at all pale by comparison. So it's no surprise that after her first, unsuccessful attempt she made another, and a year later a second grand party was held at Lisów. Once again Wanda ran about the house, once again Grandpapa Leonard took deep breaths in the garden, once again Wanda made plans and fetched things in – though the gong had survived, they had to get new festive cutlery – and once again her husband gave her the money and inspected the flowering jasmine.

Finally, the memorable day came. The weather was like glass, the air was crisp and transparent, and nothing presaged another storm – the guests strolled about in the midday breeze, enjoying the sun and the rustling leaves. The table was set with just as much dazzling artistry – by the standards of the Polish provinces, of course – as the year before. The silverware, glasses, bouquets in jardinières, napkins, candles and little name cards were all waiting in perfect order and dazzling brilliance for the ladies and gentlemen. The maid appeared in the window and just banged the gong three times – for Grandmama Wanda had decided everyone would recognise that on its own as an unmistakable summons to dinner – why run the risk of linguistic slips by the servants?

There on the threshold stood Wanda Broklowa, offering her hand to be kissed by the gentlemen and making discreet bows to the ladies, as she invited them all inside. And once they had all gone in, she closed the door, walked down the long vestibule, and entered the drawing room.

The table did not exist. Instead, in a swirl of flowers, dishes, crumpled cloths and broken glass stood a large, melancholy cow, chewing the hors d'oeuvres *extraordinaires*. Next to it, wallowing in all sorts of goodies were a sow and three piglets. The horse, who had – as horses are wont to do – thoughtlessly left the garden gate open behind him, allowing this entire primitive rabble to get inside through the French windows, was proudly strolling about the orchard, not even deigning to glance towards the manor.

The guests stood dumbstruck against the walls. The ladies fanned themselves feverishly, the gentlemen twirled their moustaches with an uncertain gesture. They were asked to step into the garden, where they were hastily served those dishes that hadn't yet been carried into the drawing room – but, admittedly had gone a little cold while the servants were chasing the piglets about the house.

As you can guess, that was Grandmama Wanda's final grand gathering. From then on she preferred intimate tea parties for a narrow circle of friends.

❧

All this, including the lightning and the livestock frolicking in the lettuce, might seem like a rural idyll, but in those days the Kielce vicinity wasn't a safe one.

For the Resurrection Mass and the New Year people shoot into the air, because the world is being born anew, it's young and weak, with no exoskeleton, and the devils have easy access to it. Things were similar for young Poland, attacked by the Bolsheviks from one direction, by West European corporations from another, and by the Bull and his gang from a third.

The Bull and his gang used to prowl about the neighbourhood, and it wasn't innocent prowling, such as walking off with a cow or having a brawl in a corner shop, the prowling typical of Lisów's traditional thieves, but out-and-out brutal banditry. Not surprisingly, when Valerian arrived from Kielce, from Mrs Wolgemut's apartment, to join his wife and in-laws, he walked down the middle of the road with a pistol in each hand, just like John Wayne.

And at this point I'd like to tell the story of the Bull and his gang, but that can't be done without first telling the tale of Redhead Henio, the Bull of my childhood.

For years on end Granny – a great lover of flowers, brilliant at arranging bouquets and designing gardens so that yellow forsythia would bloom beside white cherry plums, and the blue-and-pink striped American irises (known as pyjamas) would border the clumps of darker Siberian irises – had not just a garden in front of her house, but also a so-called 'State Forests worker's allotment' a short walk away. But the worker's allotment brought her a lot of bother too, because in the communist era the council insisted on the planting of a set quota of specific root and leaf vegetables, while Granny grew nothing but bee balm, globeflowers, asters and delphiniums; worse yet, she allowed herself other extravagances, failing to hoe every bare patch between the parsley and the lettuce, as the other allotment keepers dutifully did, but leaving the grass to grow in peace between the rhododendrons and astilbes. Eventually the two sides came to certain compromises, and Granny planted the edges of the beds with sorrel, just as if it were box, and elsewhere she made a hedge of currant bushes. From spring to autumn she weeded, pruned, watered and fertilised, with my grandfather helping her as much as he could; for although she let him water and fertilise, when it came to weeding, she didn't exactly rate his talents very highly.

'Zygmuś? Zygmuś isn't fit for it. If I say: "Zygmunt, pull out that goutweed over there, but be careful not to damage the berberis", he's sure to show me the ripped-out berberis like this, triumphantly, and say: "You're not going to tell me *this* is berberis, are you?" '

After my grandfather's death Granny still went to the allotment, but her heart was like a toy with a flat battery, and she had less and less strength to dig a plot or weed the peonies. Of course, she ambled about among the beds and cut flowers for her arrangements: tall delphiniums; aconites – she told me it was an extract from their leaves that was used to poison Socrates; 'Judas' pennies' or honesty, those strange plants that grew little green discs, in the autumn they went grey and you could shell them, revealing the silver petals; jasmine, which caused a headache if you left it in your bedroom overnight; and many, many other flowers. But for all this to emerge from the ground, to produce leaves, put out buds, blossom and bear seeds, one after another in turn, from the snowdrops to the narcissi, tulips, irises, peonies, delphiniums and nasturtiums all the way through to the autumn crocuses, for none of these plants to die, someone had to be hired.

And that was how Oktawian came to us, the common-law husband (Granny sometimes said: 'morganatic husband') of Madzia.

Oktawian arrived, picked up a spade and said: 'This has blooming well got to be dug, because if it ain't blooming well dug before the winter, it never blooming well will be.' He was paid the going rate per hour, on top of which, after a hard day's work he was given a glass of brandy wine. ('Mama,' said my sensible mother, 'there's really no point in giving Oktawian the decent cognac that we buy specially for you to have now and then for your heart when you feel unwell. I've bought some brandy wine – Oktawian won't know the difference anyway.') In parallel, Madzia (with her canny mind) kept coming to see us, bringing good milk every day, or maybe every other day, from a farmer at the marketplace in Oliwa; sometimes she left vodka to hide it from Oktawian, and took the opportunity to do some gossiping, if Granny let her get a word in edgeways.

Oliwa was – and still is – a district where two separate worlds existed side by side. On the one hand you could meet charming old ladies there, 'born of the gentry', as Granny would say, distinguished old fellows, and students trying to look like worthy young intellectuals (whatever that is supposed to mean). On the other hand, you could get a stone or a padlock thrown at your head, observe the gentlemen at the round-the-clock buffet under a chestnut tree or hear the shouts from a drinking den. Once upon a time the latter world was more widely repre-sented in Oliwa, and Granny was asked at work: 'You live in Oliwa? What have you got there, Helena, a brothel or a shebeen?' 'A brothel *and* a shebeen,' Granny would reply, for what else could she say?

But in those days the local hooligans and bandits had their own code of honour, their own laws and their own alderman; some twenty years ago, when my grandfather died, one of these picturesque local dignitaries (little hat, overcoat, bulbous nose and a tumour on the jaw) came up to Granny in the street, stood to attention, bowed and said: 'We've heard about your misfortune, madam, and we'd like to offer our deepest condolences.'

And it was these people whom Madzia knew the best; it was from her that we learnt about all the romances, carousals, bloodbaths and other scandals. One time we were even lucky enough to hear a truly shocking psychological novel in episodes (every two days, arriving with the bottle of milk), the story of Oktawian's pal Mr Gruszkiewicz, who had decided to drink himself to death because no one loved him.

'It's not surprising,' says Madzia, her prominent teeth dancing to the rhythm of her words like two rows of yellow ballerinas in *Swan Lake*. 'His children have moved away, his wife's dead and the man's unhappy, all alone in the world. And he's got no legs. So he says to my Oktawian: "Here's some cash, enough for some vodka and a funeral. I'm going to drink, and you bring me the vodka till I die." '

Every other day we heard a grisly report: 'Gruszkiewicz has been drinking for a week', 'Gruszkiewicz isn't getting up', 'Gruszkiewicz is delirious', and finally 'Gruszkiewicz is dead'.

Gruszkiewicz was dead, and Oktawian wasn't feeling too great either; it looked as if he'd been taking the odd nip with Gruszkiewicz, or maybe at the wake – in any case, one day it was he who brought us the milk, but he tripped on the front step and broke his leg. As he was already quite an age and had a fair amount of alcohol in his system, the break didn't heal properly, and in the meantime Granny's allotment was inexorably invaded by weeds. And that was when Redhead Henio appeared on the horizon. Or rather reappeared.

'Are you looking for someone to do the digging?' asked Mrs Hibner, stopping at the edge of the path and shaking her hoary head. 'Redhead Henio is just out of prison. His wife has banished him from the house, so he's homeless, poor chap. He's nowhere to sleep. I'm sure he'd willingly do the work, especially if he could live in your hut for the summer until he finds himself a place.'

Mrs Hibner, who from early youth to the age of eighty had worked as a paramedic, and had given cupping therapy and injections to our entire family for the past thirty years, evidently believed in her kindly way that anyone with no occupation was very eager to have one.

'Well,' said Granny, 'let's give it a try. Would you please ask him to come and see me next time you run into him?'

My sensible mother was not enthralled by this prospect.

'Mama,' she protested, 'I'm not sure Redhead Henio is the best idea. Heaven knows what might enter his head – he might do you harm…'

'Redhead Henio? Do me harm?' asked Granny in disbelief. 'I've known him since he was so high,' – she sliced the air with an outspread palm somewhere at hip level – 'since he was five years old. I remember it very well – I was on my way home from the radio along Kwietna Street… no, Liczmański, going up the hill, and there was that little boy, crying. He comes up to me and goes: "Boohoo, give me two zlotys, Missus, boohoo, my dad'll tan me, boohoo, 'cos he give me two zloty to get me brother a dummy and boohoo, I lost it." So Missus gave it to him. By the time I got home, Paweł was back from school, I told him about it, and he laughed at me for letting myself be fleeced by Redhead Henio, the crafty little kid from Liczmański Street. Aha, I thought, he who laughs last laughs longest. A week later I was on my way back from the radio again, the little boy came up to me again and said: "Boohoo, give me two zlotys, Missus, boohoo", etcetera. And I leaned down, looked him in the eyes and said: "Do you know who I am?" ' – at this point Granny adopted the tone of the High Priest in *Forefather's Eve** – ' "I'm Paweł's mum." All those little boys had great respect for Paweł because he was so good at fighting. He was held in very high regard. So at once Redhead Henio replied:

"You should have said so in the first place." But he didn't return the two zlotys.'

After that, Redhead Henio had continued to come and go in Granny's life. One time he brought her a stolen rubber plant, another time he defended Paweł from some yobs when they accused him of attacking them by setting a dog on them. ''E attacked you?' asked Henio. 'Eh? The dog bit through its lead to defend 'im, and you're saying 'e attacked you? I'll give you some good advice – you take back that charge. And if you don't, the clay pits in Oliwa are deep.' And then he suddenly vanished. Not like before, for a month or two, but for ten years.

And ten years on, he was back in front of Granny again.

''Ere we are,' said Redhead Henio, standing in the doorway with Fatso.

'What do you mean, "we"?'

'Me and Fatso. You wanted someone for your allotment, right? I don't work without Fatso.'

And indeed, he worked with Fatso, that is, Fatso did the digging, while Henio pointed a finger. They both set up home in the summer house, ''cos you see, Mrs Karpińska, you gotta have somewhere to live, eh?' Fatso dug among the raspberry bushes, and destroyed them, weeded the irises and destroyed them, and dug up the tulip bulbs, destroying them too. Whatever he didn't see to, he trod on while seeing to something else.

Meanwhile, Henio sunned himself.

'Henio,' Granny asked him one day in the most direct of her tones, 'what exactly were you in prison for?'

Scratching his belly, Henio shifted his gaze from Fatso digging to the blue of the sky and said: 'Hee hee, Mrs Karpińska, hee hee, they don't give you ten years for stealing, you know.'

But with time Fatso did less and less digging, and Henio did more and more drinking; Fatso clearly came to envy him, and now they both drank. On top of that, various pals, male and female, started moving in with them, drunks, drug addicts, shabby-looking ladies of easy virtue, and so on. Not surprisingly, the other allotment keepers began to fulminate against the noise, the thieving and the scattered bottles, until finally my mother took the decision to evict Redhead Henio, Fatso and the gang. She took my father with her, they drove to Oliwa, went to the allotment and categorically demanded that the summer house must be vacated, all the more since they had never officially given either Henio or Fatso, not to mention Boozy or Floozy, permission to live there.

Three times more they drove there and presented their demands, first together, then just Mum, and then Mum and Granny. It wasn't much use. Each time Redhead Henio solemnly promised that he was just about to move out, and either did nothing, or moved out and came back; meanwhile new bottles glistened in the flowerbeds, the stink behind the summer house worsened, and on its wall the black stain made by an electric heater they'd hung on a nail grew bigger.

'I thought I was going to explode,' said my mother indignantly one day. 'I was in Oliwa today, and I took Granny to the allotment. On the way we ran into Redhead Henio and Fatso, busy hauling an old TV set out of a dustbin – it had no casing, it was a total piece of junk. "What are you doing?" I asked, and Redhead Henio said they were taking it away from the allotment because they were moving out. Like hell, I thought, because they were carrying it in the opposite direction, but never mind, I told them they had to get out today, otherwise I'd call the police. "But Mrs Dehnel, we can't, because my mate 'ere's got a bad knee and 'e can't walk." "So why's he carrying a TV set?" I asked, then I said: "Anyway, I really don't care, you're to take all your things away and clean up, because I'm certainly not going to touch your filthy rubbish." "Makes you sick, does it?" "Yes, I'm afraid of catching a nasty disease, AIDS or something." "Oh no," said Henio, "you're beautiful but you're so unkind…"'

That was an error of judgement on Henio's part, as I knew well. Just a quick glance at my mother with her lips clenched and her eyes blazing was enough to tell you to drop that sort of an argument, but plainly Henio was no great connoisseur of human nature. I deeply regret that I wasn't there with Mum at the time, and didn't see her hurling abuse at Henio like a winged Fury; it doesn't happen often, but when it does, it's apocalyptic – neither Berma,* Anjelica Huston nor Mae West are a patch on her.

❧

Of course the story doesn't end with Mrs Dehnel – so beautiful but so unkind – and her fit of fury.

'I told them for once and for all,' Granny announced one day, as she bit into a slice of cheesecake from 'the count's daughter' (because the patisserie is run by Mrs X, née Y, another one born of the gentry).

'Them, meaning whom?'

'Redhead Henio. I went inside, and they were all lounging about in there, with some woman again, watching television…'

'I knew it. I knew they'd drag that TV set in there. "My mate's got a bad knee" – the hell he has! They're furnishing the place. Like newly-weds.'

'…watching television, and I came in and said: "What on

earth has got into your heads? You're to get out of here today. Be off with you!" And to make my point, I gave the television a big thump. But it was so old that it shot out a shower of sparks, something went hiss, and it died. What a fine entrance I made!'

'And then what?'

'That was it. I just put down the drops and left.'

'What drops?'

'Eye drops,' said Granny in a tone implying that it was obvious.

'Eye drops?' Mum gave Granny a searching look, as she raised a piece of cheesecake to her mouth. 'What eye drops?'

'Well, you know,' said Granny, trying to sound as casual as possible, 'that other fellow has trouble with his eyes, so I brought them some drops... after all, they are human...'

'Mama! They've taken over your summer house, they've done nothing, if you don't count the damage, the whole allotment is covered in rubbish, there are bottles all over the place, all sorts of filth and pestilence, druggies and whores... it's going to be the most popular drinking den in all Oliwa soon. And you take them eye drops! The world is coming to an end. You order them to get out and you bring them eye drops!'

'Ania...'

'Don't "Ania" me! Everyone's sick and tired of those crooks, and rightly so. There are rumours they're stealing and vandalising the other allotments. I wouldn't put it past that scumbag to stick a knife in you, Mama.'

'Don't be silly, it's just Redhead Henio. What on earth can he do to me? I've known him since he was so high...' – Granny measures off half a metre with her hand – '... and he's been swindling me ever since? Naaaah!'

'But Mama,' pleaded the wisest of all mothers, 'he's a thug, and you can't take chances with people like that.'

'I know how to deal with "people like that", as you put it. I am from Lisów, and Lisów is a bandit village. For centuries. A place of banditry and honour.'

'But Mama,' said the wariest of mothers, refusing to give in, 'that was before the war. Sixty or seventy years ago. Not now. People are different, bandits are different. They have no sense of honour. They're completely devoid of principles. That sort of person has no scruples about strangling you or dealing you a backhand blow.'

'Oh yeah? Is that so?' – at this point Granny flared up in her charming, quite inimitable way – 'Well, let me tell you something. When I was a very small child...'

'Mama!'

'We know,' I chipped in from out of shot.

'... a very small child,' said Granny, raising her voice, 'we had the most terrifying brigands prowling about in Lisów. There were plenty of criminals around there, because they'd be released from Holy Cross and settle in the district. Not just cut-throats, but political prisoners too...'

'Thanks to which,' I interrupted her, 'the peasants were exceptionally, quite exceptionally intelligent, they were tremendous thieves and they loathed the police, so they resolved any conflict among themselves. With axes.'

'Quite so. But it was after the first war that they prowled about like that. After he came to Poland, a couple of years later... about two or three years later... whenever he had to go somewhere far beyond the village, my father would walk about with a loaded pistol in each hand...'

'Just like John Wayne.'

'... just like John Wayne. Or Gary Cooper. So. It was very dangerous, but the worst of all was the Bull's gang... well, I'm not sure you could call it a gang, there were two of them, sometimes three. I know the ringleader was called the Bull, because once I was in my teens, I found some newspapers from that era in the attic, in which their exploits were described. They had several lives on their conscience – on the very day they appeared at Lisów they had killed an old woman in the next village. Or maybe she died of heart failure when they threatened her with a pistol? I can't remember. In any case, I was tiny, and as I know from my mother's account, I was lying in my cradle in the next room. My grandfather was working in his study.'

'Mama, we know this story by heart…'

'And what if you do?' The direct manner of this sort of question temporarily removes the potential for argument, so we didn't interfere in the flow of her narrative again. 'Grandfather was working in his study. It must have been summer, because it was harvest time, everyone was out in the fields, and the village was utterly deserted. And suddenly, on the dot of noon, those thugs invaded the manor house, the Bull and his accomplice, and set about rifling all the cupboards, brandishing their pistols… On a corner of the table, as Mama and Grandmama showed me afterwards, on the corner of this large oak table they piled up their booty: silver, jewellery and watches. They raked through private documents, gutted desk drawers and screamed like banshees. They kicked open the door into Grandpapa's study, but Grandpapa simply looked up from his papers, reached into his inside jacket pocket, took out his cigarette case and said…'

'Would you bandit fellows care for a cigarette?' cried Mama and I in chorus.

'… and of course they had no objections,' continued Granny, undaunted. 'The sidekick went on looting, piling it all on the corner of the drawing-room table, while the Bull sat himself down and had a smoke, having first requisitioned Grandpapa's silver cigarette case, watch and banknotes. And then my

mother, whom I cannot forgive to this very day, slid the feeble
bolt on the door of the little room where I was sleeping and
sneaked out of the house by the back door – you know that my
mother always ran instead of walking, and all the more so then
– she ran to the alarm bell and started ringing it like mad.
Everyone raised their heads from the corn and dashed towards
the village, while the bandits were off like the wind, in their
panic leaving everything they'd piled on the corner of the table.
Not long after, they were caught and given very high sentences…
but you know, I simply can't forgive Mama for leaving me
behind, because they could easily have got into my room with
a single kick at the door, and that would have been the end of
me. I had dreams about it for years after, as vivid as a real
memory: the nails falling one by one, the bolt snapping and the
bandits forcing their way in, removing me from the cradle…
ugh, even now I've got shivers down my spine at the mere
thought of it.'

Lisów was the greatest bandit village on earth. This was
because – as mentioned earlier – in his wisdom, the tsar of All
the Russias had established a famous jail at nearby Holy Cross,
where prisoners from all over the Russian Empire were locked
up, both criminal and political. And once they had served their
lengthy sentences, for their remaining years they often settled
in the area and took up a profession, which they had learnt
either while still at liberty or in jail. There were blacksmiths
and carpenters, cobblers and stove fitters, with Hungarian,
Lithuanian, Russian and Armenian surnames, and they all took
up with local lasses or widows, they had children with them,
and those children had their own children, and so it continued
through the generations. Intelligence was inherited from the

political prisoners, and a lawless streak – and their famous sense of honour – from the criminals, because these were still the honourable felons of the nineteenth century, who had a code almost as complex as the chivalric code, and certainly just as conscientiously observed.

'One time a peasant stole all the cabbages belonging to an orphan – there was this orphan girl, you see, who had nothing but a shack by the road and a cabbage patch, and you see he crept up in the middle of the night with a knife and cut off the heads of all the cabbages... when the other peasants found out about it, which happened quickly because the girl went wailing around the entire village, they held a meeting at the corner shop, a whole committee – because going to the police was a terrible stain on their honour – and they searched one cottage after another until they found the cut-off cabbages at that blackguard's place. Then they gave him such a thrashing that he couldn't get out of bed for three weeks, while his wife looked after him. Next day I arrive at the shop, which was a debating club and a tavern as well as a trading point, and one chap says to me: "We gave him a right tanning, the rascal! 'Why couldn't you go to the priest,' I says to him, 'and not the orphan? Why couldn't you go to the manor, you cur, and not to the orphan?'" And I interrupt to say: "No, he couldn't have gone to the manor, because there aren't any cabbages there." How those peasants laughed – it was quite remarkable; at once I felt accepted as one of their own, and then one of them said in a tone of the highest approval: "Miss Lala's got a rare sense of privilege, she don't turn her nose up, or put on airs." They were very good people, you see. Grandmama Wanda was horrified by the thieving. She remembered the peasants in the Ukraine who never took other people's things. She always used to tell how one day they were driving to the next estate when the branch of a fruit tree, heavy with ripe, sticky greengages, hit their coach-man in the face. "You should eat them," Grandmama told him from behind her veil, "seeing they're pushing themselves into your mouth." "I didn't plant them," he replied, "so I'm not going to eat them." But when it came to real trouble, they were cut-throats, whereas our peasants defended us against the Soviets.'

'I know, Granny, I know, I've heard it all before. I know that one time they stole something from you, you called the police, and suddenly the whole village that had always loved you and called you Lalunia blocked you like a stone wall...'

'Indeed it did. They all came and stood outside the manor house, surrounding the policeman and glaring at me, until finally I gave up and didn't lodge a complaint. And then I heard this long drawn-out "pheeeew..." The peasants relaxed, the thief relaxed, and even I relaxed.'

'I know.'

'And have you heard about the lovely fabric my Grandmama Wanda had, white piqué with a black pattern? There was a roll of it standing in the wardrobe, and now and then Granny would open the wardrobe doors to see if it had dwindled. And when my mother died, we wanted to make something out of it, because the war was on, and we couldn't get decent material for mourning clothes. So we opened the wardrobe, and fetched out the roll, but it was just wrapped in fabric, with newspapers stuffed inside. The work of Gienia, the maid. Of course she wouldn't admit it, but she was a dreadful thief, and a very cunning one too. But I've nothing against her – Aunt Ewa did her so much harm, filling her head with all that anarchist nonsense. Gienia spent all day sitting in her room, underneath those gargoyles, masks and pictures...'

'Granny, I know, but the point is that Lisów was Lisów, and Henio is Henio. And we have to get rid of him.'

'Well, maybe you're right, we must,' agreed Granny with a heavy heart.

❧

Finally, we did as we'd been advised: we lured Henio out of the summer house and fitted a padlock. When he broke the lock and went inside, it became official breaking and entering, and we could call the police. The police kicked out Henio and Co., and my mother doused the cabin in Lysol, firstly to disinfect it, and secondly to discourage further potential lodgers.

And then Henio did something that Granny couldn't forgive. As a parting shot he asked if he could use the phone, and he called the police to grass on a pal. Granny went red with rage and said: 'Shame on you. I am from a bandit village and I fully understand, but the thieves there had a sense of honour. If anyone had informed on an associate he'd be compromised for the rest of his life. Get out. I don't want to set eyes on you again. Never. You're not to cross the threshold of this house.'

❧

But that wasn't Granny's last encounter with Redhead Henio. In the spring, when the Lysol had cleared a little, the snowdrops were out, and after a severe bout of flu Granny made her first expedition to the corner shop, as if on cue Redhead Henio sprang out of the cobblestones of Liczmański Street, ran up to her and, without a word, raised his hands to her neck and seized the ends of her scarf.

'Mrs Karpińska,' he said, 'I 'eard you was ill, you've only just come out of the 'ouse, but you ain't wrapped your throat properly – do you want to catch cold again?'

VI

After shrewdly renting out Morawica, which soon mysteriously changed owner, Grandpapa Leonard was in fact a little worried, but at once he saw the next deal of a lifetime on the horizon, which, like every one of his pre-planned business deals, was a quite stunning flop. Beguiled by the magic lure of millions, right in the middle of currency reforms he insisted on selling the land at Lisów to the peasants, and on placing the gigantic sums secured through the sale in stocks and shares, in which, as we know, he had plentiful, but mixed, experience. In fairness to the family I should add that everyone advised him against it, with Aunt Ewa clamouring that this time he really should be declared legally unsound; in fact it was an old idea that had first hatched in her mind when Grandpapa Leonard leased Morawica.

'But my mother said' – here Granny's voice resonates with pride – '"You lot can do as you wish, but Lisów is officially mine. If Father wants to sell it off, he can go ahead, after all, it's his estate." And she refused to declare him legally unsound. As a result, Grandpapa sold off Lisów, all the more since the peasants seemed strangely keen on this deal and strangely rich, so quick as a flash all the land, apart from a few scraps including a hill, a soggy meadow and a morgen or two here and there, passed into new hands. Fait accompli.' (Granny always said this phrase in grand style, like a Russian prince in Monte Carlo over the roulette table.) 'Grandpapa happily minded his millions, but a week later, as inflation continued its rapid rise, he could only buy a box of matches with them. After the war, when the communists arrived and spoke of land distribution, the peasants said: "Land distribution? Ha ha, the squire did our land distribution twenty years ago!"

'Grandpapa gradually went gaga. He often sat with Uncle Maciej, examining tiny flies, ladybirds or earwigs. One time my father arrived from Kielce, and found much lamenting. The lure of millions had worked its magic on Grandpapa again, and he had sold a whole cartload of pictures, books, lacquer screens, chairs, etchings and knick-knacks to a junk dealer. My father fetched a peasant and his cart, and they caught up with the dealer: a poor, balding Jew, who, why hide it?' – here a note of deep sorrow sounds in Granny's philo-Semitic soul – 'had fooled the old man and was pleased he'd make a tidy sum. "This is what you paid," said Papa, "and this is for your trouble. Now please give the stuff back." "I bought it all from the old gentleman, I paid him for it." He started to squabble, shouting insults and threatening to call the police. "The police?" said my father. "What an excellent idea, let's call them right away. That's a capital solution because I am a lawyer, and I'm fully aware of what you'll get for cheating a man of advanced age." And the dealer backed down. My father returned his money, added a small sum, told him to shift the things onto the cart and turned for home, tinted gold by the setting sun, as proud as Agamemnon. And there sat Grandpapa Leonard in an armchair, sleeping the sleep of the just.'

❧

That was exactly how Granny remembered him – an elderly gentleman with white hair, who would go into his room, fix his gaze on his granddaughter and calmly say: 'Come on, you stinker, out of my armchair, your grandpa wants to sit down.'

Through the windows they can see the garden, and Kubuś chewing the grass. A farmhand comes in from the fields and washes his hands in a barrel. In Grandmama Wanda's room the girls from the village are making mobiles out of straw and coloured tissue paper to have something to decorate the house in winter before the Christmas holiday.

❧

And then Grandpapa Leonard died. With his black eyes, swarthy complexion and white hair, carefully arranged in the style of a marble bust. And the goddess Fortuna, who had taken care of Grandpapa Leonard throughout his variable life, casting him from the heights of her wheel into the depths, and from the depths back up to the heights, there and then decided, in her typically capricious way, for no apparent reason to take care of his granddaughter, my granny. She flapped her gilded wings, whirled her spoked wheel, flew down from clouds of whipped cream and set a star of propitious fortune on my grandmother's brow.

VII

In the meantime, Valerian Karnaukhov learnt Polish well enough to have his solicitor's diploma validated, got a job at the Revenue and Customs Office, and moved his family from Lisów to Kielce. His family meaning his wife, Irena, and daughter, Lala (officially his step-daughter). Because Romusia, Great-Grandmother Irena's daughter from her first marriage, lived separately with her husband and only came on visits.

❧

I'm pushing a trolley around the supermarket, choosing yogurts, steaks and olives, and Margot's here with me.

'You know what,' she says, at the powdered-soup section, 'at the flat I've moved into…'

'Eh?'

'…there are ghosts.'

'That's great,' I say, without batting an eyelid, because Margot is one of those people who take a respectful approach to the essence of the world and have broad, irrational horizons, thanks to which one can hold a conversation with her without superfluous phrases such as 'oh, but that's not possible' or 'aargh, how terrifying'. 'Do you happen to know whose?'

'Yes, because it was my aunt and uncle's flat. Their daughter inherited it from them, and now she rents it out.'

'And were you fond of them?'

'Very. And they liked me too.'

'So what else?'

'Nothing, we talk to each other.'

'That's great, they'll look after you.'

'You think so?'

'Sure. Ghosts like those are an asset. Have I ever told you about Romusia, my grandmother's sister?'

'No.'

'My grandmother... Fancy some chocolate? This kind, with the bubbles? White or milk?'

'Milk.'

'My grandmother had a beloved half-sister, Romusia. And Romusia had tuberculosis. Or to put it another way, my grandmother and a nasty illness both had Romusia – and the illness won. Romusia caught it in her youth from their mother, and with wavering fortunes got better and worse again – it went on for years. During the first war she survived the siege of Kalisz, where there was dreadful cold and hunger, and from then on she just declined. She married a doctor who loved her very much and did what he could to save her.'

'Did she?'

'Did she what?'

'Love him?'

'Probably not all that much. Granny hated him, because one time they came on a visit from Warsaw and she heard them quarrelling in a locked room. Roma shouted "How can you treat me like that?" and Granny thought she said: "How can you beat me like that?" She imagined him behind that door hitting Romusia, punching her with his great big fists. And she hated him. He'd bring her chocolates, but she'd scatter them on the floor and stamp on them; he'd bring her a doll and she'd throw it out of the window. But he probably wasn't all that bad. For the modest bequest he got from an uncle, he sent Roma to Italy for a cure. She went, and there she met a young consumptive, with whom she fell in love. She kept putting off her return, but then the young man died, and she came back heartbroken.

They treated her as best they could, but as they were generally clueless, the therapy was constantly being changed. For instance, she had to eat five dozen raw eggs a day; there was even a photograph of her lying in bed with a pile of egg shells... the Bolsheviks burned it in the fireplace, like most of the photos... but everyone hoped it would work. After all, her mother lived with consumption for twenty years. It's true she spent more than half the year in mountain sanatoria and was only home once in a blue moon, it's true they gave her a so-called barrel-organ...'

'A barrel-organ?'

'It's an operation: the sick lung was rolled up, like on a crank handle, to lessen its surface area. Few people survived it, but my great-grandmother did; she'd been forecast an early death, but she lasted with that ligated lung until halfway through the war, about fifteen years.'

'What about Romusia?'

'I'm just coming to that. Everyone hoped she'd get better. Until one night my granny, who was then about four years old, was woken by the sound of her mother weeping terribly. She slid out of bed, and on her tiny little feet she toddled towards the corridor. And what did she see? Her father was sitting on the bed, cuddling her mother, who couldn't stop crying, and was fitfully gasping: "This... grey, grey figure came... it stood in the doorway and said: Romusia has only a year to go... a year to live... she's going to die... on such and such a day... that's less than a year..." And he went on cuddling and hugging her, telling her over and over that it was just a dream, and hugged her again, and kissed the tears from her cheeks; a big, bald, bearded man, kissing the tears from her cheeks... But he wouldn't have been himself, he wouldn't have been the organised, rational, conscientious solicitor Valerian Karnaukhov if he hadn't written the date on a slip of paper and hidden it under

Roma, Valerian, Lala and Irena in the garden in Kielce, c. 1924.

the papers in his desk drawer. And not quite a year later, when my great-grandmother received a telegram from Warsaw telling her to come at once because Roma had declined, she knew it would be their very last encounter. The prediction was right to the very day.'

'There are fewer people over there.'

'But look how full their baskets are. Oh well, all right, better stay here. Anyway, my grandmother was five at the time, and she missed Romusia like crazy. And Romusia came to see her every night in her dreams. She'd talk, play with dolls, and after a while she'd be off. "They're waiting for me there," she'd say, "they only let me come and see you for five minutes. But I'll be back again tomorrow." Then one day she didn't come, and Granny realised she was somewhere else by now. And that was all. So Granny grew up without her sister, and actually without her mother, who spent months on end in sanatoria in the Tatras. She only saw her a couple of times a year, at Christmas and Easter, and when the foehn wind was blowing, because the foehn wind is very bad for consumptives. But even then her mother ate and slept separately, sterilised all her cutlery and dishes on a Primus stove and wouldn't let anyone kiss her. Just think, all these years later Granny once told me: "One of my worst childhood memories is of my mother coming home from the sanatorium, so I run a long way towards her to give her a hug, but she stretches out her hands to push me away and says: Don't touch me, don't touch me."'

❧

My mother brought us up just as she was brought up by Granny, and as Granny was by my great-grandfather. Dad brought us up just as he was brought up by my grandfather, and as my grandfather was by my great-grandfather. Great-Grandfather Dehnel was a legionary, member of parliament and head of a hospital; his son first joined the cadet corps, then later became an officer and a sea captain. As a result, my dad applied power play, issued orders and met with endless mutiny on board ship.

Karnaukhov, the solicitor, used to negotiate. 'I think you must brush your teeth,' he'd say, 'but if you can give me solid reasons supported by examples and can prove in debate that it's not necessary, then you won't have to brush them.' What's more, there were occasions, though maybe not on questions as basic as that one, when he did accept his daughter's arguments. As a result, once she had grown up, my grandmother's authority within the family was rigid, and she ran the entire house as she wished, on the principles of an enlightened absolute monarchy, whereas our mother found it far easier to exact various kinds of childish virtue from us, such as tidying up our building bricks and doing our homework.

So it's quite a surprise that my brother and I, tossed between two headwinds like a boat in an Italian baroque aria, did not grow up to be neurotic teenagers with a tendency towards generational rebellion.

There was just one issue on which my great-grandfather was intransigent, namely the question of diet. The doctors, the same ones who had told Roma to eat five dozen eggs a day, claimed that a child potentially at risk of consumption should eat first large quantities of fatty meat, then large quantities of rare steak, first this, then that.

'He'd stand over me with his belt,' says Granny, 'and tell me I couldn't leave the table until I'd eaten the steak. I'd cry and sulk, but I'd eat it. Anyway, he never actually spanked me for not eating. He only gave me a thorough hiding one single time – with no argument, no debate. I came into the house and tossed my shoes anywhere. "Put your shoes away neatly," said Papa, to which I replied: "Hanka can do it, that's what she's for." "No," said Papa, "Hanka's helping us because your mother is at the sanatorium and can't cook for us. You're to put away your shoes yourself, and don't you ever dare to say that Hanka is for anything. Now go and tell her you're sorry." "I won't." "You will." "No I won't." And then he gave me a slap. I cast him a reproachful look and solemnly said: "Go on, hit the Polish child, you Russki!" He went beserk. He took off his belt, threw me onto the bed and started to give me a real thrashing. I

screamed so loud that Hanka came flying in from the other
room and had to pull him off me.'

🌺

A Russki. I wonder how many of them there were in Kielce,
those white Russians? The solicitor Karnaukhov, his sister
Sasha, who had had enough of being a governess in the
Viennese homes of her former acquaintances and had come to
join her brother, some tsarist officials whom the abolition of
the empire had found outside its borders, some émigrés, and
refugees of various sorts.

'There were plenty of lawyers and judges. They'd come and
see my father to complain that the Polish Bar was refusing to let
them join its ranks. And Papa would nod, agree, and console
them, but once they'd gone he'd say he'd be surprised if any of
those scallywags ever got a job.'

'And when he talked to those Russians could you understand
what they were saying?'

'Of course. From my earliest years. Papa always said I
shouldn't learn Russian from him, because his was adulterated
by elements of Ukrainian, but from Mama, because she spoke
beautiful, literary Russian. And he learnt English from her, in
order to read the English poets in the original; Mama used to
praise him for having a large vocabulary, but whenever he
read aloud, she fled to the other room, complaining about his
dreadful accent.'

'Did he speak Polish well?'

'Oh yes, with no trouble at all. He only had a few persistent
errors in his repertoire, which were left over from the days of
his studies. For instance he said *beetle* instead of *battle*. And *two
sheeps*. But apart from that he spoke faultlessly, though with
an Eastern accent. And if he and Mama didn't want me to

understand what they were talking about, they switched to
French, the result of which was that I learnt French very
quickly, but I never let on.'

Apart from Russians there were also Jews, Germans and one
Serb, whose name was Vitek. The majority were Jews. In any
case, Mr and Mrs Karnaukhov lived on Szeroka Street, in a
large garden flat in the house of a man called Frydman, opposite the synagogue. Frydman was a devout Jew and a good
person, who made peace between my great-grandmother and
the Hassidim.

'The Hassidim? The Hassidim? I don't remember that.'

'You know, Granny, the time when the tsaddik came.'

'Oooh, yes. The tsaddik came, and lots of young Jews. And
one of them went on and on praying and dancing until he went
into a mystical trance… well, at any rate, he was having convulsions, he fell to the ground and started foaming at the mouth.
And my mother, who could see it all through the kitchen
window, ran into the street and – after all, she was the daughter
of a chemist, by her first marriage a doctor's wife and by her
second a lawyer's, with a scientific mind – rushed to revive the
boy with smelling salts. They were terribly offended – she was
blaspheming, insisting the boy had epilepsy when it was plain to
see he was communing with God. Luckily Frydman was able to
make peace somehow, and good neighbourly relations were
restored. And that winter, as every year, I gave the poor Jewish
children rides on my toboggan again. It was like this, you see:
the street was very steep, and when it froze over in the winter,
it made an ideal tobogganing slide.' (Ten years ago Granny
would unerringly have added at this point: 'But don't imagine
you're allowed to ride your toboggans down the street.
Nowadays there are cars and buses, something could happen to
you. But before the war there was only one car every
three hours, and it was safe.') 'So all day long we did as much

tobogganing as we could. And the children whose parents couldn't afford a toboggan would stand on the sidelines. But there were so many of us that if each one took someone on his or her toboggan, everyone had a ride. But no one wanted to give the Jewish children a ride, and it was always me who took pity on them, which is why the others used to call me: "Jewish auntie, Jewish auntie!" '

❧

'My parents were very fond of the Jews, and whenever there was an anti-Semitic incident my father always said: "I'd apply corporal punishment, I'd catch those students and give them a thrashing in the university courtyard," to which, although in principle she agreed with him, Mama would retort: "Because you're as black as the Black Hundreds," and she'd be seriously offended by his authoritarian views. But later she'd laugh about it, and when they went to the cinematograph, where a film about the Cossacks was being shown, she said to me with pride: "Papa's lot are galloping." When we got home Papa lounged in his armchair and said: "We Cossacks don't get attached to things, you see. We'd attack the Tatars, the Turks, the Poles, we'd loot their silks and cloth of gold, we'd put it all on, and splosh! jump into a barrel of tar." And what...'

'But there was meant to be more about the Jews.'

'It's coming, it's coming. As you know, I attended Maryla Możdżeńska's school, which, substituting for the forms at primary school, enjoyed an excellent reputation, and they accepted children from there into the gymnasium with open arms; they deliberately didn't examine us in geography and biology, because everyone knew that those subjects weren't taught at Mrs Możdżeńska's. Naturally I insisted that I would take that exam too, so they asked me why a caterpillar that feeds on leaves is green, and I said its tummy is transparent, so you can see what it has eaten through its skin. They laughed out loud at me.'

'The Jews!'

'All right, it's coming. All because Mrs Możdżeńska was an anti-Semite. At school she told us that decent Poles don't buy things from Jews, firstly because they're swindlers, and secondly they sell nothing but trash. In fact there was some truth in this second allegation, because the little Jewish shops were generally very down-at-heel, so everything was second or third rate. Do you know the one about the poor Jew who's up before the court? "Is it true that you have a shop?" the judge asks him. "I do have a shop," he says, "but day in, day out, it brings me nothing but losses." "So what on earth do you live on?" "On the fact that once a week, on the Sabbath, the shop is closed." One Sunday, as luck would have it, I'd failed to buy an exercise book in time the day before, but I knew I'd have to hand in my homework on the Monday, so I ran to the corner shop and bought one. The paper was shoddy, and the ink spattered, but never mind, next day I took my homework to the teacher and said I'd had to buy an exercise book on Sunday, but as soon as I got home I'd write out a fair copy. But she was furious! She wrote my father a note that said: "I do not wish your daughter to make purchases from Jews." And my father wrote back: "And I do not wish you to educate my daughter politically. One more attempt of this kind and I shall remove her from the school." And the fees were high, so the teacher never made a scene again.'

Who else was there? There was devout Mr Frydman, who had a large number of children and relatives. There was the factory manager, Mr Paszyc, who earned six thousand and had an automobile, Mrs Paszyc, in other words his wife, whom the workers hated, and who cruised about town in a luxury landau,

and Miss Paszyc, their astronomically lazy daughter; there was
old Mrs Sandałka, who went from house to house each day
with a basket of rolls on her back and sold them at a slightly
higher price than she bought them for wholesale at the bakery,
and every time she would gaze at my sickly-looking grandmother and say: 'Keep 'er, keep 'er, she might grow inter
somefink...' Oh, yes of course – at Lisów there were Aron and
Gołda. Aron the butcher, an extremely nasty man, who wasn't
allowed to set foot in the manor, ever since Grandmama
Wanda had sold him two calves on condition he didn't kill
them but sold them on, to let them grow bigger. Aron swore to
do that on all that's holy, then instantly butchered them in the
barn, because he couldn't even be bothered to take them to the
abattoir. And when he'd slaughtered and skinned them,
Grandmama Wanda had entered the barn, and she'd cursed
him. Whereas Gołda, Aron's wife, was a good woman, god-
fearing and hard-working. She raised his numerous children
and put up with his foul nature, and everyone agreed that she
deserved God's mercy. But as God would have it, one afternoon
she was sitting on a small bench outside her house, warming
herself in the sunshine, when a truck full of egg crates came
driving around the corner; as God would have it, one of the
crates fell off the truck and hit Gołda, killing her on the spot.
She had a lovely funeral, with a cantor, laments and an
outpouring of tears for having met with such misfortune. Who
could have known at the time what good luck she'd actually
had? The Lord God alone.

VIII

What can life have been like in Kielce in those days? To quote the famous song, *'That's how I think of Kielce, the symbolic height of horrid...'*

'God knows why,' Granny tells me, 'but people from Radom thought of Kielce as a nasty little town, though their own city had no trams. In Kielce there were trams. What was life like? Papa went to work. Mama was stuck in sanatoria, which ate up half his salary, although he didn't earn at all badly, six hundred and fifty zlotys. Aunt Sasha gave piano lessons. I went to school. Right at the start I made a dreadful faux pas, because the other little girls were standing in front of a poster, reading out loud: "tsee-nay-ma pa-la-is", and I said correctly *"cinema palais"*, because I'd learnt French when I was tiny, to eavesdrop on my parents... and they made awful fun of me. But later on I had various girlfriends. Hanka Przyłuska, for instance.'

'Is that the one who was jealous of you and played stupid pranks?'

'Yes, she was like that, you see. Just like that. She'd say: "Sit in water in your knickers, sit in water in your knickers, and I'll do it too." So I'd sit in a puddle, and she'd burst out laughing. And walk away. Always the same. But one time, I remember, she was totally dumbstruck when I said I had inspiration and was going to write a poem. "A poem? You know how to write poems?" "Yes, I do," I said, proud and pale. But we didn't have any paper with us, or a pencil; I remember there was no one at home, but somehow we got in the back way, through a vent, I mean she got in, because she was very agile, but I wasn't... so she got inside, handed me a sheet of paper, and I wrote: "The

poppies were wistfully hanging their heads, home came the
Morawica thoroughbreds…" The Morawica thoroughbreds!
Ha, if she'd known what old nags they were… For two weeks
she went about gazing at me in awe, but then she was the same
as before again.'

'For instance?'

'I can't remember. No, actually I can. As you know, my
father always negotiated with me. On all sorts of things.
Including matters of religion. Papa was an atheist, but I was an
incredibly fervent believer, as children often are. I used to go to
mass, and to church processions… So one day I remember a
lady going up to a girl of about five, who was tired of scattering
flowers and had sat down on the church steps, with her little
knees showing. The lady stopped in front of her, glaring
fiercely, suddenly tugged her dress lower and hissed at her:
"Cover up your sinful body!" To a five-year-old… I loved those
masses, I loved scattering the flowers and saying the prayers,
and I desperately wanted Papa to go to mass with me. As a
result I decided I was going to be a nun. My plan was that when
I grew up I'd go and be a missionary in Africa, or some such
faraway country; meanwhile I mortified myself, and got myself
ready for martyrdom. Hanka Przyłuska and her younger
brother tied me to a tree, picked armfuls of nettles which they
held with a cloth of some kind, and then lashed my body with
them; I went along with it all and suffered in humility, but there
was one thing I made clear: no stinging on the nose. They
could whip me, they could make my skin come up in bubbles
the size of walnuts, but anywhere except my face, especially
my nose. So what did Hanka do? Of course she stung me on
the nose, saying that if I was to be mortified, there could be no
exceptions, because when the natives caught me they wouldn't
ask how they should torture me. But at that point I broke free,
and suddenly my entire vocation for a life of humility and love

was gone; I chased off the Przyłuskis and gave them a thorough hiding, both of them.'

'Indeed, she doesn't sound terribly nice. A right little man-eating shark.'

'She was horrid, yeeees. She got it from her father, he was a nincompoop too. An officer. Papa used to make fun of him: "Mr Przyłuski with the small nose and the even smaller mind." One time, I remember, he came to visit with his wife, who was a charming person – I think Papa was a bit in love with her, platonically, but still... the visit was coming to an end, Mrs Przyłuska was in a hurry to be somewhere and had to go, when suddenly it started to rain outside. And Mr Przyłuski said: "You go home on your own, darling, because I'm in a new uniform and I don't want to get it wet." Papa was annoyed and said: "Well, if your husband's uniform is going to get wet, perhaps he'd better wait here for a while, and I shall escort you home." And he did. Another wonderful man of this kind was Mr Jaruzelski: a small, ugly little shrimp who didn't work, but lay in a hammock all day reading misogynist texts by Weininger, while Mrs Jaruzelska, a large, well-built woman, ran a tailor's shop making luxury bed linen, kept house and sometimes organised life for us as well. She always used to argue with us, because she was a National Democrat, and we sided with Piłsudski, but apart from that she was very sensible, and Papa felt sorry for her.'

And straight after Mrs Jaruzelska, Granny remembers Mr R—ski the engineer, a collector, who sat at home as if in Aladdin's cave, surrounded by treasures of every kind: porcelain, silver, pictures, rare and beautiful books, and so on; he was as jealous of his Aladdin's cave as a robber baron, or a djinn at the bottom of the ocean, jealous of the pearls munificently scattered about his underwater grotto. Everyone thereabouts had had electricity installed by then, so instead of the oil lamp smoking every night they had the light bulbs hissing every night, and cuts in the supply of energy from the power station, but engineer R—ski had no intention of letting the workmen come inside his house. Firstly because they were sure to break, smash or tread on something in the process, and secondly because they were sure to tell their low-life pals about his treasures and there'd be a break-in. My granny was a very different prospect – she had no low-life pals and was able to move about in R—ski's study full of antiquities – on top of that, she enjoyed the beautiful objects almost as much as their owner did. So naturally he was pleased when she and her father came to visit, and he let her venture among the cases and cabinets full of mysterious things, and once he even presented her with a lovely little cup, which was later lost in the turmoil of history, thanks to which, like Miłosz, 'porcelain troubled us most'...*

What didn't trouble us... what about the Amati?

My great-grandfather learnt to play the violin at the age of forty. He got an Amati violin from Misha de Sicard when Misha bought himself – for money from the chain of banks – a Stradivarius. Valerian didn't play at all badly, except perhaps for a few tricky pieces, such as the *Kujawiak* by Wieniawski,* for instance. But on the whole he coped pretty well, and often invited amateur musician friends to join him for musical evenings. Mr Rommel, for example.

'Mr Rommel was of German origin, and spoke Polish badly; he always called *prymulki* – primulas – *prunelki*. He used to come to our house to play violin duets with Papa. And he was the father of Margerytka. You know that. And another girl too, though she was pockmarked and ugly. But Margerytka was exquisite, just terribly tall. For those days, because nowadays she'd probably have become a model. But people always said of her: "Poor thing, where's she going to find a husband?" And then...'

'No, no, no. That story comes later.'

'Oh yes,' says Granny, 'that comes later... well, all right. Who else used to drop by? Mr... what was his name... ah, I can't remember. Papa used to give him the hares he hunted at Lisów, because there were always too many of them. And one day, I can't remember why, Papa needed hare skins, so he asked that gentleman if he could bring him some. "Well, you know, sir, a skin like that is a costly item..." says the man. And then Papa said: "I hope you won't charge me more than I charge you for the hares." And the man was thoroughly ashamed. But usually it all went like clockwork, Papa and his friends played the violin, and Aunt Sasha accompanied them on the piano. Meanwhile Mama would shut herself in the other room and say to me in secret: "Goodness, how that aunt of yours thumps the ivories." At home there was endless bickering about music, especially between Mama and Aunt Sasha, because they had both studied at the conservatory and were both fanatical about their own national composers: with Aunt Sasha it was always "Tchaikovsky, Tchaikovsky", and with Mama it was "Chopin, Chopin". Mama played in Polish, Aunt Sasha played in Russian, and no one should ever make the bold claim that music is a universal language; as a result Mama used to say "Sasha's thumping the ivories," and Aunt Sasha would say: "Irena's plonking away," and then my father would have to make peace between them, going from one room to the other and hearing out their solemn musical arguments. In any case, after Romusia died, Mama insisted she'd never sit at the piano again; Papa tried to persuade her endlessly, explaining over and over again that it wouldn't do Roma any good, but all in vain. Anyway, that caused the scandal at the Kościeńskis.'

'What scandal?'

'Once a year, in summer, we went to Mr Kościeński's house. He was the president of the Revenue and Customs Office, who invited the more senior of his underlings to his home and threw a festive dinner party for them. In the drawing room... which was square... just a moment...' Granny grows pensive and frowns. 'Yes, it was square. And there was a large square rug in the middle of it, with a cat sitting in one corner. The Kościeńskis had a cat and a dog. The dog was a Basset hound; tubby, ugly and stinky. From the moment the dinner started it kept nervously looking around, waddling up and down the room, casting glances at the cat, and waddling about again. Everyone exchanged greetings, sat down at the table and began to swap rumours and gossip. And the dog waddled and glanced, glanced and waddled. Whereas the cat... the cat was calm. Dignified. It sat up straight at the top of the rug, right in the corner, like a little Egyptian goddess...'

'Bastet.'

'No, a Basset hound. The cat just sat there, only moving its head ever so slightly now and then. Finally the dog couldn't hold back, it went up to the table and started begging. How repulsively it fawned, how it slobbered, how the saliva trickled from the corners of its mouth... And then the cat moved from its corner, softly padding along, went up to the dog, bopped it on the nose and went back to its place. For the rest of the dinner it sat perfectly straight, while the dog waddled around the room with its head drooping, not daring to approach the table again.'

'What about the scandal?' I asked, taking control, so Granny wouldn't stop halfway through the story.

'Oh yes, the scandal. Well, quite. One time there was a young man at the dinner, a cousin of Mr Kościeński. A cousin who, apparently, had just entered society and was quite determined to show off his best side. But the side he chose turned out to be rather unsuitable. I don't deny that he may have been a charming fellow, he may have been superb at whist and even better at bridge, perhaps he was a keen tennis player or stamp collector, but it so happened that he insisted on playing the piano. Would you fetch some jam to have with our tea?'

I go into the kitchen and bring back a jar.

'SOUR CHERRY 87. No, 89.'

'Give it here, I'll open it, I have strong hands.'

'Granny...'

'I do, it's from playing the piano... but hold on, after the dinner everyone was invited into the music room, where rows of chairs were already waiting, arranged in a semi-circle. We were obsequiously herded as close as possible to the instrument, and then, pallid and perspiring, the self-conscious young man sat down at the keyboard and started to play. I was eight years old at the time... maybe nine... no matter – in any case I already knew by then that he wasn't doing it properly. He was making mistakes, thumping away and murdering the tempo. He finished the first piece. Then a nocturne. A polonaise. Two mazurkas. My mother was sitting next to me, with an agonised look on her face, and finally she asked: "Excuse me, may I please make a request?" A murmur of approval ran through the room. The Revenue and Customs Office officials and their official wives wildly applauded the president's young relative, and smilingly awaited a request for a waltz or a prelude. "Could the young man please stop playing?" And she left the room. My father went purple and headed after her, justifying her on the way by saying that since Romusia's death she wouldn't play, the piano reminded her of her daughter, he was

terribly sorry and it was getting late... what a scandal! Hand
me that jar.'

'As you wish.'

'At school I was useless at gymnastics because I was always
weak, but I was always the best in the class on the beam. Strong
hands from playing the piano.'

'But Granny, you never played the piano...'

'What do you mean? Of course I did, but then I gave it up.
Because of Aunt Sasha.'

'Why because of Aunt Sasha?'

'Because it was she who taught me. In Russian. She'd fetch
out these horrifically boring scores, books of exercises, Czerny's
for instance, though Czerny wasn't the worst by far... well, you
know, the sort of thing that makes your fingers refuse to move,
utterly charmless... and she told me to play those. But I
rebelled, because I wanted to play something pretty. After all,
there are so many pretty pieces for learning to play the piano.'

'Like Bach's *Inventions*, for example.'

'Exactly. I adamantly refused to play those boring, ugly
things, but insisted on trying Chopin's *Scherzo in B minor*
immediately. Aunt Sasha said I was a silly little chit... give me
some more of that jam... thank you... she said I was a silly
little chit and it was too hard for me, but I started to learn it.
But I soon got to a point where at one and the same time the
left hand has to play two tones, and the right has to play three,
and I went terribly wrong, so I lost my temper and said I didn't
care two hoots about Chopin, and gave up the piano. After
that I studied singing.'

'Was that with Aunt Sasha too?'

'No, with Mrs Klamrzyńska. Mrs Klamrzyńska was a friend
of my parents who had once been a prima donna at the imperial opera in St Petersburg. One time she came to visit, and she
told me to sing something. So I did, and she said: "Mr and Mrs

Karnaukhov, Lala has a superb voice, naturally attuned. She sings in the mask..." – that means' – Granny shows me, opening her mouth wide – 'right here, into the palate. "Please send her to me next week for an audition." And I went. Mrs Klamrzyńska spent an hour enthusing about my beautiful singing, and insisted I apply for music school without fail, then finally she said: "As long as you don't catch cold in the week ahead, because your throat is softened now. And if anything were to get into your vocal cords, it'd be the end." And of course two days later I was lying in bed with a temperature, and that was the end of my voice.'

'Was that the time the concierge came?'

'No, that was another time, when I was sick with pneumonia. I lay in a fever for three weeks, delirious. I remember Dr Grzybowski coming and telling my father: "O God, O God, I attended Miss Roma when she was ill, I watched her fade away. And now for Mrs Karnaukhova to lose a second child... O God, O God, what a misfortune... I shall do everything, please believe me, I shall do everything I possibly can for the child to get better." And he came three times a day, sounded me, percussed me and listened to my chest. One day I finally wake up from such a morbid dream... it's dark, the blinds are down, and I'm so tired that it's all the same to me if I pull through or not, I just want it to end. My right hand has slipped from the bed and it's hanging down, but I haven't the strength to raise it. It feels heavier and heavier. I'm too weak to tell anyone about it or to ask for help. And just then the concierge comes in and says: "Mr Karnaukhov, downstairs we've lit the votive candles and we're praying for a gentle demise for little Miss Lalusia." And when I heard her say that I thought to myself: "Ha, I'll give you a gentle demise, just you wait!" I gathered all my strength, raised my hand, laid it on the bedding, and fainted. When I came to, Dr Grzybowski was there. They were taking my

temperature. And I'm lying there with my eyes closed, pretending to be asleep. The doctor says: "Now we'll see. If it has fallen
below thirty-eight, it's too big a jump, her heart won't hold out.
But if it has stayed higher, we can be hopeful. Praise be to God,
it's thirty-eight point three." After that I was on the mend. But
even so, for about a month they fed me on beef extract, the
kind that's made by boiling the stock into a thick, viscous jelly,
a highly nutritious brew, and I was given a teaspoonful of it
morning, noon and night, because the body wouldn't be able
to take a larger amount than that. And then they sat me under
the cherry tree on a deckchair, feeding me increasing doses of
beef extract from day to day. But of course I was soon bored of
sitting there, and I decided to go out of the garden. I got up
from the deckchair, went into the street and suddenly felt
weak. A lady noticed me and said: "Lord, child, you've gone
completely grey..." And boom! I fainted. They carried me
home, brought me round, and once I was over it they yelled at
me for getting up to such silliness. And I had to spend another
two weeks on the deckchair.'

'Under the cherry tree?'

'Under the cherry tree. Finally they let me walk about. First
it was once around the garden, then a few circuits, and eventually I went out into the city. I'm walking along, and there's
some building work, under scaffolding. As I'm walking past
below, suddenly I hear: "Watch out," and just at that moment I
feel something brushing my arm. It turned out a workman had
let go of a large iron bar, which had come sailing down from a
height of three floors and fallen with a mighty crash right next
to me... ba-boom! So I look, I was wearing a blue dress with
puffed sleeves, and there's a rust-coloured scar on one of them.
That's nice, I think, that's the second time death has been out
to get me. The best thing I can do is go home. And just then a

large cart drove out at me, very nearly running me over; it was a real miracle that a lady pulled me by the arm and saved me. Oh dear, I think to myself, third time lucky – now that I've already fainted, a bar has fallen on me and a cart drove into me, I'm going to have peace and quiet for the next few decades. And indeed I did. Except that I've always had a weak heart since then.'

'Isn't that from your father? Didn't he have a prob—'

'No, no, my father was as strong as an ox, except that in early youth he'd had cholera. He survived, but for four weeks he ran a temperature of over forty degrees, which completely ruined his heart. And very often, especially in summer, at Lisów, he used to have a "mini attack", and he'd end up lying on the road or out in the fields somewhere where he'd gone for a walk. The peasants would run in shouting: "The Counsellor's had a fall," so Mama or I would grab the nitro-glycerine and rush to his aid, but we usually met him on the road, calmly walking home, always in a capital mood.'

Because in summer they always went to Lisów. Meanwhile Morawica had passed into other hands, those of Mr and Ms Pawlik, who, as their common surname implies, were not exactly aristocrats. My grandfather Zygmunt (who doesn't yet have a place in this story) called such people 'arrivistes'. Almost as soon as they'd taken possession of the estate they lowered the daily rates for the hired labourers.

Counsellor Karnaukhov and his wife were sitting on the porch at the Morawica manor house, drinking coffee, tea, or maybe kvass, and listening with all ears as Mr Pawlik boasted of various innovations that would save him a pretty penny.

'For instance, there are some houses behind the village that were built by the squire, and theoretically we should be getting rent from them, but for years this has been scandalously neglected by successive owners. All that money! But we've set to work, checked the books, and now we're demanding monthly rents from the tenants.'

'Do you happen to have a mill here?'

'Yes, I do.'

'Is it insured against fire?'

'No.'

'Then get it insured.'

'Weeell, Counsellor…'

'Get it insured, because the peasants will burn it down.'

He didn't get it insured. The peasants burned it down.

*

Even closer, on the very next hill, was a hamlet known as Lisów B. There, in a tiny little manor house, dwelled Squire Libiszowski, a dreadful gambler, roisterer and wastrel, whose brother had given him a small remnant of land, nothing but sand really, with the proviso that he could not sell, pawn or gamble it away. He ran it badly, and was as poor as a church mouse, but he told the peasants to call him 'Squire' and to kiss his hand through the sleeve.

A peasant called Milewski, who sometimes helped out at our Lisów manor, once went to Libiszowski's place to weed the carrots, or maybe to sell some carrots, I can't remember which, but I know it was to do with carrots, because the squire didn't pay Milewski, but merely said to him: 'Do you know, Milewski, you are a Polish nobleman, the name Milewski belongs to the Korwin clan, it's Korwin-Milewski.' 'Ha,' Milewski told Valerian, 'he paid me for the carrots with membership of the Korwin clan.'

*

A little further off there were two German estates. One belonged to two brothers, and the other to Mr Hess ('nephew of the famous Hess, but not Höss,' Granny always says, comically stressing the *e* and the *ö*, 'the one who went to Britain, not the Auschwitz one'). The two brothers were legendary for their good management, for they even had surfaced roads in the forest. Whereas all the girls gazed after young Mr Hess, because he was incredibly handsome, over two metres tall, a Polish officer and, above all, wealthy and single. He often visited Counsellor Karnaukhov to seek his advice on various administrative matters, and personal ones too; they'd sit over a glass of strong drink and discuss the world at large.

'But my dear sir, you should get married,' said my great-grandfather.

'I should, but please don't be offended, I'd like to have a German wife.'

'Well, what's the problem? Go to Germany and come back with a wife.'

'I said German, not Nazi. Those women have gone mad. Everyone's gone mad there. I want a normal German girl.'

'Aren't you afraid war will break out?'

'And then what?'

'Well, what about the fact that as a Polish officer you'll have to fight against your own people?'

'I hope,' he muttered, which no one noticed at the time, 'the Poles will have enough tact not to send me to the western front.'

❧

Further off again, in Jędrzejów, was the estate of the Przypkowski family, the ones who were famous for collecting clocks. Their entire house was like one big museum – although

not like the Royal Castle in Warsaw, where I once actually saw
a lady custodian run diagonally across the gallery to shout at a
German tourist who had sat down on a 1970s stool: 'Pleess,
pleess,' – she said in broken English, making desperate upward
hand gestures – 'eets or-eedg-eenal, eets or-eedg-eenal!' For at the
Przypkowskis you could touch everything – including the
broken pane of glass in the door, supplied with a little note
saying: 'This glass was broken by a Russian soldier in 1864', and
any of the ancient clocks, of which some fired a salute, others
were totally flat, and yet others imitated birds or plants, and
you even could sit down on a piece of furniture labelled: 'On
this stool sat the Grand Emperor Napoleon during the retreat
of his troops from Moscow in 1812.' And the exact date.

Old Mr Przypkowski was a collector, a scholar and a clock-
maker, and his son was a sculptor and Germanophile. Before
the actual war, when everyone rushed to join Polish–British or
Polish–French friendship associations, he had signed up for the
Polish–German Society of Friends. He said that when he had
visited the colonies, he had formed the opinion that the British
are rogues and beasts: they drove the blacks off the pavement
with whips, tormented them and treated them like slaves; he
preferred German order, Schiller, Goethe and Hitler.

※

Granny comes into my room in the morning and looks at my
portrait of Basia.

'Very like you, except your nose is different.'

'Granny, it's not a self-portrait – it's Basia.'

'What? It can't be. It's nothing like her.'

'What do you mean?' I say, getting out of bed and, wrapped
in my duvet, join Granny in front of the easel.

'It's not her. And I know what I'm talking about.'

'How come?' I ask angrily, though I know I shouldn't.

'How come? For starters I was brought up in a house full of paintings. Not only did my grandparents have lots of beautiful works of art, but when she was sent to Italy for therapy, Romusia used to write to me almost every day, and she made a big effort to include with each letter a postcard of a different work of art. Those postcards, I remember, hung above my bed afterwards. And Papa painted, so did Aunt Ewa... Aunt Ewa did it in her own crazy way, supposedly the right way, but you know... one time, for instance, she repainted Grandpapa Leonard's little Japanese cabinet...'

'Paint a Japanese cabinet! What barbarism!'

'But that cabinet wasn't at all pretty. And she painted a manor house on it, just like ours, except that there was a giant frog sitting on the flowerbed at the front, and it looked as if it was just about to swallow the house in a single gulp. Whereas Papa painted very correctly and very much in the Russian style. For instance he'd paint a copper bowl half-full of water, so that it looked real. As well as that he adored Stanisławski, and sometimes did little landscapes like his... there were lots of them lying about the house – one of his botched pictures was even made into a dustpan. He befriended painters; I remember the time a friend of his who was a professor at the Academy in Warsaw came by, and I sat to one side and sketched him. He had a very distinctive profile... wait a moment, I'll draw it for you' – at this point Granny takes out a paper napkin, splits it into three layers, and on one of them she draws a bulging forehead, an aquiline nose and a prominent chin – 'there, like that. When that professor saw my drawing, he said: "My dear man, she must go to the Academy..."'

'People were always trying to educate you.'

'So it seems. So Papa sent me for drawing and painting lessons, but I didn't want to paint copper bowls half-full of water and I rebelled.'

'Granny, may I go and have a wash now?'

'All right.'

'I'll be straight down to breakfast and you can tell me the rest.'

❧

'No, Granny, I can slice my own tomato. Would you like me to blanch and skin one for you? All right. Now you can tell me more about the family.'

'About the family? Well, for example... we lived with Aunt Sasha, who was famous for her beautiful hair. One day I went into her room, and there was Aunt Sasha, bald, with just a tiny mouse tail on the top of her head, and her hair was lying on the dressing table. It gave me a dreadful shock. Quite unlike Mama, who had the most beautiful hair, which she wore braided into two long plaits, down to her ankles, as thick as your wrist at the top and like a man's thumb at the ends, but even so, once a month when she unplaited it to give it a wash, she'd say: "Hmm, there's so little left of my hair... nothing but mouse tails."'

'"Mouse tails"? Weren't there some "bumper cheeses" too?'

'It was Grandmother Wanda who said "bumper cheeses" when she happened to go into Róża's room and saw her bust. "Bumper cheeses", like wedges of *twaróg*. I only ever saw Aunt Róża in the holidays, when she came to Lisów with her children, Alinka and Zdziszek' – at this point Granny casts a look of thunder across the sandwiches – 'who was the bane of my childhood.'

'Was he the one who tried to give you a soaking?'

'Oh, what didn't he do? First of all, he doused me in the pond, secondly he often used to pretend he was drowning, while I stood at the water's edge, screaming... he was an excellent swimmer, so he could stay underwater for a really long time, and every time I let myself be taken in. But then how old was I? About seven? Thirdly, he used to call me Cockatoo. And I was terribly annoyed by that, as a child would be. He used to take my favourite doll and stick it at the top of a huge lime tree that grew behind the house, and then he'd say he'd give it back to me if I let him call me Cockatoo... and you know what my tree-climbing was like... just one single time I climbed the pear tree at Lisów, because it had a long, horizontal bough that was easy to clamber onto, but then I was afraid to come down and I had to wait until Papa came home from work in Kielce – meanwhile all the village children gathered around the pear tree and laughed at me for not being able to get down. So Zdziszek would take away my doll, Tosia, hang her on a terribly high branch and say: "Tell me your name is Cockatoo and I'll get her down." Whereas Alinka always rescued me; she could climb trees as nimbly as Zdziszek, and she fetched Tosia down. Once when they came in late autumn, he threw Tosia into the icy water and I tried my best to get her out, but I slipped and fell in. Luckily Alinka pulled me out...'

'You got on all right with Alinka.'

'Oh, certainly. She pulled me out and carried me home, but even so I caught pneumonia. That was when the servant came and said she was praying for a gentle demise. What else was there about that Zdziszek...? Oh yes, of course, he bet me I wouldn't go to the graveyard at night. He said I'd be too scared. And I always was contrary, so I waited until it got dark, slipped out through the window in my night shirt... it was summer, so I didn't feel cold. But somehow my father had found out about it all, about the bet, and he knew that Zdziszek was waiting for

me at the graveyard, wrapped in a sheet. So he got there first,
and tore a strip off Zdziszek, saying he was almost a grown
man, and here he was, frightening a child, because at the time
I was only seven or eight... and then he found me and took me
home. I got a worse fright from my father than from the ghosts
I was expecting to see... but if I had seen Zdziszek like that in
the sheet, who knows what might have happened? A nervous
shock or something. And while we're on the topic, it's curious
that both Alinka and Zdziszek were so odd... she loved to
defend and save me, she climbed trees like a monkey and
wasn't afraid of anything. And he went about in extraordinary
flowery shirts, wore lipstick, and couldn't bear girls – in time he
started appearing in the company of various peculiar friends,
well, you know. I think it was all because of their mother –
Róża was so frigid, she probably only married General
Szymiczek to please her parents.'

'And then what? What became of them?'

'The Germans killed Alinka during the war, and Zdziszek
was already dead before it. He was swimming in the sea off
Varna and he got cramp. He drowned' – Granny smiles
ominously – 'what an ironical fate – he was always fooling me
into thinking he was drowning, he was such a joker, he played
so many pranks, and then he drowned.'

'Wearing lipstick and a flowery shirt. Hmm. But you had
other cousins, didn't you?'

'Yes, the little Mechs, Aunt Ewa's children. Little... well, not
so little in fact. I never knew Staś Mech, because he died in
Lwów at a very early age, only twelve or so. He's buried in the
Eaglets Cemetery. He died in hospital, endlessly crying: "Mama,
mama!" And my aunt was on her way to him, apparently in a
terrific hurry, but she had to see to some business along the
way. And he died before she got there.'

'Damn that Mechowa woman!'

Róża and Irena, c. 1920.

'Oh, certainly. It was because of her that Uncle Mech lost his job as the provincial governor of Volhynia. He had an important post, and his wife got up to various larks. For instance she went about town with a stork and a piglet on a lead.'

'Didn't they try to bite each other?'

'No, well, I don't know. Maybe she took them out separately.

Or various important guests would arrive for the Volhynia Fair, which was a terribly important event in those days, it was a big deal, like the Poznań Fair, but agricultural... so the guests would arrive, my uncle would invite them to the house for a festive dinner, and she'd receive them in her dressing gown. There was an awful scandal; here were all these fine gentlemen, presidents and representatives, and here she was in her dressing gown. And a threadbare one too. She was batty, why hide the fact? Everyone knew. Eventually they told my uncle he'd have to resign. And no wonder. He asked if they were unhappy with his work, and they replied that they were very pleased with it, but not with his wife.'

'All right, but there was a second child too.'

'What second child?'

'Staś's sister.'

'Wandzia? Wandzia Mechówna* was my favourite cousin. She had an exquisite voice, crystal clear. She inherited it from an aunt on her father's side, who was a famous prima donna. Unfortunately she didn't inherit her ear for music. I remember Wandzia coming to Lisów and walking about the garden, singing The King Went Out to War, while I sat in the window and listened to her, because she had such a lovely voice. She sang it a hundred times, and each time it sounded different. That's a talent too. And I never learnt to sing The King Went Out to War, because as the Russians say, I'd overlearnt it and kept blundering. You know what... give it a flick.'

'Sorry?'

'Give it a flick. Press the button!' said Granny, sounding irritated. 'The radio. It's almost twelve, that programme's on... you know, it's also a terrible irony to have such an exquisite voice and no ear for music. If there was an instrument leading her, it was less of a problem, but *a cappella*... utter despair. Even so she made some recordings – my aunt arranged it for her through a friend... and she chose the sort of pieces where the instrument led the whole time, so she sang purely. We heard it later on the radio. But when I think about her walking around the garden, in the sunshine, and how I listened to that wretched The King Went Out..., it makes my stomach churn. She probably would have achieved some sort of fame eventually, because her voice really was phenomenal, but she died during the war. The Germans tortured her in Pawiak prison.'

'So nothing but saintly virgins and saintly youths?'

'No, not really, Zdziszek was no saint. And Wandzia wasn't a virgin because she had a husband.'

'A husband? I've never heard of him before.'

'What do you mean? First she had a fiancé and rashly told her mother about him. Aunt Ewa was furious, and did such a lot of meddling, sending out letters, blackening her own daughter in the eyes of the other family and so on that it all fell through. So the second time Wandzia didn't say a word, and only informed her the day before the wedding.'

'That was very decent of her too. In her place I wouldn't have told her at all.'

'But she did. And then, during the sublime ceremony of entering into matrimony, right there in the middle of the church Aunt Ewa's knicker elastic broke. And her knickers fell to the floor. Providence' – said Granny in a solemn tone, 'chooses the most curious paths for itself. Now hush, it's the news.'

And so Granny peremptorily cuts short her reminiscences in favour of the news from Afghanistan, Bosnia or Otwock. Meanwhile I'm left behind in those idyllic surroundings, in the cloud of golden dust she has raised – it's just as if I were sitting in the window at the Lisów manor house, in a window that certainly no longer exists, leaning my elbows on the smooth wooden windowsill. The white transparents are ripening, or maybe the sweet cherries, or perhaps nothing is ripening yet, but in the tall grass, which here and there is darker, taller and greener, strolls Wandzia Mechówna, a lovely young girl, singing The King Went Out to War, but horribly out of tune.

Well, the war came by itself, and there was no special need to go out to it.

❧

'Is that all about the family?'

'On the whole, yeees… what else is there? Maciej? Uncle Maciej was usually meek and mild, but occasionally he went berserk. He once attacked my father when they were out for a walk by the pond and tried to drown him. They were right by the edge, so it was shallow, but you don't need much water to drown someone if you push his head into the ooze. Luckily Papa was very strong and broke free of Uncle Maciej, who then recovered his wits and apologised to him profusely; since my grandfather's death Papa had been the only member of the family who could calm him down. Another time my parents went out to the theatre, but Mama stopped halfway, because she had a bad presentiment. She turned back, went into the house, and there was Uncle Maciej, smothering me with some coats.'

'What do you mean, "smothering you with some coats"?'

'The usual way,' says Granny, as if a usual way of smothering someone with coats actually existed, 'he'd thrown me into the wardrobe, covered me with coats and was smothering me. They only just saved me. After that they never left me alone with him again.'

'What about your grandmother?'

'My grandmother was fit and healthy. She could still genu-flect at the age of ninety. In any case, her life was lived in peace.'

'And that reminds me, you're not yet ninety, but you're already refusing to look after yourself and you haven't put your teeth in.'

Granny casts me a reproachful look and says: 'I spent all my holidays at Lisów...'

'Granny, you haven't put your teeth in.'

'Shush, you little brat,' says Granny, whom everyone nags for not wearing her teeth, but she couldn't care two hoots what anyone says.

'But Granny, a sophisticated lady...'

'Don't give me your "sophisticated lady". They're uncom-fortable. I spent all my summer holidays at Lisów, right up to September, because it was always beautiful there in September, so I went back to school a month later. It was at Lisów that Papa taught me to shoot.'

'You learnt to shoot?'

'Learnt? I was extremely good at it. I always did have excel-lent vision and strong hands...'

'... from playing the piano.'

'Yes. And as there were three revolvers at home, there was always something to practise with.'

'Why as many as three?'

'Papa had had two of them for ages, and he took the third one away from a man he knew. It was this young fellow, a bit silly and a bit of a tearaway. Papa once went to pay him a visit, because they'd just had a new child, and somehow it was appropriate. "You know what, Counsellor," says the fellow, "I got a licence and bought myself a revolver,"' and he fetches it out, shows the guests, waves it about, and so on. My father says: "Please handle it with care, a gun is not a toy." "It's all right, it's not loaded." "My dear sir, I beg you…" and just then there was a loud bang. Everyone jumped from their seats, terri-fied, people were screaming, the wife ran to the cradle, and the bullet had actually hit the cradle and smashed the back of it, just above the baby's head. "How much did you pay for that pistol?" asked Papa. "Right, here's the money. Please be so kind as to hand me the gun and don't buy yourself another until you're ready to have one."'

'And what happened to the pistols later on?'

'We gave them all to the partisans at the start of the war. But I was telling you about Lisów.'

'You were.'

'Did I mention the doll?'

'No.'

'That was earlier, when I was still very small. Papa gave me such a lovely doll, who opened her eyes and did a wee. God, how fond I was of that doll… one day we went to Lisów, and typically for me, I invited the village children to play, because I always had a complex about being the little squire's daughter from the manor who has everything, while other children have nothing. So we played with the doll for some time, and then suddenly the children said they were hungry. So I ran into the house to fetch them some bread and butter. I came back, and neither the children nor the doll were there. Then I went in tears from cottage to cottage with Papa, but all in vain. I never saw her again.'

And suddenly I'm struck by this curious feature of life; seventy years on, Granny, who remembers less and less, is still upset about a doll from her childhood, which ended long ago, from a house that was gone long ago, from an era that was over long ago; I never cried as much for any of my childhood loves as for an orange plastic crocodile, superb at swimming in the

bathtub, which my parents inadvertently threw away one day
while painting the bathroom. But meanwhile Granny is telling
a different story.

'... I have nothing against those children. For what did they
have to play with? A pipe whittled from bark. Waldorff, the
music critic, lost his job at *Przekrój* magazine for many years
because he wrote about his childhood memory of shepherd
boys playing on pipes, but since all the shepherd boys had gone
to be ministers, there was no one left to play them in the Polish
countryside. The children at Lisów were so talented... just
before the war, I remember, the teacher said to me: "Madam,
all these kids should go to college, but who here can afford it?"
Only Stefan Wrona – God, what a handsome man he was –
only Stefan became an officer. I remember him riding at the
head of his unit during a military parade in Kielce, all the
women were making eyes at him, and he bowed to me... so
handsome, in his uniform, on horseback... and then what? A
friend from school told me that Stefan had got into an affair
with a woman, of whom there were rumours... well, in any
case, he contracted syphilis. I remember how one time he came
to the manor, and of course we invited him, as an equal, to
afternoon tea. He sat there looking so haggard, he hardly
moved. And he asked me for a rug, because it was the evening
and his legs were cold. How humiliated he must have felt, such
a hero, asking for a rug... not long after he went to the front,
he was captured and killed at Katyń. And there was one more,
I can't remember his name, but it may have been... Kostrzyk.
Or maybe not? My father sent him to high school. He would
have gone on to college, but the war broke out and he had to
take care of his family. One day the Germans caught him with
tobacco – everyone in the village planted tobacco, although it
was strictly against the regulations. So the gendarmes caught
him, started screaming at him and hit him in the face. If he'd

been an ordinary peasant he'd have put his tail between his legs and just endured it, but he felt himself to be intelligentsia, and hit the gendarme back. They beat him to death so cruelly with their rifle butts that his mother had trouble recognising the remains – he was just a bloody mess.'

'But Granny, you're on to the war already – I haven't finished asking about your childhood and youth.'

'What else would you like to know?'

'About school.'

'About school... Papa used to come and fetch me from school, and I always hated it, because as soon as he saw him the janitor would call out: "Miss Bieniecka, your grandpa's come for you." And no wonder – Papa was over fifty and bald as a billiard ball, which he actually found embarrassing, so he always tried to wear a hat. Within the bounds of reason. But sometimes someone paid him a compliment, like the man at the railway station, whose job it was to make sure the passengers had platform tickets, and who said to Papa: "There's no need for me to check up on you, sir, I can see that you're a gentleman, pure and simple. Because you've got that look about you, sir. I can see it at once."'

'But you were going to tell me about your school, not about your school from your father's point of view.'

'About my school? I was a very good pupil, I was usually second or third in the class, because I had problems with gymnastics. And I used to argue with the priest...'

'Really? You did, after practising to be a nun and a martyr?'

'Yes. Because Papa spent such a long time telling me: "Child, these are matters of freedom of conscience and no one can be converted by force. Arm yourself with patience. And remember that you might end up changing your views on these matters one day." And of course I shouted, took offence and simply felt sad. But yes, little by little, I started to find various places in the Bible which I thought totally at odds with the rest, especially with Christ's teachings. What I found the most shocking was that the Virgin Mary knew Herod's soldiers were going to slaughter all the boys in Bethlehem, but she didn't tell the other mothers. For me that was unacceptable. So at the religion class I asked the priest how it was possible, and he explained that otherwise the Holy Family wouldn't have managed to escape to Egypt. That wasn't enough for me. I started questioning and probing, until finally I lost my faith. Of course the priest loved carping at me over various piffling details, so I had to know the prayers, rules of the catechism and songs etcetera, best of all in the class. He was just waiting for me to put a foot wrong, but in vain.'

'And what other teachers did you have problems with?'

'With several. Different things with each of them.'

'For instance?'

'Well, my worst problems were with the new headmistress. I was very fond of the old one, but she retired. She was a nice, distinguished lady. Whereas the new one was a primitive boor, who screamed at the pupils, barked orders instead of having conversations and was altogether the wrong person in the wrong place, to such a degree that one time one of the mothers couldn't restrain herself and slapped her in the face. I had subtler methods. One time she was taking a biology lesson with us and she wrote on the board: "the hemisferes of the brain", with an *f*. She'd simply made a mistake, probably because she was trying so hard to write each letter artistically. Of course I carefully copied it all out in my exercise book. She came up to me and asked: "What's this? How do we write the word *hemisphere*?" To which I replied: "When the old head was here we wrote it with a *ph*, but with the new one it's like this..." – and I pointed at the board, where it stood as large as life, in black and white... well, in white on black, "hemisferes".

You can imagine how fond of me she was after that. She fought with me to the very last class. But there was one thing about her that I liked: we had a campaign at our school to bring breakfast for our less well-off schoolmates. And one day the headmistress saw one of the girls donating a dry roll with no filling. "Did you get a dry roll for breakfast, eh? No? Yours is with ham, is it? All right, you can eat the dry one, and the ham roll can go to your poorer schoolmates."'

'Nice.'

'Yes, it was nice. But apart from that she was a primitive boor. Quite unlike the Latin teacher, Mrs Staszowa – she was very well mannered, but terribly harsh. I wasn't afraid of her, because at first I was pretty good at Latin, and I got her used to the idea that I knew it all. As a result she never questioned me in class, but called up all the other girls in turn, and they'd spend such a long time stammering over Caesar or Livy that finally I'd hear: "Laaaala, now you tell them what it's all about." Then I'd stand up and speak without any effort, because it had already been translated by the others. Until suddenly one time in the final school-certificate class she asked me to translate without warning. And I didn't react. She was dumbfounded. "Lala, stand up, please," she said. "What do you mean, you can't do it?" Well, I told her I couldn't do it, plain and simple, that for ages she'd never asked me, and I hadn't studied just for the sake of studying. She gave me three weeks to get on top of it; the school holidays were just coming up. And just imagine, I did it. And passed with top marks. Yes. She had various funny phrases, such as: "Why are you hopping about like a flea on a chessboard?" Why on a chessboard I have no idea, but that's what she used to say.'

Lala as a schoolgirl, c. 1935.

Whether she translated well or not, Lala Bieniecka was given a classical education. No wonder that when I was small, instead of fairy tales she told me Greek myths; at bath time she told me about Achilles in the waters of the River Styx; in the garden about Narcissus and Adonis; at the marketplace about Hermes, and about Nessus, Odysseus or the Stymphalian birds whenever and wherever. And about Augeas when she wanted to make me tidy up my toys. Other heroes appeared too: Hamlet, Roland, King Jan Sobieski and his inseparable wife Marysieńka, Queen Bona poisoning her daughter-in-law Barbara Radziwiłł, and in time Emma Bovary, Hans Castorp and Baron de Charlus too, but by this stage we were telling each other the stories.

So during my childhood in Oliwa everything was a little different, with Oedipus, Bruges and the Russian ballets in the background. We communicated in language removed from the reality of the local streets – Kwietna, Liczmański, Podhalańska and beyond; removed from the reality of Gdańsk, Pomerania, Poland, and most of the Western and Eastern world: we talked in allusions to family stories, books we'd both read, and family tribal catchphrases. It was often hard for anyone from the outside to understand us; but wasn't that partly the point?

When my friend Richard came to stay from Vienna, Granny got into her usual flap, saying: 'Where shall I put him?' and then the other flap that goes: 'How am I going to communicate with him?'

'Well, you know... either in English or in German. He speaks excellent English. And pretty tolerable German too.'

'What about French?'

'No. Nor Russian either, to pre-empt your next question.'

'Scandalous,' sighed Granny. 'Oh well, we'll have to find a way.'

🌺

'Well, Richard,' I asked on day three, 'how's it going on the communication front?'

'When I understand, I smile and nod my head. And when I

don't, I make a sad little dog face,' he said, making a sad little dog face.

'Aha.'

Luckily, most of the time we were either touring churches and museums, or discussing various serious subjects, things like time and space, because Richard knows about them and I don't, or vice versa, how to paint pearls and how to build up suspense, because Richard doesn't know about those, or else we discussed topics on which we're both ignorant. But sometimes I had to leave him on his own for a while with Granny, who, largely cut off from our conversations by the language barrier, was plainly sulking.

Either way, when I went into the kitchen to make the tea, for instance, just in case, I did my best to keep my ears open, because you never know... As ever, the teapot was standing on top of the electric kettle ('Because it warms up. The pot must be heated, so that's where it's always put'; if ever I failed to apply this new tradition, Granny made a hoo-ha). There's a residue on the glasses, pale brown and grey streaks of limescale and tea, flavourless in fact (or maybe even enriching the flavour, at any rate with no odour or yuk), but to the eye of an aseptic young Austrian they might be horrifying. So I give them a good scrub. I can hear Granny's voice from the sitting room, more and more resonant, filled with certainty and mission. There's no question she's explaining something. I must hurry up, because who knows where this will lead?

So I buck up, tip Richard's favourite tea (pepper and cinnamon) into the pot, I redouble my efforts, polish the teaspoons, and finally enter the sitting room, where Granny, decoratively sprawling in her armchair, is reaching the zenith of her narrative, the mystical heights of eloquence.

'The Capitol, the Capitol,' she cries, waving arms given wings by her classical education. Now and then a gaggling noise comes into it, and as if that weren't enough, she adds some other scenes of a significance that I don't recognise.

On the other side of the table Richard is making his sad little dog face.

'Jacek,' says Granny, turning to me with a dignified gesture, 'I'm trying to tell him that we converse like a goose and a piglet.' An untranslatable Polish idiom, but how very apt.

With a view to the safety of the tea and the polished glasses, I set down the tray on the table, and then ask: 'But what was the meaning of that pantomime?'

'You what? The geese! The Capitoline geese! By night, the barbarians were approaching the walls of Rome' – at this point Granny makes sweeping movements to draw the Eternal City in the air – 'I can't remember which ones...'

'Never mind, there were plenty of them. Then what?'

But Granny is already climbing up the imaginary slopes of one of the seven hills; time and again, with furrowed brows the Gauls cross the stretch between armchair and table. Suddenly – here are the geese, making a racket, flapping their wings and gaggling away, until invisible feathers are sailing onto the invisible floors of the Capitol; the awakened Romans leap into combat – Granny jostles the armchairs and raises a clenched fist at a non-existent sword. The geese have saved Rome.

'Goose,' says Granny solemnly. 'Goose,' she repeats, staring searchingly at Richard.

As I give him a brief explanation of the meaning of the phrase 'to converse like a goose with a piglet' he never loses the sad little dog face, which he has retained throughout Granny's ballet. It also comes to light that he doesn't know the story of the Capitoline geese, but he's more than happy to broaden his horizons, like any nice, intelligent, well-mannered Austrian boy. The *son et lumière* is at an end.

'He's never heard of the Capitoline geese? Incredible.'

'I don't think he had a classical education. It might be easier through Donald Duck – poultry's all the same, isn't it?'

Luckily, feeling exempt from the obligation for further explanations, Granny abandons the idea of depicting piglets and sits down for a cup of tea.

❧

'All right, you didn't like the headmistress, and you weren't wild about the Latin teacher either. Whom did you like?'

'Weeell, Garbacik. Garbacik was my favourite teacher. The history master. An incredibly intelligent man, he was a professor later on, in Kraków I think, but I'm not sure; he died recently, I saw a note in *Przekrój* about it. He lived a good many years too. But he didn't look as if he was going to last that long. He was from a simple family, he'd only just graduated, thin as a rail, poor as a church mouse, he always went about in the same suit with trailing trouser legs, all baggy at the knees, hanging in folds. One time, I remember, we were sitting in the classroom before his lesson and I drew a cartoon of him on the board, looking gaunt, with those saggy trousers. He came in, saw it, smiled, and said: "Yes indeed, it has gone too far, these trousers really are worn out," and from then on he came to school in his only Sunday-best suit. My God, how profusely I apologised, how we all begged and implored him... but no, he stuck to his guns. I felt awfully silly, awfully silly... One time, I remember, I decided to wear something provocative for May the First, something red, and as I had nothing entirely red, I put on a red scarf with white spots. Garbacik came in, took one look at me and said: "Ah, what heroism... well, well. Fancy donning a red scarf for my lesson! With white spots too! For my lesson!" He was a bit of a socialist' – Granny fills in – 'and at the same time he had some sympathy for Mussolini, because he'd been to Italy, and he told us about their public works. "Anyone who has made those lazy Italians work", he said, "is a great man. He's drained the Pontine marshes, built roads, introduced order…" Later he got over it. Either way, he was a superb teacher, very good at encouraging each of us to work… there was a girl in our class whom we all called Herringirl, because she stank awfully of herrings, I have no idea why. She was perfectly clean, and she washed, but always smelled of herrings… and she wasn't very bright. So just imagine, one day Garbacik called her up to answer a question in class, so she stammered away, and when she was done he said: "Miss…" what was she called? oh, never mind, "Miss Whatsit. Miss Whatsit has considered the matter from a very interesting perspective…" And from that day on Herringirl swotted away at history like mad. She went on getting Fs in every other subject, but in history she got nothing but As. Such an excellent teacher. And then there was the story of the C grade. He read us the marks for the term and said that one of us had a C for conduct. In those days a C for conduct at a girls' school was a real scandal. I don't know what you had to do to get a C. The girls were horrified, they came to me and said: "Listen, Garbacik likes you, you go and see him and ask who got a C." So I go and ask, and he says: "Don't you know? Can't you guess?" So I come up with something, saying maybe this girl, because she was seen at a ball at the officer's club, or that one, because one time she wore make-up at a school event. "No. You really don't know who got the C?" I had no idea. "It's you." I was speechless. "Me?" And he looks at me, nods and says: "Do you have to keep waging war on the headmistress? Why do you do that? And you find it surprising."'

'So… hmm, he was a bit of a… conformist.'

'Nooo. Garbacik fought with the headmistress too, just as I did, but more subtly. I remember when I was taking my school-certificate Polish oral and he was one of the examiners. I gave spotless answers, and then the headmistress, who was determined to flunk me, asked a question about contemporary literature. Professor Garbacik leapt from his seat and started to protest that it wasn't in the curriculum, but then he remembered that a month earlier I'd had an hour-long paper on it in the Polish class, and he sat down. And I answered from memory, word perfect, I simply recited my paper, and that was that. Finally I got to a point where I'd forgotten something, the title of a book, so I said: "But here perhaps you would help me, Headmistress, because my memory fails me." "No, that's enough", she muttered, and Garbacik couldn't stop himself, he leapt to his feet again and kissed me on both cheeks. Just before the war she threw him out of the school, and he went straight off to the university. What a mind.'

Apart from fights with the headmistress, in collaboration with a friend from the parallel boys' gymnasium Granny edited a well-regarded school literary journal, spiced up with opinion columns, inspiring poetry and personal views; the friend was madly in love with Granny, but he was two months younger, so she never even glanced at him. That passed with age, once he was a fully grown man – and along the way had become a fully grown writer, then toured half the world, finally to die of heart disease in a southern city, at the foot of a volcano – but that's another story. For the time being let's leave him in a classroom, where he has laid a sheet of paper on a desk that's dark blue with ink stains, and is drawing Lala Bieniecka in the shape of a caryatid, as 'the mainstay of Kielce culture', or striding along with a scowl on his face and Freud's *Introduction to Psychoanalysis* under his arm. In any case, one way or another, he was going to be famous in the future.

'We even ran a school postal service: anyone could drop a

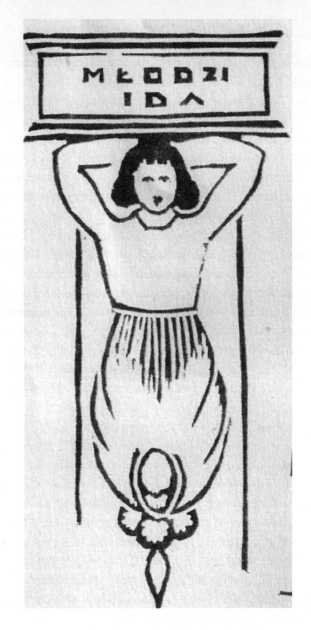

*Lala as the mainstay of Kielce culture,
an illustration from the cultural journal* Młodzi Idą *('The Young Are
Coming') by Gustaw Herling-Grudziński, c. 1935.*

letter to the editors into a special mailbox, then we read them together, and often replied within the journal. Once, I remember, we got a piece of paper with two vulgar words, starting with a *p* and a *c*, printed on it with a stamp cut out of a potato. Mr Garbacik, who used to help us to prepare the journal, cast an eye at it, crumpled it up and threw it aside, but I read it all. A couple of weeks later I was sitting with my parents and my aunt at dinner – I remember we had Little Russian borscht, and suddenly Mama said: "Valerian, I saw a strange word on a fence today, *cunt* or something like that. What does it mean? Is it short for something? The name of a political party?" Papa went purple and choked on his soup, and straight after that he had an even worse choking fit, because he'd noticed that I'd gone red too. But Mama was like that – for instance, she never would have used the word *burdel*, literally meaning a brothel, to describe chaos, but whenever she saw a mess, she'd say: "What a terrible *bardak*", because she thought it was a nice Russian word for disorder, even though it means a brothel too.'

No wonder my great-grandfather Valerian choked on his hot borscht – like any gourmet, he had his eccentricities; he loved to eat his soup piping hot, ideally straight from the pan. He himself was a superb cook, but was extremely fond of special treats. He loved to feast on all sorts of goodies. The doctors had told him to go on a diet because of his heart, but he said he'd rather live another ten years eating what he liked than twenty denying himself everything he liked, reduced to nothing but boiled carrots. 'He forced me to eat olives, but I couldn't stand them. And to drink dry wine with dinner. I would have preferred sweet wine, but Papa said: "Surely you don't want sweet wine? because if that's what you'd prefer, you won't get any…" He was fond of fish; I only once saw him give a woman a hard time – when a lady shopkeeper promised to get him fresh lampreys, but forgot all about it and sold them to someone else. My God, how he ranted… And those dinners, with my father swallowing piping hot soup, and there were always some guests, not just acquaintances but total strangers… Because you see, Papa had this habit, whenever he saw miserable-looking jobless people in the street – and those were the years of the great economic crash, so there were plenty of miserable jobless people in the streets – he would invite them home for dinner, and when they left he'd press more food on them as well. Or clothes. He couldn't bear new clothes. I remember a time when Mama insisted that he buy a new spring coat, because his old one was looking shabby, and didn't suit the dignity of his position. He griped and whined, but he did as she asked. And the very next day, as he was walking down the street, a workman renovating a house spilled some paint and splashed the new coat. "What's your size? Maybe this coat will be of more use to you than to me?" And there and then he gave it to him, and came home very happy, because he had an excuse to wear his old coat. It's a good thing he didn't bring that particular workman home with him for dinner. Mama merely insisted that he should tell her in advance, but he would say: "I've only just met them, I didn't know whom I would see along the way, how many of them there would be and if they'd be hungry." Or that gentleman, what was he called, the young engineer. He worked at a design office, in fact he earned a pretty good living, but as bad luck would have it, his wife fell seriously ill and he needed money for medicine. So he withdrew some funds from the company, with the honest intention of paying it back out of his next wage packet; unfortunately, the books were inspected just at that time and the money was found to be missing from the safe. There was a dreadful scandal, the fellow was fired from his job and from then on no one would shake hands with him – all that was said about him was "embezzler, embezzler!" On top of that his wife died. It was a hopeless situation. So what did my parents do? They regularly invited him to dinner, so that he wouldn't sit fretting at home in an empty flat.'

'And whenever dinner was late…'

'… and whenever dinner was late, Papa would fetch his violin and play one of the pieces he'd never mastered, such as Wieniawski's *Kujawiak*, which had some tricky passages… and Mama, who hated music that was off-key and always claimed a wrong note caused her physical pain, would fly out of the kitchen, shouting: "I'm almost there, I'm almost there, but for God's sake, stop playing." What else do you need for your notes?'

'The Japanese.'

'Aaah yes, the Japanese…'

The Japanese was called whatever, because Granny can't remember Japanese names, well, unless perhaps they're attached to a pair of talented hands playing in the Chopin piano competition. Either way, this Japanese fellow did have very agile hands, but he didn't play the piano – he extracted teeth.

'Look at this, Irenka,' said Counsellor Karnaukhov from behind his newspaper, 'that Japanese fellow is still in Warsaw. It says in the *Courier* that all of society has been going to him… people in the arts and government ministers. Even the prime minister went.'

'And? Did he have a tooth extracted?'

'Yes. Apparently he was very pleased with it.'

'Well, I never.'

Or: 'They've written about the Japanese again.'

'What Japanese?'

'The one who extracts teeth painlessly. He puts pressure on nerves in the jaw and pulls the tooth out like a cork.'

'Oh, Valerian, it hurts just to think about it! Please!'

It's curious that my great-grandfather was so fascinated by the oriental dentist, because he never had any trouble with his own teeth, until at the age of sixty-plus he broke a molar while – as usual – cracking open walnut shells. Either way, one morning he exclaimed: 'Irenka! The Japanese has come to Kielce. He'll be dining with us tomorrow.'

My poor great-grandmother, accustomed to never knowing how many people were coming to dinner, because Valerian might meet an acquaintance in the street, or a jobless person who hadn't had a bite to eat for two days... and so on, shrugged and just muttered that as he was a dentist he might not want to eat sweets. But Japanese food – not for love nor money, and what about Gienia – for the love of God, where on earth was she going to find Japanese food...

'It doesn't matter as long as it's tasty,' mumbled my hospitable great-grandfather in reply, optimistically flashing his bald spot as he leaned over some papers.

'So he came to dinner,' says Granny, nibbling at a slice of apple cake as she sits back in her battered old armchair, unfolding itself like a catafalque, in which both her grandpapa Leonard, her grandmama Wanda, and her mother died; 'he was small, he had a bowler hat and a walking cane, and slanted eyes. He spoke Russian, German and English, he bowed to left and right, talked about putting pressure on the nerves in the jaw, and with a persistence worthy of a better cause the wretched man ate dishes as alien to his palate as stuffed cabbage leaves, potato dumplings, and also Little Russian borscht. Until suddenly—' At this point Granny pauses.

'... he left the room,' I say.

'How do you know? Yes, he left the room. So you know this story? He went to the outhouse, because we didn't yet have an indoor lavatory in those days. Papa apologised to him for such poor conditions, said this, that and the other, down there to the left, then makes a dash for the coat rack and the umbrella stand, taps on the man's bowler hat, and tries unscrewing his cane – and yes, it can be unscrewed, and there inside it are some little notes and microfilms. Because the Japanese was a spy – while he was extracting teeth he took the opportunity to pump all those twittering generals and ministers for information, he pumped the daughters of bankers and company directors, even Supreme Court judges, MPs and senators, skilfully, not blatantly, oh no, after all, he was a polite, educated Japanese. So then he came back from the outhouse, saw Papa holding the unscrewed cane and tried to make a run for it, but whoosh! Papa grabbed him by the collar and dragged him off to the police, and they took him on wherever necessary, to counter-intelligence, I expect. And then Gienia heated up the stuffed cabbage leaves and we finished dinner.'

❀

At roughly this point in time the story of Margerytka took place, so we can now go back to the moment when I interrupted Granny (here I must confess that in reality, when I said: 'That story comes later,' Granny didn't actually stop telling it; she did say: 'Oh yes, that comes later...' but she told it to the end, merely complaining that I kept butting in). 'One evening Mr Rommel came to call. But this time, after playing a few pieces with your great-grandfather, he didn't talk about his *prunelki* but about his older daughter, Margerytka, and more to the point, about Mr Hess. So one night Margerytka was going to a ball. Mr Hess was going to the same ball too, but at the last minute he had decided to stay at home. His friends came along and said: "Listen, have a shave, dress up and come with us. Why waste your youth sitting at home? You're coming with us in the car... Zula will be there, and Marynia, and Margerytka." "Margerytka? Who's Margerytka?" "What do you mean, who? Mr Rommel the gardener's daughter. Look out of the window, she's sitting in the car." So he looked out, and fell in love instantly – she was so beautiful... a tall blonde, very tall; in any case, tall enough for it to be considered a flaw, but Hess was two point four metres tall. When he asked why she had such an unusual name and they replied "because she's German", there was no going back. In a wild rush he shaved, dressed and left. They danced the whole night away, and six weeks later they were married.'

The same cannot be said for Granny's classmate, Jadzia Żarnowska, who was like a character from a nineteenth-century drama; as lovely as a dream, she had flaxen hair in plaits, and eyes as blue as cornflowers. Her father was the son of the nobility, suffering from consumption, and her mother was a peasant girl, in good health. They fell in love. The grandfather of the future Jadzia, a despotic aristocrat, was against their marriage, but they defied him and married. The young nobleman moved to a country cottage, and there he died. The mother raised the girl on her own; combining refined aristocratic features and rural vigour, she grew up to be a goddess. A son of the nobility fell in love with her, times had changed, there weren't any despots now, so there was an engagement, rings, and a perfect idyll. But then it all broke down, and I start to feel emotional, even though I've heard it a hundred times before. 'The wedding was all arranged, but the groom's parents hadn't yet met the bride's mother; this had to be seen to as fast as possible, so there was an exchange of letters to plan a meeting. And then in one of his messages Jadzia read: "Do ask your mother not to wear a headscarf because it looks a bit too rustic... bla bla bla... I love you very much..." She took off the ring, put it in an envelope and sent it back.'

So for the hundredth time I'm moved, and for the hundredth time Granny ruins it for me by adding that the young man apologised profusely, and they did in fact live happily ever after.

Which means that once again we've reached matters of the heart, and gradually we must accept the fact that at this point in the narrative my granny has grown up enough to warrant, as she would put it, an admirer. And so we come to Julek.

IX

In fact it's hard for me to refer to Julek as anything but 'Julek', though if I had known him I'm sure I'd have addressed him formally, as 'Mr Rogoziński', with a respectful bow. But he only exists for me as the young man from Granny's stories, as part of a shiny photographic plate with a view of the Lisów garden, as a set of anecdotes, and finally as several hundred or several thousand pages of French novels in translation. I should really only mention Julek after Adzio, and before Zygmunt, in other words my grandfather; apart from that there are a few other men's names that Granny mentions with relish, just as people used to utter the names of a few favourite hotels in Biarritz or Marienbad, but let's skip them for now.

Adzio – short for Adolf – was a poet, and Granny's first boyfriend. He succeeded in taking her by storm on the literary front – that is, by having some serious journals publish his serious poems dedicated (with full sincerity) to his beloved – poems teeming with artful similes, byzantine splendours, forgotten deities and mythical beasts. And with flushed cheeks, amid a gaggle of girlfriends in the school corridor, Granny would read these serious poems in the serious journals. This was in the days when the written word still carried some weight and it was easier to kill, seduce or invigorate with it than it is today, and as Lala Bieniecka was, so they said, a mainstay of Kielce culture, to whom the printed word spoke forcefully and radiantly, she soon began to appear here and there in the company of a small, inconspicuous student, crowned with a hairstyle the popularity of which would soon be curtailed by an equally inconspicuous Austrian painter who shared his first name.

'Because you see, Adzio was from a poor, a very poor family. His father worked for the railway, his mother toiled away at home, and there were three sisters. And they had two tiny rooms in a level-crossing attendant's cottage, because it seems his father was a level-crossing attendant; the parents and the three sisters crowded into one tiny room, while Adzio lived in the other, because Adzio was a genius, he had to have room to work, and silence, and peace, and the whole house went about on tiptoes when he was writing, reading German novels or translating. And when he went off to college in Warsaw, the parents worked their already bleeding fingers to the bone to support him; luckily he had lodgings at a friend's house free of charge, that is in exchange for German conversation, because he really did know the language extremely well. The friend was amiable, but not terribly bright, and he idolised Adzio; he carried his books, cooked and cleaned for him, until finally of his own accord he had practically become his servant. They only communicated in the language of Goethe, so I couldn't understand them very well, but from the tone and from the few words I was able to catch of their artful conversation, using all the tenses and moods, with particular regard for the impera-tive, I realised that Adzio treated that Krzyś or Tadzio rather shabbily. Later on, after I'd broken up with Adzio, I quite often used to see that friend of his in town – looking pale, stooping, and casting people a nervous, feverish look. I heard that he moved away from Warsaw, but I don't know for sure.'

'After I'd broken up with Adzio' – because breaking up with Adzio was inevitable. Granny did in fact go on reading poems dedicated to her in serious journals, and sixty years on she could still remember several lines from a funeral poem written

on the death of Marshal Piłsudski* – about a lioness of snow,
perishing in the sunlight on the railings, and Thanatos walking
across the roofs – but enduring the constant scenes, the furious
fits of jealousy and hysteria, including throwing himself on the
floor and banging his fists against the parquet, was most definitely not my granny's style.

'Until one day I went to a ball with him, and before it to a
spiritualist séance, because that was very fashionable at the
time, all those whirling tables, mediums, summoning up
spirits, linking hands and so on. There sat my girlfriends and I,
one beside another, around a table, with a small saucer and a
round alphabet chart on it... I can't remember how it worked,
but when one of the girls shook or moved the saucer somehow, the letters were picked out of the circle one by one.
Naturally we asked for the names of our future husbands –
one girl was told Ludwik, another got Antoni or Piotr, yet
another got Janusz or maybe Marian, but when I asked, the
saucer whirled away like mad, spelling out the sentence: "Fear
not, sweetheart, it will be OK". You can imagine how they
laughed at me, saying I'd be either an old maid or a kept
woman. And then we went to the ball, where in literary
company Adzio began to pontificate that inspiration was vital,
but a woman, a muse, was non-essential, just a way of
off-loading an impulse that hampers free creativity, and such
like. But everyone knew he was saying this in the presence of
his official muse and girlfriend. They tried to find a way to
restrain him, to get him off the subject, until finally Julek
asked me to dance – because somehow Julek was the only
person Adzio wasn't jealous of – I don't actually know why,
perhaps he thought he was ugly? So Julek put his arms around
me, brought his lips close to my ear and said: "Fear not, sweetheart, it will be OK."' And then things moved at lightning

speed – as usual in my granny's life; in later days of glory her friends used to call her Hurricane Helena, and said it was no accident that typhoons are called by women's names.

'I waited until Adzio had passed all his exams, because he had a weak heart and a rather neurotic temperament, and then I told him I'd had enough of him; I said I might call on him from time to time, but he wasn't to call on me… because you see, I could always leave, if he started making one of his rumpuses, but I couldn't so easily throw him out of my place… and that was that. Six months later I ran into him in the street and only recognised him when he bowed to me. And that convinced me that I was completely over it.

'When I told Mama that I was seeing a charming young man called Julian Rogoziński, she stopped in the middle of the kitchen, because she was busy with some cooking, giving the servant instructions at the time, so she waved a large wooden spoon about and said: "Rogoziński? Rogoziński? Isn't that the young scoundrel who failed to graduate from high school for four years?" Because you need to know that at the Kielce high school there was a fashion for the boys in the graduation class to cut small squares into their school caps with penknives and then sew them back together again with thick pink cord in running stitch. But Julek had done it at once in the first year, on top of which he walked about with a cane and wore a monocle – in short, my mother had plenty of reason to suppose her daughter had become enamoured of an ass.'

❧

Apart from the charm and the cap Julek had a mummy too.

' "Your mother has such southern looks, that black hair and olive skin… is Mrs Rogozińska Greek, or Spanish perhaps?" he was often asked. And, shoving his hat to the back of his head, he would say: "Mummy? Yes, she's Gweek, yes, Spanish. On one side her granny was a Glaubitzer and on the other a Braumann." Because he sought out all the grandmothers and great-grandmothers in his genealogical tree – in fact his mummy's name was Kirchner and it's true that she wasn't exactly Aryan... but she didn't have Semitic features... she was just a tall, slender, handsome woman. Beautiful hair. She was very young when she married Mr Rogoziński, the manager of a factory making bentwood furniture, he was charming and elegant, with family connections that made an impression, being... my God, I've totally forgotten. Anyway, Julek's great-grandfather, or maybe his great-great-grandfather, was a man called Fraget who made silver-plated tableware, knives and forks... And this Fraget, who was an ordinary member of the gentry, but who made a fortune, married, with all that wealth, into the noble Mirski family, who were as poor as church mice, but with a ducal title. And later on Julek took me to see various Counts Krasiński as his official fiancée... Anyway, one time we went to the grave of this Fraget together, and there was a ceramic portrait on it, you see, and just imagine – it was the spitting image of Julek, the same features, the same facial expression; we were stunned by the likeness. And look how curiously it all fits together – from early childhood he was drawn to everything French, he learnt the language in a flash and first translated poetry when he was still at high school... true, he was a duffer at mathematics, and during his graduation exam the teacher had to prompt him to remember the formula for the surface area of a circle, but by the time he took the exams he already had a series of publications in various journals to his name, and somehow they pushed him through... The similarity to Fraget and the Francophilia, well, it was incredible...'

'What about Mr Rogoziński?'

'What?'

'Mr Rogoziński. There was a mummy, but was there a daddy to make up the pair?'

'No. I never met him – not even Julek had met him, for the simple reason that he was a posthumous child. His father suffered from severe renal tuberculosis and had to have a kidney surgically removed. Unfortunately, the surgeon was either old or absent-minded – in any case, he took out the healthy kidney and left the ailing one, and Mr Rogoziński died in the prime of life after several weeks in his death throes, but didn't live to see his son. And as the widow of this paragon of virtue, Julek's mummy resolved never to marry again, out of respect for the memory of the deceased. However, that didn't prevent her from having the occasional admirer – it seems her husband's memory suffered less on this front, and Mummy was a young and extremely alluring woman.'

And so here comes the story of Karczówka. It's on its way, because Granny is nervously adjusting the bedspread or the phloxes in the vase.

'One time she happened to be receiving one of these lovers, when Julek, aged about ten or twelve, went into her bedroom and saw her *in flagrante*. Shocked, he rushed out of the house in his nightshirt, barefoot, in the middle of the night, and ran to Karczówka, a hill beyond the town. They only found him the next morning, frozen to the bone, wet with dew. As a result he had various complications later on, and he used to go to see a psychoanalyst. And when he told her that he had a fiancée, she replied: "A fiancée? Very good, bring her here, we'll see if she's right for you." And he did. At first I sat there feeling very anxious, but then we started to talk…'

'So not without reason did Gutek draw you with *An Introduction to Psychoanalysis* under your arm…'

'Not without reason. Finally, after an hour she said: "You couldn't have done better. Rarely does one come upon such an internally well-organised personality."'

❧

His literary talents, lovely lips and remarkable intelligence were not Julek's only merits. For example, he talked in his sleep. What's more, he did it in verse, one poem a night, and in alphabetical order. Her chronicles record the ones starting with B and M:

> *Buttons are often distressingly prone*
> *to coming unfastened on their own.*
> *And trousers loathe this mean deceit*
> *that makes them fall down in the street.*
>
> *Melons are big and greasy fruits,*
> *Melons are closely related to sprouts.*

'I didn't believe he did it in his sleep,' says Granny, stretched in a comfortable pose in her armchair, with a glass of tea; naturally, as befits a half-Russian, Granny drinks her tea from a glass, often with a small saucer of cherry or raspberry jam on the side, 'but one time I tried saying: "Julek, roll onto your left side. Go on, roll over. Good. Now do it again. And again…" until he fell out of bed and woke up. Slightly bruised,' adds Granny with a mischievous smile, 'so maybe he wasn't pretending. Although he was quite prepared to make greater sacrifices than that for the sake of a practical joke. Do you know the story about the saints? Yes, you do. Of course you do. A lady came to call on my parents, who was terribly devout, and we unwisely left her on

her own with Julek, come what may, my official fiancé. And he
says to her: "Ah, Madam, I've just been to Rome." The lady
oohed and aahed, blushing in admiration. "Oh, how marvel-
lous! And what did you see there? Did you see the pope, the
tombs of the martyrs and the Appian Way?" "Oh, yes," replies
Julek, "and the wonderful antiquities, you see, the churches and
museums..." "Why yes, you are a man of art..." "The art may
be one thing, but the profound religious experiences are on
quite another level..." The lady goes pink. "Although Madam, I
must say that here I did discern a somewhat discordant note.
Nay, indeed, such a thing is possible. Just imagine if you please,
the Vatican has no money. The Holy Father is almost bankrupt.
The appropriate setting for the liturgy, the papal court, the charitable activities – it all consumes a vast amount of cash. In view
of which, one of the cardinals came up with an idea that, after
some initial hesitation, has now been implemented. It allows
film stars to buy themselves advertising space on the altars."
The lady goes pale. "Of course, the more popular the saint, the
higher the price. The apostles sell like hot cakes. Valentino is
there as John the Evangelist, Greta Garbo is St Teresa, our Pola
Negri has taken Mary Magdalene, Lilian Gish is St Catherine,
and Clark Gable is St Sebastian. And you know what, as one
goes about the places of worship in Rome, finding a star or a
starlet on every altar, it does rather interfere with one's prayers.
Even if we know we're offering a supplication to St Jude the
Apostle, and not Errol Flynn." He recited all this with the stony
expression of Buster Keaton, in other words St Jerome, merci-
lessly staring into the lady's eyes, while she suffered flushed
cheeks, palpitations and silent spasms. Anyway, she never
showed up at our house again.'

❧

'What's on television tonight? *A Streetcar Named Desire*. Noo, I'm not going to watch it, there's a Chopin concert on the radio. I remember travelling by streetcar with Julek – he called to me from the other end of the carriage: "Come hither, dear heart", or some such old-fashioned phrase, and everyone looked at us. In one of Chmielewska's crime novels* there was a man who had learnt Polish from Wujek's sixteenth-century translation of the Bible, and it was very comical. In fact, at Lisów there was a Wujek Bible lying on a side table, with beautiful illustrations by Doré, featuring angels, prophets, patriarchs…'

'And what became of it?' I ask sacramentally.

'Oh, that very thin paper is perfect for rolling cigarettes. The Soviets took it.'

❧

'Once one of Julek's friends told me how they got pretty tipsy and somehow ended up at his flat together. The maid opened the door. The boy was sloshed and started rambling away at her, but Julek said: "Don't even try talking to her. She's clueless about French literature."

'The same maid, probably not in an act of revenge, but more likely out of goodwill, once rearranged his entire library in his absence by colour and size: books in purple covers from large to small, blue ones from large to small, green ones, and so on. It took him about a month to reorganise that mess.'

❧

'Eventually, I was very much the official fiancée. Julek regularly took me to the "Zodiac", one of the favourite cafes of the literary world, where I once had a moment of glory, which he enjoyed with me, when Gombrowicz* came in, and from the

Julian Rogoziński as a young man.

doorway shouted to the entire room, pointing at me with his outstretched finger at the end of his outstretched hand, aiming that hand and that finger at me: "Who, oh who is this beautiful schoolgirl?" Julek went about proud as a peacock all week... Another time we're sitting there, and in comes Pawełek Hertz.* He was as handsome as a young Rameses, slender, with large black eyes and raven-black hair, and with it skin as pale as ivory... a vision. He minces along, swinging his hips, and drapes himself across a row of chairs. So there we sit, and then he goes to the telephone and says into the receiver loud enough for everyone to hear, simply everyone: "Jarosław"' – who can imitate Granny's faultless pronunciation of the ł in the name "Jarosław"; and who knows how on earth to render it in print! – '"*do* come and see me tonight. I have such *lovely* new pyjamas, you *must* see me in them. Without fail." Of course everyone knew at once that he was talking to the great writer Iwaszkiewicz.* And next day, in the social diary section of the literary journal *Wiadomości Literackie* there were these three lines from a little poem:

> Mummy, through a pair of specs,
> cast a glance at young Pawełek,
> and then she uttered: Fie!

'And no one knew what it was about except for a handful of regulars at the "Zodiac" and their friends.'

'What about the araucaria?'

'Well, yes, as I'm on the subject of where Julek took me, I should tell you about that too. As his very official fiancée – although my father still hadn't agreed to the wedding because he wanted me to finish my studies first – he presented me to his family, including Count and Countess Krasiński. And there,

before I'd had a chance to open my mouth, on the very thresh-
old I knocked over a tall guéridon, quite idiotically positioned,
I'll have you know – you tell me, a guéridon on the threshold?
And on it there was...'

'An araucaria,' I said, unable to stop myself from uttering
that word; it has a similar flavour to words like marabou, Kama
sutra, encaustic or Tarquinian.

'Yes, that's it, an araucaria. And of course I made a dreadful
gaffe, because I knocked the araucaria off the guéridon. And as
if that weren't bad enough, I made an even more terrible blun-
der, because I threw myself headlong and caught it in mid-air,
instead of letting it fall to the floor, smash to bits and spatter
earth in all directions. Then I was presented to the aunts, who
amid the smiles and casual conversation were staring at me like
a Martian... and later on there was a dinner, and for dessert we
had a delicious crème brûlée that tasted so exquisite that I took
the liberty of asking for a second helping. Deep down I reckoned the araucaria had already done its work, as far as burying
my social position went, so I might as well enjoy another
portion. And after I'd eaten it I found that my head was slightly,
ever so slightly spinning, because it was laced with alcohol.
Julek politely asked me not to demand a third helping, and
somehow the evening came to an end, as if propelled with long
poles by the entire company.'

X

I went off to university in Warsaw solidly equipped by Granny with a rich supply of chronicles, a collection of tales about what college life in Warsaw is really like. In fact it was a lecture in instalments (the reprint of which starts here and ends about a dozen pages further on), delivered over many afternoons and evenings in late summer, as we were picking flowers at the allotment to make bouquets or as we were coming home late at night, savaged by mosquitoes, burdened by kilos of windfall apples, and replete with the flavour of raspberries and wild strawberries ripening all day long, dug out from under intense green leaves.

'My first accommodation was found by my friend Basia. Basia was a lovely girl, with black hair, so black it was dark blue, with rainbows running through it... but why deny it, as the daughter of ardent National Democrats she had definite political views and corresponding boyfriends from the National Radical Camp.* And it was she who found us a landlady who may have been pure in race, but was dirty in the flesh, charged us extra for each minute of a hot shower, constantly made a fuss about us using electricity when we were studying in the evenings, and so on and so forth. And then Kingfisher came to our rescue – she was Julek's cousin, who had befriended Mr Luksemburg. Mr Luksemburg, a Supreme Court judge, resided with his wife and servants in a large flat on Czacki Street, not far from the university, and it seemed he would have no objection to taking in two nice, pretty students as lodgers.

'He received us in the drawing room. Handsome, elegant, with superb manners, Mr Luksemburg was fond of a joke and was very open-handed. He said that as friends of his friends we must feel like guests in his home, so there was no need for us to worry about rent. He only had a few modest demands: from such and such an hour we weren't to appear in the drawing room, because that was the time of day when he liked to walk about naked. And a couple of other injunctions of this kind; perhaps it gave him pleasure to pose as Bluebeard. Of course a week later it was quite clear that the entire conversation had been a joke, but it made an indelible impression on Basia.

'As a high-ranking civil servant, Mr Luksemburg had a very high salary, and on top of that he increased his income by writing, in collaboration with a lady, crime novels in instalments for the daily press, but he blew most of it at the races, so the house was not particularly affluent, and poor Mrs Luksemburg performed real miracles to keep it up to standard. So we did in fact pay rent, but to the wife, in secret from her husband, for whom we were permanent guests.

'Apart from the master and his wife and us there were the servants too – a young maid, who was rather clumsy and none too bright, but a good sort, and Antonina, the old servant, who acted as housekeeper, ran the whole set-up and constantly bickered with the mistress, a meek and gentle woman. Antonina's advantage lay in the fact that she could always say, and often did: "I was here many years before you, Madam, so please believe that I'm right," which could be just as good an argument in discussing a recipe for Easter cake as having the kitchen pipes replaced. Because Antonina was bla-bla years old and then some, from the days of the first Mrs Luksemburg, and knew every nook and cranny of the house.

'The first Mrs Luksemburg was a highly intelligent, ambitious and well-educated woman. She was fully aware that her young husband was too idle to study voluntarily for his law exams of his own accord, so she spent hour after hour quizzing him on every possible codex and statute. Eventually, although her degree was in Polish literature, she knew the law just as well as he did, if not better. Every morning she woke him up at six, dragged him out of bed, made him get washed and dressed, quickly served him a hearty breakfast, and then locked him in a small room with his textbooks. She let him out for an hour-long test, and then shut him in again. And so it continued for weeks on end.

'Finally Mr Luksemburg passed his last exam, happily went to get drunk with his colleagues and came home just before dawn. And to play a prank on him, a silly trick, his wife woke him up at six. He got up, washed, had his breakfast as every day, in a lethargic state; finally he opened his textbooks, and only then did it dawn on him that he hadn't a single line in them left to learn, not a single paragraph. He got up from the table, went straight to his wife and demanded a divorce.

'No wonder the second Mrs Luksemburg was quiet and meek. How very often I heard her trying to appease her husband, as he yelled over his newspaper: "Idiot! Moron!" and then did it again over the telephone into the remote ear of the lady with whom he wrote the crime novels by turns: "You'd have to be mad to leave the hero in a situation like that, and what am I to do now, you wretched woman, what on earth got into that female head of yours, dear madam?" And his wife would tug at his arm and whisper: "But Towser, it won't do, Towser, stop shouting at the lady, I implore you..." Apart from that, she floated about the house looking crestfallen, because not only did she have a hard time coping with the eternally leaking budget, on top of that Antonina treated her at best like an expendable waif, like a necessary evil. We consoled her as best we could, and the extra few zlotys she received from us were of some help to her in the everyday struggle against this strange, luxurious privation. Either way, we were both more than satisfied. Mr Luksemburg held lengthy debates with Basia about her world view and would ask: "So tell me, the Jews are to blame for everything, eh? The cost of living, the poor state of the roads, and the government instability too?" And with unwavering faith Basia would explain to him, word by word, as if reciting from an NRC brochure. "And tell me, Miss Barbara," Mr Luksemburg would ask, "have you never met a Jew who would do you a favour disinterestedly? Always nothing but that deplorable desire for profit?" And she would say yes, of course, yes, indeed. And there they'd sit in the drawing room, in the yellow lamplight. Now and then Mr Luksemburg would turn to me and cast a knowing smile, I would wink just as knowingly, choking back laughter, and I'd pretend to be reading something closely. Whenever one of Basia's beaux called, he'd say: "Miss Barbara, I hear in the receiver a voice brimming with love for the fatherland." As far as I know, he escaped from Poland in 1939 along with the government, via Zaleszczyki. From the West he wrote to his wife, and sent divorce papers – as an Aryan she could have had terrible problems if she didn't divorce. I heard that after the war they got back together and lived long and happily.

'Though I have no idea what happened to Antonina. But first I have to tell you about the ring. My mother, as you know, had a lot of lovely jewellery. And when I went off to Warsaw... that's a point, do remember that your mother's to give you some smart clothes to take with you... when I went off to Warsaw, she gave me a beautiful ring, an antique made in Amsterdam, with a large sapphire surrounded by tiny diamonds, so I'd have something for grand outings. So I only wore it for special occasions, and guarded it with my life. Until one day after returning from a ball at the writers' union, I think, next morning I looked in my little jewellery box, and the ring wasn't there. I could remember taking it off the night before and putting it somewhere – on the table, on the chest of drawers? I'd been so sleepy – and the ring had vanished. One servant started looking for it, so did the other, we shifted all the furniture and shook out pockets – nothing. Finally I went to the post office and sent a telegram to Kielce: "Something terrible has happened. Lala." The reply comes from my mother: "What's wrong? Pregnant or sick? Mama." I went back to the post office: "I've lost my sapphire ring. Lala." And another reply: "So what, silly, is your finger getting cold?"

'And six months later Antonina suddenly disappeared. They spent a few days searching for her, making inquiries and worrying that maybe she'd been the victim of a crime or something – until down in the cellar they found two fur coats, some silver, and some bundles full of valuable knick-knacks, all prepared ahead of time to be carried off. Evidently she'd been afraid something would give her away and had legged it with nothing but the lightest things – including, I'd swear it, my ring made in Amsterdam with the sapphire surrounded by tiny diamonds. I suspect she survived the war. People like that usually survive.'

❧

'Judge Luksemburg was of course an exceptional Jew. Most of the Jews in Warsaw lived in poverty in Nalewki, trading in anything they could in hundreds of teeny little shops, inhabiting crowded basements and shabby tenements, arguing in the streets and pushing their way along the pavements. Every month I always put aside a little money, and before going home for Easter, Christmas or the long vacation, I went shopping. How good they were at bargaining! Who on earth can do that today? No one. I remember, one time I came to a shop where they had such a lovely hat... Black and white, incredibly smart, but so what, as it cost about fifty zlotys. Well, never mind. The salesman says: "Do try it on, my dear young lady, take a look at yourself, what a wonder!" I say I haven't the money, I can't afford it, to which he says: "Money? Why worry about money? Money's the least problem." I try it on, he's delighted, smiling, dancing, flapping about, beaming. I put it down. He puts it in my hands. I put it down. He laughs again. "Sir," I say at last, "I have such and such a number of zlotys, of which I need x amount for my ticket, x for food for the journey, and that leaves fifteen zlotys. I simply can't afford this hat." But he wraps it up and says: "So fifteen it is. You will say you bought it from me, you'll tell everyone. You look so lovely in this hat, why not go about in it, show yourself in it? And I'll make up the difference on some ugly old bird." '

❦

When Granny started to lose her memory, suddenly everything was from somewhere. A pair of plimsolls for example, bought – so she claimed – on Żabia Street in Warsaw. Before the war.

'There's still a price,' she says, showing a fluorescent green label, 'sixty zlotys. That was a lot of money, my father couldn't stop wondering why I spent so much on shoes, because he always went about in any old pair and had to keep changing them.'

'They're Chinese plimsolls bought last year in Oliwa.'

'What do you mean, Chinese?'

'All right,' I said, glancing at them, 'I take it back, they're Brazilian.'

If things weren't from Żabia Street in Warsaw, they were from Lisów, inherited from Grandmama Wanda, from her grandfather or her father.

And incidentally, I thought, isn't she right to say that? All these things belonged to the deceased; they're part of the great community of orphaned objects, and does it matter by whom exactly they were orphaned? They're from the past, like her entire life; and what on earth is gained by clinging to dates and facts?

I made Granny a folder for photographs of Julek, my grandfather, my great-grandfather and Uncle Paweł.

'Take Paweł out,' she said, 'all the others are dead. I don't want him to become one of the dead.'

What a house, what a life full of the departed. And almost everyone is here, in photographs, in things and mementos.

❧

'And do be sure to go and visit my apartment,' Granny said in parting, winking at me. Her apartment, meaning the Royal Castle. Because after a year at Mr and Mrs Luksemburg's, Granny made a lot of changes in her life – she changed faculty from Law to Romance Studies and moved in with Uncle Kazimierz Brokl, a custodian at the Royal Castle.

'My uncle got his job when Mrs Mościcka sacked the previous custodian.'

'Mrs Mościcka? Not her husband, the president? The one who didn't like the melons at Morawica?'

'Yes, Mrs. You see, President Mościcki married a much younger woman... a disagreeable creature. Very disagreeable. She bossed the castle staff around like anything, changed some of the furnishings and did some redecorating. One day they summoned the custodian to say they were redoing the upstairs bathroom and needed his consent. "What idiot chose these tiles?" he exclaimed, when he saw the interior. "Madam President." And an hour later when he passed the president in the stairwell and greeted him politely, the president gave no reply. Not a word – he just walked on. "Mr President, don't you know me?" "Indeed I do," said Mościcki. "From the very worst side." And so they fired him. That was why my uncle didn't want to take the job, but the sacked custodian implored him to.'

'And thanks to that you lived in the Royal Castle?'

'Thanks to that. In all my life I never lived in worse conditions. Because they were rooms for the servants of King Stanisław.' If I raised my arm, I could touch the ceiling. But then my aunt and uncle were both small. What's more, my uncle was very good-looking too... Aunt Adi wasn't all that pretty, but she loved him terrifically. At the dinner table she always held his hand, and he responded to those caresses of hers, automatically somehow; I think he found it a bit tedious after all those years. Aunt Adi was a German and she spoke very comical Polish. She used to pass some rather original judgements in that broken Polish of hers.'

'Such as?'

'Such as the one about the "yooterus", when her daughter, Jasia, abandoned her fiancé. She'd had the fiancé for years, and he was handsome, intelligent and well mannered; until suddenly, two months before the wedding, she met young Sulkiewicz. Sulkiewicz was the son of Black Michał, a Tatar, who had once brought a Tatar cavalry unit to Piłsudski's aid; he was terribly funny because he had bandy legs, like the typical lancer...'

'Black Michał or his son?'

'The son, the son. He was a lancer too. And his name was Michał too. But he was a redhead. For a Tatar that's peculiar. He was as ugly as sin, let's be frank about it. And the official fiancé was a paragon, apart perhaps from the fact that he had a funny surname, Piegża, I think. But it was a good Lithuanian name. Next door to my uncle lived the chief of protocol, also from a good Lithuanian family – his name was Kupciełło. Mrs Kupciełło was a woman of great beauty, with hair so black that dark-blue rainbows ran through it, and she had dark-blue eyes to go with it, and skin like ivory: almost white, not like a corpse, but like porcelain. She was as thick as two short planks. Witkacy* adored painting her, and there were well over ten of those portraits hanging in the corridor at the castle; I don't know what happened to them, but they probably went up in flames in 1939. However, I wasn't talking about Mrs Kupciełło, but that Piegża fellow, whom Jasia dropped.'

'She dropped him?'

'Yes. For the ugly Michał. And she was so beautiful... she had the loveliest bust I've ever seen. At first I felt a bit sorry for her, but I think they must have been united by some incredible, chemical passion; after they got married, they sometimes came to dinner at my uncle and aunt's. They'd sit and eat, and chat, until suddenly they'd look at each other, go red and say: "We must go now," and rush off to bed at breakneck speed. And then Aunt Adi would say: "Vun must make a dee-tsizion, do I sink for my yooterus or does my yooterus sink for me?" And other things of the kind. She told us about her cousin, who had stayed in Germany, and at first had climbed up the Nazi Party struc-tures, but then somehow had fallen out of favour. She said he was a prisoner in his own home, spied on by the gardener, the chauffeur and the maids... One time she came to visit him, but he couldn't talk to her alone at all; finally they drove out to a lake, where they managed to get rid of the servants for a while, so he was able tell her all about the terrible poverty in Germany, because everything went to heavy industry, about the storm troopers, the denunciations, and so on. But at once the chauf-feur appeared, and the cousin had to move on to neutral topics. We listened to this as if it were a cock-and-bull story, and we didn't entirely believe Aunt Adi. But with hindsight...'

'What else about the castle?'

'What can I say? I never went on a tour of it, because my uncle was always saying: "You can't go around the place without a guide – let's make a date when I have more time, and I'll show you every last corner." And the result was that we never did. Just like Julek, who beat it into my head that Boy-Żeleński's* translations of Proust are no good because he breaks the original rhythm and loses a lot of the effect, so I should wait until he'd translated the whole thing himself. But he only ever translated the last volume. Oh well, never mind. The castle. At the end of the corridor lived Mrs Żeromska* and her daughter, and we walked past on tiptoes, because it was like walking past the widow and child of Słowacki, or Mickiewicz;* Żeromski meant the world to our generation. The fact that privately he behaved like a rat was quite another matter, but for most Poles he was an unquestioned authority on moral, social and political issues. And there were peasants from Lisów standing outside the castle.'

'What?'

'Because the Lisów peasants were often very tall and very handsome, so they took them for the guard of honour. Just imagine, they went off to the army as adult men, and when they came back to the village they were twenty centimetres taller. Their trousers reached halfway down their calves. They'd finally been able to eat their fill. What's more, one of them once saved me from a pest. A fellow in the tram tried to accost me, I told him to get lost, I got off the tram, and boarded another, but he was still after me the whole time – I changed trams again, and yet again. Finally, I was outside the castle, and there in the sentry box stood young Osman, who saluted me, and then I said: "Please get rid of this man – he has chased me halfway across town." When the fellow saw what was coming to him he was off like a shot. And another time Mr Kościeński's nephew tried to rape me.'

'The man from the Revenue and Customs Office, whose cat bopped the dog on the nose?'

'The very same. Papa had asked me to deliver something to the nephew from his uncle. So we fixed a time, and he invited me to his place... it never occurred to me that he might want something from me... there were in fact rumours about him, they said he was a bon vivant and that he had... syphilis, you see, but our acquaintance was of such an official nature... so in I go, and he locks the door, then says he set it all up specially to have me fall into his arms, etcetera, on and on he rambles, drooling. I yelled at him that I was going to start screaming, and he said: "Scream away, no one can hear you here." Then I ran up to the window and said I'd throw myself out—'

'Gosh, just like Lucretia. But without the knife.'

'And it worked. "You fool," he said to me, exactly like our parish priest. And he let me go. Not long after I ran into Mr Kościeński on a train. I told him everything, and he said: "My dear girl, he's such a prankster, he loves a good joke." I was speechless, simply speechless. Oh, and that reminds me of my father. My theoretical father, Bieniecki. I had occasion to meet up with him from time to time. After all, in a certain sense he was a friend of the family and, at least in official terms, he was my father. So one time we met at the Brokls, he came to visit me. A friend of mine from high school happened to be there. So I introduced them to each other: "My father, Kazimierz Bieniecki, my friend, Tuśka Rośnicka", and they both turned crimson. At once I realised. He was well over sixty by then, can you imagine? She was twentysomething. But then he always did have success with women.'

❧

'Apart from Bieniecki I used to meet up with Romusia's

husband too. Or rather her widower. We ran into each other by chance… he invited me to his home, and I agreed, not because I had any great affection for him, but because I felt ashamed of having thrown away the chocolates and the dolls he had brought me long ago. So I paid a visit. A terribly ugly woman opened the door to me, who looked like a Mongol maid, a skivvy of the worst kind; but it turned out that this was his wife, a former nurse at his consulting room. They had two little sons who were ugly too.'

'Granny!'

'Now what is it? Really! And just imagine, as I walk about their house, the wife and the children are looking at me in a strange way… and all over the place there are photographs of Romusia. In a scarf, in a hat, in a ball dress, in bed, in an armchair, in a light dress, in a dark dress, everywhere, absolutely everywhere, in all sorts of poses and from all sorts of years. I drank up my tea, said goodbye and left the house; on the way to the tram I thought about that woman, the poor wife.'

❧

After moving to the castle, Granny transferred to the Romance Studies faculty, where Julek was a student. It was then, after some anti-Semitic incidents, that they introduced Jewish benches in the lecture rooms at Warsaw University.

'And those Jewish girls, because in our faculty it was mostly girls, protested by standing against the walls during all the lectures. The most wretched of all was Mania Paszyc, whom I remembered from Kielce, because Aunt Sasha was meant to teach her to play the piano… The Paszyc family were unimaginably rich, he was the director of a Belgian or French power station… as you know, after the first war lots of Western factories were built in Poland, which twenty years later would pass

into state ownership, but while they were foreign they charged
rip-off prices for everything, and the employees were paid very
high salaries, not to mention a director like that; he was said to
have a monthly income of six thousand, which was a tremendous amount of money – so he had a car, lots of servants, a
large house. Mania's mother was a rather unlovable creature,
a typical nouveau riche, who did everything to make sure
every zloty earned by her husband was plain to see. She drove
about Kielce in a carriage with a pack of poodles wearing red
bows; as soon as the Germans invaded, someone gave her
away. But that's not what I want to talk about. Mania Paszyc,
brought up in luxury and comfort, was quite simply an incredibly lazy girl; when Aunt Sasha came for the first lesson, Mania
was assigned a maid to turn the pages of the music for her; so
Aunt Sasha said that if Mania was going to be her pupil, unfortunately she would not only have to turn the pages herself, but
also strike the keyboard. And just imagine, that wretched idler,
who never did a thing, went from class to class thanks to her
father's money, and went to college to become a match that
was not just rich but also symbolically educated, but here she
was, having to stand against the wall for hours on end. She
would slump and lean against it, snivelling. The other girls
would cast her deeply pitiful looks. And I of course, who used
to give the Jewish children rides on my toboggan, sat down on
the Jewish benches.' At this point Granny smiles, as if she'd
pulled a fast one on history; naturally, my granny, who all her
life was a beacon of enlightenment, the daughter of a lawyer,
was bound to go and sit on the Jewish benches. 'Those girls
ran up, and one after another they cried: "Fellow student,
we're not sitting down, we're protesting!" And I said I was
protesting too, because I wasn't a Jew. After me, Julek changed
seats too, and so did Booby. Booby was a friend of Julek's –
someone had once given him that name, and it had stuck, no

one ever called him anything else. It's funny, but I can't remember what his real name was, I'm not sure I ever knew it. And, funniest of all, he was a highly intelligent, sensitive boy, that Booby fellow. We sat there through every year, up to the final lectures, when the university was closed, because anti-Semitic riots had erupted again, several professors had been publicly insulted, one had had a spittoon thrown at him, and there were gangs of those NRC men with voices brimming with love for the motherland loitering in the courtyard. One time I'm walking along, and just imagine, here are five brawny students with big sticks, getting ready to beat up this small, skinny Jew in spectacles... So I go straight up to them and say: "Well, bravo, what heroes, five against one – you could have found yourself a smaller one though, or a girl, chivalrous medieval knights in the flesh, it's plain to see!" They come at me with those sticks, one's about to strike, but another grabs him by the arm and says: "Stop, I know her." I look at him, and it's the son of my teacher from my pre-war primary school, the one who didn't want me to buy things at Jewish shops. And sounding outraged and disgusted he says to me: "Well, I never would have expected to meet you in these circumstances." And I say: "As for me, I had every expectation of meeting you in exactly these circumstances," and turned on my heel. But I had the satisfaction that the poor Jewish boy had got away from them! I was supposed to be taking my final exam in October, I'd have defended my dissertation... hmm, but the war broke out.'

'And did Julek pass them all?'

'Long before. He was working, translating. My God, what a man he was... I'd come to see him, we'd have a bit of a cuddle, and then he'd suddenly get up and say: "Sorry, Lalunia, but I have to translate another ten pages." And he'd do it.'

'And did you get bored?'

'Bored? Not at all! He had a superb library...' (I've forgotten I'm dealing with the mainstay of Kielce culture.) 'And he worked on and on like that, but even so he never earned much. Did I tell you about the time we went to the writers' ball? A huge gala, I made myself a little tailcoat specially for the occasion' – at this point I tried to conjure up a mental picture of Granny as a pre-war *savante*, but somehow it didn't really work – 'and there were crowds and crowds and crowds of people – and excellent food. But as you know, writers, all starving, impoverished, how ravenously they went for it... Julek was busy talking, so I tried to get him some food, but all I managed to rescue was a pear. A pear, can you imagine! I don't think I've ever gone so hungry at a party, maybe only at the Shah of Persia's.'

But Granny must have been busy at the table too, because that was when she had her first taste of turkey in Malaga wine... half a century later, I remember it clear as day, she came back from a birthday party full of joy, because the hostess had made the famous turkey in Malaga wine, familiar to us all from her story about the writers' ball and the pear. What's more, the hostess had a recipe, thanks to which I can provide it here – after all, it is part of the great narrative too.

Sear the turkey breasts lightly in a frying pan without letting them release too much of their flavour, and then boil them in water. Remove, and to the reserved water add an equal amount of sweet wine. Then add as much fruit jelly (e.g. sour cherry or blackcurrant – the main thing is for it to be bland in taste and red in colour) as you need for that amount of liquid. Place slices of turkey breast in deep plates, scatter them liber-ally with raisins and pour on the jelly. Lay grapes on top (whole or halved, best of all red, because the colour matches), and put them in the fridge. There's probably a grander recipe for this, but that's exactly how turkey in Malaga wine is prepared in our house.

❧

Meanwhile Julek was working at the editorial office of a journal, let's call it *Parnassus*, run by the phenomenally rich and extremely well-educated son of Jewish factory owners. For Granny, who gave the Jewish children toboggan rides etcetera, it wasn't the slightest problem – whereas the fact that Mr N. was known for his... Greek proclivities, and Julek was a very handsome young man, did prompt certain reservations.

'But ultimately nothing happened,' Granny would say in elaboration of this story, 'because N never propositioned Julek. He satisfied himself with the cleaners, the servants and couriers... My God, there was no finer editorial office in Warsaw as far as the beauty of the staff was concerned... Either way, there wasn't much money in it, so my father categorically refused to let us get married until I had finished my studies.'

'But you never did.'

'No, I didn't – in fact I only had one exam left, but the university was closed because of the anti-Semitic incidents. But by then I had the most difficult exams behind me.'

'For instance?'

'The hardest was with Professor Jarra, but that was in the law faculty. Jarra was said to be a monstrous pedant who asked agonising questions and failed everyone... so they all swotted away like mad, but you needed to understand, not swot. So I got there, passed the exam, and Jarra stood up from behind his desk, came over and kissed me on the brow, saying: "I haven't had a student like you for years." The other hard one I had was with Kotarbiński. Kotarbiński didn't take the classes himself, but had his assistant Bolesław Miciński do it for him. What an intelligent person he was! The lessons consisted entirely of him sitting at the lectern, while I sat on a bench, and we swapped comments over the heads of the other students, who had no idea what we were on about. I went to the exam excellently well prepared, but the professor had some other classes and would only start to examine us at six in the evening. So all day we waited, I helped everyone and explained the subject, because I was the best at it, until one of the girls actually said: "Don't talk so much, or what you're saying will fly out of your head." I laughed. The professor came, apologised profusely, and said we could come back the next day, but I preferred to take the exam at once. I went in, and as soon as he asked the first question my mind was a complete blank. A black hole. But I answered the second one easily, and the third one too, so then I said: "Excuse me, Professor, but I do know the answer to the first question, I was just a bit nervous at the start…" "No, no, let's not worry about it… you've got a B." I was furious. Next day I saw Miciński, and he said: "So could the professor find a high enough mark for you, Miss Bieniecka?" "Oh yes," I replied, "a B." He was terribly surprised.' And here the narrative wanders off down various professor-related byways; at once we get the tale of the famous botany professor from Poznań, what was he called, who went on an expedition with his students and fell into a bog; up run the students, crying: "Professor, Professor, hold on, sir!" and he says: "Water lilies? So high up? It is patently obvious that I must have stepped into some mud"; and then comes another absent-minded fellow, this time an architect, who was in the habit of keeping his hand in his left pocket, and important items, such as keys or documents, in his right, so in his left pocket he always had a note that said: "Your keys are in the right one."

'Very well,' I interrupt Granny's flow, because I too could go
on about mad professors ad infinitum, 'so much for the university, what about the vacations?'

'In the vacations I went to the mountains. Once I went to the
seaside, in 1938. My father always gave me a fixed sum of
money, and depending how thriftily I managed it, I could stay a
longer or shorter time. So I lodged in the Free City of Danzig,
because it was much cheaper there, but I ate my meals across
the border in Poland, because there in turn the food was much
better, not margarine and ersatz stuff... The German woman,
or rather the citizen of Danzig from whom I rented a room,
was very agreeable. One day, I remember, there was some sort
of Nazi festivity, and there were flags with swastikas hanging
all over the city. "What's it for?" I asked. "Ooh, it's probably
because some little Nazi has done a nice healthy poo." Joking
apart, things were already getting hot then. I remember standing in the Polish Post Office building, when several of those
bruisers came in and started to jabber in German. And of
course I said: "This is the Polish post office and here we speak
in Polish." And that set them off. They came at me, to beat me
up. Just then some young scouting types appeared out of
nowhere, they leapt over the counter and came to my defence,
and as there were more of them, the other lot went off. And
the scouts said: "What on earth do you think you're doing? We
have problems here the whole time, people being beaten up,
postboxes smashed, brawls, and you're pouring oil on the fire?"
I can't tell you how stupid I felt.'

'And where exactly did you live?'

'I can't remember. But I do remember coming to Oliwa. I
remember Liczmański Street, which was called something
completely different in those days...'

'Jahnstrasse.'

'Yes? In any case... Liczmański Street was simply idyllic, like all Oliwa. Every house had a wrought-iron fence, with fancy spikes on top... do you know the kind I mean?'

'Yes, there are still a few of those.'

'A few. In the 1960s they said they were a bourgeois leftover, and had them replaced with wire netting. But before the war those fences were everywhere, with cascades of variously coloured rambling roses pouring through them at every point; the gardens had the most beautiful shrubs with variegated leaves, white, yellow, striped, spotted... The Germans were terribly restrictive when it came to maintaining the greenery. If anyone didn't bother to grow flowers, they made them pay a fine, and a high one. No wonder Oliwa was like one big garden. I was delighted by it, delighted, until I ran out of money. I sent Papa a telegram and he promised to send me some money by railway, but it didn't get there. And then an old railwayman came up to me and said: "I keep seeing you here every day, young lady, looking worried – is there something wrong?" So I told him that Papa had sent me some money, but it still hadn't come, and I had nothing to live on. And then that railwayman said to me: "If you please, Miss, let's make a deal: I will lend you the money, and you will give it back to me when your transfer comes. But don't forget that if you should let me down, I'll never give anyone else this sort of help, and that gives you a major responsibility, because the next person who comes to me might be in very great need." Luckily the next day my money came and I could pay back the debt. I wonder what happened to that man a year later? Did they arrest him and send him to a camp, like the other Poles? Did they shoot him at once? Or maybe he survived the war? Probably not – people as good as that rarely have enough sheer nerve to survive... For the next vacation I went to the mountains. And came back before the time was up.'

XI

'Everyone knew there was going to be a war. I don't think anyone had illusions. "There's going to be war," they said over the borscht, "Oh yes, that's right," they replied over the cheese-cake, "And I think there will indeed be war," someone would add, sipping the evening drop of brandy. But when I came home from Zakopane two weeks early, my father yelled at me for wasting the September sunshine by believing in stuff and nonsense. "Papa," I said, "I had trouble finding a seat on any train at all, they're leaving the station one after another, jammed full, every man jack is fleeing to Warsaw, Łódź or Kraków, the holidaymakers are going home, and they're buying up every last item in the shops." And as I believed in stuff and nonsense, I had brought home a suitcase packed to bursting with butter, sugar, buck-wheat, vanilla, packets of coffee, tea and cocoa – in short, whatever by some miracle was still obtainable by serving your time in a long queue. Thanks to that we had some supplies for the first few weeks of the war. What's more, when the Germans invaded, the government issued public messages on the radio and in the press in which they implored the citizens not to close their accounts at the National Bank, because the reserves were visibly melting away. The banks were under worse siege than the borders. And then my father said: "The Poles can take their savings out, but I can't. They'll say 'he's a Russki, he's not patri-otic enough'." And so we lost all our money.'

❧

Each of us has different recurring nightmares. I, for instance, always dream that I come home, but instead of stairs there's nothing but blue rubber banisters that I must climb to reach the tenth floor. Granny dreams about the bandits who steal her out of the cradle amid the deafening clanging of the bell. She dreams of her mother's terror – in another, darker version of the bright story that she often tells at teatime, the story of Grandpapa Leonard and the robbers, maybe it's just an accident that this version hasn't been exploited by history; or maybe it has been, maybe it's happening in parallel in another branch of time and space? The bandits tug at the door, large splinters fly off the frame, the bolt snaps, they run in, shoot, and seize the child from the cradle. Whereas my mother dreams about my grandmother's memories – enormous aeroplanes that come flying over the city, the whistle of bombs and the rumble of houses collapsing.

'It's such a strange, wailing sound, completely unlike other aeroplanes,' she used to say, before she heard a huge military Galaxy at the airport, which flew in to Poland with President Bush's entourage in 1989. 'Incredible,' she said afterwards, 'a sort of dismal wail that I heard before I saw the plane... for a moment I thought I was in my dream, I know that low rumble so well... it's the first time I've heard it apart from in my dreams – terrifying, it made me go weak at the knees.'

But it's not just her fear or just her dream. Seventy years ago, my great-grandmother Irena was lying in bed with an appalling migraine and, without opening her eyes, she said: 'and there's that terrible noise again, intensifying... I don't know, I don't know, it keeps repeating, it's such torment, time and again I can hear that racket under my temples, getting louder by the moment, I can't stand it' – and she clenched her fists so hard her knuckles went white.

'It's all right, it's all right. I'll give you my special "valerian" treatment,' said great-grandfather Valerian, covering her brow with his large, heavy paws, capable of removing any pain. 'Is it like aeroplanes? Like armoured cars?'

'Neither armoured cars nor aeroplanes.'

In August 1939 she heard that ringing noise inside her head for the last time, and then September came, and early one morning she exclaimed: 'The sound I keep hearing all the time... that's it!'

And along the road came some large German Panzers.

❦

Everyone, including ninety-year-old Grandmama Wanda, fled the manor house and ran across the fields to the appropriate place, meaning to Chmielnik, because in Chmielnik there was a monastery with thick stone walls. Off they ran, but suddenly my great-grandmother Irena turned on her heel and raced home again, claiming that running away from home without a survival kit was idiocy. She dashed indoors, and then, listening intently to the wail of the tanks, she wrapped in an eiderdown various objects essential in time of war (how many of those skills we have lost – who among us would now know what to pack, and even if he did know, who would be able to gather it all together in ten minutes?), and with a heavy bundle on her back, but with a lighter heart, she set off for Chmielnik.

'I saw Mama running across the stubble, and I saw a German plane flying over her, coming near, closer and closer... my heart stopped and leapt to my throat, because for the first few days they fired from the planes at everyone, at women and children, at shepherd boys in the mountains; in the West they wrote about it in the newspapers, pictures were printed and Hitler backed off, as if to say "Germania fought nobly and fairly". And suddenly the plane wasn't firing, but flying into the air. Mama told me at the time that she had seen his face. Maybe he was checking it was a woman, and hadn't fired, maybe his conscience had pricked him at the last moment, or maybe he was simply a decent man. I don't know. Because you did come across honest Germans... Throughout the war I never met a single truly beastly German; everyone who was billeted at our house was very nice, although we repaid them for it as badly as we possibly could; obviously, they were the occupying force. If it were put like that, people would certainly be outraged and say that I collaborated, or something of the kind, because really, the Germans never did anything terrible to me personally; that was my good fortune, I had more luck than common sense. Whenever something dreadful happened, when the Jews were herded through the village, when young Kostrzyk was attacked, I wasn't there, and besides, those things were done by strange, other Germans, not our ones at the manor house.'

✿

But it's time for the Germans to invade, because so far they've only flown over in planes and driven by in tanks.

'The bombardment ended, the tanks went off somewhere else, leaving deep ruts behind them, and a decision was made to go back to the manor. Not long after, the infantry appeared. We sat in a state of panic: the family, the holidaymakers, the servants, all huddled in one spot to brighten our mood. We're looking at the Germans, and they're looking at us. Suddenly we can hear bombs. Two soldiers jump into the bushes, and a third grabs the small daughter of one of the ladies who've been renting a room in the farm workers' block. The little girl struggles, and cries, but the German throws her to the ground and lies on top of her. The panic is mixed with joy, because it's the Polish air force... Wow! the Polish air force! But all the Polish planes were stranded at the air fields, entirely destroyed – apart from this small private one, whose owner had loaded a few bombs on board and flown off to rout the Teutons. He flew around for a while, dropping his bombs, but there was an anti-aircraft gun in the bushes and a quarter of an hour later he was shot down. The soldier apologised to the lady for seizing her daughter, but, as he explained, he was strong and beefy, and if anything had happened, the shrapnel would have wedged in his big body, and wouldn't have scratched the little girl. Then he gave the child some chocolate – we didn't have that kind in Poland at the time: wartime, nasty and cheap, with an after-taste of rancid grease and chocolate substitute. And he said he had a small daughter of the same age.

'Everyone tried to ignore him and not admit the thought that perhaps he was a thoroughly good and decent human being. That he could be human at all.'

Whenever we accuse Granny of being obstinate, we always hear: 'Grandmama's genes', and she makes a serious face, 'Grandmama's genes'.

And naturally we know perfectly well which genes and which story is on its way – approaching in great strides.

'Do you know…' Granny starts.

'Yes, we do. By heart,' we reply, patently helpless.

'You do? Well then, listen. When the Germans arrived at Lisów, each person behaved differently. I don't know if I've told you, but the manor had always been full of rugs, some of them very valuable; Grandpapa Leonard had bought them in the days of his prosperity; one of them, I remember, was identical to one of the rugs in the Royal Castle in Warsaw, except that ours was more valuable…'

'Why was it more valuable?'

'Because when a rug is made, sometimes there isn't enough wool and you have to tie on extra threads, and the shades are always slightly different, so then there's a small corner that's a touch lighter or a touch darker; our carpet had the smaller one, and the one at the castle's was bigger, but never mind about that. Most of the rugs were hung above a sofa or a couch, pinned up with tacks, so Aunt Ewa or Aunt Sasha went through all the rooms holding a cane, went up to each couch in turn, and used the handle of the cane to take down the rugs, sending the tacks flying about the room; swish-flick and it was done, the rug lay safely hidden behind the couch. Meanwhile my hair went dark from nerves, and Mama got going with the broom, because Gienia was busy with something, and started to sweep the hall, study, drawing room, everything, thoroughly. "They'll come in," she said, "and say Polish pigs live here. It has to be as clean as the home of the tidiest Frau." And come in they did. They drove up to the manor, tethered the ordinary horses under the trees, and put the captain's in the cowshed, from which they evicted the cow. They lorded it about in the courtyard, garden and rooms. And then there was an incident. Grandmama Wanda, my ninety-year-old grandmother, who usually toddled about in an old widow's housecoat and shabby shoes, hunch-backed and indolent, appeared dressed in the splendour of the Kiev salons of 1900; exactly as she was depicted in the portrait hanging above the fireplace. A full-length, dark taffeta silk dress, with folds, tucks and frills, in one hand a cane, in the other an ostrich-feather fan, and a golden hairnet dotted with pearls. She went into Grandpapa's study. There on the desk sat a German officer, with his legs crossed, casually rapping his crop against his shining boots. And Grandmama said to him, in Polish of course, because she didn't know any foreign languages – she was devoid of any linguistic skills, she lived in Kiev for twenty-five years without a word of Russian, and she spoke execrable French – so in Polish, not giving a damn that the German couldn't understand a thing, she said: "Sir, if you haven't been taught that when a lady is standing you are not free to sit, then you might at least sit on a chair and not on the desk, because this piece of furniture is for a different purpose." At this point she swished her cane in the air, almost hurling him off the desk as she pointed at the armchair, then she raised her lorgnette to her eyes and handed him a wad of documents, with some huge wax seals hanging from them. "Here are papers from Archduke Ferdinand stating that my property is exempt from all requisition, both in time of war and peace." The officer took a look, read the papers, began to laugh softly and then to justify himself, saying that in the Reich there were no dukes any more, now there was the Third Reich and one Führer, and unfortunately these documents were without value. But he stood to attention before Grandmama, and to the day he and his soldiers left, he always bowed to her with great respect.'

'Shall I make some tea?'

'Yes, when I've finished. So then, emboldened by my grandmother's success, I raced into the orchard. I had learnt that you have to scream at Germans. I went on screaming to the end of the war. At the Russkies too. Remember,' – here Granny turned to face us all with the look of Anna the Prophetess – 'if any army ever invades, you have to scream, but firmly, not hysterically. Right. So I went out to the orchard, and asked in a sharp tone if any of them spoke French or Russian. One of them could, a white Russian; he was dim-witted, and had no one to latch on to but the Nazis. I point and say: "Your horses?" "Ours," he replies. "And who let you tie your horses to the trees? Don't you know they chew the bark and then the tree dies? Take them out of here this minute and tie them to the fenceposts. Immediately!"'

This was always my favourite moment in the story. Granny rose up in her armchair, her eyes burning in their dark frames like poisonous pearls in black-lip oysters, as for the hundredth time with a hand stretched out towards the TV set or the piano, depending on the circumstances, she flushed the German cavalry out of Lisów's garden of paradise.

'And did they take them out?' I ask as a matter of form in gratitude for her masterful performance in the role of a cherub with a golden sword.

'Indeed they did. They took them out. And then I said: "Now get that horse out of the cowshed and put the cow back in there, or she'll freeze." And the soldier boy said: "But please Miss, that's the Captain's horse, the Captain is a dreadful man, he'll be angry." "Let him be angry," I say, "as long as he takes his horse out of the cowshed." "But Miss, you don't understand, he does dreadful things, the Captain, to him killing a person is like killing a fly" – and throws himself at my feet. "*Barynia*,"* he squeaks in Russian, "*barynia*, he'll take that horse into the salon." "So where is this captain of yours? I'll talk to him myself." And he escorted me; the captain was beefy, a fine strapping fellow, though with the occupying army. He spoke French, that was a good start. "Please remove your horse from the cowshed and take him to the stable. The cowshed has to be for my cow." "Why so? Keep your cow in the stable." "The stable is large and the cow will freeze in there." "And my horse won't?" "Does your horse produce milk?" He thought and thought, and told them to take the horse out to the stable. We went into the manor together, because he wanted to choose rooms for his quarters. "Well I never," he said, looking around, "well I never. I never expected to find so many beautiful pictures, so many wonderful books, such exquisitely furnished interiors in a Polish home." And I thought to myself: "You bastard, you scum, what did you think? That you'd come to Poland and find Mongol yurts and polar bears?" so then I replied: "And do you know, I never expected a German to notice." "One all," he said, and smiled broadly.'

XII

Meanwhile Julek was stuck in Warsaw under bombardment.

Well, it has to be said that Julek was never a hero. As his reincarnation, I can only add from myself that I understand him fully. Whenever he found out about my grandmother's capers – arguing with the Germans, helping the partisans, various dangerous escapades – he went deathly pale and hid away in his room with Anatole France.* But he wasn't afraid of the shells – maybe because their ingenious trajectories came straight from mathematics, which for Julek was wrapped in a black mantle of magic and unfathomable mystery. The bullet and the bomb belonged to the realm of blind fate and abstraction.

'During the siege of Warsaw, when there were bombs falling around him, and everyone was sitting in the cellars, Julek stayed at home in his room. "If I'm going to die of the stink and lack of air in there, I'd rather die in my own flat," he said. So there he is, sitting in an armchair, reading the newspaper, while the city burns. Suddenly he hears a "psssst" and a crash. And that's because a piece of shrapnel has fallen through the window, made a hole in the newspaper and lodged in the brass leg of a tall lamp, just above Julek's head. "And I can't even remember", he said, "how I ended up in the cellar." '

Either way, this was a minor triumph for Granny, who was always afraid of shells (maybe because she was better at maths, or maybe not).

'Julek said there was nothing surprising about that, because I could outtalk a German, but not a bomb.'

To be frank, I'm not entirely sure from which flat and down to which cellar Julek ran that time, but I suspect it happened at his Auntie Chyczewska's house.

For as well as a mummy, Julek had an auntie, Mrs Chyczewska, famous for her poor and rather asymmetrical figure, which was even the topic of one of Julek's famous little rhymes – though I can't say if he uttered it in his sleep or while he was awake:

> It takes no flair
> to kill a hare,
> What makes it easy to sit on a drum?
> My aunt Chyczewska's crooked bum.

Auntie Chyczewska's daughter was Kingfisher. She had a large dose of Armenian blood, and maybe that was why a huge, pointed nose protruded from the middle of her face, the origin of her nickname, which naturally was Julek's idea too.

Kingfisher's flat was extremely beautifully furnished, because Kingfisher's mate was an art historian and furniture restorer; he worked for various state institutions, which from time to time sold him some of the shabbier items for tuppence-halfpenny, and then he restored them, transforming them into real gems.

On the table stood a large turquoise bowl full of pomegranates – everywhere there were compositions and arrangements, accents and proportions.

'You know, I made a dreadful faux pas,' Granny tells me, 'because one wing of the cupboard was open, and I could see a Hutsul shirt, exquisitely embroidered in turquoise on a red background. The sleeve had slipped down, and was hanging almost to the ground, so I reached out a hand to tidy it, but Kingfisher hissed: "Leave it, it's meant to be like that." I'd gone to see her because Papa had said that as well as the Amati from Misha de Sicard he had a superb violin that was perfectly good enough for someone of his abilities, so it would be a good idea to sell the Amati. I took the violin to Warsaw, and it was due to be shown to an expert, but I didn't want to keep it at my flat, because it was a worry – there were so many people hanging about at the castle, besides which my room was tiny, something might fall and crush it... so Julek suggested I take it to Kingfisher's. There it lay, waiting for the expert. And there it went up in flames during the first few days of the bombardment, along with the Hutsul shirt, the bowl of pomegranates, the Empire chaise longue, several Louis Philippes, a Biedermeier sofa, all the rhythms and arrangements.

While de Sicard's Amati was burning in its case, a number of streets away Uncle Brokl was carrying paintings, candelabras, pieces of frescoes cut out of the walls, armchairs and sculptures out of the Royal Castle; but as he was hauling off a vase made of malachite, a bomb fell into the courtyard and killed him on the spot. He was buried nearby, in the place where pieces of the old Sigismund's column* are lying.

When the Germans entered Warsaw and occupied all the public offices, Aunt Adi went to insist on an allowance. The official looks at her papers and says: 'But dear Madam, you are a citizen of the German Reich, you are due a special allowance from the state.'

To which Aunt Adi says: 'I am Poleesh. I followed my huzbant to Ziberia and now your German bomb hez killed my huzbant. I do not vont your allowanz, I vont an allowanz for my murdered huzbant.'

They gave her the allowance, but her daughter Jasia was terrified they would come and shoot her for this audacity, whereas she wasn't in the least bit scared to have some rescued national relics on the shelves between the books, such as the hearts of Tadeusz Kościuszko, Emilia Plater* and the like.

'And Lorentz,' says Granny about the powerful National Museum director famous for recovering art looted in the war, 'didn't write a word about Brokl. What a louse. After the war he plundered the whole of Poland, and carted off to Warsaw every collection found by the army. The museum experts called him a second Goering.'

Now I open Lorentz's book, *The Fight for the Assets of Culture*, and indeed, all it says about Kazimierz Brokl, who was after all custodian of the Royal Castle, is that he was killed on 17 September while removing works of art from the burning building. Not much. Nor could I discover the fate of the portraits of the beautiful Mrs Kupciełło, whom Witkacy had drawn so many times; they probably went up in flames with the castle, because it didn't occur to anyone at the time that a malachite vase or a stucco skirting board would be easier to reconstruct from photographs than those daubs of Witkacy's.

❧

To make the times more interesting Julek was mobilised, and Granny had hysterics. 'Yes,' she shouted at her father, 'yes, you forbade me to marry him, and now what? He'll be killed. He won't come back, he'll be killed, and I won't even be a widow!' Her father said: 'He won't be killed. I give you my word of honour.' And as he was a gentleman, he kept his word, and

Julek came home from Warsaw; all the fighting he did was to spend one week in the forest, so he was dirty and unshaven.

And once he had turned up at Kielce, there was no question of postponing the wedding any longer. People drove down to Lisów, the family managed to put together some sort of food and gave a wedding party.

'Aaaah, what a wedding! I swapped some of the butter I'd brought from Zakopane, and it was only thanks to that we had a turkey… what a shame it was shabbier than many a simple little country wedding. But what could we do? We had to invite the entire village, because no one ever failed to invite me to their wedding; we set up trestle tables in the courtyard in front of the house, served everything we could afford, and somehow it went on until evening.'

❧

A few days later the house was occupied by the Germans as their billet, and Granny fell ill with inflammation of the heart and once again very nearly died, to which she became so inured that even now, thank heavens, although it's as if everything in her has been completely used up, as if whole parts of her brain have died away, she is still alive and still smiling.

The Lisów manor house wasn't large – of course there was the drawing room, where my great-great-grandmother Wanda resided; it was about sixty square metres, and Aunt Ewa's room was about twenty, but they couldn't be relocated. The only thing left was to empty out my great-great-grandfather's former study and the junk room – and so the broken furniture, old screens and annuals found their way onto the rubbish heap.

From the windows of Granny's room there was a broad view of the fields and meadows, set in a white frame between the wardrobe and the clock. The sun was shining, and in its light the village children went running about those fields and meadows with black ostrich-feather fans pinned to their arms.

❧

But Granny went on and on lying there. Silence. The ticking of the clock, spots of light on the glassware and the porcelain; only very occasionally could she hear the Germans' soft footsteps sneaking down the corridor to listen to the radio. Because gradually it was becoming apparent that in spite of all, Lisów was going to be an oasis of peace during the second great war.

'People would be ready to think I was *Volksdeutsch*, I was always so full of praise for our Germans, but we only got decent ones there. Maybe because the local Gestapo officer broke his leg four days after arriving, and as luck would have it, the mighty machinery of wartime bureaucracy somehow overlooked this fact, thanks to which we were never assigned a replacement to the very end of the war. Those Wehrmacht soldiers sat around at our place, and all of them to a man used to listen to the foreign radio, but in secret, terrified the others would inform on him. One of them would come in, and from my room I could hear the radio hopping between channels and the announcer's voice, then another one would come in, the first one would switch it off abruptly and turn the knob to cover his tracks, so you couldn't tell which radio station it was... then he'd leave and the other one would switch on the radio and turn the knob... to the very end of the war they never felt brave enough to listen to it together.'

❧

'At our place at Lisów everything was full of calcium and sele-
nium – the earth, the water and the air, so the peasants never
did any singing. Of course they had some sort of ditties.
When the women were working in the fields, now and then
one of them got up and sang something like: "For no one do I
cry, saving Mikołaj, 'e strained the stock and burned 'is...
sock." And the older they were, the bawdier the rhyme. But
apart from that, as a rule they only had instrumental music; of
course, they played fabulously at the weddings, they played
beautifully, but they never sang because their throats were
eaten away. But on the other hand, they never suffered from
cancer, and the doctor told me that if I'd lived there for all that
time I'd never get it either. Well, anyway, making soup with
that water was impossible, because with all those minerals in
it some of the vegetables were soon cooked to a pulp, and
some were almost raw, so it came out a mess. In any case
Grandmama Wanda didn't know how to cook and none of her
maids could cook either, so my father always used to say: "At
the Brokls even the turkey is revolting," because Papa was a
great gourmet. But not even a master chef could have made
good soup with that water.

'And while I was ill, for some time Julek made the dinners.
Dinner as dinners go, the second course was quite tasty, but the
soups! What soups! They were wonderful, everything cooked
to perfection, absolutely delicious, full of flavour. He refused to
betray his secret, but he was proud as a peacock. One day he
told me: "Today I'm going to fix you a Lucullan feast!" And he
kept adding one, then a second, then a third ingredient, bringing me some to try now and then, until he'd thrown in so many
things it became inedible. But anyway, apart from that one time
when he went overboard, his soups were exquisite. Finally, with
a lot of caresses and mock threats I got him to reveal the secret

of his recipe to me. And he said: "You know what, I don't really know why my soups come out so well. I fetch water from the barrel, I peel…" "From the barrel?" I asked. "Yes, the one under the house." It was the rainwater barrel, where our farm help Bakalarczyk used to wash the muck off his hands when he came in from the field. It was full of mosquito larvae, and if you put your hand close to the water's surface they went "trrr-rrr" deep down and were gone in an instant – not to mention how many even tinier beasties were swarming about in there.

    'And quick as a flash we went back to our nasty Lisów soups.'

'The war didn't look likely to end soon, so we'd have to sit it out in the country, where it was easier to feed ourselves and have a safer life. We had to get to grips with the farm more seriously, be inventive and toughen up, and of course it all came down to me, because Grandmama Wanda was an old lady, my mother was a pianist, my father was a broken-down lawyer, and Julek was a bookworm… and to make matters worse, here I was, lying sick for the third week in a row. First of all, as I lay in bed for hours on end, I realised we should definitely buy a cow. So, willy nilly, I summoned Julek, told him to fetch the gold chain with moonstones from my grandmother's dressing table, quite ugly really, but long, so there was plenty of gold in it, and I told him: "There you are, go and sell that at the jeweller's and buy a cow at the market tomorrow." Julek sat on the bed, took the chain, looked at it, sighed heavily and nodded, which was supposed to mean he would go and do the selling and buying.

    'Next morning he came and peeped in through my open window, bathed in sunlight, because it was late September or maybe early October – anyway, it was very warm. "Well?" I ask,

"Did you buy a cow?" "Yes," he says. "And what's she like?" I
ask. "Has she got a big udder?" Julek gives me a searching look
and says: "You know what… I didn't really get all that close a
look at her udder. But she has such lovely red curls round her
head!" My God, what despair! The cow was so thin I was afraid
to touch her in case she fell over. Her udder was like a dried-up
prune, and it looked as if she wouldn't last long. She did indeed
have red curls. Apart from that, the peasant who sold her had
persuaded Julek she was in calf, but she was all skin and bone.
Well, anyway, we fed her up, made a fuss of her, and what do
you know? Not only did she give birth to a lovely little heifer,
but she produced such good milk that the people at the dairy
told us to add water, because when the Germans saw that
percentage of fat in the records they'd make it the norm. And
who would have thought it from those curls, eh?

'And after that I got better – that may be putting it a bit
grandly, but I got up from my bed and walked to the window.
One of the Germans was sitting on the porch polishing his
boots, saw me, and started shouting that the Fräulein had
recovered. They all ran up and congratulated me, smiling and
singing. I didn't know why they were so damned pleased. And
then it turned out the Captain had forbidden them to talk loud,
sing while shaving or while not shaving, or stamp their feet. It's
hard not to stamp in army boots, so they'd gone about in
carpet slippers or slid around on floor cloths – all that just
because the Fräulein was sick. And now that I was well, one of
them, who said he played in a symphony orchestra in Hamburg,
took a harmonica out of his pocket and began to play Mozart.'

XIII

What else happened in the first few days of the war?

Young Mr Hess reported for duty in the uniform of a Polish reserve officer, fought, and was taken captive by the German army. Somehow his uncle got him off the hook, and not a hair on his head was harmed, but it has to be admitted that he behaved beautifully. Not so the two brothers from the neighbouring property, the ones who had surfaced roads in the forests. Now there were German tanks smoothly driving along those roads.

Some sad gentlemen knocked at engineer R—ski's door and ordered him to pack up his collections. Later on some porters came and took away the silverware, porcelain, paintings and books, all carefully stored in boxes. But they didn't take the pistol, which engineer R—ski fired into his own head after their departure. He was buried by the graveyard wall, as suicides always are.

Young Mr Przypkowski, the Germanophile, carved a medallion with a double profile of the conquerors of the Jews, Titus and Goebbels. He sent it to him as a present.

My great-great-grandmother Wanda disappeared. In utter dismay, everyone looked for her all over the manor, in the meadows, and in the neighbouring villages, until a few hours later she came back from Kielce in the carriage, brimming with good humour and said: 'I have reached the age of ninety without ever having a permanent wave. So I decided to give it a try.'

And there's the story about the doctors. In Kielce there were two renowned surgeons. One of them was a distinguished physician, graduate of a famous university, a universally respected man. The problem lay in the fact that he wasn't a very good surgeon, not to mention the fact that with age his memory declined badly, so there were anecdotes going around about watches, scalpels and scissors that he had sewn up in his patients' bellies out of sheer carelessness. The other was an excellent doctor, but had never actually gained a medical education; during the first war he had been taken on as a 'body snatcher' in the army, and had only done a first-aid course. But he had such a flair for cutting and sewing, such dexterous hands, such natural talent, that they soon started letting him operate; in any case, as usual there was a lack of people at the front. And he had been so well trained, on what were after all the most difficult cases, that he soon took the lead in his... in the unit, as the best surgeon.'

'But he never went to medical school?'

'Not at all. He got himself some dodgy documents, and for years he treated patients and worked at the hospital in Kielce like a normal doctor. But he never did learn much about the ethics of the profession. He took money for everything. I remember the time when I was waiting to see him, and there was a poor old woman in tears, who had brought in her husband with appendicitis. "I ain't got no money." "You can pay with a calf." "I'll bring it, doctor, for sure, but please operate on 'im." "Once you bring the calf, he can have the operation." She went home for the calf, but her husband died in the waiting room. "Have you no shame?" I said. "Couldn't you have got on with the operation?" To which he said: "Are you out of your mind? He'd have died on my table and she wouldn't have given me the calf. And where would that leave me?" What a swine. Finally someone exposed him as just an ordinary paramedic, and not a "BMedSci." The case went to court, but he must have had some well-placed patients, in any case he was allowed to go on operating, as if he really had completed his practical studies.'

'It's like the baptism of blood among martyrs. If they hadn't been baptised, their martyr's blood washed away their sins. I love that sort of theological gem. Then what?'

'During the German offensive an officer grabbed him in the street and ordered him to run to the station, where there were wounded men. And he said: "Not in my wildest dreams. I'm not going to go looking for trouble." At which the officer took his revolver from its holster and said: "You'll go." "No." And the officer shot him.'

'What about the other doctor?'

'The other doctor saved people heroically, dragging them away from under fire, racing around like mad, dressing wounds. And later, when the Germans had taken the city and the shooting had long since stopped, on his way home the doctor was hit in the head by a random bullet.'

'And then there was Dr Poznański too.'

'Poznański? Yes... but I can't remember.'

❧

I shall tell this story for Granny. I'm doing more and more of the telling for her. In her mind, it's all going to pieces, blurring, coming apart.

Granny's deterioration was most evident in the disintegration of her narrative. At first there were just some small pieces missing ('What's happening to me? I can't remember, I can't remember anything any more... for goodness' sake, who staged *Summer in Nohant** in 1938? It was one of Nina Andrycz's* first roles, she was stunningly beautiful in those days, stunningly... I can't remember'), then bits of stories began to disappear, some of the details were muddled and no one knew where the plum tree stood, and where the cherry, what was the colour of Mrs X's dress on one particular evening, and so on; typically, Granny sorted out the narrative by supplementing it with imagination, in other words matter of a different nature. In time, whole stories started to vanish, or worse yet, some were mixed up with others, resulting in some unusual contaminations and absurd collisions.

'What a shame I haven't got a car...'

'Granny, you've never had a driving licence.'

'How can you say that?'

'It's true. You've never even ridden a bike. What lovely magnolias.' (We're out for a walk in the park in Oliwa, where she took me so many times in my childhood; now the roles are gradually reversing.) 'Don't you remember? You always had trouble with labyrinthitis.'

'A bicycle is another matter. I did have a driving licence, and I used to drive.'

'When?' asks my mother in an inquisitorial tone, deeply convinced that Granny must be given proof of her mistake, and once that's done, she's sure to get it into her head and keep it there. 'Can you tell me when you had a driving licence? It wasn't before the war. Your father didn't have a car.'

'Yes, he did. In the Ukraine. One time the peasants chased him with wooden stakes...'

'It was your grandfather who had a car in the Ukraine, Grandpapa Leonard, not your father.'

'Then it was after the war.'

'Mama, Daddy had his first car in the 1980s when Paweł bought it for him.'

'So did Uncle Paweł buy him his first car?' I ask.

'Yes. Your grandfather was seventy at the time. Before that of course he rode a motorbike for a very long time and had a car and driver when he worked for the State Forests, but he only had a car of his own after the age of seventy. Anyway,' says my mother to my grandmother, 'you couldn't have had a car before Daddy did. Don't make things up.'

'I used to drive, and that's that.'

And so on, and now nothing pleases us, not even the magnolias, because Mum is set on proving to Granny her lack of logic, and Granny keeps finding new loopholes in the narrative, as befits the daughter of a lawyer.

Mum had started taking her to various doctors, buying medicines 'with the beautiful names of Greek nymphs', as the poet puts it* (or something of the kind), but it wasn't of much use. More and more often I was arguing with Granny about her actual experiences, until finally she would lose her temper and say derisively: 'Yes, because of course you know better.'

'What's this?' I once asked, finding some little white pills in a remote corner of the kitchen.

'Meeeeh, some sort of medicine. Your mother gives them to me, but I don't think they help.'

'But why are they in here?'

'Because she checks to see if I'm taking them. She counts them on a slip of paper. So every day I put one pill aside.'

'But Granny…!'

And so on. But going back to Dr Poznański, he was a reputable surgeon too. Apart from that, he was a Jew, but so 'un-Jewish' looking that he decided not to reveal his origins. He and his family simply didn't move into the ghetto, and he went on practising his profession.

Until one day, he was in his consulting room when he heard loud knocking at the door. He heard one of his sons running to open it to the client, and then he heard some shouting in German. He got up, buttoned his jacket and went into the hall. There stood several soldiers, one of them holding a wounded dog in his arms. It turned out the partisans had tried to assassinate a Nazi dignitary, and though their shots had missed him, they had seriously wounded his beloved bitch.

Although Dr Poznański's appearance did nothing to betray

his origins, his son's most definitely did. Let us leave them like that for a moment: the doctor, his son with the prominent ears and the sorrow of centuries in his eyes, the soldiers, the dog and the general's or commander's adjutant. What can happen? What did happen, if this story is worth telling? For I wouldn't be repeating it here if it were about to end in the death of the doctor, his son, or both at once. And indeed, it didn't end like that at all. Let's allow them to move again, let's allow them to think and talk. The adjutant thinks: 'The dog might survive. What's one Jew to me, or several Jews, or even a hundred Jews? What matters is the dog.'

And he says: 'I don't think there's anything we need to explain to each other. It's a simple matter: if you operate on the dog and she survives, you will survive too. If not, you and your entire family will go up against the wall.'

And Dr Poznański and his entire family survived. It seems improbable, but it really did happen. The man who valued the life of a dog higher than the life of a man, at the same time respected his promise and kept it. God moves in mysterious ways, and terrible is His irony.

❧

Meanwhile, the life of the Karnaukhov family (or rather the Karnaukhov and Rogoziński families, now that Lala and Julek were married) had shifted to Lisów. Living in the countryside meant greater safety and better supplies, and besides, it was the only way for everyone to live together: Granny, her parents, Aunt Sasha, Aunt Ewa, Uncle Maciej, my great-great-grand-mother Wanda and Julek. In fact there were grim incidents that took place in the countryside too, but the peasants defended the manor, and no mistake.

'One night the partisans came, tired and dirty. "Is this Lisów

B?" So I sleepily rub my eyes and say: "No, it's Lisów A." "Then we're sorry to have bothered you – the villagers won't let us take advantage." I offered them some food, but they politely declined it. They left, bowing and thanking non-stop. There was a large basket of apples in the hall, so I said at least take some apples, but they said no – "the villagers won't let us." Finally, when I just about forced them, they took one or two apples each and stuffed them into their pockets. They didn't want more than that. But at Lisów B, at the Libiszowskis' house – in the plural now, because the niece of Mr Libiszowski the wastrel had come to live there – oooh, things were different there. The partisans stayed the whole night, demanded to be fed and entertained, and stripped the place bare, even taking the furniture – to a point where the family had to hide their clothes in the bread oven. But old Mr Libiszowski told them to call him "Squire" and to kiss his hand through his sleeve. Yeees. At the very start of the war he asked my father: "Have you installed shutters yet?" "Shutters? What for?" "What do you mean?" snapped Libiszowski. "To defend you against the peasants." But our peasants liked us.'

'If anyone had let me cheat and rob them as much as the Brokls let those peasants, I'd have liked him too.'

'They were aware of that. One day my father went to see Milewski...'

'Milewski was the intelligent peasant who knew the world?'

'Yes, Milewski was highly intelligent and amusing, and he was worldly-wise too, because he'd been in the tsarist army for years and had fought against the Japanese. Before the war, whenever we spent the holidays at Lisów, we bought our milk from him. So that day my father went to see Milewski, to tell him we wouldn't be getting milk from him any more, because until then he had sent us a can each day... oh yes, one time such a beautiful girl brought the milk that my father got up early especially to open the door to her and feast his eyes on

LALA   197

her; the local race was very handsome in Lisów... so Papa went
to see Milewski and said that because of the war, the crisis, for
lack of money and so on. And Milewski replied: "Counsellor,
I've lived off you for fifteen years. It won't do me any harm to
have you live off me for a while", and he kept sending us milk
to the very end of the war.'

'But they went on stealing too... Do you remember the time
they stole the straw?'

'Hmmm, the time they stole the straw... what happened?'

'You were lying sick. But when you got up, and went to the
barn, it turned out all the straw was gone. And there had been
more of it than ever, it was a bumper year, the whole top level
of the barn was packed right up to the roof. So you went down
to the village club, in other words the corner shop, you stood
in the doorway and you said...'

'I said: "While I was sick in bed, you stole all my straw."
Silence. "Not all of it," says one of them. "All of it," I reply
calmly' (and Granny's voice rings with just the same sepulchral, death-knell solemnity as at the time, making the word
'straw' sound like 'diamonds'). 'They looked at each other and
one of them says: "It's not possible." "Come on then, come
and see." They came, like a committee, went in, checked,
and looked around the empty barn. "Dammit all," says one,
"whoever took the rest is scum." They nodded, apologised, and
the next day they brought me a whole cart of straw from the
Liegenschaft.' Dirty, it's true, but never mind. They'd bought it
back and delivered it. And we had firewood from the Germans.'

'From the Germans?'

'Yes, because one time a German transport arrived, I think
they were going around the countryside requisitioning animals
that exceeded the limits, hidden timber and tobacco. I look, and
they've got so much wood... and at the house we had none,
everything was missing, it was cold, so I went up to the vehicle,

grabbed a few logs and flew home with them. And the Germans came after me. Not those unfamiliar ones, but ours. I raced into the drawing room, tossed the logs to the floor and whoosh, under the armchair... no, under the pouf that stood below the window. In those days it was upholstered with material at the bottom that reached down to the ground, so nothing showed. "What are you doing?" shout the Germans. "What are you doing with that wood?" And feeling remorseful, I say that there's no wood in the house. "Have you gone crazy, doing things like that in front of unfamiliar soldiers? Do you want them to accuse you of stealing the property of the Thousand-Year Reich? You should have told us there was nothing for the fire." And from them on they brought us firewood.'

❧

Granny has often repeated that she has always had more luck than common sense, and that if she had told the truth about her Germans, she would have been accused of being *Volksdeutsch* – ethnically German.

And indeed, the Germans billeted at Lisów were not blood-thirsty beasts, but ordinary middle-class people with very respectable German manners. One had protected the little girl during the bombing, another played Mozart on the mouth organ and maintained that in his home city he was a member of the philharmonic orchestra. ('Later a telegram came for him, to say that his wife and daughter had been killed when their city was bombarded; next day I saw them taking him and others to the eastern front; he was sitting in the back of the lorry, looking grey-green, staring into space; that's how I remember him.') The captain borrowed books about art, the red-haired NCO helped in the house, and Apollo-with-the-braces fell in love with Granny.

'Weeell, Apollo-with-the-braces was a divinely handsome man. He looked exactly like the Apollo Belvedere, he had a perfect figure and aristocratic features. Except that he was very scruffy and always had his braces hanging down on either side. He followed me like a dog, mooning about with a dopy expression, and was eager to do every job in the house: he washed up, cleaned the cutlery, peeled the potatoes... And he was an occupying soldier! Finally I told the red-haired NCO that the situation was ridiculous, because I was after all a married woman and Julek didn't have to put up with Apollo, but on the other hand, if they ever did have a fight the result would be a real catastrophe, so the red-haired NCO had a chat with him. For a while Apollo went about looking sad, but in time he came to terms with it – anyway, he was quite catastrophically stupid.'

❧

Paris surrendered without a fight.

Julek defended it – as the treasure house of culture, the Louvre, the churches, the priceless manuscripts, the genius loci; this way the remains of European civilisation had been saved.

Granny attacked it – Warsaw had been burned down, but not sold, and the French were cowards and rogues.

As they were walking down the street, car after car full of drunken Germans drove past, celebrating the victory. And from the opposite direction a small boy of about ten came towards them; he had his hands in his pockets and was softly whistling the Marseillaise.

'You see,' said Granny, 'that one little imp has more courage than all the French put together.'

❧

'What did you live on during the war?'

'On selling Grandmama Wanda's jewellery. Apart from that we had a cow, two cows. And hens, but they all died off when there was fowl pest. I had one who was such a darling, she used to waddle about the house, I called her Tufty; when she fell sick, she came to me, tilted her little head, nestled in my arms and died there. We had a sheepdog too.'

'Was that Trop?'

'No, Trop was before the war, he was Papa's hunting dog. A hunting dog, but he was very tender towards small creatures. The duck used to leave her ducklings with him. She'd come up, quacking, he'd look at her as if he understood, then she'd leave all her babies and go off to see to her business; and he'd stay behind with the ducklings, keeping them safe between his outstretched paws – if one of them tried to leave, he'd gather it back to the middle again. Then the mother would come back, and he'd let the ducklings go, until the next time. So when I saw the same thing in a Disney film later on I laughed tremendously. But during the war we had a different dog.'

'But Granny, I asked how you kept the house going.'

'Aha. Well, we still had a bit of land, so we planted potatoes. The peasants wondered how on earth I did it, because one summer I planted them too late, and on top, so they shouldn't have done well at any price (the peasants said they'd be the size of peas and dry as a bone); but all summer it bucketed down, so while everyone else's potatoes rotted, mine grew beautifully. The next year I planted the other way around, on soggy ground and too early, so once again the peasants tapped at their foreheads, saying it would all rot. And guess what? It was a blazing hot summer, everyone else's potatoes dried out, but mine grew into whoppers. "Those as 'ave been to school 'ave been to school," one of them said.'

'And you all lived on potatoes?'

'There was no choice. But there was dreadful privation, and problems with everything. One morning I heated up yesterday's coffee, and it turned out to be delicious, we all liked the taste of it, because it was just as if it had been sweetened, though there wasn't any sugar. After breakfast I opened the pot, and it was full of cockroaches; all night they'd been getting inside and drowning in there, hence the sweet taste. So I asked Uncle Maciej – he was the only one I told – and together we set about tracking down the cockroaches; we finally found their nest behind the kindling twigs by the stove and squashed as many of them as we could. But there was something worse than cockroaches, namely Aunt Ewa. She was always throwing her weight about, griping and telling us off. One time she actually turned to my mother and said: "Yes, you don't remember any more, but in 1912 I had specially set some cream aside for my coffee but you stole it and drank it." And so on. She had a large room at Lisów, where she hung up those plaster casts of the Notre Dame gargoyles she'd brought back from Paris, and various other bits of Satanic paraphernalia. At any rate, the general rural masses in the form of the village women were afraid to put their noses around the door. But Aunt Ewa had a passion for taking on young maids and stringing them along, instilling a revolutionary miasma in them, a proper Madame Defarge in the countryside. She had become infected with the same miasma in Kiev, where she'd hung about with some student anarchists, read atheist pamphlets and stuffed her head with global theories. And then for the rest of her life she mixed it with her own bile and fed the maids on it. Even worse, she used to fraternise with the common folk, for instance she'd lie down under the pear tree with the resting farmhands and chat away to them like that, lounging on the grass. And then they'd come to me, spit on the ground and say: "Be she a lady? Be she a lady? Lying under a tree with the peasants? That's no lady,

Miss Lalusia, that's a ninny." Or she'd be walking down the road, see a pregnant woman along the way and say to her: "Hey, Maciejowa,* how many children is it now? That's the ninth, isn't it? I don't let my Żołka" – Żołka was her little dog – "I don't let her have it away with the local hounds, but look at you, an old woman, and you're still at it." And Maciejowa shielded her belly with an open palm, like this, crossed herself three times with the other one, and spat to ward off evil. Can you imagine talking like that, and in the countryside? Apparently she spouted something else as well, about the Virgin Mary, you get the idea. I explained to them that she was mad, and that it was divine retribution, but what a thorn in my flesh she was. It's quite another matter that they really did go about pregnant all the time there, I used to wonder about it too – one time I asked a woman who had fourteen children if it wasn't hard for her to manage, and I remember, she gave me such a beautiful reply: "Yes, it is hard, but if you bain't got no kids, your hands are so empty…" '

🌺

Meanwhile Uncle Maciej, with his schizophrenia and his excellent grasp of German, also turned out to be dangerous. One morning he was taking a stroll in front of the house. As luck would have it, one of the Germans happened to be shaving, and he poured the soapy water out of the window so inopportunely that he soaked Uncle Maciej from head to foot. As Uncle Maciej had studied in Munich, and had learnt a thing or two from his fellow students, he gave the officer such a dressing-down that it cut him to the quick. And it led to an international incident. The red-haired NCO came to mediate, and explained that they weren't bothered, they knew Uncle Maciej was mentally deficient, but it was a serious matter, because some

other Germans from outside had seen it happen, and Uncle
Maciej would have to get a grip on himself and apologise. Poor
syphilitic, schizophrenic Uncle Maciej! He went into the room
and stood in the doorway, while the scolded German politely
got up from his armchair, nodded and said: '*Gut, gut,*' and thus
the whole matter was closed.

※

Julek wasn't terribly comfortable either. The peasants had little
respect for him. Why deny it – in those days, what could a man
of letters, a translator from French, mean to a peasant, even a
highly intelligent one? Here Granny interrupts me, shouting:
    'Oh, he could mean a very great deal – these were the Lisów
peasants! They respected books, and anyone who respects
books respects writers too. Take Big Tarapata, for instance. Big
Tarapata (he was over two metres tall, as opposed to Little
Tarapatka) was a carpenter. He had severe asthma and his work
wasn't a great success, so he made rather a poor living. But he
loved books. He used to come to the manor to borrow them,
one after another; he always returned them in perfect condition – sometimes it was as if they were in a better state than
before – but maybe books are like that? If you read them with
feeling, they repay you by looking spruce? Anyway, Big Tarapata
always brought them in his giant paws, bowed before the
library door and went inside as if it were a cathedral. He'd
spend ages looking around, carefully choosing what to read
next, and then breathing heavily, as asthmatics do, he'd go
home to his cottage. Sometimes he'd stay another quarter of
an hour or so, holding a learned debate with my father. He
made very interesting observations, from which his exceptional
intelligence and sensitivity were immediately apparent. But he
didn't respect Julek, not because he was a man of letters, but

because he was from the city, and hadn't a clue about rural
proprieties. Whenever we needed, let's say, to get the ploughing done, and I sent him off to the village to bring back a
peasant with his horses, he'd come home an hour later and say
that he hadn't been able to win any of them round because
they were all so busy. But he did it like this: he'd go in, say
"Good morning" and put the question. Then I'd have to go
myself. I'd call in at the first cottage to hand, start by having a
long chat with the housewife – about the weather, about the
children, about the hens, about their health, then another long
chat with the man of the house about the same things, and
right at the very end, with one foot out of the door, I'd ask if
perhaps he'd have some time tomorrow to come up with his
horse and do our ploughing. And the peasant would say that of
course he'd come and do it. Because first you had to talk to
people, and not just shoot from the hip. In the countryside
people aren't in a hurry, courtesy is at a high premium. Like
everyone who's impoverished and badly treated, the peasants
attach great importance to their dignity.'

XIV

It's night. We were going to play *Talisman*, but Basia's sitting on the bed, painting her nails.

'So, are you going to say the same thing as last time? That I look like a five-year-old who's painted her tootsies with Mummy's nail polish?'

'Mummy the Stripper,' I rounded out the image. 'Of course. Anyone who saw your tootsies would say the same.'

Because it's true – though her physique is not in the least bit childlike, Basia has tiny hands and feet, small and adorable extremities that look as if they've been transplanted from a pre-schooler.

'So tell me, who supported your granny during the war? Julek?'

'Basia, that's not the right question. The question is: "Whom did your granny support during the war?" Her father, mother, grandmother, Aunt Sasha, Aunt Ewa, Uncle Maciej and Julek. And two houses, meaning the manor at Lisów and the flat in Kielce. The flat in Kielce only for some time, because it was within the borders of the area that became the ghetto, so the Germans took possession of it, and gave the family an "ex-Jewish" flat as compensation.'

'And did they live there?'

'No, they kept some things there, but they lived at Lisów; anyway, towards the end of the war the house it was in burned down and everything went up in smoke. But there's a good story to do with the move.'

'What's that?'

'As you know, my great-grandmother...'

'Irena?'

'....yeees, Irena, was fluent in several languages, including German. So when she found out that their flat and all their property, the furniture, books and personal objects, had been seized by the German authorities, she decided to call on the Gestapo and kick up a fuss in her faultless German. Naturally, they did their level best to dissuade her from this plan, but you know the women in my family... She dressed smartly, probably crossed herself before leaving, but discreetly, so no one would notice, and went. And as you know the women in my family, you also know that she couldn't possibly fail. She did kick up a fuss, and the Gestapo... funny, that – I'm talking about the Gestapo as if it were a person, but of course it was a whole series of officials, caretakers, security guards and so on... well, no matter. The Gestapo issued her with a permit to say that she had the right to take all the household goods and move them to the new place. On top of that they assigned her a young officer, who was to see to all the formalities; and so my great-grandmother walked across the city with a Gestapo officer, and shortly after with her daughter too, one on one side, the other on the other – indescribably awkward. Along the way they hired a cart, so the group was joined by a peasant with a wagon and two porters, and so all together they headed across the city, went through the ghetto gate, reached the front of the synagogue, which had probably been demolished by then, or maybe just desecrated – "just" is nice... When they entered the flat, they found it had been badly looted already. The door of one of the Kiev wardrobes had been broken off with a bayonet, although the key was still in the lock; following through, my great-grandmother made another big scene, and demanded compensation. The officer, who was young, courte-ous and slightly shocked, promised her one of the wardrobes requisitioned from the Jews, without its contents, of course, so once the porters had loaded the furniture onto the cart, he escorted the two of them, Granny and her mother, into one of the neighbouring flats, where with a lordly gesture he showed them an equally plundered interior and encouraged them to pick out a wardrobe for themselves; then he gave orders for it to be emptied and carried out to the cart. They watched as he went into the other room, walked up to the desk, and with deft sleight of hand took a nice little inkwell, or maybe a clock. He pinched it. But they did some stealing too. Because Granny instructed the porters to carry the new wardrobe out on the double, with everything still inside it; at the same time she sent a boy – who knows, maybe one of the little Frydmans – to seek out the owners and tell them she'd rescued two fur coats and two quilts for them. And it worked, so soon the fur coats and quilts were lying innocently among the pieces of furniture, when suddenly Granny remembered that she'd seen a pair of warm socks hanging from an open chest of drawers, which the Birnbaums, Goldmans, Sztajns, or whatever they might have been called, would certainly find useful in the winter. She grabbed the socks, and was on the point of stuffing them into her pocket, when the officer emerged from the next room, cast her a look of contempt, shook his head, and beckoning with his gloved hand, told her to put them back in place, then he went outside, glanced at the cart and gave orders for one of the fur coats and one of the quilts to be removed. Why one of each? Maybe he wasn't sure which flat they really came from, or maybe he wanted to make Granny his partner in crime, or perhaps he'd taken a fancy to one of the coats, but not the other? I don't know. He clicked his heels, smiled disdainfully, and left. And Granny felt stupid, because she'd promised the neighbours more than that, and now she had to explain herself like a fool. "To this day I wonder", she once told me, "whether they believed I was only able to rescue those items, or whether they thought I had robbed them." '

Basia and I are sitting on the bed. Her nails are dry. It's three in the morning, and any moment now Granny's likely to walk in and say: 'I don't know about you, but I'm going for a pee,' or: 'Decadence and debauchery.' We're supposed to be playing that game of *Talisman*, but the storytelling's going too well, and another thought comes back to me.

'But the incident with the Germans who brought the water from the well occurred at the old flat.'

'I get the feeling we're not going to play.'

'We can. Set out the board.'

'No, no. I prefer to listen.'

'It was at the very start of the war. It was a rare occasion when Granny was spending the night in Kielce, alone, because her parents had already moved to Lisów. Evening. Thumping at the door. She opens it, and there are two Germans. One speaks Polish, a Silesian or something.'

'And what does he say?'

'He says they have to wash and they're temporarily commandeering the bathroom.'

'Or rather its utility. Its ablutility.'

'In fact you should say its lack of utility, because there wasn't any water. They complained, so Granny showed them the buckets and said: "Bring some up, there's a pump in the courtyard." So they took the buckets and dutifully set off for the pump. And Granny, being a vigorous, patriotically minded Polish lass, set off for the crêpe paper and white cardboard supply, promptly cut out a white eagle and a profile of Marshal Piłsudski, draped them with a tissue-paper flag, and hung her occasional composition above the bed. The Germans came back, had their wash, noticed the composition and said: "That wasn't here before." And Granny defiantly replied: "No, it wasn't, but it is now." They burst into laughter, and the Silesian said: "Pisudzki was *gut, gut,* if Pisudzki lived there would not be the war." They said thank you and goodbye, which Granny dismissed with a growl. Then they exchanged glances again and said: "And do you know who we are? Geheime Staatspolizei" – and seeing that she didn't understand, they added: "Ge-sta-po. Ha ha ha!" And they were gone.'

'Anyway, while Granny was cutting out the paper eagle, and her mother was arguing about the wardrobe, Mummy Rogozińska, née Kirchner, by never admitting her ethnic origin at all, not only lived peacefully (or at least as peacefully as one could in those days), but also had a German gendarme put behind bars.'

For it so happened that a highly intoxicated gendarme reeled up below the house where Mummy lived, and started to cause a row, accosting women and making trouble, brandishing a pistol. Either he was very drunk, or else he liked middle-aged ladies, in any case he was distinctly inflamed by his feelings for Mummy, who happened to cross the street just then; he ran up to her, grabbed her by the arm and would surely have dragged her into a gateway if not for the speedy action of the German police. The gendarme was handcuffed, a crowd formed, it was a sensation, with Mummy at the centre of all the fuss. Next day she was summoned as a witness, so she dutifully appeared at the hearing and showed her bruises; for you need to know that Mummy had incredibly delicate skin, and any more-than-average grip left dreadful contusions. 'Here,' said Mummy, showing her arm, in a fit of righteous indignation, 'here and here. *Suuuch* bad bruises.' And the gendarme ended up behind bars. Or maybe at the front? Who can ever know…?

At about this time, when Mummy incriminated the gendarme
in Kielce, and the Germans fetched their own water in metal
buckets and argued about Piłsudski, a new priest appeared at
Lisów, or rather a priestlet, straight from the seminary. And
high time too, because the old parish priest, busy making
babies for the village women and minding his orchard, was ever
more neglectful of his flock; free to do as he liked, he had lost
all sense of tact.

'Whenever Grandmama Wanda had palpitations, she absolutely had to have some communion wine. Our house was full
of wine, but she insisted on the communion kind; whether out
of piety, or because she had a special taste for it, I don't know,
but she'd be swooning and gasping: "Ah, ah, I'm fainting, ah, I
feel so weak." So of course I had to dash off to the presbytery,
and the priest always gave me half a bottle or a bottle, then
back I'd go, down the hill and up again, pour Grandmama
Wanda a glass of it and she'd recover. But one time the priest
grabbed me by the blouse and started to fondle me. He was
pushing sixty. "You seem to have made a mistake, Father," I
cried, but he just carried on. So I said: "I'm going straight to the
window and I'm going to scream." "You little fool," he hissed,
and opened the door. "The wine," I said, so he furiously
handed me a bottle and almost threw me out by force.'

The curate, tall and lean, seemed ideally made to be a
bishop's secretary – neat, taciturn, dignified, as if pre-destined
to glide about silently in a black cassock behind the rustling
silks of a cardinal's attire. Or so it seemed to Granny as she
gazed at him, sitting on the porch at the manor, sipping a cup
of tea. The Brokls were splendidly suited to this timeless mano-
rial order of the day: holding parties, inviting the priest to
afternoon tea, having informal conversations. It came around

to the Jews. 'It's terrible what the Germans are doing to them,'
he said, as if reciting a set lesson from the seminary, 'but one
must admit that in a way it will solve the Jewish question...' Oh
dear, how badly he misfired... Grandmama Wanda may not
have paid special attention to these words, but fiery lakes
of sulphur blazed in her granddaughter's eyes; first she
delivered a lengthy philippic, and then, without a moment's
hesitation, she sent the curate packing and forbade him to
show his face at the manor ever again. It really was a pretty
scandalous incident, by Lisów standards, but those were scandalous times. Besides, now everyone knew who was in charge
at the manor; my granny may have been beautiful and intelligent, but – and everyone was aware of this too – meek and mild
she was not.

❧

Ghettoes had not yet been established in every town, so Jews
were still seen here and there, but more and more rarely. That
was when on the road to Chmielnik Granny saw a young
Jewish woman standing in the rain, with a baby in her arms. 'O
my God,' she said, 'you must hide, get out of sight, the
Germans are locking up Jews and killing them...' But the
woman didn't react; she merely shrugged. 'Then at least let me
take the child,' said Granny without a second thought. 'I'll look
after him, I'll keep him safe, why not at least save the child?' But
she shielded the baby with her hand, spat against the evil eye
and started cursing, get away from me, evil spirit. Three days
later they set up a ghetto in Chmielnik too.

❧

'Meanwhile Milewski's wife died, and as his daughter was

married by now and had work enough with her own husband and her own cottage, he decided to get married again. He chose himself a woman who was pretty, but as stupid as a stone. And no wonder,' adds Granny, 'because she was from another village. So one day this woman arrives on a rack wagon stacked with all manner of goods. What wasn't there? She had a table, some cupboards, chests of drawers, bedding, china, chairs, lamps, and clothing. And she says she bought it all for a song, she's laughing away, because like everyone in Lisów, they're in dire poverty. Then Milewski comes out of his cottage, looks at it all and barks: "Where did you get that from? Was it from the Jews? You so-and-so, you want to get rich on human injustice?" He called the whole village together, heaped all the things into one big pile and set it alight, and then he whacked the woman with a stick, he beat her black and blue, while screaming the worst possible abuse. The people stood stock-still, watching in silence, just nodding. Once the pyre had gone out, they went back to their homes.'

XV

O my granny's beloved Jews, olive-skinned Jews, sons of rabbis and grandsons of tsaddiks, O you black-eyed Pharaohs, O you beautiful Jews, ugly Jews, Jews from little groceries and butcher's shops, Jews from the twelve generations of Israel, even if you never knew the kaddish by heart! O you Jews, you Jewesses in wigs, Jewesses with lapdogs in your arms, in furs and gemstone necklaces, Jewesses standing by the wall in the university lecture room, Jewesses walking with baskets of bread, Jewesses going 'I told you so, my life! knock on wood, what a charming young lady, God bless,' O Jewish girl with babe in arms, O Jews forcibly herded through Lisów, O race chosen by God and by my granny!

One day, and it was a hot summer's day, a day when the limestone dust wafting along the roads was even whiter than usual, a day when bees buzzed noisily over the clover and rainbow-bellied flies whirled green and gold above a muddy stream, boggily strung the length of the road, drying up in the scorching heat, and also a day when wasps droned in the sour nests of fallen apples… one day the goddess Fortuna, whose descents to the region of Mitteleuropa had been even rarer and more fickle in recent times, unfurled her wings that shone with gold leaf, flew down to the roof of the Lisów manor, then took my granny by the hair and put her on board the bus to Kielce, where Granny had nothing to do at the time, and found herself wondering why in that heat she'd suddenly had the urge to jolt along those chalky roads.

And in the evening – without the help of the goddess and her swiftly spinning wheel – Granny came home along the same chalky roads, which were still as hot as a lizard's belly from the day-long heat. On she walked, taking confident steps – just as one does on a very familiar path, where each stone has had its fixed place since time began, circumscribed with the blood of five-year-old knees and seven-year-old elbows. On the hill stood the manor house in a crown of trees, trees black against a sky already darkening, but still faintly illumined by a soft glow, trees outlined in ink against crimson – apple trees heavy with fruit, twisted cherry trees and gnarled greengages. And that was when Granny saw – yes, saw and not heard – the silence, the great silence, intensifying in the trees, silence solid enough to cut into large blocks and haul on a wooden sledge, down into quarries of quiet, where maybe one day someone would buy them to sculpt a mute David or a Pietà.

One lamp was burning in the kitchen, one in the drawing room. Granny opened the door, went into the hall, put down her basket containing a few odds and ends she'd brought from the Kielce flat and straightened a crooked picture painted by her father – but the silence was omnipresent: bloated, shapeless and set solid. In the drawing room everyone was sitting in total speechlessness, at a distance from one another – and not occupied with anything at all; no pipe smoking, no leafing through old annuals of magazines, no embroidery or painting watercolours, no looking for a phrase that would render the melody of a phrase by Anatole France. No one was even making tea. Their faces were green and their hands waxen, lying flat on the armrests of their chairs and the table top. Their silence was black, as if words had yet to be invented.

For that day the Jews had been herded through the village.

The Jews were ashen and bloodied. The Jews had no hope. The Messiah had not come to the Jews that day, neither in Lisów nor in Staszów, but in the forest, where they were shot above ditches as long and as wide as dead seas. For food and water the Jews gave away gold, clothing, watches – whatever a person had. The principle was simple – one forfeit for the soldier, one for the seller. In fact there were some – and don't think it won't have been recorded in the Book of Life – who wanted nothing in exchange for bread, and nothing in exchange for apples fragrant with grass and sunshine.

With tinware mugs and a pot of cold water from the well, Maciejowa went from one to another, filling her lap with scarves, rings, compacts – whatever a person had. A boy of no more than twenty, who had already paid an earring as his forfeit to a Ukrainian, was trying to hand her a beautiful, thick woollen sweater, a good sweater, bought by his loving mother when the boy went away to study, bought from a trustworthy source, a thickly woven sweater, a good sweater – a hand, a hand, a mug, a transaction on the move, while being herded by rifle butts. But the Ukrainian, who had a weakness for forfeits, seized the sweater too.

'Well?' barked Maciejowa. 'What'll you give me now?'

The boy stopped, holding the tin mug, cold from the water, my God, it was as cold as in the well, and said he had nothing else; he'd only had the sweater, and now he had nothing left.

And Maciejowa knocked the mug from his hand.

❧

The next day was Sunday. That morning, the women hung beads around their necks and laced their corsets, the peasants polished their shoes and combed their hair. The curate was finishing writing his sermon, scribbling something over and over on pages torn from an exercise book. Inspecting herself in the dressing-table mirror less coyly than usual, Grandmama Wanda draped her shoulders with the black shawl of her stately widowhood, which stood out strikingly dark in the patron's pew, right beside

the altar covered in snow-white ruffles of Richelieu lace. The bell
rang at the door from the vestry, silence fell, the sublime Latin
syllables followed one another in the steadfast order of the
liturgy like herds of docile animals in golden caparisons. And
then the priest, that thin, nervous priest with the pale face and
the prominent Adam's apple, that patched-together priestlet
entered the pulpit as if dragged by the hair by invisible angels;
not a word did he say about the workers in the vineyard, or
about the mustard seed, or about the wise and foolish virgins. He
cast his gaze down the nave, across the painted ceiling, over the
stucco cherubs and the lacy flounces, and then he glanced at the
crucifix, as if mentally weighing the size of the blasphemy that
he was about to utter – and then he opened his mouth.

'Woman, I'm speaking to you, woman, whose name I shan't
even utter, for fear of sinning in a holy place… have you never
heard the words of our Lord Jesus Christ, that whatever we do
to the least of His brothers we also do to Him? And that he
who hands a mug of fresh water to the least of His brothers
shall not lose his reward? I tell you, woman, if Golgotha had
been in the Miechów forest, and if the Lord had gone to this
Golgotha, you would have knocked the mug of water from His
hand. And that you have already done. May God forgive you,'
he said more quietly, 'I cannot.'

And he stepped down from the pulpit pale, his eyes burning
like two holy candles at a funeral rite, after the lessons he'd
learnt at the seminary – and the smooth currents of Latin took
him back into their possession, all the way to the *Ite, missa est*.

That evening the priest received an invitation to dinner from
the manor.

✿

Fortuna may have spared Granny the sight of the herded Jews, but she didn't spare her the sight of the executed Kaczor and his wife, though she did provide sterling support on this occasion.

'Oh,' says Granny, glancing at Mateusz flirtatiously, 'I always did have more luck than common sense. And what happened with Kaczor was this: before the war my grandmother used to rent rooms in the farm workers' block to summer vacationers; whenever we came on holiday from Kielce, we always lived in there, though for our meals we walked over to the manor. But during the war all sorts of people lived in the farm workers' block – there were so many victims of fire, people who were lost or in hiding at the time that it wasn't hard to find tenants. Among others the new head of the dairy lived there, Mr Kaczor, with his wife and child. Mrs Kaczorowa was a stunning beauty, like an Italian Madonna, but with very fair hair, enormous blue eyes and lashes as long as a cow's. She was as dense as a doorpost...'

At this point Mateusz gives me a knowing look, and I know that when we leave he'll say to me: 'My God, how well your granny tells a story! "She was as dense as a doorpost"!'

'... and they had done pretty well; my father even sold Mr Kaczor his gold watch. Evidently the Germans also noticed that Mr Kaczor was doing rather too well for himself, so they came to arrest him. Anyway, it must have been to do with financial finagling of some kind, because they seized all his property, and they never did that to political offenders. As soon as Kaczor caught sight of them, he tried to leg it through the window, and in that window they shot him dead. Then along comes Mrs Kaczorowa the Madonna, in floods of tears, with their tiny baby in her arms, and says to the soldiers: "Jesus Christ, Jesus Christ, they've killed my darling husband, Jesus Christ, kill me too... what am I to do all alone with the child, what am I going to do, Jesus Christ, kill me, kill me..." So they politely answered: "All right, go and give the child to someone to keep it for you and come right back to us." She handed it over to someone, went back, and they shot her dead beside her husband, then sat in the window and calmly waited for the gendarmes. And along come the partisans – they bypass Julek: "We're here to see the lady," they say. "Maybe I can help…" "No, we're here to see the lady. Miss Lala, Miss Lala," they say, "a terrible thing has happened, Kaczor had sixteen forged Kennkarten in his jacket pocket for the lads – if the Krauts get hold of them, they'll round them up in a trice." '

'So what did you do?' asks Mateusz.

'I said I'd see what could be done. So I search out a very small basket and go over to the farm workers' block. Two soldiers bar my way, saying it's *verboten* and I can't go through until the gendarmes arrive, because there are two corpses lying there. So I say I don't give a fig about their corpses, but I have to make the jam today. It's my jam-making day and that's final. "So what's up?" they ask, "not enough trees in the orchard?" And I say the plums that grow just here are special. Special, my foot – they were still completely green, so green it made my heart bleed to pick them. They let me through, you see. Russkies would either have clouted me or shot me, but not Germans – as soon as they heard there was a plan, the Germans knew the plan had to be obeyed and they let me through. I'd deliberately taken the little basket so that I'd have to keep going back for more. So I pick one little basketful, a second, and a third. They ask why I've got such a small one, and I say it's because I know how much sugar to use per basketful. Russkies would have told me to go and fetch a large basket and do the measuring at home, but the Germans believed me right away. So there they sit in the window, it's blazing hot, and I'm picking plums. Finally they ask if I'd fetch them some water. And I say no, but that down the hill, by the road there's a little shop, and they can buy themselves orangeade there. One of them was a Silesian, he translated for the other, and then they started to argue which of them would go. So I say I'm picking plums here anyway, so I can keep an eye on their corpses. They exchanged glances, finally they nodded and off they went. Quick as a flash, I went up to the window and hopped inside. The Kaczors were lying on the floor in pools of blood, so I had to lift him up – and he was a big fellow – to remove the Kennkarten from his inside jacket pocket. I also peeped in a drawer and took out my father's gold watch, and the Kaczors' gold wedding rings as well, so at least there'd be something for the child.'

'And what happened to the child?'

'Its aunt was supposed to come for it, that nitwit's sister.'

'And then what, did you run off to the partisans?'

'Nothing of the kind. I hid the Kennkarten under a layer of plums, sat in the window and calmly waited for the soldiers. They came back, said thank you, I did two more trips to and fro with the basket to cover my tracks, and that was that.'

'Granny, tell Mateusz about the sister too.'

'Oh, yes, the sister came – she was just as stupid or even worse. She took the child, and I drew her aside, gave her the watch and the rings and said: "At least have these for the child, I managed to get them out of their room." To which she said: "Oh, my sister always had such lovely hats – could you go back again and fetch me the hats?" The village women were outraged that her sister had been shot, but all she could think of was those hats. Anyway, I didn't envy the child.'

'What about the plums?'

'I binned the lot,' says Granny, laughing. 'There was nothing to be done with them. Though Aunt Sasha used to make jam with deseeded currants. She'd sit and pick out all the seeds, one by one, with a hair pin.'

'Tell me, Basia,' I say one day, 'where do you think they come from, all those great-great-grandmothers, great-grandmothers and great-aunts of ours who smuggled priests across the partition borders under their crinolines, hid fugitives and went to balls dressed in mourning for the nation? Where did those mothers come from, who bid farewell to their insurgent sons in January or December, only to go to large, empty stations months later to collect their coffins, with their names marked crookedly in chalk?'

But Basia doesn't know. For how could anyone know? All those women, who look exactly as we imagine them based on family legend – women with knitted brows, clenched, narrow lips and hair rolled into tight buns, but also the ones who didn't look like that – slender, gracile, squeezed into corsets, doe-eyed and swan-necked, like angels, who followed their husbands to Siberia and fled through a window at night to escape the marauding mob, carrying a child, a scapular and a bundle of jewels? As if someone had hewn them from hard wood, like stakes for mooring galleons or like wayside crosses that the roads hold on to, to avoid going astray... they are all of this breed. Basia and I wander the memories, as if wandering the Natural History Museum in London – where Basia, riveted to the spot by the sight of a fossilised reptile, once said in Polish: 'Jezus, Maria...' ('Jesus, Mary...') and a man behind her added in Polish but with an English accent: '... Józefie święty' ('and Joseph'), then vanished – as if wandering a vast museum of breeds that are extinct, forgotten giants.

Such as my friend's great-great-grandmother, who in 1863 was left at her husband's estate with two tiny children. The soldiers tied her by the lily-white wrists to a gun carriage and dragged her around the courtyard until she gave up the ghost. They would have killed the children too, but the servant smeared their faces with coal dust and led them out by a side door as her own.

Or my great-great-great-grandmother Michalina Karpińska, who smuggled the priest, Father Brzóska, across the partition border under her crinoline.

Great-great-grandmother Wanda Broklowa, who raced with the relay horses and saved her husband from the firing squad.

Another friend's great-aunt, who jumped out of a window in 1945, taking two children with her, after a peasant warned her that at night they'd come and slaughter the whole manor. She got away through the woods. To this day all the villagers think they have her on their conscience, but no one knows who actually killed her.

The wife of Uncle Eugeniusz, who miraculously managed to buy potatoes during the revolutionary famine.

The aunt who in 1943 was guillotined in Breslau for running a Polish paper called *The White Eagle*. In a letter from the death cell she wrote about God, Poland, to whom to give her watch and to whom to give her dress.

Aunt Dziunia, lighting one cigarette off another as she tells me: 'I learnt to smoke during the Uprising, you see. Everyone smoked, so I did too. We were building a barricade, so I let the lads take our grand piano from the drawing room. How furious Mama was with me, how she shouted, how she wailed… and guess what? Three days later a bomb came crashing into the drawing room – there wouldn't have been anything left of the piano but splinters anyway, so in the event, at least it came in handy…'

The Karpińska aunts and their private drawing school, their adopted would-have-been mothers-in-law, their dead fiancés, their rather bitter spinsterhood and boundless grief.

And Faulkner can put away his *Unvanquished*, because these women have been unvanquished for centuries, one after another, brigantines on stormy waters.

XVI

And then everyone began to die off. 'One winter's day they came running from the shop to say the Counsellor had had a turn. We raced there, but Papa was already dead. We were told he'd picked up a loaf of bread, pushed forward with the money, raised his hand and said "I'm paying," then sunk to the floor. The funeral was in Kielce. It was shockingly cold, snowing, minus twenty. And would you know it, in that awful weather about fifteen peasants came on foot from Lisów. They'd always liked him very much and often used to say: "The Counsellor says that if a peasant rips out a fence post 'cos he's nothing to burn in the stove he's a thief, but if an official steals tens of thousands of zlotys he's merely an embezzler." Besides, it was after all he who'd got them a licence, so the corner shop could sell alcohol, though Mama had a dreadful grudge against him for it. After that, every time the peasants hacked each other up with axes, Mama would say it was his fault. "Weeell, if they're going to drink," he'd reply, "then let it be decent vodka, and not moonshine." On the other hand, in the second year of the war, when Papa was sitting on a bench outside the house and one of the peasants came and sat down with him, later Papa said: "Before the war he'd never have taken the liberty." But he didn't say it resentfully, just thoughtfully.'

And those peasants came and did their share of standing in the cold. But they weren't the only ones – half the city turned out for the funeral, and suddenly it became apparent that Valerian Karnaukhov had a large number of friends and acquaintances; quite unfamiliar-looking people came, who told how he had given them free advice on writing applications,

Valerian Karnaukhov at an advanced age, Kielce, c. 1935.

how he had waived part or all of his fee if he could see the client was poor. Despite the filthy weather, such a large crowd gathered at the cemetery that the Germans sent troops to make sure the funeral wasn't a demonstration in disguise, or an illegal assembly. Poor Big Tarapata attended too, despite his asthma. How much time he'd spent discussing things with the Counsellor, how many books he'd borrowed from his library… and now he was standing by his coffin, as if struck by lightning, totally devastated, in a suit with sleeves that were too short, and Granny hadn't the heart to tell him that the suit, which his niece had brought him, had come in its time from a wardrobe at the manor and had once belonged to the Counsellor, his great big body lying so peacefully in the coffin, lying so peacefully...

💮

A year later, in 1943, my great-grandmother Irena died.

'Mama got up one day feeling rather out of sorts, shrivelled and cold. She went about all day in her dressing gown, unwashed, with dark rings around her eyes; the weather was filthy. I told her it must be because of all the rain, and that she should lie down. She lay down, and never got up again. The priest refused to bury her the Catholic way because she was a divorcee and a convert. I implored him, but it was no good. He wouldn't do it. They buried her under the graveyard wall. And only the young priest, I remember, stood in the presbytery window and drew a great sweeping cross above the coffin. I went to her grave for two or three months, but then I sensed it was empty, I could tell that she wasn't there. And I went home feeling calm.'

💮

Hanging in a thin gilded frame (O darkened gold, the hue of bygone Europe!) above my great-great-grandmother Wanda's bed there was a papal blessing, which guaranteed that if, on the point of death, one sort of sighed through it – if I've got the right idea, through the glass, the gilded frame and the multi-coloured lithographic print – to God, then all one's sins would be absolved. A heavenly safe-conduct pass. I don't know if Grandmama Wanda sighed into it on the point of death – when she heard that Irena was dead, she broke down entirely. The

night after the funeral she fell out of bed and crawled across
the floor – she was found by the door in the morning, chilled
to the bone; she let herself be picked up, a ninety-year-old bird
skeleton, and set down in an armchair. And there she died –
who knows, maybe her face was turned towards the papal
lithograph? Maybe she was thinking of the countless afternoons when she'd gone onto the porch and the village women
had asked her, the lady of the manor, to tell them about her
'ordy-ance' with the Holy Father; when she'd coyly simpered,
affecting modesty, they'd asked her again and again, so finally
she'd vanished into her room and come back fifteen minutes
later, wearing a black dress from the year... let's say, 1903, and
a black mantilla, sparkling with precious jewels, and told them
in detail, room by room, about the papal chambers, and how
she'd kissed the pope's gloved hand. My great-great-grandmother, the penniless gentlewoman brought up in a convent,
whom Fortuna had raised to the heights, to limousines and
audiences, to dinner services and silverware, before shooting
her down to Lisów, where sitting up straight, in pleats of black
silk and lace from half a century ago, she held forth to the
village biddies on the audience with the pope, generously paid
for – a fact she passed over in discreet silence – by her husband's
silver roubles. For the thousandth time the women's
jaws dropped, and they crossed themselves as she took the
lithograph off the wall, brought it onto the porch, and translated the blessing word by word from Latin, which she'd
studied at the convent school; after a while she removed this
remarkable relic from their sight, the outward sign of Divine
Providence watching over the lady of the manor.

Yes, maybe that's what my great-great-grandmother Wanda
was thinking of, as she sat in her armchair on the last day of her
life; maybe, sensing that the end was near, she fixed her gaze on
the papal blessing. Though I'm sure that as she lay in the

armchair, with death sprouting in her tissues, she was numb with pain. For which reason an envious sceptic might cast doubt on her salvation.

❧

A little later on, the young priest got involved in some underground activities. Soon after that, a fabulous scene took place, straight out of a film, when the Germans came for the priest; a cart was already in place below the window facing the garden, ready to convey him to a place of safety, so he threw out a valise, jumped from the window and lay down flat on the hay. Just at that very moment the soldiers hammered on the front door of the presbytery and went running around the courtyard.

After a time, a breathless boy came racing into the manor and gasped: 'Miss Lala, the Germans want to take away the priest.'

'God forbid, they haven't caught him already, have they?'

'No, they haven't, 'cos he escaped them, but he's had to hide until evening.'

'Where is he?'

'In the forest. He'll have to be brought some grub.'

Then the boy ran off to warn others.

'And then what?' I ask Granny. 'Did you take him some food?'

'Yes, he spent about two or three days hiding in the forest; how scared I was at the time! There were juniper bushes all over the place, and every juniper, if it's high enough, looks like a person. But the priest wasn't there. I don't know what happened next, but as far as I remember he survived the war.'

'When I was at Lisów, Tarapatka told me it was he who took the priest away in the cart below the window.'

'Maybe it was. But what can he remember? He's very old.'

XVII

I think that if Julek could have had children, and if the woman on the road hadn't been holding her baby daughter so tightly in her arms, I wouldn't be here at all, or I would have been completely different, burlier perhaps, with olive skin and large eyes. And if my grandfather had had speedier sperm I'd have been the same as I am, but Julek would have been my official grandfather. But that's not what happened. And that's how Zygmunt Karpiński, the forester, appears in this story.

❧

Zygmunt Karpiński was a forester, to all intents and purposes. Of course he really had completed the relevant studies, after eleven years, just like his father, uncle and grandfather, but – as Granny often put it – he was a whole trunk full of wasted talents: a pianist, an inventor and other things. That was one of the reasons why the forestry was only superficial. So what was the other? Well, it was that my grandfather toured the forestry district on behalf of the Home Army;* he worked for Sabotage Command gathering the wreckage of German V-1 and V-2 missiles that had blown up over the woods, made drawings of them and sent them to London on microfilm. Luckily he was much shrewder than a certain Japanese dentist, and no one ever exposed him at a dinner party.

Now he is nothing but a collection of photos. The finest ones are always out on the table, the chest of drawers, or above Granny's bed. 'Now tell me, he was an extremely handsome man, wasn't he?!' There Granddad coexists on peaceful terms

with Julek, Valerian Karnaukhov, my mother, my uncle, my
brother, my cousins and the rest of the family. But in those days
there was no love lost between him and Julek.

'You're writing a book about me? Oh, I'm sure you'll drag
out all the horror stories.'

'Why?'

'Because if I were writing it, that's what I'd do.'

'Such as?'

'Well, all that cheating on Julek, and in general.'

I run off to make tea or fetch the gingerbread.

'When your grandfather came and asked me if he could live in
the house, he didn't charm me straight away. Oh, no, it wasn't
love at first sight. Of course I regarded him as a handsome man,
and a well-bred person, but he only won my heart one afternoon when I was making the dinner. I asked him to pass the
salt, which was standing on the sideboard just behind him, and
he said: "I'm sorry, I would pass it to you at once, but the cat
has settled on my lap and I can't push her off or she'll be
mortally offended." And then he endeared himself to me for
being so inept when he came and said: "Excuse me, I don't
know how it happened, but I washed my shirts and now they're
coming apart in my hands." "How did you wash them?" I
asked. "The usual way," he replied. "I got a bowl, filled it with
water, threw in a box of powder and washed them." So I took
him for a good breeder.'

'And how did Julek react?'

'At first he didn't know a thing, but later on… I'd always told
him I wanted to have children, but after those operations for
TB, he—'

'What operations?'

'Well, for renal tuberculosis. But they thought it was something to do with the testicles and they operated on him. Didn't I tell you? He was cut up by a Warsaw surgeon who did all his operations without anaesthetic because he reckoned it healed better that way.'

'And did it?'

'Yes, but when I saw Julek after the treatment he was grey-green all over, the colour of clay.'

'And that was why he couldn't have children?'

'Yes, that was it. So when he guessed – after all, he was never exactly lacking in intelligence and perceptiveness – he demanded an explanation. And I gave him one. There was still an awkward situation, because the charwomen had just arrived at the house and I couldn't talk to him freely until they left in the evening. I told him the man was a breeder, he'd make me a child, and that would be that. He wasn't thrilled, but he understood me. You know, he loved me very much indeed.'

'And then what happened?'

'Nothing. Your grandfather and I did try, we tried and tried and tried, but nothing happened. He had to leave for Warsaw, because he had duties towards his country, and his wife too, but he promised he'd be back.'

❧

Granny waited, for her pregnancy and her forester. But nothing happened.

One day on the tram in Kielce she ran into Mrs Hess and her children.

'The boy tried to give me his seat, but I said: "No thank you, you young Germans can sit down." And Margerytka looked at me and asked: "Why did you say that? What harm have I ever done you? Am I sitting in the section for Germans? How am I to blame for having German descent? I've never taken advantage of it, I'm not hurting anyone." And it made me feel very sad, I apologised to her and we started chatting about this and that. She had two children, a boy and a girl, who looked much older than they were because they had inherited their height from both parents, so it had multiplied, and at thirteen the boy looked eighteen and was one metre eighty tall.'

'Like for Jews.'

'What?'

'They're under an obligation to marry – anyone who spends his life in a state of celibacy commits a sin against God's commandments, so they all have to get married. And as in any society there are hunchbacks, ugly people, dwarves and giants, who have trouble finding a suitable partner, they end up with marriages between dwarves, uglymugs and imbeciles, and the features inherited from the parents intensify in the children and grandchildren.'

'Indeed so. That's why there are such intelligent Jews and such astronomically stupid ones. But anyway it's curious that you compared the Hesses with the Jews – it's obvious you weren't alive during the war, because in those days that sort of association would never have entered your head, you simply wouldn't have had a connection between those neurons – they were two separate planets.'

❧

We still need a short interlude before my grandfather-to-be returns from his then wife in Warsaw to his future wife in Lisów. So let's tell the kidnapping story.

'Do something!' shouted the Germans from the threshold. 'Do something!'

Like the partisans, just like the partisans; Granny seems to have been the only publicly available mover and shaker at Lisów. 'What is it?'

'Two Germans came from Kielce, a colonel and a lieutenant, and they kidnapped Helenka. In a car.'

'Helenka Chuzia.'

'The dark girl with long hair, the pretty one.'

'What do you mean, "kidnapped" her?'

'They kidnapped her. They took her from home. It's a scandal, it's a kidnapping in Mitteleuropa.'

And off they ran to the radio station to broadcast, complain about and counteract the scandal. Granny's opinion of Helenka's virtue was not highly inflated, to say the least, and she harboured some vague suspicions about what had really happened, but just in case, she went to the little shop to make enquiries. Typically, Helenka had got into the car quite freely and without the use of any form of compulsion; the colonel and the lieutenant had tried to outdo each other in their efforts to be courteous and to pinch her bottom. Now all three were sure to be hanging out together in some secluded spot, passing the time by pursuing some simple pleasures.

Meanwhile the red-haired NCO and his colleague came back from the radio station disconcerted, because they too had found out Helenka had not really been kidnapped.

'Has she gone mad? Doesn't she know what the partisans do to gals like that?' (They didn't really say 'gals', they must have tossed in a stronger word.) 'They shave their heads. Pity about her plaits.'

And Granny went to see old man Chuzia, and he said: 'Ach, there'll be no trace on the girl, like a tank gone through water, but she'll bring home a big pot of lard.'

❦

So much for the interlude.

Meanwhile my grandfather comes back on stage; by a strange quirk of fate he began to spend more and more time in the Kielce area, and was more than willing to stop off at Lisów. Julek went about the house muttering: 'It's the roll-up man again', because before the war there was a company making cigarette papers that had a picture of a robust, ruddy peasant with an impressive moustache on the wrappers.

Once in a while Granddad, who didn't know at the time that one day he would be my grandfather, set about his breeding activity. The village began to talk about it. When I went to Lisów a few years ago and talked to a trembling old man called Tarapatka ('Tarapatka?' asks Granny. 'The young one, Józek?' but to me he wasn't young – he was nearly eighty, showing the black stumps of his teeth when he smiled), he leaned forward a fraction, winked at me and said: 'Ah, but your granny was a goer...'

'I don't understand.'

'Well... hee hee... for quite a time she... for quite a time, you could say she had two husbands...'

The whole village knew, but Julek pretended not to. What Granny didn't know, however, was that Granddad kept his technical drawings of the remains of blown-up V-1s and V-2s in the Sommerfeld upright piano. And no one, absolutely no one knew that Granddad was a secret agent. Because Granddad was good at it. One day, two fellows came out of the forest, not partisans, just a couple of tramps. They said they were from the AK and had come to requisition Granddad's bike.

'The AK? What's that?'

'What do you mean? The AK – the Home Army.'

*Zygmunt Karpiński as the
roll-up man, c. 1942.*

'What army's that? The Polish army was defeated in autumn 1939.'

'What planet are you from? You know – the army, the partisans, the boys in the woods...'

'Well I never. Well, in that case I'd ask you to leave me a receipt to prove I didn't give you the bike but you took it from me by force. Just in case.'

They tapped their fingers against their heads, but wrote out the receipt.

Because Granddad knew how to be an agent, unlike the boy who a month or two after Poland was occupied started going about the village in a uniform jacket, breeches and riding boots, encouraging the other lads to join the partisans. They did, but two weeks later the whole lot, including the ringleader in the riding boots, were captured by the Germans because someone had betrayed the entire group.

After all, there were collaborators too. Chuzia, for instance.

'Yes, because Chuzia came from miles away, near Bydgoszcz,' says Granny. 'A foreign immigrant – that's how Chuzia's old woman referred to her husband, because she was rich, and had land, while he was on his uppers. "I'm me, my child is mine, my own flesh and blood, but he's a foreign immigrant." He went about in a white sheepskin coat with a swastika on his arm. Everyone wanted to do him in – they used to plot and say that as soon as the war ended... and then the war did end, but nothing happened, he just put his tail between his legs and they never did get even with him. It was over and done with – that was the way in Lisów.'

Mr F. the teacher's son was quite another matter. Mr F. was such a decent man, known for his kind heart and immense erudition, respected throughout Kielce. But so what, if he didn't know how to bring up his son? So the boys came for the

son with a sentence for collaborating; the father opened the
door to them and asked what was the matter. They were just
young lads – Mr F. had taught them at school not so long ago.
And they spilled the beans.

'I see,' said Mr F. 'Do you mind waiting for just a moment?
I'd like to say goodbye to my son.'

He went into the other room and shut the door behind him.
The boys waited in the drawing room, and then they heard a
shot. Seconds later Mr F. emerged looking pale and said: 'You
needn't bother now.'

They checked, because they had to – that was their job, and
then they left.

There was also that Serb, Vitek, who went to collaborate
with the Germans straight away. A man like any other, he had
his contacts and connections (some people claimed they were
criminal ones), but that wasn't what the Germans liked about
him – it was his incredible visual memory. 'Once I was walking
down the street with Julek and suddenly I could feel this fellow
staring at me. I looked round at him and he just ran his eyes
over my face; I felt as if a hand had run down me, yes, it was
like the touch of a cold hand – it made shivers go down my
spine. And Julek said: "That was Vitek, the one who, you
know…" At the very start of the war he founded a partisan
group, just boys from good homes, and then he betrayed them
all. He got the death sentence for that. For a while he went on
living quietly with a classmate of mine, a White Russian girl
called Tushka. They used to sit out on the balcony upstairs,
looking down at the city that belonged to them, looking out
at the new Fatherland. One day a car drove up and Vitek got a
burst of gunfire from an automatic. He was taken straight to
Dr Poznański who, typically, operated as best he could, because
he knew his life and the lives of his entire family depended on

it. "Luckily the bullets went past", he said. Fourteen bullets, and each one had gone past something. Past his spine, past his brain, past his lungs, past his liver, and so on. And Vitek survived, and went on betraying people, went on collaborating even more ferociously than before. Then they made another attempt on him and he ended up under Dr Poznański's scalpel again; this time Poznański told the Germans: "Gentlemen, I am a doctor, not a miracle worker. He will live, but he won't be much use to you any more." And he told the man from the underground: "He could have pulled through like the first time, but this time I made an effort. He won't do you any harm. He'll only be capable of sitting in a wheelchair. I don't even know if he'll be able to talk." And that was how Vitek remained – silent, put out in the sunny doorway on the balcony by his lover, where to his heart's content he could gaze at the Fatherland, until it collapsed like a colossus with feet of clay.'

The romance began to flourish, with breaks for Granddad's trips, but flourish it did, because the child was apparently refusing to be conceived, and Julek was no hero.

Meanwhile, somehow Granddad's wife Ala found out the whole story, or at least part of it (it reminds me of when H.G. Wells had a lover, and one day his wife came into the room and said: 'I know everything!' 'Really?' replied Wells. 'When was the Battle of Salamis?') and wrote my grandmother a short but pithy letter saying that for obvious reasons she did not wish her husband to visit Lisów any more.

'Granny,' I ask, 'do you remember the letter from Ala Sasim?'

But she can't remember it any more. A few days ago she was sitting at the table with us and suddenly asked Mama: 'Ania, am

I getting everything in a muddle, or did I have a very active sex life?'

So I must fill in for Granny with what I remember from her tales of old. 'And do you know what those idiots cooked up?' she said.

'What idiots?'

'Julek and Zygmunt of course. Men! They sat down together and wrote that they did not wish her to send me insulting letters full of insinuations that bore no relation to reality, and so on and so forth, in the same sort of tone, so that any woman could have guessed what was going on. Maybe she would have had trouble understanding why Julek signed the letter too, but never mind.'

'Then what happened?'

'Nothing. They sent it. And proud and pale, showed me the rough draft. And I was furious with them – I got on the bus, then a train and went to Warsaw. In Warsaw I managed to find Ala's uncle, and by fibbing, ducking and diving, in a roundabout way I explained that Zygmunt and Julek had written a stupid letter, and that under no circumstances must it reach her hands, and so on. He looked at me rather strangely, but took me to her flat and persuaded the caretaker to open her letterbox for us, and then we ripped the envelope into tiny pieces. And a very good thing too, because a month later the Uprising broke out and Ala was killed. I can just imagine how Zygmunt would have kicked himself for the rest of his life if that letter had reached her then.'

🌸

'The Germans knew all about the Uprising. Zygmunt went to Warsaw in great secrecy, because he received a telegram saying "Aunt Ania sick has Aunt Frania left for Kraków" or something equally nonsensical. It brings a lump to my throat. And down the main road the Germans were on their way, whole herds of them. "What are you doing?" I asked an officer who'd been talking to our Germans, "where are you going?" "To Warsaw. Haven't you heard there's going to be an uprising there?"'

But Granddad was already in Warsaw.

❧

Strange – all his life he was so reticent... once I asked Dad what Granddad Zygmunt was like.

'If I had to define my father-in-law in a single phrase, it'd be "heh-hem".'

He died when I was eleven, and I know nothing about him. I don't know what his wartime pseudonym was, where he crept through the sewers to and from in Warsaw, where he fought, whom he killed and whom he saved. I remember him weeping when the Insurgents' memorial was unveiled, and how he defended Miron Białoszewski,* saying he wrote the truth about what the Uprising was like: dirty and smelly, a big mess in lots of cellars, but heroic in spite of all.

One day he was on his way to a People's Army* meeting at a shelter in the basement of a building that he could see in the distance amid the ruins of the street. On and on he walked, with that house ahead of him, where his wife and her mother were sitting in the cellar; apparently he adored his mother-in-law more than his wife. Just then a bomb fell, and the blast threw him to the ground. When he came to, he was deaf in one ear and had gravel embedded in his left cheek, and the building simply wasn't there.

Then he kept firing and running, went through the sewers, was taken captive and injured his spine when he spent three days being transported with lots of other POWs, crammed into a lorry and unable to move. He ended up at a camp, then another one, and yet another one.

He said Murnau was really something – a show camp for the Red Cross. They had everything. Only in the final period did they starve, because problems with transport began and there wasn't even enough food for the guards. But before that... the prisoners were sending food parcels home. And when everyone despised Białoszewski for his *Memoir*..., just as earlier they had despised Andrzej Munk for his film *Eroica*,* Granddad said: 'That's just what it was like in the camp. One man cut the fingers off another fellow's glove because they were lying on his bit of the table. Then he said he'd do it to the actual fingers too.'

XVIII

At the same time, while Granddad Zygmunt was starving in Murnau, the invincible Soviet army marched into Polish territory and began its glorious offensive. In January the front arrived. Yes, arrived, because it is a sort of movable feast, a shifting mass event. First come the announcements – flares and gunfire, and then a lot of commotion.

Granny and Julek reacted to the first announcements wisely, meaning that they packed up all the most necessary objects, then lugged a large chest down from the attic and filled it with the most valuable items in Grandpapa Leonard's collections. I don't know exactly what was included – probably engravings, pictures and family keepsakes, but above all books; whenever my mother talks about a fire or other domestic calamity, she always says: 'It can all be rebuilt, but the books... the pictures and books – you'll never get them back.' That sort of statement is in the blood, so I'm sure the chest did indeed contain some beautiful old editions with very fine pages and elaborately embossed covers, unearthed from the stalls of Parisian second-hand booksellers and at antique auctions by Leonard Brokl in the days of his prosperity. And once they had filled the chest, they grabbed it on either side and hauled it into a flowerbed, in case the manor house were to collapse under fire. Then they rolled up the rugs and laid them under the hay in the loft above the barn. The battle was getting closer.

The red-haired NCO stood in the doorway, buttoned up to the neck, and said the captain and his adjutant hadn't left, because it was their duty to hold on to the radio station for as long as possible, but he had entrusted his men to the NCO, with orders to walk through the forests and fields, so they'd end up in the hands of the Americans – the Americans without fail, and not the Russkies. He also said: 'We were given an order to throw grenades behind ourselves into all the houses where we've been living. But the captain forbade us to carry it out.' In the neighbouring village, Maleszowa, three hundred people were killed, because the Germans obeyed the order there – Germans who'd been just as amicable as our ones. They'd given the children chocolate too. The NCO and the captain's adjutant passed each other in the doorway. And once again I'm staring into the eye of the storm – in the tremendous whirl of the offensive and in the tremendous whirl of this tangled tale now and then there are places and moments as smooth as a metal sheet untouched by an etching needle.

In wind-tossed snow, in splashes of mud and the thunder of cannon fire, like a clear glass figure, I can see the German captain; I don't know if he was the one who said he'd never expected to find so many books and so many beautiful pictures in a Polish home, or someone completely different. Either way, I can see him, standing up straight in his smart, well-cut uniform, officer of a defeated army, scion of the Munich middle class, of Prussian Junkers or patricians from Lübeck, translucent, yes, translucent, because that's what people are like a few hours before death; now he knows it all – he has spent the past five years in a squalid village in the east, where the peasants called him a Kraut and the masters called him an occupier, but however hard he had tried, so it would have remained; the front is relentlessly advancing, the Russians will shoot him like a dog, because they're not going to dance around with prisoners and other such trappings of civilisation. He need not make any decisions – he knows he'll stay put at the radio station to the end. He need not say a thing – he has given his men their final orders, and watches through the window as they walk towards the woods. He sees no occupation ahead of him other than death. And that's when he summons the adjutant, hands him the Rembrandt album he borrowed, and tells him to take it back to the manor.

❧

Like Lisów's other inhabitants, Granny and Julek decided to flee to Chmielnik, site of the old monastery with thick stone walls. Meanwhile, by now the fighting was extremely close; the peasants fled in panic, dragging cows on ropes and carrying the remains of their belongings wrapped in eiderdowns rescued from houses engulfed by fire; a German whose head had been blown off by a shell ran right across the yard; on and on he ran, until he hit the coping around the well and tumbled in; moments later, a felt-booted leg flew past from left to right.

❧

In Chmielnik it was night – thick walls, the roar of gunfire and a horde of runaways, each with a quilt, some pots and all the usual clobber common to refugees in every place and time. Among them was Mrs Bartlowa, wife of the pre-war prime minister, a very decent man, though she was an extremely nasty woman; arriving with her daughter, as soon as she entered the monastery she treated it like her own property; she took possession of the only solid bed, occupied the kitchen and rationed the space. As they were simple peasants, and she was the prime minister's wife, the people were almost on their knees before her. One of the men was wounded, and one of the women was in labour.

'We have to boil a pot of water,' said Granny to Mrs Bartlowa.

'What on earth do these people imagine? This is not a soup kitchen! No one's going to do any cooking for them.'

'But it's for a baby.'

'The baby can drink it cold. I'm far too busy to have to cook for these brats as well.'

'But it's no problem for me to help these people,' Granny replied, 'my crown will not fall from my head. But yours is evidently at risk of slipping, Mrs Bartlowa.'

And the woman was speechless.

'We're going to need the bed too – this lady is in labour.'

'A mattress will do for her.'

Julek helped lug the mattress into place. Luckily a midwife was found, who agreed to deliver the baby, but on one condition: 'I can't see a thing, so someone must stand here with a candle. And they'll have to stand by the window, in plain sight of the snipers.'

And Granny stood by the window holding a candle.

I don't know if the baby was a boy or a girl, but I do know what Granny dreamed about that night. She dreamed of a tank on a frozen flowerbed, heavily standing astride the chest full of books. She got up feeling shocked, and instantly wanted to run back home. The fighting had tailed off.

❧

The first thing she saw when she got home was a tank, standing on top of the chest. The wind was scattering frozen pages about the garden.

'Couldn't you have stopped it somewhere else?' she asked a soldier.

'That was the easiest way,' he said, shrugging. 'There's a war on.'

❧

Lisów turned out to be utterly wrecked. Lisów, meaning the village, because the church and the manor house still stood unshakably on the two hills, as God ordained; except that a shell had smashed a hole in one of the drawing-room windows, fallen inside without exploding, and was now lying among the furniture like a large cuckoo's egg. There were occasional bullet marks on the plaster, several dented sheets of copper in the cemetery, and a few broken roof tiles in the garden. The village houses were quite another matter; the fiercest fighting had happened along the road; the ridges of their roofs burning like matches, one after another the suns on the sunburst-shaped gables were setting in a red blaze. Shells had demolished the workers' blocks and burned the coach house down to the ground. In the entire village only two cottages were left; it was a miracle that only three people were killed – a small child, a woman who went back for a cooking pot, and a peasant leading a horse out of the barn. But everywhere lay the bodies of fallen soldiers.

❧

The Soviets gathered up the corpses: Germans in one heap, their own in another, and then they told the priest to bury the lot.

'But the priest refused, because they were Bolsheviks and non-believers, and he wasn't going to bury non-believers in a Catholic graveyard. At which the officer pulled his pistol from its holster, put it to the priest's temple and said: "Oh yes you will. The Orthodox ones with an Orthodox cross, and the rest with a red star." And he buried them. At the time I said: "I'm sorry that when my mother died I didn't put a pistol to the priest's head. She'd be lying in a decent grave and not by the graveyard wall." '

❧

Among the corpses lay the captain and his adjutant, who the day before had clicked his heels in farewell, after returning the Rembrandt album.

❧

'I understand you killing Krauts,' said Granny, 'but why a dog? What harm has my dog done you?'
    'Oh, but the Krauts train those dogs to jump under tanks with grenades.'

❧

By the road stood a burned-out tank, with four charred bodies inside it. 'They were small. Like little black dollies.'

❧

Just as the Germans had occupied the manor five-and-a-half years earlier, so now the Russians took possession of it. Except that this time the whole house was packed with people, because Granny took everyone under her roof, and there was a family sitting in every corner: the Sabats, the Tarapatas, the Osmans, the Iwanskis, the Kuzios and the Rogozińskis. Because now Lala and Julek – or rather Mr and Mrs Rogoziński – were the local teachers, sheltering like the rest at the manor, apparently abandoned by the bloodsucking squire. No one made a special agreement on this matter with anyone else, but as the Soviets went from room to room, looking for wealthy landowners and bourgeois elements, and asked questions about the patently white-handed couple, every peasant said the same: the teacher and the lady teacher. Only one of them slipped up, not out of spite, but stupidity; later on, the others gave him a thrashing, just as they'd beaten the man who stole the orphan's cabbages all those years ago.

❦

On the other hand, they came close to shooting Milewski dead. They'd found a china cup in his cottage – porcelain means bourgeois. I'm not sure if I remember rightly – maybe I invented it, or maybe Granny did, because it seems extremely unlikely in view of his foot-stamping sanctimony, but it was the one and only thing he had kept for himself from the 'ex-Jewish property' brought by his wife from Kielce or Staszów.

❦

But while the Germans were interested in rooms (*Lebensraum* in miniature), the Russians were more taken with things (the doctrine of abolishing private property). They trailed about the manor and the farmyard, with Granny in their wake, removing from their hands knives and spoons (they never took forks), plates, glasses, picture frames, and all sorts of other items. And they gave them back meekly, without much argument – maybe it was the vodka that had this effect on them, maybe tiredness, maybe Granny's beautiful Russian, or maybe her bossy character, but in any case, as soon as they heard: '*Nazad!*' – 'Put it back!' in Russian, they even hauled the piano back into the drawing room, though just on the point of throwing it down the porch steps (*'Eto vashe? My dumali, shto eto germanskoye'* – 'It's yours? We thought it was German'). However, this did nothing to stop them from fuelling the stove with the photographs, ripping pages from the Bible to roll their cigarettes, cutting out the face from a portrait of Aunt Ewa's daughter Wanda ('What the hell have you done, you swine? The Germans tortured that girl to death, and that was her mother's only memento...' *'Nishto, nishto* – Never mind, never mind,' he replied, hiding the canvas under his arm, *'ya budu vsyem gavaril, shto eto maya dyevushka* – I'll tell everyone she was my girl') and chopping the rugs into insoles for their boots. ('But to give them their due, they stole the most valuable rugs whole.')

And suddenly, amid all this pandemonium, a very smart NKVD man appeared; carried along on the stormy waves of the front, he was travelling with numerous chests full of wood shavings.

'I was walking down the corridor,' said Granny in the days when she still remembered this scene, 'when I saw him in the drawing room, kneeling down to remove the Brokls' Sunday-best dinner service from the etagere...'

'And to look at?'

'The NKVD man?'

'The dinner service.'

'Cobalt blue with gold, and a little pastoral scene at the bottom of each cup and in the middle of each saucer, in pearly grey, each one different. The NKVD man calmly took one cup after another, one plate after another, and packed them into the chest with the shavings. And then I had a sort of presentiment; so far I'd gone up to each of those Russkies and deprived him of whatever he was stealing without a second thought. But this time I didn't. I just took a look and walked past, as if there were nothing wrong. Next day I saw him going to wash at the well, with a towel draped over his arm. "Look, just look at him," I said to Julek, "isn't he squeaky clean?" and the man said: "I advise you to be careful with such comments. I can understand every word, I'm a Pole." Then it occurred to me that a Pole who's in the NKVD must already be such a total bastard that if I'd attracted his attention the day before, he'd have taken his pistol from its holster and shot me dead on the spot.'

❧

'One of them said: "All this is yours? You've been very stupid. You should have taken the most valuable things from all over the house, put them in one room and sat there guarding it, so no one could pinch it." But everything came apart, pouring out in a broad stream straight into the soldiers' rucksacks and the peasants' bundles – of course they were depressed by the catastrophe of the front passing through, but they hadn't forgotten that Lisów was a bandit village.'

❧

'If only the Russkies had merely thieved, but they raped too. After the war, a doctor in Białystok told me how many abortions he'd performed in those days, how many girls he'd treated for syphilis, for gonorrhoea, how many dreadful tales he'd heard… Anyway, even at our place, in the neighbouring village, there was this one girl who was a real virago, and when all the other women ran off to the forest she said she wasn't afraid of the Russkies, and stayed behind. Along they came, she was in the barn at the time, and they set upon her – she whacked them on the head, in the face, as hard as she could, but finally they got the better of her; they left her so badly mutilated that no one knows if she was still alive when they left the barn, which they set on fire as a parting shot. Besides, they very nearly raped me too.'

'Whaaat?' I ask, choking on a piece of gingerbread. 'That's the first I've heard of it.'

'That's impossible. Don't you know about the time Gienia and I were on our way home at night and the Russkies gave us a lift in their truck?'

'No.'

'They offered to drop us off, and like idiots, we agreed. Into the lion's jaws. So off we go, there's an accordion playing, there's vodka, they start making a move on us. We say no, and they come on stronger; finally I screamed at one of them: "Bravo. The Germans told us the Russki barbarians would come and rape us!" "And you were fool enough to believe them?" "No," I said, wounding his pride, "I was fool enough *not* to believe them." And thank God, they threw us out of the truck.'

And then they marched off to Berlin.

'But Jacek, how they sang! Once, I remember, one of their trucks broke down and five lads worked to repair it. My God, how they sang!'

So like Granny.

🌹

'We had to get on with life. We had to bake bread. But there wasn't any grain or flour in the entire village. I went to ask Gienia, but she said she hadn't any either. Finally I got hold of some. But then I saw that Gienia was making bread as well. She turned out to have a whole box of flour, but she'd been too mean to share it. I looked straight at her and said: "I know you've always stolen from us, you've told us lies and slandered us. I've always known, and I've tried to forgive you. But to refuse us flour for bread is a dreadful sin. I curse you." And you know what? The next time she went to fetch flour, she reached in a little deeper and found the whole lot had gone mouldy.'

But now there was bread. Granny shared it among the Sabats, Osmans, Kuzios and others, sat down on the porch with Julek and set about eating.

'You know what,' she said, 'given an unlimited supply of bread and butter, one could be perfectly happy.'

XIX

The war ended. And Granny and Julek, appropriately for young people brought up on Żeromski, began work in the field, because 'this is what Poland is'* and so on. They found jobs at the Department of Culture in Kielce and were given staff accommodation, which as far as I know consisted of some large rooms that had been absurdly divided; their inlaid floors had been given a coat of black oil paint, which of course made Granny's blood boil – she immediately scraped off the paint and polished the floor, while hissing the word 'Savages!' They played the role of intellectuals and well-bred people, and naturally they did it extremely well. They weren't really experts on anything in particular, but they did have some broad general knowledge, thanks to which they were capable of dealing with a number of important tasks.

'But what did they actually do?' asks Basia.

Granny spends a while trying her best to bring back the memories, and then she says: 'I did know, I did, but I can't entirely remember – we did something there, we travelled about.' Luckily she gives up, and listens to what I have to say.

'For instance, Julek travelled about the villages, gathering the remains of scattered collections, because, unlike many of the newly appointed officials, he could distinguish an escritoire from a Buczacz tapestry,* and a cuirass from a canvas by Wyczółkowski.* In one village there was a manor house that had been home to a great collector of Chinese ceramics. They arrived to find the house had been looted, and the ceramics scattered about the village. Ducks were drinking from beautiful goldfish tanks, a woman was feeding her husband and children on Ming plates, and there was a nobly glistening Tang vase stuck on a fence post. Luckily Julek went to see the local teacher, who told him the village was suffering from a lack of school equipment. The children had no exercise books, erasers, pencils or textbooks. So he drove to the city, came back with a large box full of assorted school items and announced that anyone who brought in something that had come from the manor house would be given a notebook or a pencil sharpener. So those kids went all over the place, and brought in various odds and ends of china, furniture and books, which Julek swapped for copies of Falski's ABC.'

'I'd do the same swap too.'

'Ha! They're probably languishing at the back of a museum storeroom now, or else they were given away to some Party bigwig. Like the Witkacys in the museum, those pastels... did I tell you?'

'No.'

'Kasia went to Z. to look for her beloved Witkacys, but the people at the museum told her they weren't there. "What do you mean? They must be here!" So they caved in, and took her down to the basement, and there in a damp corner behind a cupboard, propped against a water pipe, were Witkacy's pastels. And you know Kasia – she made such a big fuss that the earth shook; she screamed at them that she herself was related to the artist, and so on, that it simply wouldn't do, it was a scandal, etcetera. And they were so terrified that they put on an exhibition.'

'But tell me more about Julek – it's interesting.'

'Ah, well, there's also the time he went to the palace that belonged to the noble Wielopolski family, who were margraves by title, to requisition their bloodsucking landowner's library. The general situation was that the last generation of

Wielopolskis had gone to the dogs on a grand scale. This was plain to see, not just from the solid fence that the Margrave had had built across the courtyard to keep the peasantry from looking at his wife, but also the library shelves. While earlier generations had collected some real literary treasures, spending a fortune on them, for the last few years before the war the only titles to have appeared in the catalogue were some trashy novels by the likes of Mniszkówna...'

'Or Courths-Mahler,' adds Granny, who has suddenly come to life for a moment because she has seen a box of Jaffa cakes on the table.

'Exactly. What's more, they guarded the library like Aladdin's cave, they wouldn't let any scholars make use of it, they wouldn't let anyone near those treasures, though they never even glanced at them. The one exception was a young student who had got the job of librarian there, and was paid a miserably low salary to catalogue the collections. He alone in the entire palace loved those books, he was the only one who cared about them. So no wonder he hid as many of the most valuable items as he could, stuffing them into various hidey-holes, nooks and crannies, and then with despair in his eyes he watched as Julek methodically found and emptied each of these hiding places. Finally Julek supervised the packing of the books into large boxes; he called the librarian aside and said: "Why don't you come and see us off when we clear out of here?" The librarian came and wasn't disappointed, because Julek had the box containing the most valuable books, the ones that had been hidden, placed at the back of the truck, and as they drove away he kicked it off, leaving it to the man as a souvenir. And that student's name was Gerard Labuda.'

'The professor?'

'The famous professor. The very same.'

'And what about your granny?'

'Granny began another affair.'

Meanwhile Granny's not listening at all, thereby missing the opportunity to find out what her life was like in the past, because all her attention is focused on the Jaffa cakes.

'Granny,' I say, putting the box aside, 'that's enough. They'll make you sick. If you're hungry, I'll make you a sandwich.'

'Bah, a sandwich... I'm not hungry, I just fancy a Jaffa cake.'

'I can see that – you've eaten half the packet already. That's enough for now. Really.'

Granny sighs, and with a pained look she capitulates.

'But what affair?'

'With Janusz Szymański.'

'Do I know him?' asks Basia.

'Not yet. Nor does Granny either. Janusz Szymański was a sound designer, one of the best in Poland, and as they were setting up a radio station in Kielce then, he was marched in to help. He was housed in the same absurdly carved-up apartment as Granny and Julek. Granny didn't notice him at all, because one, she had a husband, though ultimately that wasn't such a major obstacle, and two, she was worrying about her forester, of whom there was still no news. But Janusz Szymański was a stunningly handsome man, and he fell in love with Granny on the spot.'

'Then what?'

'Granny went about Poland in her usual way, bearing the beacon of enlightenment. For instance, she wrangled with some stuffed suits who'd instructed her to go to Silesia and buy a piano for a concert hall. So Granny went, looked around, and instead of buying any old piano, added some more cash from state funds and bought a Blüthner, a Bechstein, a Bösendorf or something of the kind from a solid German home. When she got back they made a fuss, saying why had she spent so much money when she could have got an excellent, Polish "Calisia" piano. But most of them were unsophisticated boors. In those days Granny wrote articles – I once found some in a cupboard – film reviews, and so on. A review of *Jolly Fellows*,* for example.'

'It's a beautiful film,' says Granny, still chewing up the last Jaffa cake with her gums. 'The piglets wallowed in their food just like at Grandmama Wanda's party.'

'You see, in those days Granny was having a flirtation with the new order. Julek's friends used to ask: "Listen, is she serious about it? Or has she just gone crazy for a while and it'll pass? We don't know whether to take offence and break off relations, or wait." "Just wait, she's gone crazy and it'll pass." And it did pass. After some trouble with the censors, when a jobsworth who didn't speak Polish all that well, and if at all, with a strong accent—'

'From across the Eastern border?'

'More like from Nalewki Street…' so he started to cross out something she'd written, and to make a fuss, saying: "This sentence, Comrade, has spoilt your entire article," to which Granny said: "I am no comrade of yours, Sir – to you I am Mrs Rogozińska." "Mr and Mrs, ladies and gentlemen," he replied angrily, "that was before the war. I suppose you'd like to go on wearing hats as well?" "Yes indeed, but the wind is very strong in Kielce – it blows my hats off." And that was the end of her flirtation. Then they wanted her to sign up for the PPR – the Polish Worker's Party, as the Communist Party was called – but she said she was already in the PPS – the Polish Socialist Party – and had been since before the war. They cajoled and threatened her, but to no effect.'

'I always did have more luck than common sense.'

'That's true too. Another time she and Julek started up a theatre group, but the authorities took away their rehearsal room to make it into a club room for workers who had to hold political meetings. Because a worker who attends political meetings is a good worker. Julek went to argue the case and encountered another blockhead, or it may have been the same one. And they got so heated that the man pushed Julek, Julek's wallet fell out of his pocket, and out of the wallet slipped his Polish–Soviet Friendship Association membership card, because in those days they handed out those cards to anyone who worked for the city council. "Aaaaa...", stammered the decision maker, embarrassed for having roughed up a Polish–Soviet friend, "aaaa... so you're in the Friendship Association?" Naturally, being no one's fool, Julek went straight into character and said in a superior tone: "Almost from the very start. What did you expect, Comrade?" And the hall remained a theatre, not a club room.'

'So what about your granny's admirer?'

'Janusz, you mean? One day he came to see Julek and said: "You've got to let me go because I can't bear to be here any longer." Julek was alarmed and asked him what was wrong – was the accommodation unsuitable, or the salary too small, or was he missing his wife...'

'He had a wife?'

'Yes, but she was somewhere else – he'd been planning to fetch her, but then he fell in love and somehow became less keen on the idea. So anyway, Julek asked a few questions, and Janusz said: "No, the flat and the job both suit me fine, it's just that I've fallen in love with your wife, but I've no chance of success. It's making me unhappy." Julek came proudly sailing into the house and cried from the threshold: "Thanks to you I'm losing my best employee," in his usual way, with emphasis. Granny asked what was up, and he explained. Men are such idiots. And from that day on, Granny cast a more favourable eye on the neighbour in the next room, which must surely have added spice to their living arrangements.'

❧

'So what about your grandfather?'

'All right, be patient. No one knew a thing. He'd gone to the camp after the Uprising and hadn't been seen again. Silence. No letters. Granny went on sighing. After all, those were times when people either turned up, or else they showed completely different faces. At the time, there was a move to condemn the young Przypkowski for collaboration – the man who made the double profile of Titus and Goebbels. And who do you think came to his defence? The Jews. Because it turned out that throughout the war he'd kept sixty people safe in his astronomical observatory, just a step away from the manor house, which was partly occupied by the Germans. Meanwhile, old Mr Przypkowski had spent the entire war saving writers, musicians and painters. He'd invited them to Jędrzejów, put them on the scales and refused to let them leave the estate until they'd gained the ten or fifteen kilos they needed. At about this time Granny met the beautiful Rachela Frydmanówna in the street; she was the only member of her entire family to have survived, not counting the Frydman who'd left for Palestine years ago, or maybe the United States. Half the Jewish boys in the county had been in love with Rachela, and so had the Piotrkowice squire's son, until his father knocked it out of his head. At night they dreamed of her pitch-black hair and eyes as deep as wells, her pure white hands and pearly teeth. She had survived doing forced labour; she'd worked at an arms factory, twelve hours a day amid mercury fumes. When she came back, people hardly recognised her. Her hair had faded, her teeth were yellow, her eyes dull. And her hands? No one knows, because from then on she always wore long black gloves, right up to the elbows. But who cared, now that there were no more Jewish boys to admire Rachela?

It was not just a time of discovery, but also a time of balls; in those days people loved to hold dance parties, which wasn't surprising, after all those years... A ball was held for the culture department employees, at which now and then a guy asked Granny to dance, and now and then a girl went past her and said: 'Helena, are you blind? Janusz only has eyes for you,' or 'All you care about is that forester – why don't you send him to blazes?' or 'Do stop torturing Janusz.' They left the ball, he came after Granny, then there were bunches of roses, sitting in the park at night, kisses on a bench. The suggestion that maybe, soon, tomorrow at the latest.

But next day Granny came home with the housemaid and heard Chopin coming through the windows, so she said: 'Aha, Aunt Ewa has arrived.'

'Mrs Mechowa doesn't play that piece,' replied the house-maid, which says a lot for her knowledge of the Polish musical canon.

And it was my future grandfather, who meanwhile had managed to get out of the German camp, feed up on American supplies, arrive in Poland, en route temporarily be manager of a cannery in Ustka (naturally, he was fired when he loudly objected to the victorious Red Army carting the machinery away), stay with his mother and little sisters a while, and finally show his face without so much as attempting to send a letter or telegram in advance. 'You nitwit,' said Granny when she learnt the truth. 'Am I to understand I'm too late?' replied my grand-father. 'Not quite, no. But it was a close call.'

'What a mess.'

'Yes, as you can tell, the situation had become intolerable. It was like this: there's Granny, sitting beside Julek, but gazing lovingly at Zygmunt, who's on the other side of the table. And into the mix comes Janusz, who makes eyes at Lala all the time, says "I'm sorry" and leaves, only to come back shortly after with a large bouquet of red carnations. So there they sit together, Granny puts the flowers in a vase, they talk and drink cups of tea as if everything were fine.

'What did they talk about?'

'Love. But nothing specific, just love in general, you know what I mean… though of course they all know what's up. Each of them says what the word "love" means to them, they talk about women too… Julek's bound to be the winner – he's a man of words, isn't he? My grandfather certainly isn't, he finds it hard to speechify… in theory I should be on Julek's side in this conversation, for one because I'm his next incarnation, and two he's the legitimate husband, and I like that sort of thing to be in order, but I'm backing my grandfather because I know he's just about to put his foot in it.'

'How?'

'I can't remember exactly, but he got himself into trouble.'

'What sort of trouble?'

'What sort of trouble?' asks Granny, like an echo – naturally, she's listening to my story as if it's news to her.

'Trouble trying to explain. That the relationship between a man and a woman is a sort of two-in-oneness, and in this two-in-oneness… and so on. Julek sort of laughed, but nervously. Janusz couldn't bear it and quietly withdrew. Then my grandfather took his leave, because he couldn't stay the night at the Rogozińskis', not least because Mummy Rogozińska had somehow learnt of his arrival from the others, and – out of concern for her daughter-in-law's virtue and her son's happiness – had made him promise to spend the night at her house. So Janusz has gone, Zygmunt is leaving, and Julek is staying. He looks at the bouquet, and all the carnations have wilted. "Oho," he says, "your Two-in-Oneness has peed into

Zygmunt, Lala, Julek and the dog, on the porch at Lisów, c. 1942.

Janusz's vase." So you can see the situation was impossible. But it can wait a while.'

'So what now? Are you going to tell me what happened to Lisów?'

'Yes, quite – I haven't got round to it yet. Formally the house and the scrap of land belonged to Granny and her mother's siblings: Aunt Róża, Aunt Ewa and Uncle Maciej. All three died at a rapid rate: Róża I'm not sure when, Ewa among the nurses and lunatics at the Morawica manor, now converted into a hospital, the house she had once argued about, and as for Maciej... he was probably carried off at last by complications to do with syphilis, though there is a suicide drifting about in my head – I can't remember the details. As a result, Granny was left the sole owner of the entire place and, a bit like Queen Jadwiga, Emilia Plater, or a heroine out of Żeromski,* she gifted the house to the peasants, leaving it up to them to patch the roof and the hole made by a shell under one of the windows, and turn the place into a school – since they were so clever, and the pre-war teacher had said that all of them should go to university. And what did those clever Lisów peasants do? Well, Gienia Iwańska, Aunt Ewa's former maid, and her husband stood there wielding axes and said the house was hers. And the villagers put their tails between their legs. They gave way. Can you imagine? Every last house was gutted, there was nowhere for people to live, and those two grabbed the manor. If only they had actually moved in, but... watch out, this is where the landowner's blood in me starts to boil... I don't think they had the nerve to occupy the master's rooms, because they built a place next to the manor, which thanks to the holes in the roof got wet, decayed, went mouldy and fell apart with age. A few months ago I dug out a file marked "Lisów", where there's a ton of old papers, including the original deed of sale, thanks to which you can see how many silver roubles the Brokls paid to buy the property from someone called Samuel or Izaak; and among the extracts and copies there's also a letter from Grandmama Wanda's maid, a very respectable woman, asking for intercession before the court. She writes that Gienia had started clamouring that she'd been bullied by feudal bloodsuckers for years on end, for which she should be given the manor house by way of compensation. In fact she had only worked there for three or four years...'

'... but actually she was the one who'd been bullied.'

'Bullied or not...'

'That's not what I meant.'

'Oh yes, I see, you mean it was Wanda's maid who'd been bullied, by Gienia. You see what a schemer she was? No wonder she had those yellow tiger's eyes.'

'And did your granny ever go back to Lisów after that?'

'Yes, first with a military transport, then with the children, in 1950 or 1951. And the peasants went on sending her money for renting the land until the 1960s.'

'What military transport was that?'

'Aah, for that we'll have to go back to her work in the field.'

❧

'In 1945 or 1946 my grandmother went west to the Recovered Territories,* where she witnessed some terrible things,' I tell Piotr, while sitting in his room, watching over his shoulder as he crushes enemy empires on the computer; Piotr is a genuine Danziger, and a Prussian patriot too – he's proud to say that his family once had a bakery on Mariacka Street, and if we arrange to meet at the Upland Gate,* he always says 'under the horse's tail', for an equestrian statue of Kaiser Wilhelm once stood there. Everything German strikes a tender chord in him, though he never loses his reason, unlike another friend of mine, who told me: 'I can offer you my hand with a clean conscience because you are sub-Nordic,' and another time, listening to a piece of Haydn or Beethoven: 'Can you see the Teutonic flags flying over liberated Eastern Prussia?'... Piotr pauses the game and turns to look at me, so my tale has clearly caught his interest.

'Granny was coerced into joining a military expedition by Mr Sasim, brother of my grandfather's first wife.'

'She and her mother were killed when their house was destroyed in the Warsaw Uprising, right?'

'That's the one. Mr Sasim was the provincial governor, deputy governor, or senior official – either way he represented the local authority. Unlike many other apparatchiks of the time when the new regime took over, he was a thoroughly honest man. Granny once saw the underside of his grey jacket lapel and it was a deep navy blue. She told him at the time that a man in his position who wears such worn-out clothing is a miracle on a national scale. Sasim greatly liked and respected her, so when he heard that Colonel S., a communist warlord and later one of the men behind the Kielce pogrom,* was going to Silesia with his henchmen, he asked if she would agree to go along as an impartial observer. Colonel S. was furious of course, but there wasn't much he could say.'

'So then what?'

'They went by military transport, in lorries. By then the Germans had been given orders to evacuate into the Reich, but they still had the right to stay in Poland for a short time to see to the formalities. Meanwhile, the colonel drove into a city, Legnica I think it was, spotted a teenage boy carrying a casket of some kind, and without saying a word he shot him in the head – he didn't even stop the car. Granny was petrified, because if that was how he treated people who had done him no harm, what value would he place on her life, tasked as she was with poking her nose into his business? She witnessed many of these executions. Finally she got a grip on herself and made a scene, but Colonel S. just laughed in her face and said: "I'm in charge here, I am." That evening a banquet was held for the Russian and Polish top brass in the drawing room of a looted mansion. After a few drinks, the Soviet general had a very enjoyable chat with Granny, then got up and did a tour of the table, collecting a flower from each place setting to make a small bouquet that he finally presented to her. "How very Russian – to take from all and give to one." "Have you ever served time?" he asked. "No." "Ooh, then your turn is yet to come."'

'Nice one.'

'Though it didn't work out that way. Yes. From Legnica I think they went to Wrocław, or another big city where the

governor was a friend of Sasim's. They were all taken to an
audience with him, including my grandmother – despite vocif-
erous protest from Colonel S.; what's more, as they were
waiting in the corridor, a secretary emerged from the governor's office and said: "The governor would like to speak with
Mrs Rogozińska." Mrs Rogozińska described the atrocities
committed by the Poles so precisely that once Colonel S. had
entered the governor's office, looking daggers at Granny in the
doorway, once he had taken a seat and heard the accusations,
and then replied: "I'd advise you not to have a go at me. My
boys are here too," the governor calmly answered: "Your boys
are not here – they're in the city jail, under the professional
supervision of my boys." And not only did he make the colonel
apologise to my grandmother for all the impertinence she'd
heard, but also to repair all the damage that could be repaired.
So much for Colonel S. But there was also Mr Ż., or let's
call him Żeremski. Mr Żeremski had received from some
colleagues a government order to organise transports of food
to devastated villages. Right from the start when Granny met
him at Sasim's, he made the worst possible impression on her
– especially because of his smart clothes. In those days everyone went about in what they had, in pre-war overcoats, jackets
with threadbare elbows, altered frocks and battledress, but Mr
Żeremski went about in a perfectly cut white suit, beautiful
shoes and dark glasses. He was from another planet – more like
a playboy from Monte Carlo than a reliable entrepreneur,
saving peasant families from starvation by the sweat of his
brow, in the name of People's Poland. For some time Żeremski
disappeared from Granny's field of view, but not long after, she
received a letter from the Lisów peasants, complaining that
they'd been given a far smaller amount of regulation corn,
flour and sugar than the newspapers had promised.'
   'Then what?'

'What do you think? Granny went to see Sasim and said:
"Listen, I trust them more than I trust myself – if this is what
they're saying, Żeremski must have misappropriated funds.
Please look into it." Sasim set up a committee, but it failed to
confirm any malpractice. At Granny's request, he set up
another committee, which also cleared Mr Żeremski of the
charges; it was only the third committee (either an honest one,
or else he had no cash left for the bribes) that discovered
massive embezzlement and sent Żeremski to prison for a good
few years. But someone had to deliver the extra food. So
Granny did it. Can you remember the happiest day in your life?'

'Yes. No. I'm not sure.'

'I'm not sure either, but Granny can remember hers. She
told me it was the day when she arrived in Lisów at the head of
the transport, and was welcomed by the peasants as their
saviour. "This is for you," she said, and they said: 'Please give
some to the community."'

'"The community"?'

'Yes, meaning the next village, home to the local administration. Granny said no, the food was just for them, but they
insisted: "You'll give it us and be off, but we're staying here."
So they donated part of it to the community. Granny spent all
day standing on the truck, distributing flour, sugar, buckwheat
and corn into sacks, while the people came up to receive it as
calmly as can be, without any arguing, as if they were part of
a great, sacred ritual. They took the food, bowed, exchanged a
few words and were gone. "And at dusk", Granny told me,
"you could see smoke rising over the whole village. Back in
their half-restored cottages the women were baking tarts
sprinkled with sugar. Then I saw a mother coming along the
road with a small child at her side, shyly sticking its fingers
into a small bag of sugar, blissfully absorbed in eating the
sweet crystals."'

✿

On another occasion I tell the same story to Basia, and at this point our eyes mist over. So Basis quickly says: 'But I want to hear about Julek and your grandmother, and about your grandfather too.'

'Well, let's go back to them. Where did I stop?'

'The situation was impossible.'

'That's right. The situation was impossible. So what on earth could the Rogozińskis do? Go away to Belgium.'

XX

'What do you mean, Belgium?'

'You know, the place between France and Holland.'

'But how did they end up there?'

'From Poland.'

'This is starting to sound like the gravediggers' scene in *Hamlet*,' says Basia in a cautionary tone.

'Well, all right. It was that Julek was offered the post of cultural attaché at the Polish diplomatic mission in Belgium. At first the communists wanted to show that they weren't sending nothing but dimwits from the Party ranks, but worldly intellectuals. They gave them various non-essential posts and put them on show in the European capitals, then suddenly recalled them to Poland and replaced them with their own people. Yes. So Granny gave away the Lisów house to be a school, locked up the Kielce flat, entrusted the keys to a friend (who in their absence removed from the flat almost all Grandpapa Leonard's art books, a small inlaid table and many other things, but that's another story). They said goodbye to Janusz, the forester and Mummy, and were off.'

At this point I'm forced to abandon Basia, sitting at the table in Oliwa, keenly listening to stories about my grandmother's colourful sex life; I'm moving to a completely different storytelling session – it's about the same events, but as told to another person.

It's a few years earlier, and Mateusz is sitting at exactly the same table in Oliwa. This morning, at my parents' house, I asked if he wanted to go into the city centre to see the Memling painting* at the National, or maybe to Słupsk* where they have a collection of Witkacys – though I'm afraid it doesn't include any portraits of the beautiful Mrs Kupciełło, which must have burned up in the corridor of the Royal Castle in Warsaw – and Mateusz said that, if at all possible, he'd like to go to Oliwa and listen to more of my grandmother's stories. So I called Granny and said: 'Granny, doll yourself up a treat.'

Granny dolls herself up, we take the bus, then a tram, and now here we are, sitting over a stack of assorted documents.

'Oh, look,' I say, 'look at this. An invitation from the Shah of Persia to a reception at the Persian embassy.'

'Oh,' says Granny disdainfully, 'it was rather dull. We thought they were going to give us something special and delicious, but all they served were some tiny cakes with oodles of nuts and honey. It wasn't bad, but it didn't fill me up.'

'But better than Bartych's biscuits?'

'Ooh, miles better. I'll never forget Bartych's biscuits as long as I live. You see,' she says, turning to Mateusz, 'Bartych was the only Jew I've ever met who fitted all the anti-Semitic stereotypes to a T. An utter blackguard, he really was. He was the envoy in Belgium, my husband's boss.'

'Julek's boss,' I add.

'The envoy was what's now the ambassador. Well. One time we travelled to Belgium together, and we had a stop in Germany on the way. After the war the Germans were miserably poor, and the food was atrocious. At the station restaurant they served us coffee, or rather some appalling dishwater, and to go with it some little biscuits, as hard as dog food. So I picked one up in my fingers, at which Mr Bartych said: "Where are your manners? They've provided a fork for these biscuits." To which I replied that the biscuits are as hard as rocks, and it won't be possible to spear them with the fork. "A civilised person can do it," said Mr Bartych snootily, and then he tried… his biscuit skittered about the plate, bounced off something, flew in the air and landed down the cleavage of a lady at the next table. He was crippled with embarrassment, then cringingly apologised and simpered away like mad, but he couldn't erase the bad impression. From that day on he hated me.' At this point Granny made a slight move, and after a pause she muttered: 'Maria Janion.'

'Sorry?' asked Mateusz in surprise; I didn't ask, because firstly I knew that Granny keeps a tiny mirror by her armchair, and secondly I already knew that lately she's been worrying that she looks like the literary critic, Maria Janion.

'Tell Mateusz about the landlady,' I suggest; I have to be quick to head off potential digressions about Granny's looks, now and in the past.

'The landlady? All right. Our landlady, Madame Dupont, was very dirty, and very charming. She went about in a stained, unbuttoned negligée, edged in frayed lace, till four in the afternoon, and she always had a large, overfed, hairy dog with her, just as scruffy as she was. From her general manner, and from the photographs set out here and there of skimpily dressed, heavily painted young ladies we concluded that in the past, or perhaps even the pluperfect, she had been a prostitute, and later a brothel-keeper. The war can't have done too much harm to her business, but perhaps she'd wearied of the profession in her old age and chosen instead to buy herself an apartment house with the nest egg she'd put aside, to live in peace off the rental income. Either way, as in de Maupassant and French literature in general, the prostitute was the most respectable landlady we encountered there. The commercial attaché, Mr Gęsiński, for example, lodged in the house of a dreadful old hag who switched off his hot water during "too long" baths and made him pay a tax for using the staircase. The old hag would lurk in her sitting room, listening out for Mr Gęsiński or his guests whenever they went up or down the stairs, and then added the cost to his bill. But Madame Dupont was charming, except that she told us to carry out a large rubbish bin, too heavy for me to lift – I was very ill in those days, you see... and Julek rarely had the time, and besides... anyway, there was another tenant on our floor too. One day Julek asked: "Why is it just me that has to take out the rubbish, when that gentleman never does?" "But my dear sir, that gentleman is a real baron," replied Madame Dupont, indignantly waving the lacy sleeves of her pink negligée. "Surely you don't expect a baron to take out the rubbish?" Julek took it on the chin, but a few days later he approached Madame Dupont again, and right up front, playing the innocent, playing the Dupont, he said: "Madam, do you know where the baron got his title? Eh? Because I have discovered the entire truth" – at this point he shifted to a conspiratorial whisper – "he bought it. Bought it! And where did he get the money? From the white slave trade. Imagine if you please, he persuaded poor country girls that he'd give them work in the big city, decent jobs as servants, nursemaids or shop assistants. And then he sold them to brothels. The poor little things." And from that day on we never took the rubbish out again. But every two or three days the tenant from next door went flying up and down the stairs with the bin, to my and Julek's great delight.'

'Tell him about the carrots too,' I remind her, just like a prompter, ensuring that the show runs smoothly and the audience leaves the theatre truly dazzled.

'The carrots? One day I go to the vegetable market in Brussels. I buy this, that and the other, and finally a bunch of carrots from an old biddy. Realising from my accent that I'm not local, she asks where I'm from. I say I'm from Warsaw. "That's in Russia, isn't it?" "No," I say, "it's in Poland." "Poland? Not Russia?" "No, Poland." "Oh yes," she adds after a long pause for thought, "maybe it is in Poland. I heard that the war didn't spare you." "Indeed, we had a good deal of suffering," I reply. To which she says: "Yes, yes. Here in Brussels too we had plenty going on! Terrible losses. On my street alone eleven houses had their windows smashed," and she gives me a sympathetic look. I try to pay, but she says: "No, as you're from Warsaw you needn't pay," and for ruined Warsaw she gave me a bunch of carrots.'

'Was Belgium destroyed too?'

'Belgium? Get away! Belgium was probably the least damaged of all the countries involved in the war. Neither the Germans nor the Allies ruined it. The Belgian king surrendered and collaborated with the occupiers, so the resistance movement, which probably fitted on a single sofa, tied a scarf over the eyes of his father's statue and wrote on the plinth: "We're blindfolding you so you don't have to gaze upon your son's disgrace." Meanwhile the queen and the heirs to the throne escaped to Britain and gave the Allies some uranium deposits in the Congo, thanks to which they could build the atom bomb. No wonder the queen was so greatly respected later on. After the war she went back to Belgium in a blaze of glory. Whereas the king fled, and after some time, when he wanted to come back too, he found a banner on the border saying: "There's no place for you in Belgium." And he ordered his chauffeur to turn around. But, to tell the truth, he served the country pretty well. I remember looking through an art book once, and saying to a Belgian: "What superb quality! Didn't the Germans destroy your printing industry?" "Destroy it?" he said, laughing. "They created it for us." Indeed, in Belgium they had everything: power, water, electricity, furniture, food and medicine. And on top of that they had lots of wonderful musicians, firstly because they preferred to come and give concerts in Brussels, where they were guaranteed a decent night's sleep and a good feed, and secondly because the Belgian queen was a famous music lover. You've heard of the Queen Elisabeth Competition? Well, there you are. I saw her many times, because I went to concerts on a weekly basis, sometimes twice a week. And she was always in the royal box. She never stopped applauding, and the court clapped with her, and so did the rest of the audience too. She'd stand up, so would the ministers, secretaries, etcetera, and soon there'd be a standing ovation. The performer would play an encore, and the ovation would continue. So he'd play another encore, and another, until finally the chief of diplomatic protocol would lean over to the queen and whisper that the pianist was on the point of fainting, because how could he not come out from behind the wings and play another encore when the queen was on her feet, applauding?'

'So who performed there in those days?'

'Ah, whom didn't I hear in those days! We even had Schnabel, who used to play for Hitler, so he wasn't paid the normal wages, just a modest little fee. They claimed that if he were totally banned from performing, not only he would lose by it, but so would the whole of European culture, so they let him go on playing, but almost all his earnings went to war orphans. I often used to go with Countess Delidekirk.' (God alone knows how I'm supposed to spell that name.) 'What a beautiful woman she was... she had a daughter who was famed for her beauty throughout Brussels; I remember going to a reception at Madame Delidekirk's and being delighted by that girl. A stunner. And then her mother came and stood next to her... and there was no comparison. Of course the daughter still looked pretty, but just pretty, whereas the mother... out of this world. What's more, she laughed her head off when she found out we lived on her street, because we really did live on Rue Général Delidekirk, named after an ancestor of hers. And how she laughed – it made her look even more beautiful.'

'How did you meet her, Granny?'

'The countess? Her husband worked at the Polish embassy. In fact he was her common-law husband, because it was her second marriage, and for some procedural, property-related reasons to do with inheriting the goods and title, he was her sacramental, though not fully legitimate husband. His name was Blochman.'

'Who?' asks Matcusz, whose thoughts have wandered.

'Her husband. He was a Polish Jew, a pianist. During the war he escaped to Belgium. He went into hiding, and for ages he starved terribly, but one day he noticed that each evening the shopkeepers poured whole vats of milk into the drains because it had gone sour. The Belgians are unfamiliar with soured milk or sour cream, and they think it's harmful, or at least inedible. So Blochman asked if instead of pouring the milk away they might leave it for him. And so he survived the entire war on soured milk. So much for Belgium.'

'There's the bidet too.'

'Oh yes, of course – the bidet. The thing about the bidet was that when we moved into Madame Dupont's house a new bidet had just been installed. But there was no refrigerator. So I used the old bidet, and the new, as yet virgin one, served me as a fridge, that's right. I used to put the butter, vegetables and whatever else in there, and keep a very thin stream of cold water running. One day I'm standing in the shop with Basia, my colleague from the diplomatic mission. "Look," she says, "what nice cream." "Ooh, I'd buy some, but I've still got plenty in the bidet." And behind me I hear a loud "hee hee hee," and there are some officers in battledress, Poles. They thought the proletarian females had got hold of some unfamiliar appliances.'

'It's not surprising,' I say. 'Recently I read somewhere that after the war a new Polish ambassador was installed in Sweden. When they sent a carriage for him, he muscled his way onto the box, next to the coachman. They had to force him down from there and get him to sit inside.'

'Yes, yes. I used to know a man like that, a good poet, but a very bad politician, Ozga-Michalski was his name. That was in Białystok. He was from the countryside, and bragged about it a lot, but he was also extremely sensitive and educated. One day I come to see him, and he's got a hen tied to the upright piano. So I ask: "What's she doing here?" and he says: "You know what, in the city they're saying the yobs have shoved their way into the masters' rooms and are feeding their cows out of grand pianos. So I didn't want to break ranks, but I haven't got a grand piano, only this one, and my flat's too small for a cow, so I just tied a hen to it." A very smart fellow. Unfortunately, he didn't restrict himself to writing poetry. Oh well, never mind. You asked about Belgium.'

'Yes, yes. What else is there?'

'Where?'

'In your head. In your memory.'

'What else did we do in Belgium… we used to go to parties, best of all to the Russian embassy, because those were the most lavish; one always had to drink a glass of olive oil before leaving the house to avoid getting drunk. In the Soviet Union the poverty was extreme, but there they had champagne, grapes, sturgeon, caviar, superb wines, delicious sweets and, above all, piroshkies; long queues would form at the table, and everyone kept whispering nothing but "piroshkies, piroshkies" to each other. Whereas at the British embassy it was all very neat but very shabby. Everyone, including the ambassador, went about in corduroy or tweed jackets with leather patches on the elbows, saying: "We don't know about Russia, but after the war Britain is a very poor country and we can't afford such extravagance." But apart from the parties Belgium is a terribly boring country. And the Belgians are appallingly stupid and uninteresting…'

'Granny has always taught us that all people are equal, regardless of religion, sex or nationality,' I say to Mateusz under my breath. 'And she has always added: "Apart from the Belgians and the Belarussians – the former have no common sense or imagination, and the latter have no honour or history."'

But I can see Granny's reproachful look, so I shut up. 'Just imagine a country,' she says, 'where everyone has a duty to wash the pavement in front of their house once a week. But they all do it on a different day, one on Friday, another on Tuesday, yet another on Saturday, and so on, which means it's never clean, because as soon as someone has cleaned up his bit, they track in mud from next door. Or take the residential houses in Brussels. When I saw those streets I stopped wondering why Corbusier came up with those little boxes of his, because every house in the city is different – each of them has its own ornaments and decorations, with no rhyme or reason, and on top of that each one is painted a different gaudy colour. It's enough to make you go boss-eyed. We used to get out of there just to give our eyes a rest.'

'Where did you go, for instance?'

'One time we went to Bruges, where I saw one of the most beautiful things I've ever seen; we went on a tour of an exquisite Gothic convent – well, all of Bruges is Gothic and exquisite, but that convent is particularly fine – and we found our way into the cloisters. And the entire green in the middle was covered in tall grass, like a meadow, and in among the blades of grass there were masses of narcissi, snow-white narcissi in bloom. And above the narcissi the nuns' white cornettes went floating by, because there were nuns strolling about the place, alone or in pairs, reading their breviaries. Bruges, the narcissi amid the sunlit grass, and those cornettes... and there was Gałczyński too.'

'What's that about Gałczyński?' asks Mateusz from his armchair.

'What do you mean? Julek and I tried to persuade him to go back to Poland. But somehow he wasn't in much of a hurry. It

was a strange meeting... very odd. He came along with his
lover, a frightful virago, large and tall, a real Amazon, wearing
battledress, who thought of herself as ethereal and soulful, and
she kept saying: "Konstanty and I", "me and Konstanty".'

'And what did Gałczyński say?' Mateusz asks.

'At first he spoke normally, but then he started declaiming.
As if talking, but improvising poems about yearning for his
homeland and the tough life of an intellectual in exile. That
was too hard to swallow, because much as I love his poetry, in
conversation that sort of silliness sounded terribly artificial and
pretentious.'

'Then what?' I ask.

'We did persuade him – in fact we weren't the only ones, and
as you know, he took the ship back in Poland, with the virago.'

'Then what?' asks Mateusz.

'All I've read,' I interject, 'is that he arrived in Gdańsk and
slept with her at the house of some acquaintances, and it was
awkward, because his wife was waiting for him, Silver Natalia,'
but here he was with that creature. So the lady of the house
says: "I've made up this bed for you, Sir, and that one for you,
Miss; I'm terribly sorry but we haven't enough space to give you
separate bedrooms..." "Why bother?" said Gałczyński. "We're
going to sleep together anyway." But I don't know what
happened next.'

'I do, though I didn't actually witness it. I know from Mr and
Mrs M., because Natalia was at their house for supper at the
time. Along comes her daughter Kira and says: "Mama, Papa
has arrived. With a lady." And she says: "With a lady, you say?
Aha, then let's go and see her." Of course it's an uncomfortable
situation, somehow they sit there and talk, and the virago
keeps saying: "Because Konstanty and I", "me and Konstanty",
"we writers", "we poets", "we artists", until finally she said:
"Because you are such a homebird, but Konstanty and I understand each other because we are..." but she didn't finish,

because at that Gałczyński said: "What? What did you say? Natalia? A homebird?" and whop! he threw her down the stairs. And that wasn't easy to do to such a large creature.'

'Was anything broken?'

'You mean bones? No. But if you mean life – absolutely. He'd convinced the girl she could write, but she was utterly incapable, she only ever produced some wretched doggerel, but she saw herself as his muse and inspiration. By the time we got home, she was yesterday's news.'

'When did you go home?'

'After a year, a year and a half perhaps. By then the communists had shown that they had non-Party intellectuals in stock, and that was enough, they sent them all back. Anyway, Bartych hated us with a passion. First because of the biscuit. And then on a trip away, he got into my room, pretending the shower in his one was broken, or some such excuse, but he didn't go into the bathroom, he just sat down on my bed and started to chat me up, wanting to have a fling with me. I sent him packing. From then on, we were daggers drawn.'

It was during those final days in Belgium that Granny and Julek read in an illustrated magazine about the misfortune that had befallen Margerytka Rommlówna and her husband, Mr Hess. Their teenage son had ended up in the dubious company of some "veterans" who spent a long time patiently explaining the grand theses of Nazism to him, until they had explained them so precisely that he put on an SS uniform, wrote a farewell letter ("Father, you have betrayed the ideals of the Führer, I cannot live with this stain on my honour"), and shot himself in the mouth.

'And so it goes. Those two had always behaved decently, so of course fate had to do them harm,' concludes Granny in a melancholy tone. She reaches for the little mirror on the shelf, glances into it, frowns, and puts it back.

XXI

On their return, Granny and Julek divorced.

'We were sitting in a large bay window in the courthouse corridor, waiting for the hearing; Julek was telling a funny story and we started to laugh like mad. Just then the judge came past and said: "Well, in this case I can see the marriage has totally and utterly broken down." But he gave us our divorce.'

And as there was a divorce, there had to be a wedding too; in fact there were two.

'You know what Julek was like. He insisted that your grandfather and I must be his witnesses, and he and his wife must be ours.'

'So he found himself a wife too?'

'Of course. "What's good for the goose..." She'd suffered a great tragedy, because some thugs had killed her husband, leaving her alone with a small son, and Julek was unhappy too, so somewhere along the line they'd grown close. And as for that double wedding! Your grandfather turned up his nose, she probably did too, and I thought it was idiotic... but it gave him such joy... The man at the registry office was amazed by all these machinations.'

'What about the honeymoon?'

'The honeymoon! That too! As you remember, your grandfather was a forester. And foresters had such low salaries that in the statistical yearbooks the column marked "average salary" had an asterisk and a note that said: "not re. foresters", so they wouldn't reduce it. We went to a forestry lodge. Next morning Julek shows up and says: "Hello, I came to see how you're doing."'

'He must have really loved you!'

'What could I do? Oh well, later on he and Zygmunt grew to like each other very much...'

'They'd have had a hard time if they didn't.'

'Very funny. And he really was extremely fond of the children. He treated them a bit like his own. He used to call Ania "Balalaika", and Pawełek "Piccolo". And there were those dedications in the books he translated... this one, for instance, fetch it down from the shelf, would you? *The Unknown Masterpiece*.* Oh, look: "For the authors of two known masterpieces, Lala and Zygmuś, from Julek." Anyway, all the dedications are like that.'

❧

After the wedding my grandparents settled in Siedlce, which was where the Karpińskis had lived since 1918 when they fled from Bila Tserkva.* My grandfather worked for the State Forests, and Granny was either seriously ill, or giving birth to one of her two children. Like this, Stalinism gave them a wide berth – and a good thing too, because with her tendencies to express her thoughts frankly she probably wouldn't have remained on this side of the Urals for long. As for my grandfather, as I've already said, he was a born conspirator, so after the war no one had the least idea that he'd worked for Kedyw, the Home Army's sabotage unit (if it had come out, he would have been sent on the same expedition east); he did in fact admit to having been in the Home Army, but he got away with it. He was partly helped by the fact that his first wife had fought for the People's Army, and at one time my grandfather himself had been a communist believer, and was accepted into the Party before the revolution. In fact he was only eight or nine at the time, and was sworn in because he'd gone after his older sisters, and on their trail he'd ended up at a clandestine meeting, but then goodwill does count for something.

And in a way, just like his sisters, for a very long time my grandfather did think of himself as a genuine communist, which meant more or less that he always put the good of the community in first place. And he sniffed out all sorts of plots and swindles, but no one liked that in the least, no one at all. That spotless honesty of his was always getting him beaten up, whenever he exposed some dubious hunting activities or illegal tree felling, selling timber on the side and profiteering; every time he was transferred to another department, and if he blew the whistle on something really serious, he was relocated to another city.

🌺

In Siedlce my grandfather diligently planned the afforestation, exterminated pests and carried on with his inventing. In particular he worked on a sower for very small seeds; and as amid the post-war poverty there was still a lack of suitable raw materials for making prototypes, the special chute through which the seeds were dispensed was artfully carved out of a stale baguette. The sower was a huge success, and as it was for very small seeds, it's no wonder that my mother arrived at this time, and a year later, her brother Paweł was born. Both came with major problems – my mother rebelled throughout the pregnancy (the doctor claimed there were no complications known to science that she did not present), but finally was born quickly, healthy and bonny. In his turn my uncle was quiet and peaceful throughout the pregnancy, but the delivery was so difficult that Granny entered a state of clinical death. The doctors suspected that the child couldn't be saved, removed it with forceps (none too gently, so Granny concluded from the effects) and were amazed to find he was alive. Meanwhile, Lala Karpińska went through a tunnel and walked about a heavenly garden, picking large poppies and talking to a luminous angel. 'But I have to go back to earth, because I have Ania there, my baby daughter, and now there's no one to look after her...' And she went back. As they were bringing her round, she kept whispering: 'Don't wake me, don't wake me, it's so lovely here, such beautiful flowers.' To which the doctor said: 'What the fuck' – oops, I'd never have written that for a hundred zlotys if he hadn't said it – 'are you on about? What flowers? You've got a son, he's alive.'

❧

'Me?' says my mother. 'Of course I hated my brother. Like every older child. One time Mama came into the room and caught me with a fork in my hand. I was trying to poke his eyes out.'

❧

At this point, whether it fits into my narrative or not, the story of Doctor Z. comes in, the incredibly handsome – as Granny always stressed – gynaecologist: an olive-skinned, hazel-eyed southerner with a shock of white hair, though only just over thirty. During the Warsaw Uprising, in a shelter at a residential house, he had delivered his wife's baby. By Caesarean section. He used brandy as disinfectant, and made the incision with a penknife. His wife and baby daughter survived, but his hair went white, just like Grandpapa Leonard when he faced the tsarist firing squad.

❧

I don't know how many people my Karpiński grandfather

killed – in the Uprising, before that in the partisans, and possibly afterwards too, during the liberation of the camp. Grandfather Dehnel shot down four planes from the deck of his battleship, and got a Virtuti Militari medal* for it; he must have had – how many people? Eight, or twelve, on his conscience? One of the planes exploded in mid-air because the bullets hit a bomb it was carrying; another one crashed onto a nearby sandbank. In the break between one barrage of gunfire and the next the Poles went to reconnoitre; they searched the wreckage – the pilot had been killed, so had the rest of the crew, but under one of the seats they found an unharmed bottle of cognac and some chocolate. 'We took the cognac for ourselves and gave the chocolate to the ordinary seamen.' Did they ever shoot anyone dead while looking them in the eyes, did they ever slit anyone's throat, or did they just fire bullets at small shapes in the distance?

❧

Granny was in the middle of reading a literary journal – it was a few months after the second birth – when she heard the most terrible screaming, full of genuine horror, coming from the nursery. It was my grandfather – otherwise a real hero who had survived a thing or two – screaming like that, so it must be something serious. Terrified, Granny runs to the playpen, and there sits my mother (in fairness I should add that she was only about eighteen months old), smearing poo on her own head, with my grandfather staring at her, as if at a Dantean scene, screaming away.

❧

'The poverty was appalling,' says Granny, or rather used to say, when she still remembered anything, 'so your grandfather took on an awful lot of odd jobs of every possible kind – he slaved away like an ox. One time I remember seeing a man in the street, dressed exactly like Zygmuś, but all huddled up, shrunken, plodding along. I look at him, and it *is* Zygmuś. "Go straight home," I say. "No more odd jobs for the next few days or you'll pop your clogs." But even so he was always riding his motorbike here and there, doing forestry work, inventing things, saving money from his daily expenses allowance, but it was still never enough. One time, when your mother was about four, we hadn't the money to buy her a pair of little red boots' – isn't the power of Granny's storytelling incredible? After more than fifty years that moment is still alive in her mind, when she left the shop with a sign saying 'Cobbler', 'Shoes' or maybe 'Footwear' feeling sad that she hadn't bought the little red boots, and as for the little red boots, just right for a four-year-old, there they stood on display, totally unaware that long after they had turned to dust, like Charlemagne's shoes or Alexander's sandals, people would still be reading about them in a thousand or two thousand copies of this book – 'and that was when your grandfather gave up smoking. He sat down at his desk, calculated how much he spent each month on cigarettes, and said: "I can't have a situation where I haven't the money to buy my daughter a pair of boots," smoked his last one, hid the packet in a drawer (to be tempting, to be available) and never smoked again to his dying day. And Ala, his first wife, was always complaining that he cared about nothing but "cards and the piano, cards and the piano"; she didn't want children with him because she thought he was an eternal kid who'd never be mature enough for such a big responsibility. Ha!'

'Granddad was terribly henpecked by Granny, wasn't he, Mum?' I ask in an affirmative tone.

'Certainly not,' protests my mother.

'What do you mean? Granny ran the entire house, was in charge of everything whatsoever, made a fuss about a broken glass or about overcooked potatoes, and when he finally sat down to a game of chess with our dad or with that fellow—'

' "Loverboy"?'

'Yes, that's the one, with "Loverboy". Her name for him alone is proof that she didn't particularly like him coming to play chess... so whenever Granddad sat down at the chessboard, at once he'd hear: "Zygmu-uuś!" and Granny would call him away to bang in a nail, do some cleaning or carry out some other essential handicraft. I remember that very well.'

'Well, yeees, but your grandfather did have a large degree of freedom, various hobbies...'

'A large degree of freedom! It's as if I were listening to Granny. Such as?'

'Photography, hunting... Granny never interfered with that.'

'He took photographs professionally, of sawflies, pine beauty moths and other pests, but if he took a picture of Granny she'd start shouting that she looked too big in the... well,' I say, pointing meaningfully, 'that he hadn't caught her celestial beauty at its best.'

'What about the hunting?'

'How much of it was there? Once a month, and anyway he dropped it very quickly when he shot a roe deer.'

'No,' says Mum more precisely, 'when he shot a roe deer and saw its tears, he stopped shooting roe deer. But he still hunted the occasional wild boar. It's quite another matter that he did it rarely, and every time Granny made a face. Like the chess with "Loverboy".'

'Do you remember how he used to fall asleep in front of the TV, and Granny would call: "Zygmuś, go to bed. Zygmuś!" '

'Of course I do. And Dad would mutter: "I'm not asleep, I'm tapping my foot" – he'd developed a habit of dozing off and tapping his foot to cover his tracks.'

'If Granny hadn't been so bossy, he'd never have done that. But you must admit, when they listened to the Chopin piano competitions and argued about who played better and who played worse...' – I pause for a moment – 'then they were quite extraordinary.'

'Well, you know, your grandfather played the piano beautifully. Beautifully. I remember that from childhood. He stopped after having meningitis; he only just survived it.'

'Was that the time he was infected by the bison?'

'Not directly – he got it from ticks. Yes. It was a very severe form of the illness, he only just made it. When she saw him in hospital, Mama almost fainted. Just in case, before she went into the ward the doctor had warned her that she'd see a living corpse in there; he also said that a great deal depended on her reaction. But she knew how to act in that sort of situation, and in other ones too, so at once she said: "You could be looking better, but never mind. The main thing is that the doctor says you're past the critical stage and everything's going to be fine." Later on Papa admitted to her that he'd looked into her face very carefully, and tried to tell something from her eyes. But he couldn't. And in the next bed lay a peasant, who also had meningitis, but the usual kind, following an axe fight; he asked the orderly what was wrong with him, heard the answer, was shocked and whispered: "Folks die of that," and two days later he was a goner. Your grandfather pulled through, but for a year he couldn't hold a needle between two fingers, let alone play the piano. And he never did any more inventing. Well, maybe

Lala, photographed by Zygmunt Karpiński, c. 1953.

I'm exaggerating. He did keep his flair for oddities... like the table for instance,' says Mama, pointing at the kitchen table.

'What about it?'

'Well, it's a folding table. Granddad made it.'

'Folding? I've sat at it for twenty-two years... what do you mean?'

'All right, move the plates and the glasses. Now lift it up.'

'Being surprised anew is the joy of sages.'

❧

After working in Siedlce for several years my grandfather discovered a scam at the forestry commission, to do with illegal hunting, and was transferred to Białystok, where Granny – after happily sitting out the worst of Stalinism having children – started to work in parallel for the department of culture and for the radio. What didn't she do there... she wrote concert reviews, organised Christmas parties for children (taking the opportunity to feed up some starving artists, whom she commissioned to make toys and Christmas-tree decorations), and finally she toured the local villages collecting folklore. And there was heaps of it, because the villages were occupied by Lithuanians, Belarusians, Ukrainians, Poles, Old Believers, impoverished gentry and others too. At the Ukrainian ones they sang, beautifully, in several parts – it was enough for four of the women to get together on the road and they'd sing in four parts; and when they got a bit tipsy, they'd take a good look around and change the repertoire to the songs of Bandera's nationalists,* just to spite the Polaks. At the gentry villages* they worked the land wearing gloves, but even so they were awfully dirty and – as Granny was always saying – they boiled milk in the kettle.

'I was given this basket,' says Granny, 'when I did a feature

on one of those villages, I can't remember its name. They were
desperately poor, and when I wrote about them weaving the
most beautiful straw mats, they were showered in orders. They
came to the city and gave me that as a present.'

❧

'Mum, do we really want to leave the straw mats there?' I asked
during our umpteenth general tidy-up; we have tidy-ups
because Mum was born on a Monday at seven a.m., and I was
born on Labour Day. Not so the rest of the family – they're not
born labourers, so it's always the same. We'll be painting the
hall, and my father will be playing a computer game, so we
hear nothing but: 'Ha! I've beaten the Persians,' or 'I've discovered iron.' Or we'll be emptying out the wardrobes in Oliwa,
and Granny will say: 'I don't know what you want to do with
those wardrobes.' 'Mama, the clothes you haven't worn for
years take up more space than all the clothes we have in our
four-person family.' 'Surely not!'

'Well?'

'Did you say something?'

'Yes, I asked if we really want to leave the straw mats hanging above the sofa beds.'

'Preferably we don't really want to move them.'

'You used to wonder…' I said, and sat down on the couch,
'… how come Granny's so fond of all these folksy things?'

Latching on to the idea of a break, Mum sat down beside
me.

'I'd say your grandmother's tastes require a whole separate
essay.'

'Should I take notes?'

'You might want to. There's always been a terrible mess at
her place, and lots of knick-knacks: in Siedlce, in Białystok and

in Oliwa. Because that's what it was like at Lisów, and once upon a time in Kiev.'

'There something in what you say. Do you remember what Wojtek once said about our flat? That the day will come when we wake up in the stairwell, pushed out by all the objects. Anyway, it's the same at my place in Warsaw. Radek says my collection of curios is expansive. And Wiktor winces at the fact that instead of buying something valuable at the antiques market once in a blue moon and restoring it to top condition, I prefer to bring home all those bits and pieces of junk. I can tell them it's all because it was like that at Morena,* in Oliwa, in Białystok, in Siedlce, in Kielce, at Lisów, at Morawica and in Kiev. Like a list of biblical patriarchs.'

And it's true. The flat in Oliwa is like an island surrounded by the waters of various seas, each of which has been tossing different shells, starfish and seaweeds onto the shore for years. From one direction the remains of former glory came drifting – a bronze candelabra, a large mirror, several photographs; from another, the Kielce furniture from the 1930s, bourgeois practicality, a solid dresser, an upright piano and a clock; from a third, the Karpińskis' paintings, the sad inselbergs of what was once a pretty decent collection; from a fourth came the folk obsession, in two varieties: the one inherited from Wanda Broklowa, who decorated the manor-house interior with straw-and-tissue-paper mobiles, and Granny's personal one, which bid her to fraternise with the peasants, record Belarusian folklore and give away Lisów for a school; all this splashes about in a deluge of 'temporary shortages of commodities', which made it necessary to keep inventing new uses for old things, to give the bottom half of a dressing table a coat of paint and make it into a small desk, change the dresser into kitchen cupboards, and partition the children's room with a plywood wall unit.

'Because there's nothing worse than having something and then losing it. I remember when Mrs... Mrs, well, I can't remember her name, told me that before the first war she had been a somebody. "I am not from plain stock," she said, "I belong to the more colourful kind – I had a flat in the house on the corner, with six windows on one side, six on the other, and net curtains in all of them!"'

So says Granny. And then, pensively picking the wilting geraniums and bunching them into a silvery-pink posy, she adds: 'Grandpapa Leonard went bankrupt twice. I lost two houses, and so many things, pictures and books. So as soon as I had money I immediately spent it. But your grandfather didn't – your grandfather was a practical person. Once, when we were still in Białystok, I dashed home from the marketplace to tell him they had some beautiful peasant kilim rugs there. They're lovely, made of wool, I say, and your grandfather says no, they cost so much, no and that's final, God in heaven, a kilim – you can't sit on it or eat it. No, no, and thrice no. So off I went, and for exactly the same money, to the last penny, I bought myself a hat. And to give him his due, your grandfather never begrudged me the money for that sort of thing. So I came home and told him I'd spent the same money. "Do you like it?" he asked. "Not really," I said. "Neither do I." I tossed the hat into the wardrobe, and never put it on again. Another time I wanted to buy curtains, because we had awful nets. And again he said no. He was quite insistent. Overnight they revalued the currency, and we lost all our savings. And I was far more pleased that I'd been proved right than concerned about the savings, because it wasn't much anyway, a laughable sum. And from then on Zygmunt never protested when I bought something for the house.'

But I don't know if this little story was just tacked on the end of 'there's nothing worse than having something and then losing it'. And I think about Lisów, about Julek, about my grandfather, about things and places. I pretend to be reading a magazine, and as I casually flip the pages, I tot up what I myself have lost, what I might lose, and what I shall lose.

'Something tells me,' says Granny, 'there'll be fewer cherries this year.'

And the black velvet drapes gently close over what's been and gone. What remains are the cherries, larkspur and tea.

'I've never been able to understand,' I tell my mother as we're sipping our tea (we've decided to extend our break and sit in the dust a while, having a bit of a chat), 'why it is, that for all her sophisticated taste, Granny managed to lug home so many frightful objects.'

'Oooh yes, that's right – on the one hand she bought such beautiful glassware, and on the other she adored porcelite crockery.'

'What about the red pans in the kitchen?'

'And the bathroom with the orange plastic containers?'

'It was even better than that,' I remind her, 'willow-green and orange.'

'Oh, yeees. But the reason for her passion for such items was her lack of a dowry. She had a complex, because when she married Julek, the war was on, and she could only dream of a trousseau. That's why all her life she's been accumulating vast numbers of dinner plates, side plates, saucepans, towels and bedclothes. Did you know that when I married your father I didn't buy a thing? I just took spare items from the cupboards. But Granny promptly made up for it.'

'But where does the love of porcelite come from?'

'For one thing, there wasn't much in the shops. And it's also a form of rebellion. She couldn't bear fancy decorations,

Secession style, embroidery and lace, because Lisów was stuffed with things like that.'

'So on the one hand we have continuity where the habit of accumulating things is concerned, and on the other a dislike of patterns?'

'Of fine patterns, yes. You see, the straw mats hanging above the sofa beds are direct descendants of the kilims and rugs that hung above the beds in Kielce and at Lisów.'

'What about the glassware?'

'The glassware came from Grandpapa Leonard's mania for collecting things. And as Granny could never afford to collect paintings and Sèvre porcelain, she collected art books and glassware instead.'

We stop talking. And for a while we sit in peace, staring at tier upon tier of coloured vases, bowls and goblets, covering – along with the books – almost every wall of the flat. We gaze as if seeing them for the first time. A transparent jug with a honey-coloured base and a long handle; a purple flagon, sapphire-blue carafes, Egyptian glass, turquoise or brown, as fragile as soap bubbles; splashes of ruby red and cobalt blue, ripples of green and yellow.

'I've always liked that urn,' I say, pointing out a violet flagon with a lid.

'And I like the green frosted one. Do you remember the time you broke the Venetian glass vase?'

'Only from what I've been told – it was turquoise and I didn't mean to do it.'

'Uh-huh. And you cried like anything. So Granny wasn't at all angry with you, she just wanted to comfort you.'

'Because it was the first beautiful thing I ever destroyed.'

And, forgetting about the straw mats and the porcelite crockery, forgetting matters of taste and inheritance, we sit and gaze into the kaleidoscope, just like children.

❧

But that's enough of the glass bead game. Let's return to the main narrative.

'In Białystok there was also the famous Master Leon Hanek. Master Leon Hanek was a conductor, and each week there were posters for the Philharmonic on all the advertising pillars, with the name "Hanek" written large, next to a slightly smaller "Master Leon", and then in tiny print the names of the performers and composers. Not only was he a megalomaniac, he was also devoid of talent. I remember a time when a French folk song had to be sung for a radio play. Plenty of time had passed since I'd lost my voice as a child, after the lesson with Mrs Klamrzyńska, the prima donna at the tsarist opera, and I could sing pretty decently; they asked me to do it, because I knew French. I did have a slight cold, but nevertheless I agreed. To my misfortune Master Hanek insisted on accompanying me on the grand piano. And it was like *The King Went out to War* as performed by my cousin Wanda: we tried a hundred times, but he couldn't find the right key. Finally, one of the pianists from the Philharmonic arrived, found the right key in an instant, and we made the recording. But I'd given my throat such a hard time that from then on for the radio plays I only ever voiced drunken old women, banging pots around in the kitchen.'

By now Granny has forgotten another story about musical accompaniment, but luckily I can give her a hand (or rather an ear and a larynx, though a hand too, because she always gesticulates tremendously). One time, a great pianist was passing through Białystok, the star of one of the first Chopin competitions; and as she was a polite and generous star, she agreed to play at the Philharmonic on a Friday evening. But a concert of waltzes by Strauss had already been scheduled for that Friday evening.

'I'm terribly sorry,' Granny said to the programme director, 'but you'll have to postpone the waltzes. An opportunity like this won't come again.'

'But couldn't they accompany her?'

'No, no, she's going to play solo pieces, not a concerto.'

'But it doesn't matter – they could accompany her with the Strauss waltzes...'

I'm searching my memory for the connections that linked this story to others, but I can't find any graceful ligatures, so I'll have to do it edgewise, through the musical theme. Very little has stayed in my memory – just this statement that Granny repeats endlessly, like a phrase that recurs in a musical score: 'Remember once and for all: there are no greatest works of literature, no finest sculptures, no most perfect compositions or very best paintings. But the most perfect composition is Beethoven's violin concerto. *Taaa da da taaada, ti... ti...*'

But there is something else... I've got it – the *Bolero*. A first-rate conductor came along (somehow good musicians often passed through the north-eastern part of the country, probably en route to guest appearances across the eastern border), who was to conduct the *Bolero*, and he agreed to have it recorded. So he conducted, the recording was made, and he left. But when they checked the tape, the whole piece was evenly paced, without any escalation of tension, without any dizzying spiral. At this the technician said: 'Oooh, well, they played so quietly at the start, so very quietly so you couldn't hear them at all, so I turned up the sound, and then when they made a racket I turned it down...'

And in the wake of the *Bolero*, the great soprano, Halina Łukomska, springs to mind. 'One time we were sitting in a restaurant after a concert, having a talk, and I said to her: "I don't know if you remember me, but you once meowed at my place..." Consternation. Here's a top singer, and I'm on about meowing... Łukomska smiles and says: "Of course, I did meow, that's right!" Because what had happened was that before she was quite so famous, I'd invited her home for a cup of tea – that was after a concert too. So we were standing at the front door, and I found I didn't have my key. It was late in the evening, the children had already gone to bed, and Zygmuś was away on a work trip. The end. But then I said: "You know what, if my son Pawełek were to wake up, he'd let us in. But he never wakes up unless the cat meows at the door. Maybe we could try meowing?" And as you can imagine, with her superb voice, Łukomska meowed like a virtuoso. Through the door we heard Pawełek saying: "Mama, get up, the cat wants to come in." "I can't," I said, "you open the door." He got up and opened it, without even noticing that it wasn't the cat but his mother and another lady, and went back to bed. So for the rest of my life I can tell the world that I once sang a duet with Halina Łukomska.'

❧

With his large eyes and radiant smile, Pawełek looked sweet and docile, but sweet and docile he was not. At the sight of this little angel, ladies in the street would either squeal: 'What a lovely boy, what beautiful eyes, what lovely hair. As for the little girl...' – here they'd pause, looking at my future mother – 'is the little girl yours as well? Very nice,' or: 'Couldn't you have shared your lovely eyes and hair with your sister?' or else: 'What a lovely little girl,' to which Pawełek would reply: 'I'm not a girl, I'm Paweł.' Both were taught not to be scared of all the silly nonsense thought up by adults to frighten children: that Baba-Yaga the witch would come and eat them up, or that the Black Gypsy would carry them away. So whenever they heard some lady saying: 'Behave yourself at once, or the

wicked stepmother will come and get you,' Paweł would snap:
'There's no such thing as a wicked stepmother.'

He may well have looked sweet, but he came up with the
wildest ideas. At the age of six he tied a scarf over his eyes,
picked up a cellophane windmill and – like something out of
every driver's worst nightmare – walked blindly across the
main intersection in Białystok (admittedly, it was the main
intersection in Białystok fifty years ago, not the main intersection in New York fifty years later, but even so the policeman
who brought him home took him to be a total fool); at the age
of ten he walked along the cornices of buildings, and at twelve
he hid out in the cellar with a view of the pavement, and fired
his catapult at the fat thighs and buttocks of women passing
by. When he turned out to have musical talent he was sent for
piano lessons, but he preferred to wander the city and play
with dogs. 'My dear madam,' the teacher said to Granny, 'I
have more than enough of these capable but idle students.
But only one who is both capable and hard-working.' (His
name was Maksymiuk, and he went on to be a famous conductor.) 'Please leave your son in peace and let him take up
something else.'

But there is a balance in nature – my mother did well at
school, went about in white blouses and little navy-blue skirts,
and if she needed money (to buy herself paints or books) she
earned it by making clay brooches and strings of beads. There
are children of Mary, and there are children of Martha.

❧

Sometimes – and now we're approaching the end of the
Białystok stories – both children went to see the neighbours,
who kept a mushroom in a jar. The mushroom was a sort of
cure-all; it gradually grew new lobes, making it look like a

Ania and Pawełek in fancy dress, c. 1956.

small stack of stuck-together pancakes, floating in yellow liquid. Once a week the liquid was drained off and drunk, and water was added to the jar. Sometimes the mushroom was sickly, and a lobe would curl up, shrivel and fall to the bottom. The neighbours would be extremely concerned about it.

The lobe that was Białystok also fell to the bottom of the jar. My grandfather exposed yet another case of fraud, yet another scandal, yet another racket, and once again his penalty was to be transferred. He had a choice of Łódź or Gdańsk, and Granny, who hadn't forgotten the rose-bush hedges on Jahnstrasse and the front steps on Frauengasse, came up with a thousand arguments, climatic, political and sociological, and knowing her, astrological and metaphysical as well, for moving to this city, which twenty years later was to be the site of my childhood.

She spent several days and nights removing glassware from the shelves and packing it into crates filled with straw, cramming metre after metre of books into cardboard boxes, and stuffing children's clothing into bags.

'Ah, Mrs Karpińska, greetings, greetings,' an acquaintance hailed her in the street.

'Ah, Mr Rozenblatt…'

'… Różalski…'

'… Różalski, do excuse me.' He'd Polonised his name. 'How good to see you, what a nice surprise. How's the timber trade?'

'Business is business.'

'Because business,' said Granny, more zestily than Benya Krik,* 'is when one God-fearing Jew loses out to another God-fearing Jew, and, praise the Lord, they both make a profit.'

'Wise words, wise words,' said Mr Rozenblatt-Różalski, 'your mamma must have fed you on nothing but fish heads, you're so smart. But why the storm clouds on your face? God forbid you have worries?'

'Weeell, you know what it's like… We're moving away.'

'Where are you going?'

'To Gdańsk.'

'Moving house is worse than a fire. Better to marry off your daughter than move house, as we say. God forbid you're short of money?'

'Oh yes, it's tough. My husband can't stop worrying about the cost of transporting the furniture, and the new flat, and having to hire a removal van, and we've so many bits of junk…'

'Don't you worry. We have a special fund for our people, you'll get the money from us. How much?'

'But… Mr Rozen… Różalski, you've misunderstood. I'm not one of your people.'

'Did I ask if you're a Jew or did I ask how much? I understand – there's been a war, I understand, not everyone wants to come clean. I don't want to know about that, I just want to know how much.'

'Thank you, you're very kind. But I really am not a Jew. Russian on my father's side, Polish and German on my mother's. Not a drop of Jewish blood. And I'm sorry, because I like the Jews, but one way or the other, I'm a goy.'

'You like the Jews, and the Jews like you.'

'It's really very kind of you,' said Granny, looking timber-merchant Mieczysław Różalski straight in the eyes, 'but even so, I have no way to pay you back…'

'If you have a way, that's fine, and if you don't, that's also fine. The sky won't fall on our heads. You've helped us, you've done broadcasts and made recordings, so we'll help you too. Please report to this address…' – he began to write something on a slip of paper – 'When are you leaving?'

'Soon, once my husband has made all the arrangements. Two or three weeks.'

'Then come next Thursday. To this address. Goodbye, I must run. My compliments to your husband.'

'Goodbye, Mr Rozenblatt!'

'Różalski!' he called after her, and smiled.

'And the funniest thing,' she said, 'was that when they gave me the cash, at some gathering of theirs (of a sort of postwar *qahal*'), they took a photograph and sent it to me afterwards. And of all the people in it I looked the most Jewish, because I had a deep tan, some sort of make-up, jewellery... that photograph must be floating about somewhere.'

And so Granny went to Gdańsk on Jewish money, like a real anti-Semite's nightmare. They jolted their way to the place, and set about unpacking the boxes of books and glass, the remains of the Lisów furniture, the plants in flowerpots and the Christmas-tree decorations stored in old suitcases.

XXII

Devil take the house – anyone could see what sort of a house it was, built on the foundations of an old barn, and thus without a cellar, constructed by such master craftsmen that none, literally not one of the corners was a right angle, the built-in wardrobes were collapsing like card houses, and nothing met the building standards. On the other hand, the master builder was a soulful person, and perhaps that was the source of his mistakes – the result of melancholic absent-mindedness. For you need to know that once he had botched one house, he set about botching another one next door (siting it, of course, at less of a distance from the first than the regulations allowed). He appreciated that Granny was a woman of culture, and he used to come and borrow books from her.

One time he comes in and says: 'You see, ma'am, I'm looking for something about life, about life you see. Lately, for instance, I read something that went like this: she was a countess, he was a simple fellow, they fell in love, but no one would let them be together...'

And as he was summarising the life story of the simple fellow and the countess, his gaze fell upon the complete works of Shakespeare.

'Sha-kes-pea-re...' he read, and pondered. 'Hmm... I've heard of it.'

✿

So devil take the house, but what a fine garden! The beginnings of the garden, like the beginnings of every beautiful garden, lay among the Islands of the Blessed, in those ancient times, where dry, branching twigs became covered in luxuriant blossom, and a stone sprouted living shoots. Before the shards of broken roof tile had been cleared, before the lime pits had been filled, while the outdoor hearth where pitch was boiled was still black, my grandmother, the Lady of the Coloured Glass Mountains, had bought some decent earth and a cartload of manure, hired a peasant with a tractor and told him to plough the building site, where all that remained of the old garden were two walnut trees and a cherry tree. And the peasant ploughed, and the ploughing was done. And Granny marked out circular beds and rectangular plots, planted white jasmine and lilac, japonica quince, and cotoneaster with little red berries. The world took on shapes and colours, and, sitting on a cloud with a large compass in her hands, Granny carved out its foundations.

Oh, they laughed at her. 'Not likely, madam, not on all that chalk' – and I swear the chalk was not just a mythical invention, for many years later, when we dug deep in the sand pit, down to the soil, we were instantly picking out small white pebbles, so brittle that we could crush them between our fingers – 'not on all those bricks' – and indeed, there were plenty of red chips under the sandy layer – 'pigs will fly before anything'll grow there!' But Granny wasn't in the least perturbed, and with a passion true to the mythical order of things, she resurrected the remains of the Lisów garden – clumps of peonies and phlox, the elegant purple heads of monardas, and rose bushes rambling across pergolas.

And it was only Mr Mędrzecki, a tall skinny man with the sunken, glassy eyes of a philosopher, who came to the aid of my Semiramis-like* grandmother by planting flowers that suited his depressive nature – weeping willows, thorny-sprigged holly, silver spruce, cypress trees and juniper, surrounded by clumps of glossy ivy. From then on, forever and ever, a small part of the garden remained in constant shade – not just the shade of the immense lime trees growing on the other side of the fence, but the more intense, palpable shade of the grave-yard trees and ivy, which imparted a chill, even on the hottest days of the year. That was another reason why our forays into that part of the garden, where Elysian shades were surely still wandering, were extremely rare, in fact only for the purpose of performing sombre rituals.

And we very rarely saw the neighbour, mainly hunched double over a holly bush, trimming a shoot of ivy or weeding the tamarisk. One time Granny asked him to take care of us. We were each given a chocolate, a long, narrow one, curved at the ends and tapered in the middle. It was called a 'cat's tongue'. I thought this a very suitable name, because, just like a cat's tongue, it did not prompt the slightest desire to pop it into one's mouth.

'Here's the bathroom, in case of need. And this is the sitting room. Look, here's my cactus collection. I'm very fond of cactuses. They're a sort of flower that grows in very hot climates and... er... what now? A chocolate perhaps? How about another chocolate each?'

'No, thank you.'

'No, thank you.'

I could tell he was confused, and I realised that actually some adults are totally incapable of relating to children. Even I'd have been better at it.

'And what's this room?' I asked.

'That's Asia's room.'

I heard that from the day she and her mother had moved out he hadn't changed a thing in there. The toys that Asia had thought too boring to take with her to her new home were still exactly where she had put them for the very last time. There were books in straight rows, five little pictures in identical frames, hung at even intervals, and on the bed a row of lifeless dolls, dusted – I imagined – once a month, on a set day, the sixteenth, say, or the third Thursday.

'She comes here less and less often,' was all he said, and closed the door. 'It gets dusty,' he added, by way of justification, 'dust gets in from the flat.'

An hour later when Granny came to fetch us from beneath the cactus collection, where eventually we had spread out our toys, we politely said goodbye to him, just as we'd been taught at home. I never went in there again. He lived quietly and, I would say, with dignity, holding up his grizzled head with its deeply set eyes, in which more and more often a strange ardour gleamed. Surrounded by regiments of dolls, books and cactuses, like a Chinese emperor with his countless terracotta retinue, he gradually sank into ever more total gloom – while his part of the garden sank into ever deeper shade and neglect.

Anyway… the garden! What a hollow word for what stretched before my childhood home! How many places I've seen that were described by the same word, how many clumsy imitations and half-baked fakes! Not to mention the execrable fences painted in all the colours of the rainbow, every board a different one, with edging made of tyres, and rows of plastic bottles to deter moles. But those neatly hoed paths, the beds marked out with string, the symmetrical hedges, the concrete edging, the baseboards, the taps, tubes and nets… no, it was something else entirely. The Oliwa garden was a beautiful, living organism, an intricately constructed whole, a universe in miniature.

My first memories, like the first memories of mankind, are

of the garden. Two big walnut trees and a cherry tree of the same height overshadowed my childhood – the cherry from late spring, the walnuts from midsummer. And below them – some botanical treasures. Huge brick-red dahlias, hanging over the fragile slats of wooden trellises, up which roses rambled, heavy with pink, white and purple flowers. The leaves of the staghorn sumac turning red in autumn. Cherries squashed in the grass, luring swarms of wasps, and walnut shells that turned your fingers black. And finally the pram, the pram set beneath a tree, with a tiny microphone suspended on a wire from its branches; this meant that while sitting in the house at tea our parents could hear even the softest wail.

'What vagabonds,' said one lady-next-door to the other, unaware of the microphone. 'That child is dressed like a beggar... They're supposed to be civilised, my dear, they've got a car, they read books, they discuss things, day in, day out, but as for the child, he's dressed like a beggar. No lace, no bib and tucker, no fancy clothes like the worst-off children have, just any old thing, my dear, any old rompers – they're without shame.'

Or: 'Have you heard about that Paweł of theirs? You have? It's true, he's gone to Germany, for good. But who's allowed to go abroad these days, might I ask? It's spies that go abroad, my dear. Do you think they let anyone go who isn't a spy? Not likely. The secret police come and ask: "Are you going to sign? If you don't sign, you can't go." But *he*'s gone. Think he went without signing? Never in my life. That's the look of it, my dear. And what about that child? Dressed like a beggar.'

Meanwhile the wire attached to the sensitive microphone, twined among the branches of the walnut tree and the rose shoots rambling up the wall to window height – sometimes, hurrying off to a visit or a private view, Granny would prune the roses through the vent – that perfectly impartial wire brought every word uttered by the neighbours to a radio located in the sitting room, and the whole family laughed till they cried.

Yet I remember neither the rattle suspended above my pumpkin-shaped infant head, nor the inside of the pram; I only remember it as a distant shape when, blindingly white in the summer sun, it carried my precious little brother, my tiny little brother, whom I had plans to suffocate or slaughter; my little brother, who some time later showed me his deep and uncritical love by calling me Aka, the name of a divine chief from Easter Island; my little brother, who in all the photographs stood right next to me, ever so slightly leaning and nestling up to my shoulder; my little brother, who to this day calls me 'little brother'.

And so I remember it from an extremely distant viewpoint, from halfway across the then enormous garden. I must have been sitting in the sandpit, or in the shade of the jasmine bushes, and looking up for a moment, glimpsed the intense whiteness of the pram. Then I turned my gaze on a ladybird marching along a ragged yarrow leaf, or on the blue iris petals where I was conducting my detailed research into the world, discovering the answers to all my questions. Answers and questions that I've managed to wipe from memory.

❧

It was there that I observed snails mating, earwigs living under old stumps, rare plants, frogs and ladybirds.

'I love the pope,' I said one day confidently, as I stood facing his portrait, 'because he's good. And I love frogs. Because they're useful.'

❧

In the summer I'd carry a table, some crayons and paper outside.

As soon as breakfast was over and Granny had made us wash the dishes, scrub our teeth and water the high-up plants – '...don't climb onto the desk on one leg, in one go, holding the watering can – do as I do: first the little table, but not the one with wobbly legs or it might collapse, then the chair, but be careful because it's a folding one and you might slip off it if you don't stand correctly, and only then onto the desk top; and water carefully, be sure not to overdo it, or you'll soak the books...' – I'd battle away for a good quarter of an hour to carry the table down the steps, then a chair, some pieces of cardboard and crayons in innumerable plastic ice-cream containers; each time I thought up new combinations, just to try and make as few journeys up and down the steps as possible, and as a result, planning the optimal solution took me longer, far longer than the actual carrying.

Finally, up to my ankles in lush grass – where the dew had already dried while we were having our two-hour breakfast – I'd survey the scene with satisfaction. 'So I've brought everything down,' I'd think, and with the look of a general on my face I'd hold an inspection of my colourful troops, and then carefully deploy them, mindful of the sacred rules of ergonomics. Just one tiny error and I'd receive a reprimand from Granny the moment she came down into the garden.

'Children,' she'd say, 'would you please bring me a deck-chair... but what's this, why have you got the crayons on your left and the book on your right? You reach for the crayons with your right hand, and you read the book when you're not drawing, but it's in your way, so you're resting your elbow on it and bending the spine...'

Then she'd sit beneath the walnut tree, in the semi-shade, covered in bright freckles of sunlight shining through, and unfold the rustling sheets of literary journals or the softer-sounding pages of books. Apart from the buzz of insects and the singing of birds that in Granny's garden seemed to enjoy an eternal mating season, total silence reigned. Sometimes in the afternoons, coming from the woods, from beyond the hedge, sumac trees and rose bushes, we could hear the shouts of local adolescents playing football; the language they used was different from ours, and I always felt as if they belonged to another world, safely fenced off by the dark leaves of the lime trees and maples.

Granny told us we should never speak badly of them.

'Yes, indeed,' she'd say, looking up from her book, 'their behaviour should be defined as improper at the very least; but I'm sure it's not their fault.'

'They haven't been taught?'

'No, they haven't. One should show them the right path, rather than condemn them. Anyway, they do speak their language with a certain flair, don't you think? With so few words at their disposal, they manage to exchange some quite complicated ideas. I wouldn't wish you to learn your vocabulary from them, but do occasionally listen to the way they express a whole gamut of feelings through just a few variables.'

And then she'd return to her book.

The afternoon started from the hedge; gradually the grass would darken and gain a heavy fragrance, and all the shadows would wander westwards along it, flexing and stretching to the point where they lost their shapes.

'Look, Granny,' I'd say, 'today I drew two sections. *The Flagellation* and *The Crown of Thorns*.'

'Rather brutal. You've been looking at too much of the German Middle Ages.'

'Oh, it's not all like that. Take Lochner, for example. Or

Witz.* The Germans have particular ways of expressing tenderness too.'

I was seven, or maybe nine at the time. I was a precocious
child.

Sometimes I would run to fetch another deckchair, and we'd
sit under the walnut tree in the splashes of disappearing light,
talking about the world and its infinite variety. Granny would
forget to make dinner, or would simply say with disarming
sincerity: 'I loathe cooking. I've always thought I should have
had a wife. There's no job more boring than cooking.'

And after a short pause: 'Have I ever told you how Julek
made the Lucullan soup?'

❧

What was left of the old garden in the layers of my memory is
like the remains of the crumbling leaves I have sometimes
found in old copies of magazines such as *Przekrój* or *Antena*:
red, yellow and rust-coloured scraps, too meagre to be regarded
as the equivalent of a bouquet; just some vague bits of images
and snatches of sentences. Yet I know perfectly well that right
then, under the brick-red dahlias of my childhood, in the
corners of wooden boxes full of buttons, in suffocating cascades
of flowering jasmine, the primordial truth about life was
revealed to me, which I was to seek in vain for ever after.

Sometimes one of those ancient scraps turns up beneath my
fingers, or catches my ears or eyes – a sentence in which I can
hear the echo of a long-lost ritual; a fraying shred of lamé torn
from a chasuble dripping with gold, a shred that has survived
its priests, its temples and its divinity; large murals depicting
knights of yore and their ladies, those resentful, faded murals
that only exist in a blue sky filtered through the eyes of a
net of branches, in the noisy buzzing of a bumblebee in the

honeysuckle, in a decadent sprig of lily of the valley. With time
the garden grew thin. Whenever I went to see Granny after
school was over and found the whole thing poorer by one
particular tree, a clump of bushes, or a branch perhaps, I would
go up the steps, stamping louder than usual, and press the bell
a little over-insistently. Because I knew that with the replacement of every broken paving stone, with the hacking down of
every tree, with the inevitable death of each peony or rose bush
that the rampant weeds had choked, came the irrevocable
erasure of a primeval codex, the obliteration of ancient formu-
lae and epic poems, the further fading of already faded
frescoes.

And finally, one autumn afternoon as I strolled about the
garden, so much humbler and smaller than the garden of my
childhood, as I cast my gaze around the broken pergolas with
pitiful shoots of roses run wild hanging from them, as I exam-
ined the overgrown holes in the trees, reminding me of the
coal tits for whom, once upon a time in winter, cubes of fat
speared on pieces of wire were hung out on the branches, as I
shuffled through the rotting brown walnut leaves that hid the
dark autumn grass, I understood in a – no, not a dazzling flash
– in a rush of darkness, that the existence of paradise is not
self-evident, that the natural state of a garden is a wilderness
and a ruin, and that any kind of beauty is actually the result of
a fight – whether with God or with the weeds, or with the
administrator who has insisted on cutting down the honeysuckle that was rambling up the lightning conductor like one
of Bernini's columns. So here I am, this is the same I who has
so often carried an inner regret that Granny, once so strong and
brave, has been unable to protect the fragility of this world, has
failed to preserve for me the biblical verses she cited to me so
many times over in my childhood, could not save the white
jasmine arch or the clump of phlox, did not make a whip out

of cords at the very idea of concrete kerbs and the very idea of cutting down the nettles, home to the butterflies – yes, this same I grasped the shocking fragility of everything that is beautiful. If only I had been grown up enough, before Granny sank into her armchair for good and all, to defend the pyracanthas, weigelias, horsemint and winter cherry, otherwise known as Chinese lantern, the garden's destiny would not have been fulfilled as it now has.

I stood under the cherry tree and cried for a long time.

Because the gods torment mortals by only showing them the truth when they are sure they will fail to understand it.

XXIII

'What's that you're writing?' asks Granny from behind a magazine.

'A novel about you, Granny.'

'About me? About an old pest like me?'

'Why an old pest? About my wonderful grandmother.'

'Well, I was never all that wonderful. Betraying Julek like that. But if I were to write it, I'd put everything. And so?'

'And so what?'

'And so how are you getting on?'

'Disastrously. None of it holds together. Either I have to do it chronologically, but that makes no sense, because you never tell your stories chronologically, or else digressively, but then no one will be able to tell what's going on.'

'Then they'll read it twice over.'

'Well, that's one way, for sure.'

🌸

When I was thirteen or fourteen my mother gave me *The Unvanquished* for a journey to Kraków; now I think it was too early, but at the time I didn't think so at all. And then came lots more books from the mythical Yoknapatawpha County, thanks to which I waded ever more confidently through Faulkner's rugged prose, lots more white residences with columns at the front, lots of cotton fields, silver buried at night and the melancholy of burned-down plantations.

All this I understood.

I knew – from her stories – what a manor house was, with

beds full of phlox and roses, with a coach house, a stable, a workers' block and a barn. I knew – from her stories – about the formalities of rural life, about the rules of etiquette, and about customs established over the centuries. I knew – from her stories – what lavish generosity was, what balls in Kiev were like, and what it meant to take the waters. And from her stories I knew how all of it falls into ruin.

Now I'm reading the old poet, I'm reading his translation of the gnostic *Hymn of the Pearl*,* which Margot buys whenever she finds it in a second-hand bookshop, and then gives it away to her friends, because it's about Margherita, the Pearl, lying at the bottom of the ocean in the coils of the serpent's body; as I read, there I discover something that I have always known, just as each of us knows that we are all sons and daughters of the king.

Culture relies on intelligent repetition. Faulkner and the Gnostics told me once again the things that I had learnt from Granny's tales about Lisów. But in time I noticed that, over the strawberry bed, while deadheading flowers amid swarms of mosquitoes in the evening, or on the deckchair in her garden, Granny had been casually repeating the words of the greats to me. Gradually I discovered that when she told me about the mad Danish prince, or about how Thetis bathed Achilles in the Styx, when she said: 'God is either good or omnipotent,' or 'I think, therefore I am,' when she defended Judas and disagreed with God, those eternal lines, on which Europe is built, were flowing from her to me.

Sometimes she gave the sources from which she was quoting.

'Who said that?' she'd call to me from the other side of the allotment, as she trimmed the blooming lilac. 'Well? What do you mean, who? Cartesius, that's to say Descartes.'

This last word on the out breath, indignant, as if to say how could you not know that at the age of seven?

'Pascal, spelled P-A-S-C-A-L.'

Or she'd call out from the bathroom; hairdryer there, radio here: 'What was that?'

'*Andante cantabile.*'

'What do you mean, *andante cantabile*? Which one? That's not the name of a piece, it's just the tempo marking for part of one. *Andante* – slowly, from walking. There's *largo*, meaning even more slowly, there's *allegro*, meaning quickly, *presto* – the same, then there's *con brio*, with fire, briskly... what else is there... ah, *con tutta la forza*, at full strength.'

Or: '... as in de Maupassant, prostitutes are the only decent women. Jacuś,' she'd say with concern, 'have you read de Maupassant yet? Maybe it's unsuitable at your age, but I took Witkacy's *Farewell to Autumn** from my father's library when I was twelve, and read it with flushed cheeks... there were such descriptions in there – *she clasped him with the legs of her psyche*, and so on – in those days it was regarded as the height of immorality. When my father found out I'd read it, his hair stood on end, or it would have, if he hadn't been bald. But it didn't do me any harm. Whereas he sensibly noticed that by then I could read anything. And did you know that Hela Bertz...'

'Who's Hela Bertz?' I asked shyly; despite having reached the age of twelve I hadn't read *Farewell to Autumn* yet.

'What do you mean, who? The vamp Atanazy falls in love with... that Hela Bertz, in fact Bela Hertz, really did exist and really was a Jewess – she really was incredibly beautiful and interesting, her pseudonym was Czajka, and as a result her husband was called Czajnik.* They looked very comical together, because he was small and jiggled about funnily when they danced... after the war I actually met her, then I did a broadcast with her... she was well over the hill by then, she'd run to fat, soft and pudgy, like Elizabeth Taylor in her old age, a similar type, but she was still a remarkable woman. Just imagine, a tiny little flat, two small rooms, photographs, pictures and mementoes from floor to ceiling, all sorts of hidden wonders. I even took your mother with me. She loved it there, but she was quite scared of Czajka. Once a vamp, always a vamp.'

And so on, and so on, and so on.

Then came Shakespeare, Epicurus and Homer. Sometimes they spoke more beautifully, sometimes more tediously. But I was at home.

It was then, as I reverently turned the pages of *The Golden Legend*,* that I understood in a sudden flash of childish wisdom – so far, my only wisdom – that the hagiographers were wrong. They were wrong – that diligent, doubting tribe, who in between raspberry and verdigris acanthuses, between four-winged beasts and monkeys frisking in the lesser margins, had filled line after line with ink, black as their habits and, sparingly, the firebrick red proper to initials and exceptionally tormented martyrs. They were wrong – those gloomy, hooded detectives of God's grace, those spies of Providence, who, one below another, set down thousands of barriers of black letters, black words, black sentences.

To them, miracles appeared to be something exceptional – like large, tropical butterflies, flashing by in gaps between points of the compass, fragile, beautiful butterflies that ever so carefully, without damaging their wings or wiping off the iridescent dust, must be put to sleep with the honeyed ether of scholasticism and extracts from learned works, and then shut away, *in saecula saeculorum*, in pearl-encrusted, gold-plated reliquaries housing the sacred codices. And they ran about the meadows of history in flowing habits, wiping the sweat from their tonsures, they ran about with the white nets of dogmata and syllogisms, hunting down the finer specimens.

A number of them, in search of the most splendid trophies, set off across the ocean; some, tossed in coracles from one wave to the next, reached faraway lands, fragrant with musk and cassia. Others were lost for ever in the surge, and drifted for centuries across the ocean bed, chasing a phantasmagoria of undersea butterflies, until time and water had thoroughly washed them away. Yet others went insane. Years later, resting in the cells of their native monastery, wreathed in the residue of distant aromas, shamefully hiding in the folds of their habits the lewd tattoos on their forearms and sailor's chests, they would turn the key in the lock, and the dislodged brick in the wall, and spend all night long delighting in their collections of miracles. Tapping and rapping on the glass cabinets, scenting the odour of naphthalene and camphor on wings and abdomens, these hagiographers, the wretched victims of their own mania, remained for ever far more the property of the miracles they had amassed than the other way around.

Leafing through *The Golden Legend*, under the flab of pietism and chronicler's steadfast care I could sense the raw, ascetic skeleton – the obdurate obsession with discovering what mankind can achieve in a miraculous way. Yet for me at the time the miraculous was – and perhaps still is – the obvious nature of the world.

On evenings when the high summer sky was setting above the glade beyond the fence, softly creeping over the crowns of the forest, and the dew was just about to drop on the dark-green grass, lush and sure of its own blackening verdure, I would dutifully carry Granny's deckchair indoors, then the small table, the boxes of crayons, and finally a multipanel polyptych, complete with predella and finial, only just glued on with sticky tape – and then I would find the time for thought, for all day long, time had seemed inadequate, buttoned up wrong. Then, in the warm light of lamps (with shades made of upturned straw baskets), I would think about the world's splendours; and when I went to bed, my head heavy with waking dreams, I'd already be longing for tomorrow. For I knew it would be a miraculous day.

After all, there was so much going on at the time! Months and quarters went by, Christmases evolved into Easters, and Easters into Christmases. We'd hang up paper chains, and Granny would tell us how she once caught fire from the Christmas-tree candles. Her cousin, Adaś Bahr, had put out the flames.

'Your cousin, Granny? Which cousin was he?'

'On the Brokl side. A maternal cousin of my mother's. He may have been my grandfather's sister's son… No, that's not right, my grandfather didn't have any sisters. Then perhaps he was my mother's cousin's cousin, I don't know. The main thing is, he put out the fire.'

Yes, it's impossible not to concur. Not least when you stop to consider that extinguishing my highly flammable grandmother must always have been a tricky thing to do, especially in the days of her youth.

Both in Białystok and in Gdańsk several more Christmas trees went up in flames, and on one occasion the fire spread to the curtains.

'You know, I was very pleased indeed, because they were horrid. The result of your grandfather's stingy nature – he preferred material that was a few pennies cheaper, although it was as ugly as sin. And it caught fire, ha! Those hideous curtains went up in flames.'

And when at Christmas we were decorating the second tree – the first one was at our house, the second at Granny's in Oliwa... just a moment... what used to happen before then? What happened earlier on, when the whole family lived at the house in Oliwa? We boys must have been too small to hang up the glass balls and stars, trail the cotton-wool snow along the fragrant branches and gird them with coloured paper chains, which we were told commemorated all those distant ancestors who, like Grandpapa Leonard, had been sent to Siberia. Either way, once we were allowed to handle all the glass and paper, the dull and shiny baubles, year after year in the same boxes we would find the same ancient glass balls with charred bellies, the same sooty tinsel and the same wrinkled, sizzled decorations – which our parents told us to hang on the side, and which I always tried to place in the most prominent spot, because I admired their carbonised splendours – so proudly stored at the bottom of the boxes, stored in their turn at the bottom of old suitcases, stored in theirs at the back of the overhead cupboard.

Sometimes I secretly dreamed that, as in times past, the Christmas tree would burst into flames once more, and all the baubles would become equally beautiful again. But until that happened, I would tenderly gaze at the damaged ones, and hum them a little tune.

❦

The house was like a gynaeceum. Indeed, 'Loverboy' some-times came to see my grandfather for two or three games of chess, and my father was probably there every day. And yet we were looked after almost exclusively by women: Mum, Granny, aunts, female acquaintances and the neighbours' seven daughters. So if I spoke of myself in the past tense – which conjugates in Polish not just by person and number, but also gender – it was only in the feminine; my father's hackles would rise whenever he heard me use a feminine grammatical ending in reference to myself; he combatted it, fighting against a whole herd of delighted women.

'Even so, the male is the inferior of the human species,' Granny would quip at him, and withdraw from the battlefield.

Oh, those friends of Granny's, the twittering ones who brought honey-flavoured sweets (in cellophane, with a honeycomb printed on it), the ones who leaned over us! Sunken or goggle-eyed, wrinkled or plump and smooth, chatty or reticent, dressed in grey linen or wool, rattling their pearls, or else in flowery pastels, with little pleats, bows and buttons; Krysia, Wanda, Mira! Elżbieta, the sculptress, who would call from the threshold: 'What a fine head he has. I must sculpt him, I *must*!'

And, in my blissful four-year-old state, I would puff myself up as much as I could, and hold out my hands to be kissed, because Elżbieta always kissed me on every finger, one after the other, as her heavy silver chains jangled on her skinny wrists. I was a little emperor. My parents regarded it as morally corrupting. I did not. I remember badly missing those kisses later on.

One of these ladies who came to call has remained particularly vivid in my memory, although I only saw her once: the slightly

tilted tiara, sparkling with brilliants of the best cut, the black
lace frills and a fine mesh of tiny wrinkles around her quail's
eyes instantly betrayed to me this lady's true identity and what
made everyone treat her with such respect and deference, as if
the incarnation of a diamond had sat down in Granny's best
armchair. The Empress Eugenie, widow of Napoleon III and
the Second Empire, for it was she, of course, leaned over me,
peering from behind a golden lorgnette and, jabbering at me in
French, pinched me on the cheek, just as in the past she had
pinched Marcel, little Jean Cocteau and di Lampedusa. To give
the lady her due, she did her pinching with rare artlessness and
directness of manner; it seemed that Her Imperial Majesty's
only amusement since the day she became a widow was travelling about Europe and meeting chubby little writers at the
point in their lives when they were still greedier for chocolate
than flattery; she could practise her cheek-pinching techniques
on them to her heart's delight, which explained the perfection
of her bony gestures: bringing the hand close to the child's
face, and – at the culminating point – coquettishly tilting the
tiara with an impetuous shake of the head.

The fact that she visited me not on the Riviera or in Sicily,
but troubled herself to come all the way to Oliwa, to my
grandmother's best armchair, added extra splendour to this
event. We scrutinised each other with mutual sympathy and
forbearance for the rest of the company, who could not appre-
ciate the mastery of the pinch, or even take delight in the
subtler nuances of the situation. After a while – at which point
I realised that the strange sound accompanying her every
gesture and coming from the folds of her dress was the
constant jingling of small objects – from among the pleats and
lace she took out a fan, a vial of smelling salts, a tiny mirror
framed in ebony inlaid with ivory, and finally a little gold box in
which, when she opened it with a soft, dignified click, there was

just one single chocolate, destined specially for me – a praline with a miraculous, fragrant walnut half on its frosted top.

I bowed, cast another glance at the discreet spot of light in the lorgnette lenses, the sparks in the tiara and, gently led by the hand scented with chocolate, disappeared into the next room.

For many years my parents stubbornly denied being acquainted with the empress. Yet my memory of that evening – and above all that praline – was so indelible that finally they surrendered to my child's certainty.

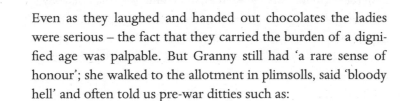

Even as they laughed and handed out chocolates the ladies were serious – the fact that they carried the burden of a dignified age was palpable. But Granny still had 'a rare sense of honour'; she walked to the allotment in plimsolls, said 'bloody hell' and often told us pre-war ditties such as:

> *Andzia dearest, Auntie warns,*
> *Do not nibble off my corns.*
> *Andzia flouts her aunt's rebukes,*
> *Chews away and promptly pukes.*

> *Do up your buttons, nothing must dangle,*
> *since Auntie's tits got caught in the mangle.*

On other occasions she'd tell us about the village women at Lisów. About the one whose husband used to thrash her with rope soaked in water, and she'd say: 'When 'e beats me with a cord, my soul feels as light as after 'oly confession.' About the one who stank from a kilometre away and was in the habit of sacramentally declaring: 'There's three times you 'ave a bath. Once when I was born, the second time for me wedding, and

the third time'll be to go to me coffin.' And finally about the
ones who had such a fierce fight they ended up before the
court: 'I calls 'er wanton, she calls me a gadabout, I shows 'er
me backside, she shows me 'er front' – for they were standing
facing each other, raising their skirts; a backside was a lesser
insult, a front a greater one – 'so if she's showing me 'er front
I says to 'er "You suffragan!" and when she seizes the stake,
when she flies at me...'

Without the least hint of embarrassment she revealed to us
the secrets of the adult world; she would make us turn away
from the television whenever someone's head was cut off, or
someone's hand was shot away (to this day I can remember
staring at the patterns on the straw mat above the couch, while
groaning sounds and gunfire came from the television), but she
had no objections to us seeing a naked body. 'Children,' she'd
call, 'children, come and see' – we'd abandon the Lego, race
into Granny's room, and there'd be an advert for Palmolive on
TV – 'Look what fine bosoms that lady has.'

'Ah,' she'd say another time, while trimming sprigs of pink,
white and purple astilbe, 'virginity brings nothing but trouble.
A virgin, or not a virgin, it's nothing but stress. They've got it
right in those primitive tribes, where the initiation... two more
of the pink ones... the initiation, that's to say the rite of passage
into adulthood, is like this: the whole village gathers around a
large phallus made of bronze or smoothed wood, they dance
and sing, and then the little girls, little because they mature
faster there, in hot countries... well, Juliet, for example, was
twelve years old... and the little girls, twelve-year-olds, let's say,
sit themselves down on the phallus and it's all over and done
with. No problems with whether you're a virgin or not,
because everyone knows you're not. And two more white
sprigs. And wouldn't it be nice to add a bit of spiraea?'

And, passing from these anthropological revelations to the

order of the day, we'd advise on whether to add some spiraea, or maybe two more stems of astilbe.

And then in the evenings, over soured milk, which had to be lumpy – oh, how I adored those sour chunks of softened porcelain – over baked apples sprinkled with sugar and cinnamon, or over a plum-spread sandwich, Granny showed me Europe.

'Aah, in Lisów the plums were different,' Granny's storytelling suddenly sneaks up on me – it was just off to one side for a moment, 'better for spread, bigger and juicier, but they came away from the stone less easily; in summer there'd be a field kitchen roaring away in the garden, with Grandmama Wanda, amid a host of servants, performing her amazing alchemy over a brick hearth, conducting whole regiments of copper cauldrons and frying pans – as you know, things don't stick as much to copper – and then a whole new generation of jams, spreads and jellies would be taken to the cellar, all carefully described and labelled, like the one hundred and forty-four thousand sealed...'*

Europe – what exactly was Europe? As I saw it in the evenings, fuddled by garden air, drained by feeding ducks and swans in the park, thrilled by the damned tumbling into the abyss in Memling's altarpiece, feeling resentful towards everyone and everything for the fact that soon I would have to go to bed, while the world stood wide open before me, laying on the counter ream after ream of twinkling mysteries.

This Europe was a casket, a jewellery box created by expert craftsmen for a spoiled child, a Europe inlaid with rosewood and mahogany, a Europe full of complex machines that I didn't have to trouble my head about, though in fact it was nice to observe their ingenious tricks; a Europe populated by little

gentlemen in tailcoats and ladies in corsets and dresses with
bustles, a Europe of violins and grand pianos, a Europe where
every object was ornamented, and superfluous things were not
denied the right to exist – thus it appeared to me in its still
intact form, the way it might have looked to my motorcar-
loving great-great-grandfather, with his sacred belief in combus-
tion, luminescence and water vapour: a Europe of glass and
gilt, like a crystal palace, festively illuminated with gas lamps,
rising skywards on invisible structures of raw brick and iron,
only to be exposed from under the layers of stucco putti and
gilded roses by two great wars.

Of course, there was bookkeeping too – for how do you
inventory all the screens and pictures, the porcelain and photos,
the houses and flats that once existed, but aren't there any
more? With people it's so much simpler – they died and went
to heaven or to hell. The aunts, great-grandmothers and
great-great-grandmothers, Mr and Mrs Korytko, all the
murdered Jews, and Gołda, killed by a falling crate of eggs. But
what about the things?

Where are the black feather fans that the Lisów children
trailed about the fields, where have they flown?

And where is Misha Sicard's Amati? Can an Amati burn to
ashes for good and all?

Or the apple tree split in two by a Russian shell – did it go on
blossoming somewhere else, did its apples go on falling into
other, unknown grass?

There must have been a paradise, well, at least a purgatory
for objects, where almost all of Lisów ended up, with the rest
of the putti and crystals of my Europe, there to sit patiently
waiting for an early second coming.

It wasn't a coherent concept, one of those fabulous notions
that children devise like a medieval compendium – I myself
created entire lands with extensive, elaborate cartographies,

kingdoms ruled by mythical dynasties, and separate races of dragons and angels – but a sort of inner conviction, which I kept hidden, even from myself, in the recesses of my mind.

I'm sorry, but I can't remember what it was that taught me to understand the whole hopelessness of transience, and with it the fact that the Europe I believed in, even if it had existed, was never to return. I realise the reader might like to be told how I broke the blue Venetian vase, and then... or how I found a dead pigeon in the park, and, word of honour, its little feet – how desperate – and then... but no. Nothing of the kind.

It was a moment of painful, glaring illumination – the only way in which we learn the things that truly matter. Perhaps I was having a stick fight with my brother, or maybe I was drawing the pink-and-turquoise wings of a herald angel, or examining the life of woodlice under an upturned stone. It doesn't matter which; but the gods opened the heavens, sent down a ray of light and showed me – as they do everyone – that everything passes. I realised that there's no purgatory for objects, that no one waits for missing letters, no one reads burned-up books, rubble doesn't turn back into houses or shards into cups from my great-great-grandmother's best dinner service. Things that are lost are not alive – they lie in the ground or fly in the air, without any tombs. I failed to parry the blow, the angel solidified on the page, and the wood-lice scuttled off. And as I well remember, I walked across the garden, taking long strides, and shouted out loud, very loud: 'Give me back my Europe!'

Then I had a fever, I went stiff all over and clenched my teeth; the healer laid his hands on me and shook them off, laid them on and shook them off, removing the temperature from me by degrees, like tiny insects from quicksilver.

XXIV

My grandfather died when I was eleven. I remember us playing with Lego bricks, as he sat in the next room, listening to old recordings of Małcużyński* playing Chopin on the radio, while being consumed by cancer, consumed by cancer with every note.

'Don't make such a racket,' Granny would say. But we'd go on playing. 'Don't make a racket.' She'd call us aside. 'Your grandfather may be listening to that for the very last time.'

That's what I remember – not the funeral, nor the wake, but Małcużyński, the chair being carried into the garden, for Granddad to sit and listen to the birds, his skinny legs being covered with a rug and Granny's impatient tone of voice when six months after the funeral I asked where Grand Cayman is: 'Say "the island" first, because I thought you were going to ask about something else.'

❧

We didn't think Granny was going to survive it. More and more often her heart refused to obey her, her stomach and liver were playing up, as if her body were rebelling against lasting any longer.

'It's a dreadful injustice,' she'd say. 'A loving couple should die together. But now I'm like the... oh, look, in this poem about an old woman. Like a dark stain on the brightly coloured carpet of the world.'*

❧

Couch grass and goutweed had throttled the dahlias and delphiniums. I went off to primary school, then high school, and finally to college, but I still paid visits to Oliwa, where time passed at its own pace (the pace of three-hour breakfasts with storytelling, of idle digressions and gradual shifts from cherries to blackcurrants and white transparents to walnuts) and the sky seemed more tangible than anywhere else.

Many a time since I've had occasion to see a huge, three-dimensional sky; over the sea and in the mountains, on the summit of Vesuvius, a sky that stretches far above the clouds; in Oliwa the sky was low, painted in early summer and autumn – especially in the daytime – a clear powder-blue. It felt as if, were I to climb to the tops of the highest lime or spruce trees and stretch the broom handle upwards, or the pole my grand-parents used to open the curtains each morning, I'd be able to touch its smooth, resonant surface, newly made and freshly washed.

In winter the sky would settle on the bare branches like thin whey, as if its underlay were releasing juice; then it looked even lower. Oliwa, with its cathedral and several little streets, the mill, the park where we fed the ducks and swans, Oliwa with its trams at one end and its zoo at the other, was topped with a miniature vault, made to measure for the needs of childhood. Even at night, criss-crossed by the branches of the walnut and cherry trees, the firmament seemed tame, like a large milk-giving animal, not the sort of alluring, distant land that in other cities, or at least in other districts of Gdańsk, kidnaps enraptured children for ever and a day, so there's nothing left of them, not a sock, a glove or a little comb.

From the time we went to school, we lived with our parents at

a different address, but they still took us to Oliwa every weekend, for all the holidays and school vacations. But only once I
was at college did I realise that neither Granny nor the place
were fated to be there for us for ever, but only for a short while.

'I've decided to stay in Oliwa for part of the summer,' I
suddenly told my mother, and the tomato fell from her hand.
She looked at me in amazement. 'How much time do I have
left to spend with Granny? How often will I have the choice of
spending August in Oliwa?'

'Well, you see… you're right, but Granny's not in a very
good way.'

I knew she was having some serious trouble with her co-
ordination, though – as I also knew, and would soon know even
better – it wasn't yet at its worst. A firm believer in the power
of the written word, my mother had spread notes about the
house saying: *Mama!!! Don't open the door to strangers!!! Only open
it to us or Monika when she comes to clean; Mama! If you want to
watch TV, pick up the remote and press the button…; Mama!
Remember to take your pills*, but Granny read less and less, and
letters made little impression on her. Until then, as throughout
her life, she'd devoured vast numbers of books; whenever I
came to see her and said: 'Have you heard about the new
Miłosz?' or 'There's a new Tokarczuk' out,' she'd invariably
reply: 'Yes, yes, it's here somewhere,' and it would be there. If
she wasn't at home, she'd either be at the allotment, or in
Oliwa's new bookshop, where she'd spend hours on end, telling stories that were gradually fading from her memory,
becoming more convoluted and muddled together, ever less
probable, further and further from the truth; three nice ladies
would sit around her, treating her to cake and tea, and showing
her the latest books in their glossy covers. If coming from the
direction of the tram, I'd make a detour just in case, and drop
in at the bookshop – from the street I'd see Granny, sitting on

Lala at the time of her retirement, c. 1995.

a small chair, nibbling cheesecake and holding forth, entirely – or so it seemed from behind the glass – without making a sound.

It all started with minor instances of self-neglect: she washed her hair less often, and instead of wearing silk blouses she'd bundle herself up in thick woollen waistcoats; she'd refuse to put in her false teeth – what battles were fought over that! How much urging there was, how much complaining, how very often Granny said: 'Stop nagging me,' how very often my mother said: 'Mama, you can't go round looking like a village idiot,' how often I heard: 'But who's going to notice I haven't got my teeth?' and 'What a fine sight – a row of black stumps. Mama, you should be ashamed.' Shabby old shoes and a nasty threadbare coat.

Gradually she stopped buying art books featuring Botticelli, Dalí and Klimt, or adding to what she called 'the mangle' – for besides looking at the illustrations she used them to press table-cloths and handkerchiefs; best of all for this purpose was a huge album of Impressionists she'd bought one year for my mother's name day, but had then said: 'Let's agree that it's your book, but it can stay at my house, because it's good for press-ing'; then with every subsequent name day, birthday and Christmas she'd say: 'I've been wondering what on earth to get you, and then it occurred to me that I could give you the *Impressionists*, what do you say?' and my mother would invari-ably reply: 'Excellent, you already gave it to me six months ago, a year ago and a year-and-a-half ago, so I'll like it this time too.' Either way, first Granny stopped buying serious fiction and poetry by little-known writers, then serious fiction and poetry by well-known writers, then art books, and then even Agatha Christie, whose crime novels shone on the shelf in a long row of black covers. So the notes with the warning messages made little impression on her. Altogether, very little did.

So that summer, when I moved to Oliwa for the whole of August, I didn't expect any fireworks of erudition or the mining of rich deposits of reminiscence. I knew all that was over. I simply did my best to be there, to watch as Granny ate her breakfast, as she laughed, and as she nodded off in her armchair. One morning I went into the bathroom and asked why it smelled of camphor; looking embarrassed, she said: 'Oooh, I keep forgetting to buy deodorant, so I'm using camphor instead.' We'd argue about whether or not she'd had a driving licence. I'd listen to her walking about at night, getting up to go to the bathroom and ferreting in the fridge, warbling through the door to ask why I wasn't in bed yet; I'd mutter back that I was working. I tried putting on a record of Charlestons from the 1920s, but Granny squawked from the kitchen that the jazz was awful, so we had a grandmother–grandson conflict dating from 1926. And then I'd put on Beethoven, best of all the *Violin Concerto*; smiling and nodding in time, Granny would sing along to the theme: *'ta da da ta da-da tiii ti…'* It didn't go as well if a different piece was playing, the *Kreutzer Sonata* for instance.

'Who's conducting it?' she'd ask.

'Conducting what?'

'The concerto,' she'd reply triumphantly. 'Furtwängler.'*

'Granny, it's the *Kreutzer Sonata*, there's no conductor, it's just for violin and piano.'

'There's always a conductor,' she'd state confidently, 'even if there are only two instruments.'

'No, that's one of the differences between chamber music and orchestral – there's no conductor. Quartets, quintets, duets – none of them have a conductor. This is Argerich and Kremer.'*

'My God,' she'd say, looking at me as if from the other shore, 'to think I had a career as a music producer, and this is what's become of me in old age.'

❦

I would settle comfortably in an armchair, immersed in the glittering past as I gazed with my eyes half-closed at the grander armchair next to it, Granny's throne, that famed Sibylline stool, the seat of Solomon with its torn upholstery, buried under layers of throws and blankets, from whose rosy plateaux Granny had delivered so many prophecies to lands and nations. Sometimes, if she was out of the room at the time, I dared to sit in it – only from its perspective did the truth seem obvious to me; merely by lounging on this antique royal pallet, on its shabby, decayed material I could see the broad vista of successive generations; on this same skeleton of wood, springs and horsehair, on these rose-patterned jacquard gores Grandpapa Leonard had died, then Grandmama Wanda and, her constant running brought to a sudden halt, the brakes pulled on her tiny footsteps, Irena Karnaukhova. As I watched the doors of each generation in turn silently closing behind me, I wondered where this gangrene-gnawed throne, this ancestral litter, this half-melted reading room, spilling its layers of diverse fabrics and ripped upholstery, this regal relic with a touch of millennial mould will be standing, and what it will look like, on the day of my death too. And, true to ancient tradition from the land of my forebears, a non-existent land, that land known as the past, whether or not I'll be sitting in it the very last time I close the covers of a book that I won't be destined to finish, or the very last time I tell an anecdote from the days of my glowing, fin-de-millennium youth; whether or not I'll be in it as I enjoy my final taste – assuming the state of my jaws, stomach and liver allow it – of turkey in Malaga wine and Christmas poppy-seed cake?

Meanwhile Granny would come back from the kitchen and relegate me to my proper place. The tea and the count's daughter's apple pie would exude aromas from the table as insistently as an advert, while Granny settled next to me, sombre as a great ark whose tablets I'd never manage to read to the end, rising above the centuries, with a rose-shaped brooch pinning her silk scarf at her throat.

❧

And here she is – the large, gilded icon of my childhood years, my Oriflamme,* carried in processions through the fields of the world, accompanied by horns of polished bronze and silver bugles; the eternal North Star, by which, with the help of Arabian astrolabes and styluses inlaid with ivory I plotted the lines of my life from the start, ever more complex, ever less simple, lines becoming tangled in alien star clusters, constellations of hostile animals.

This is how I see her, inevitably growing more distant: in billows of incense that obscure the image with a dense shroud, in revetments of tarnishing metal, under which the first layer of the painting is less and less visible – the shape of the burning eyes, the disdainful corners of the mouth and the stiff helmet of hair above the brow. Supreme, against a golden background, provided with apt comments, inscribed around her head in red paint, Granny, a lone and proud divinity, frustrated all, even the most tentative attempts by my docile grandfather to introduce polytheism – and so it was bound to be from the very start; she was born an icon, the only face on gold leaf, a face created to be the subject of a one-person cult. Her parents photographed her separately – with a doll, with plaits, with a garland of flowers – only stage props could cope with her overwhelming presence when photographed together; sometimes her picture was taken with her sister, an aunt or a friend – in just a year the plate would fade, leaving nothing but Granny's face, her black eyes burning, and an empty space where the vanished companion of colloid and silver oxide used to be.

And what had she come to, what had I come to – who years ago had put her on my youthful flags?

More and more often I'd sit in the armchair next to hers and watch as she slept, as the light from the window settled on the skin of her cheeks, sunken on either side of her toothless mouth, as her lungs worked calmly under her clothing; and instead of waking her to ask the same question yet again, and yet again hear her say: 'I can't remember,' in my thoughts I held the conversations that we used to have when she still had her memory, when every cup of tea we shared began with the words: 'I remember how…'

'I remember how Julek told me that he'd been to Paris or somewhere, and he'd changed trains in Frankfurt. Or was it Düsseldorf? Anyway, he had to wait there for several hours, so he decided to walk about the station. He's walking along, and suddenly a ginger fellow comes racing out of one of the shops with a razor in his hand, and runs straight at him. Julek was shocked, but then he hears: "Herr Rogod-gin-skee, Herr Rogod-gin-skee!" And it was the red-haired NCO, a barber by profession, who had his salon right there at the station. At once he sent his wife home for some dinner, gave Julek a haircut and a shave, and chattered the whole time as if possessed; after the battle he'd managed to do just as the captain ordered,

in other words he'd led the entire unit into the hands of the
Americans; he'd done pretty well since the war, and was leading the life of a respectable citizen. The red-haired NCO
– who'd have thought it? A station barber. Like a costume, but
then his uniform was his costume.'

'And apart from that? What else did he do?'

'The NCO?'

'No, Julek.'

'He wasn't happy with that wife of his; he did a lot of travelling, and a lot of translating. He fell in love with a Czech
woman. He told me about making dates with her, meeting up
with her and writing to her; he told me everything. He was
even going to move to Prague. And one day she didn't turn up
for their meeting; they'd made a date at a restaurant in a palace
or a museum, I can't remember the details, in any case he
walked through a long suite of connecting rooms, until he
came to the last one, where two cups had been set out on a
little table. He sat down. Just then the window flew open, a
gust of wind blew in and the cup that the woman was to drink
from was knocked to the floor.'

'And then what?'

'She never came. It turned out she was in hospital, she had
an aggressive form of cancer, and she died. He took it very
badly. And then... I don't know... He translated a great deal of
Balzac, most of what Żeleński hadn't managed to do, also
Anatole France, Stendhal, and the last volume of *Remembrance
of Things Past*. He was still as charming as ever. A couple of
years before his death he found out that what he'd been suffering from all his life was renal tuberculosis – the same illness that
had killed his father. No doctor had ever worked it out. How
much he suffered, poor man. Who knows, if he'd been treated
by wiser doctors, if he hadn't had that operation, he might have
had children, and he might still have been my husband... well,

too bad. He really was the most intelligent man I've ever met, but then your grandfather was a real hero. And a real he-man.' At this point Granny smiles suggestively.

'Reeeally?'

'Oh yes, although... You know, let's be frank, your grandfather was not perfectly faithful to me for all those years. But I always knew I was the one who mattered most to him, and that was the point. Besides, he was such a handsome man that women leapt into bed with him of their own accord. And I once told myself I'd rather have a good and handsome man who has a little fling now and then, than one who's going to be faithful to me because no other woman would dream of giving him a second glance. My mother was the same. She knew Bieniecki was cheating on her left and right, but he had so much charm, so much allure. Did you know that when I was living at the Brokls' house in my college days he once came to visit me? A friend of mine happened to be there, so I introduced them to each other, and they both went pink and looked very confused. All I said was: "I see you've met before." She was about twenty-two, he was sixty – and it was obvious they'd had a passionate affair. And while my mother had known he was cheating on her all over the place with various little flibbertigibbets, somehow she put up with it. Of course, she used to put a spoke in his wheels, shifting his secret signs, extinguishing or lighting candles in the window, or moving the flowerpots, but she tolerated it. It was only when Bieniecki took up with Mrs Korytko and no one else that she declared she'd had enough of it. She told me that one night they were out at a restaurant together, as a threesome, or maybe there were four of them. And Mrs Korytko drank herself into a stupor, went to the ladies and threw up. But she asked my mother not to let on to Bieniecki. And she didn't. I wouldn't have been such an altruist in her place.'

'But getting back to Julek…'

'There isn't much to get back to, because Julek died just after you were born. And that's why you've got his character. I'm convinced he reincarnated in you. His soul. Because he's reappeared physically in your brother Macius̀. You won't remember…'

'Of course I do.'

'All right, what?'

'I remember your friends asking why Macius̀ was so strangely dressed in the photograph, and it was a picture of Julek as a child. Oh – that's the one.'

'Yes, yes, that's it. Just imagine, his wife didn't call me to tell me he'd died. I found out from the newspapers. I wasn't even at the funeral. But whenever the entry for "Julian Rogożiński" had to be edited for an encyclopaedia or a lexicon she sent the journalist or academic to me, because she was pig ignorant. And those paintings were never returned to me.'

'What paintings?'

'They were some of Grandpapa Leonard's. One was by Paulus Potter, of some pigs, and the other was of a tavern. I'd always liked it very much, I think it was Flemish. A tavern, with a woman feeding a child outside it, and a man, Gypsies, I think. Julek liked them too, and after the divorce, when I stopped living with him, he asked if I'd lend them to him. And they fell by the wayside.'

'You're like that, you Brokls. The whole family. They should at least have gambled away a fortune at Monte Carlo, or blown it on tarts, like Kasia's great-grandfather, who frittered away two whole estates on a dancing girl in St Petersburg. But not your lot. Everything just slipped through their fingers, yours included.'

'Yes, I've lost two houses, but really, there's no point in getting attached to things.'

Thus I brought the old conversations about even older conversations back to mind.

And then one day, as I was sitting beside Granny's armchair, watching her doze and snore gently with her mouth open, it occurred to me that maybe it was meant to be like this. This quiet phase at the end, to make it easier for everyone.

I must have been about ten, or twelve, when I saw an old film on the telly, in which Spencer Tracy could cry on cue, and used this skill to stir the feelings of Katharine Hepburn, the most beautiful woman I'd ever seen. So no wonder I decided to teach myself this handy trick, in case I ever met a Katharine Hepburn. That night I lay in my upper bunk bed, on the tenth floor of our block, as the city flowed beneath me in little balls of light. And it occurred to me that the only thing capable of moving me to tears just like that, on cue, was the inevitability of Granny's death. I imagined standing by her grave... and here I should write: 'two large, hot tears, burning like fire, ran down my cheeks' (because that was roughly my idea of how to describe my feelings in those days). And then I fell asleep, half-shocked, and half-happy, as if I'd learnt a card trick.

So there I sat in the armchair, not long ago, almost now. Those 'burning tears, pouring down my fevered cheeks' didn't seem quite so attractive as in the past. Unimportant. And it crossed my mind that it was better like this – she won't depart this life as an icon, in a blaze of gold, set with precious stones, like that 'stronghold Notre Dame',* with Gombrowicz and the Shah of Persia in her retinue, but small, hunched, asking questions about my wedding, endlessly repeating the one and only story to have remained in her feeble memory, a story composed of many others, imprecise and untrue, barely a dim reflection of her erstwhile fabulous, marble-and-stained-glass narratives.

And will she be herself then? Is she still herself?

Someone told me about an old English couple in India. There at the bazaar, among stalls full of whatever they sell on stalls in India, sat a snake charmer, surrounded in the usual way by cobras that danced to the beat of the tune he was playing on his pipe. Suddenly he fainted. The cobras went crawling about the bazaar, people ran off screaming, in panic the women gathered up their children and the men reached for their knives. Just then the old Englishwoman went up to the basket, sat on the ground and started to play the pipe. The snakes went back to their places. 'We've been married for forty years, Mary,' said her husband, 'but you've never told me you knew how to charm cobras.' 'Because you never asked.'

People change, they turn inside out. Someone can like playing patience and stroking his grandchildren's heads and the spines of books – and no one knows that his favourite characters from mythology are the Furies. Someone else can spend half his life sticking together paper bags, and then becomes Dostoevsky. A serial murderer keeps a canary in his cell. But have you ever seen a siskin fall to the ground as a lump of copper? And a piece of basalt – can it suddenly turn into a metre of velvet? Change is a luxury of the human soul – which makes it hard to believe that ordinary, quiet breathing means death. Who knows, I thought, as I waited for Granny to wake up, maybe we attach souls to bodies too firmly. Perhaps during the life of a single body several souls live in it? And the old Granny has long since been walking about the Empyrean, walking in tall grass, white with narcissi, as in Bruges, which she once told me about, and someone else has taken up residence here... An incompetent understudy, who hasn't learnt the role properly, muddles the stories, insists on absurdities and, worn out by the non-stop acting, sleeps for hours on end in the armchair, in sequins of light sifted through the geranium leaves.

'Tea?'

'What?' asked Granny, awoken. 'What?'

'Tea?'

'Yes, yes please.'

'I'll put on the kettle.'

'Go ahead. There's cheesecake from the count's daughter.'

'But put your teeth in.'

'Always bullying!'

Such was our comical way of life there, in Oliwa. We say something, then there's silence, then we drift away – she into sleep, I into a book. A quarter of an hour later I wake her when I get up to put on the kettle. I come back, do some more reading, and it rains a little. The water boiled long ago.

'What about coffee?'

'Oh yes, please.'

And I make the coffee. Another quarter of an hour goes by. I bring in the cups and the cake. We do some reading. We exchange words like tokens – each of us knows what we'll hear in return, as if they were little dice made of ivory, or cards marked with golden hieroglyphs, their corrugated edges perfectly overlapping. Like a very old game, whose origins no one remembers – we don't keep score, we don't rake in the cards, we just keep endlessly laying out a series of self-generating elements. And that is all we need.

XXV

Once, sometimes twice a week my brother's friend Monika
came by, officially to earn some extra money cleaning, but
really to take care of Granny and, while doing the dusting or
washing up, to listen to her foggy stories. Together we staged
some minor revolutions. We eliminated all the dusty little
bunches of dried-out, half-decayed flowers, of which I counted
nigh on thirty in the sitting room alone; we spread a large sheet
of paper on the floor and carried out a selection to decide
which were still fit for purpose, while Granny either sat there
with a glum look on her face, as if to say we were bullying her,
or else she quipped: 'If we're tidying up, let's do it properly –
throw this out too!' and she'd abruptly toss away a sprig of
cotoneaster or delphinium.

We also conducted a campaign, doomed in advance to failure, to throw out all sorts of things, such as the red caps from
tubes of fish-roe paste, which Granny collected and arranged in
little pyramids on top of the fridge, because they were red, and
all the pots, jugs and saucepans in the kitchen had been red for
ages; of course we did it in stages, one pyramid level at a time,
to cover our tracks, for this sort of operation demands a very
subtle approach. At other times we threw away the rotting fruit,
yogurts and cheese spreads that had taken on a life of their own.
This was probably the biggest source of trouble, for even if
Granny agreed that something was no longer edible, she'd insist
on saving it, in yet another saucer that she kept on the kitchen
worktop, earmarked 'for the cats'; then she'd forget to take it
with her when she went outside, and so the worktop was gradually taken over by a growing collection of cat dishes, stinking

of carrion and secreting horrible miasmas. We tolerated this mortuary until the incident with the putrid chicken breast that Granny had decided to cook for our lunch; I went up to the frying pan, sniffed it and squawked out loud: 'Throw it away!' Only to hear the obvious objection: 'But it's perfectly all right.' After lengthy negotiations by the so-called Karnaukhov method we reached agreement that the spoiled meat would in this case go to the cats – but Granny had already put some food in their bowl, so we didn't bother to take it outside at once. Next day when I came back from the city, I found Granny cooking another wonder-dish using the same chicken breast. At once I adopted an accusatory tone; Granny dug in her heels. 'All right, eat it,' I said, 'go ahead and poison yourself.' And she ate it. I tossed the rest away, and all the other cat offerings, slimy cheese spreads and other horrors too.

❧

For our lives were not exactly a pure idyll; take for example the time when something was wrong with my ear. I kept pacing to and fro, complaining, because I hadn't the strength for any sensible activities. Finally I decided to do a lot of washing-up. Granny sat down at the kitchen table and made a remark. But I was deaf in one ear, and there was water roaring in the other. So I turned off the tap and said: 'Sorry?'

'Hasn't it turned out nice today?'

'Oh, yes.'

I turned the tap on, regulated the water, started washing up again, and very soon the same thing happened again. I turned off the tap and said: 'Sorry?'

'But the forecast said it would rain.'

I told her I couldn't hear, so she should only talk to me if it was something really important, because every time she spoke

I had to turn off the water, ask her to repeat it, give a perfunctory reply, and then regulate the water again. But we could have a chat later, I said, once I'd finished the washing-up.

I turned on the tap. I regulated the water. She piped up again. I turned off the tap.

'Sorry?'

'So I'm not to speak any more? You won't let me?'

'No, Granny, that's not what I said...'

And it happened again. The fourth, fifth and sixth time I repeated myself less calmly. Finally, the twelfth time, I seriously lost my temper. But Granny still went on. I picked up one of the plates and smashed it to the floor so hard that the pieces went flying all over the kitchen. And it helped; both me, because at once I started looking for the dustpan and brush and the broken bits of plate, and Granny, because it finally got through to her that I'd reached the end of my tether.

'Aha,' she said quietly, 'I thought Paweł was the jumpiest person in the family, but you are too. A pity you broke a soup plate,' she added after a pause, 'there are fewer of those – you should have smashed a dinner plate.'

I apologised. I counted the soup plates and the dinner plates. And what do you know? There was an equal number of both.

We spent the rest of the day pleasantly.

And yet – I thought to myself, as I lay in bed that night – she did it with morbid malice, because the things she was saying were absurdly trivial. And she mumbled, to make it harder for me to hear her. She probably doesn't realise, but the passive resistance that has become her weapon against the entire family has sown in her subconscious a latent childish tendency to act out of spite all the time. Day after day she's told she shouldn't put the chain on the inner door; it's pointless anyway, and if anything were to happen – fingers crossed – it would get in the way of help. So what does Granny do each night? She calls out to tell me with satisfaction: 'I'm going to put on the chain.' And she does it. I explain, I take it off, and we go to bed. I think she puts it on again in the night, I must check.

❧

First Basia came from Kraków; Mateusz arrived a few days later – but before that, Basia and I took the tram into Gdańsk for a tour of the Gothic churches and to go to St Dominic's Fair, and when we got back we were greeted by a thunderous: 'Couldn't be later, could you, you little brats!' and Granny complained at length and with relish that we'd left her all day long without company.

For she was very fond of company. In fact my mother, the voice of conscience, had hammered it into my head: 'Jacek, you must remember that Granny is very weak, she can hardly do a thing, you mustn't expect her to make you meals, or to wash up after you... and don't pester her...'

Pester her! Who's pestering whom? She started by tormenting Basia, using the regular set of resources with which she usually scares my girlfriends away, in other words 'the wedding package'. From the word go.

'Granny, this is Basia.'

'And when are you getting married?'

'Sorry?' asked Basia in surprise.

'When's the wedding?'

And then of course:

'But how am I to put you up?'

'In the first place, we'll sort it out ourselves, and secondly there's no problem, there are two beds in the little room, I've already found the sheets.'

'Both of you in the one room? Decadence and debauchery,'

declares Granny with a gleam in her eyes, and then adds: 'Have fun, you two.'

And so on, again and again.

'Well then, so do you want her?' (To which Basia said: 'Maybe you should be asking me.')

Or: 'Such a lovely girl, don't give it a second thought, just get married.'

Or: 'Look how nicely she's buttering the bread. The perfect wife.'

And none of our explanations, insistence or assurances that we were just good friends were of any use. Granny played her games anyway, and suddenly, in the confidential whisper of a 'best fwend' drawled into Basia's ear: 'Just you take care. It looks to me as if Jacek's in love with you. He'll make you a baby, and then what?'

❧

Over breakfast we were presented with various maxims about life. Out of the blue, with sandwich in hand, midway to her mouth, Granny would suddenly stop and say gloomily: 'Everything changes. Everything that lived has died. Even Jadzia Kontrymówna.'

Or if one of us yet again complained that he couldn't find a sharp knife we'd hear: 'My life…' – a theatrical pause – 'has been passing by in the shadow of blunt knives…' – another pause – 'if one of them is sharpened, in five or six years it's blunt again.'

'Jacek,' Basia asks me one night, as we're sitting on the bed together (very virtuously, as every night, like Tristan and Isolde divided by the favourite game of our childhood, and our teen-age years too, in other words *Talisman* with all five boards), 'who was Jadzia Kontrymówna?'

'I haven't the faintest idea. Someone who lived and died. I've never heard of her. But we can ask tomorrow at breakfast.'

And we do.

'Jadzia Kontrymówna? What do you mean, "who"? Mrs Jaruzelska's niece. She lived in Lithuania, and there were various, you know, anti-Polish incidents there, what's more her stepfather hated Poles with a passion, so Mrs Jaruzelska took her in and brought her up.'

'And what happened to her after that?' asks Basia.

'What do you mean?' I mutter. 'She died.'

'Aaah, but a good deal happened before that. She was active in the underground. She was terribly tall, the tallest girl in the city.'

'Like Margerytka Rommlówna?'

'Taller, but not as pretty. And the Germans shot her. They saw she was the height of a ladder, and they shot her, because they must have thought she was dangerous.'

We go on eating. Suddenly Granny says: 'And where are the others?'

'What others?'

'What? Did I dream there were three people? Weren't there some children?'

'There's you,' explains Basia, 'and us two. That's three people.'

'Ah,' says Granny, and we can see from her face that she's busily computing, 'I've got something wrong.'

And what pathos there was in it, in her embarrassment about going gaga; she was aware of her own disintegration, and sometimes she'd suddenly say: 'Old age is so awful, so humiliating.'

I felt sorry for her, I felt so dreadfully sorry for her, and at the same time I couldn't accept the circumstances: keeping decomposing leftovers for cats, hoarding plastic bags, eating rotten tomatoes and rancid butter. And the whole time, like Ophelia talking about Hamlet, I kept repeating: 'What a noble mind...'

We frittered away an entire day on taking pictures, supposedly 'for the back cover of your book', though in fact mainly for pleasure. Pictures in the ruins of a gutted shed, furnished to look like a gentleman's study (except with collapsing walls and no roof); pictures with a monocle made from a metal-rimmed watch face; 'Valentino' pictures (in a white Versace shirt, staring pensively into the distance...). At the heart of it all was Basia's joy, in the heat, among all the props and side tables brought downstairs; Basia's joy as a professional photographer, sitting with her legs apart on a set of folding steps, or on a small table, making the face of a poker player at work, now unmoved, now excited by the shot.

'You know what, let's take your picture in this purple cape. Change into it and lie on the grass, and I'll climb the walnut tree to take the photographs from above.'

I lay on the ground, almost naked, dressed only in the purple, Lenten vestment that I had once bought at an antique fair; I must have looked like a mad priest whose wits had been addled by celibacy. Watching us from a window, Granny had the best view.

'You should go there,' she shouted, 'over there, higher up.'

'Yes,' replied Basia patiently, 'but that branch is three metres away from me.'

'It's easy. I once climbed that walnut tree, so I know. There were more branches, it's true, but you can do it now, too.'

'Granny,' I shouted up from below, 'you've never climbed this tree!'

'What *are* you saying? I have too.'

'Granny!'

'There were more branches.'

'Yeees,' – at this point I thought of the right tactic – 'of course. There was a long, low, vertical branch, wasn't there?'

'That's right. I have a perfect memory of climbing up that branch.'

'Yes, Granny, except that it was a branch of the pear tree at Lisów, which you scrambled up, but you couldn't get down again, and all the village children came running to make fun of you.'

※

But the main attraction was still involuntary sex, meaning Granny's notions about our clandestine intercourse. In the final count, someone had to be sleeping with someone else, and there was always an element of conspiracy involved. At first, only Basia was there, so there were fewer, not to say very few opportunities. But even so there was plenty to be said. Like the time when Basia was feeling ill, and lay down on the couch in the middle of the day. Granny went in, surveyed the scene, and rounded on me, her voice trembling: 'You know what's going on, don't you? She's giving birth! She's having your child.'

Another time she came into our room at four in the morning, announcing herself in the usual way: 'What are you doing? I'm going for a pee.' We had just finished our game (Basia was the Sorceress and I was the Black Elf). Basia was reading, and I was asleep.

'Why aren't you asleep?'

'I'm reading, Mrs Karpińska.'

'And why are you reading?'

'Because I like to read.'

'And why is he asleep?'

'He was tired, so he went to sleep.'

Then in a mischievous tone Granny said: 'Tired? I wonder why?!'

That's what it was like when only Basia was there, but as soon as Mateusz joined us, lots of new possibilities arose. First of all, right from the off: 'But how am I to put you all up?'

'It's quite straightforward. Mateusz will have one bed, and Basia and I will share the other. We're used to it, because she always shared my bed when she came to see me in Warsaw. Somehow no harm came of it.'

'Decadence and debauchery.'

And of course next morning Granny came into the room with a question on her lips.

'Did you all sleep in here?' And to Basia, inquisitorially: 'Who did you sleep with?'

'What do you think?'

'With Jacek. He's thinner, so there's more room. The other one's too fat.'

'You see?' said Basia, laughing. 'That's telling you, Mateusz!'

'And you and Jacek slept like that, under a single duvet?'

'Yes.'

'And has he made you a baby?'

'No.'

'What a slacker.' I got a telling-off too.

Another time Basia was washing up, Mateusz is in the bathroom, and I've gone shopping.

'Who's that coughing in the bathroom, Basia? Is it your lover?'

'My lover?'

'You know, Mateusz.'

'But Mateusz isn't my lover. I slept with Jacek, didn't I?'

'Aha! That's just a facade.'

Finally Basia couldn't take any more and set off home, but not without a parting shot; when she got up first in the morning to pack, Granny was toddling about the house and said: 'Where are the boys?'

'They're asleep.'

'Ah, so you've worn them out, have you?'

As soon as Basia left, at once Mateusz too began to drop hints about having work to do at home, missing his sister and saying he had to go. But as the prospect of being left alone with Granny didn't amuse me much, I dissuaded him from that plan; Granny backed me up too, because she'd always loved the company of handsome men, and she regarded Mateusz as one, something we discovered by chance, when she gave the right answer to one of my questions, such as: 'Who composed the *Eroica*?' or 'Who wrote *The Charterhouse of Parma*?'

'Well done, Madam,' I exclaimed, 'you've won a Fiat Cinquecento with windscreen wipers and a handsome chauffeur.'

'I'd rather have the Cinquecento than the chauffeur,' replied Granny, and after a pause she asked: 'So what are you doing today?'

'Us? Mateusz is going to an audition. Then he's going home.'

'Well I never, the handsome chauffeur's going home. But why not stay two days more?'

But it had all been planned, the ticket bought, the flowers fetched. We were sitting at the table, while the August late afternoon buzzed around us. And suddenly as I watched,

Granny gripped the tabletop, then slowly slumped, as her hands relentlessly slid along both edges. I grabbed her, propped her with one arm, and reached for the water with the other… meanwhile all that was left of Granny was her body, or so it seemed; a heavy body that, with me trying to support it, fell to the floor. I heard some mumbling, I tried saying something to her, and pouring water into her mouth, just to make contact. Despite all the panic, the thing that stuck in my mind was that her last words before losing consciousness had been: 'Jesus Christ'. Luckily they weren't her last words ever.

There she lay on the ground; Mateusz, who was packing in the next room, came running in response to my shouts and we tried to bring her round; I put frost from the fridge on her, patted and pinched her, we also raised her arms and legs to let the blood flow to her heart, then I called my parents and an ambulance.

It's curious that now I'm reminded of a certain theatrical quality to it all, and it was doubly theatrical, firstly because it was a dramatic, serious event – I was as shocked as can be, distressed and bewildered, like the hero of a tragedy, and secondly because there was an element of acting in it. My hands were shaking; usually I'd have tried to stop it, but in this case I thought it in some way appropriate. The same thing went for my muddled sentences. It might have seemed as if I were doing it consciously. God forbid! It was a while before I found a moment to wonder about it – but it's true, I really did have a sense of being on stage; in fact, that may have been what allowed me to act so quickly and efficiently.

Granny slowly regained consciousness, and started to insist on trying to get up by herself, but it ended badly; after a while we helped her up from the kitchen floor and walked her to the sofa in the sitting room. In her damp dress, feeble, vomiting into a bowl, she stirred infinite love and sympathy in me – and also joy that she had returned to her body as herself, more or less as Granny.

Fifteen minutes later my parents and the ambulance arrived. It turned out she was dehydrated, and she had to be taken to hospital for observation for several days.

In her absence Monika and I had a bit of a clean-up – we chucked out almost everything from the kitchen cupboards (plaster filler, wallpaper paste, shoe polish, anti-rust products, mouldy paints), and Mum cleared the seeds and insect sprays from a cupboard in the sitting room. In the process we came upon some piles of photographs and papers. Articles Granny had written dating from 1945, reviews, notebooks with her impressions of concerts, posters featuring 'Master Leon Hanek', and drafts for radio broadcasts. And as well as those we found the diary of Lala Bieniecka, aged eleven. Oh what a thrilling find – everything that had died came back to life again. Even Jadzia Kontrymówna.

On the title page it said: *H. Bieniecka*
Underneath, at an angle, in flowery writing: *NOTEBOOK*
Over the page (again at an angle): *Lala Bieniecka's Diary*
And further on:

11.IV 1930
On the first day of the holidays I had an appendix attack, so today I'm still in bed, but I'll probably get up tomorrow. Today I found out that Jadzia is ill; I knew nothing about it. Mrs Jaruzelska was at our house the day before yesterday and spoke of it, but I was asleep at the time. Jadzia has bronchitis. I feel very sorry for her, because she was meant to be going to visit her friend W. Baranowska. This morning I asked Zosia to give me her life-saving book, as it can teach me various things that the

Lala Bieniecka's diary, c. 1930.

older girls study at the R. Cr. I read the part about dressing minor wounds, and was waiting for Jadzia when I found out she's ill. Today a Chinese man came to our house, from whom Papa bought a packet of tea and a lovely string of beads. The Chinese man was terribly funny; he looked at my ring and asked if I'm married...

12.IV Sunday
Today I got out of bed. Auntie almost fainted in fright at the sight of me; she told me to put on about fifty sweaters, woollen stockings and so on. But I didn't put on a single one of them. This

*morning the weather was bad, it was cloudy, the sky is complain-
ing about its ugly robes and weeping tears of rain. This evening I
went to see Lilka Kasterska. At her house there were* [here the
word *several* has been deleted] *two boys and one girl. Lilka's
sister Nusia wasn't well. She had a headache, and felt bad about
going to lie down while we were there. The boys were very nice.
They had a sort of freedom about them. At table they served
cupcakes and tarts, but I couldn't eat any of it. Then we played
various games. At half past seven I went home. I got a book from
Lilka called 'Therapy' (?) and I read it, then I went to sleep.*

19.IV 1931

[the date is wrong, either here or above; *This morning has
been* deleted] *Today I had a drawing spree. In the morning I
started drawing and painting. I made three postcards. At six
Papa came back from the city. We started talking. 'Today I met
Zosia Baranowska,' said Papa. I shuddered. 'Jadzia is very
sick,' he went on. 'What's wrong with her?' I quickly asked.
'Flu.' It all went dark before my eyes. Flu! Poor Jadzia!*

*I had a pang of heartache. When I was ill in bed Jadzia came
to see me every day. And now I'm not going to be able to go and
see her. Right now I can't go out anywhere at all, and later they
probably won't let me in to see her because flu is contagious. My
poor darling Jadzia! And everyone's jolly here, as if nothing
were wrong at all! Papa says it so calmly: 'Jadzia's very ill!
She's got flu!' I couldn't calm down. So Jadzia's really ill! When
she was coming to see me she was already coughing a bit. She
could have caught an even worse cold from all the walking.*

15th.

*When I got up in the morning at once I set about drawing. I drew
a little boy. At 12 o'clock lots of snow fell just like in the winter.
Big fluffy snowflakes came flying to the ground like feathers. The*

*sky was covered in heavy, dark clouds. A few minutes later it
hailed. Pearls rolled to the ground. Pearls and tears. The cloudy
weather had a depressing effect on people. And my soul felt heavy.
Because Jadzia my darling Jadzia is sick. Sad and dejected, I sat
down at the table. My thoughts were interrupted by a loud, pierc-
ing ring at the door, I jumped to my feet and ran to open it. After
completing the formalities, I read the address. Valerian K. Esq.
for Lala. Overjoyed I unsealed the package and saw... a lovely
little bag from Zakopane from Mama and a pencil shaped like an
umbrella. I was immensely pleased. Oh, how weak the human
soul is! In an instant I forgot about Jadzia, about everything...
But eventually Jadzia will be well again. In the evening Hania,
Lucyna, Idzia and Władek and Tania came to my house. Hania
inspected my jewellery and then we played cards. When everyone
had gone home I read a book, and then Sala Frydman came. And
we talked over supper until 10.30.*

19th.
*Today I had guests for my birthday. We had a fabulous time
playing. There was Tusia, Basia, Lila, Fela and Idzia. Tusia
dances beautifully. So do Fela and Baśka. But Lila's like an
elephant.*

It was very jolly, and then they went off home.

And that's it. After that came Miscellaneous, including the
following list (in a column):

*6 collars. (1 with hemstitch). 2 night shirts. 5 day shirts. 6 pairs
of knickers. 2 pillowcases. 3 small pillowcases (4). 2 napkins. 3
towels. 2 brassieres. 3 bed sheets. 1 quilt cover. 1 undersheet. 6
handkerchiefs. prayer book* [the page ends; after that, one
after another] *pearls, coral beads, blue beads. 1 ring. soap and
(part?) box with thread, yarn etc. spoons, knife, fork, teaspoon,*

soup plate, dinner plate, dessert bowl, for compote, pickler, chamber pot, tin mug small mug from Tania, writing paper, pencil case, paints, dominoes, game, sketchbook, Polish Storybook, Twardowski, notebook, identity card and R. Cr. card.

On the opposite page:

Polish
Reader for class IV Wojciech Grammar. Repeats. Spelling: Szoler-Bogacki IIIb. Set book The Iliad.
Latin

Frenc
Reader. Gramm

Over the page (in a column):

Maths. Geography Nature Religion History
Some doodles and Latin words.

A little further on:

8–9 a.m. do hair etc.
9–10 buy Xmas tree
10½–12 to Jadzia
12¼–1½ make gingerbread
1½–2½ tidy toys
lunch
to Karbowniczka
Decorate Xmas tree
Buy with the 10 zl.
Get ready for next day, dress etc.
Write letters

Then a few drawings (a self-portrait done up to look like a film star; then a little boy, captioned 'Child and butterfly') and in other, adult (or more adult) handwriting:

Remember to tell Staś Wolski about the dream in which I was dying, he cried and said 'you won't die darling' and Aunt Sasha asked what does 'darling' mean?

XXVI

'So how are you feeling?' I asked sacramentally, when I went to see her in hospital.

'Eeee...'

The thing bothering her most was probably the old bag snoring in the next bed. By comparison, a Canadian lumberjack is as quiet as a mouse; never in my life have I heard a woman snore so loud. Now and then Granny said: 'It's the same at night. I haven't slept a wink,' and then giggled.

I read her the extracts from Lala Bieniecka's diary. She could remember the events, but had a harder time with some of the people.

'So who was Staś Wolski?'

'Staś Wolski? No idea.' The fog descends on cities.

I sat there, I hugged her, and stroked her hands. And yet I couldn't bear it for more than forty minutes. Other visitors were only there for a quarter of an hour; but even so it felt to me like a crime to leave so soon.

❧

After leaving the hospital she was weak and indolent, as if wading through treacle. On top of that her bladder had totally rebelled. We had to buy her nappies – Granny, who'd always felt so sorry for her old neighbour suffering from Parkinson's.

'I'm going back to my infancy,' she said on the way to bed.

She started to remind us of a broken machine: mind, plumbing, biological clock... I was shocked by the constant physiological display, the dropping of all barriers of shame; I'd

look at her and she'd seem – how banal it sounds – like a child;
I couldn't bear the constant reminders: have a pee, put on your
nappy, but do put on your nappy, you see, didn't I tell you, no,
don't touch that, give it to me, I'll clean up… one evening the
phone rang and she emerged from the bathroom with no
pyjama bottoms, then stood there, looking so wretched as she
talked to my mother; I thought she'd covered her nether
regions and was holding a piece of toilet paper, but then I saw
that it was just pressed between her naked thighs. I'd never seen
her naked before – and suddenly I felt so sorry for her that I just
muttered 'Goodnight' and went off to bed.

She'd also developed a sort of egomania. It was she who had
climbed the walnut tree, she had blocked the broken window
in the shed with a heavy door, she had directed *The Threepenny
Opera*.

We're looking at a reproduction of Vermeer's *Woman in Blue
Reading a Letter* that's hanging above the chest of drawers, and
Granny, pointing at one of my mother's paintings, says: 'And
that girl is based on the same one. Do you know who painted
her?'

'Mum.'

'No, I did.'

'But Granny, Mum painted this one, and those two as well.'

'Those two, yes, but not this one. Your mother painted the
landscape, but I painted these two women, the stony one and
the lively one.'

I even neglected my diary, because somehow I wasn't able to
write it all down. But then I told myself it was no good, this
was important, really important, and I wrote:

*Monika came with a large bouquet of gerberas for Granny.
She's horrified too. More clashes with Granny (because she still
has a lie-down during the day): 'Have you put on your nappy?'*

'Not yet.' 'Then put it on, please.' In a while it's the same thing. And again. Finally I come in, and the nappy is lying unfolded on the duvet. 'That's not good enough.' 'She's bullying me, I'll complain to Mama.' And so on, ad infinitum. I come in. 'Have you put it on?' – and Granny makes some Brownian motion under the duvet: 'I'm putting it on.'

Everything's on the outside, like exposed tissue.

She comes out of the bathroom. 'I look at myself in the mirror and it makes me feel weak. How much I've aged because of the hospital.' 'But Granny, you haven't changed at all,' I say, truthfully. 'Ah, that's just love talking through you, you don't notice, but I can see it.' And straight after she stands before the mirror and says flirtatiously: 'The one thing I have left are my lovely legs. They've even got thinner lately.'

And what am I to stifle – laughter or tears?

The summer ended, and I had to move away to Warsaw. Monika moved in with Granny and bickered with her day and night, to get her to go to the bathroom, put on her nappy, take her medicine, not go out in the sun, and so on and so on. And apart from her full-time job at home, she had college too, so my mother still had to come every day and, depending on Monika's plans, get Granny up, make her lunch or put her to bed.

❧

Whenever I came home from Warsaw for the weekend or the holidays I always visited Granny, although it increasingly felt as if I were visiting an empty shell, which she hadn't occupied for ages; and yet now and then a sudden flash would testify to the fact that this really was the same person who had told me the Greek myths, argued with the German soldiers and lain in her cradle while the Bull and his gang were looting the manor house at Lisów.

And so, every three weeks, I wrote something like this in my diary, for instance:

Yesterday I was at Granny and Monika's – everything's all right, though her plumbing is still broken, but it probably can't be fixed. On the bright side, Granny had her teeth in, was taken out for a walk, etc., and as well as that, Monika responds to every attempt at defiance or griping by saying: 'But Mrs Karpińska, we agreed that I'm the boss here, didn't we?' And that's that.

Or:

Granny's getting worse: she's apathetic, touchy, and spends all day long either dozing, or sitting without moving, responding in monosyllables. She wets herself. We're sitting at table, and Mum says: 'Mama, put in your teeth.'

Granny looks, blinks, and starts to arrange on her hand the tablets that are lying ready by her plate.

'Mama, what are you doing?'

'I'm picking up my teeth.'

'Those are teeth?'

'Some teeth, some tablets...'

In the evening I'm channel-hopping. There's a programme with three superannuated nymphomaniacs who'll tell you all about sex. Between them sits a disgusting sight, a guy of about sixty, covered in tattoos and piercings – at least ten in each brow, in his lips, ears and nostrils too. He's sitting there naked, with everything on show, because he's got piercings down there too. He starts fingering his scrotum to show them. I change channel. 'Show me those testicles,' says Granny.

'*Granny!*'
'*Show me, I want to see.*'

In the spring, probably in March or so:

I arrived home and I had a nightmare: I return to the house with shopping from the market in Oliwa, but oddly, by a roundabout route, because part of it went through the woods on Podhalańska Street. I get back to the house, Granny's sitting on the sofa, there's a yellow glow coming from the windows, and I can see Granny's face in this warm light.

'*You know what,*' *she says,* '*I'm bored with life. I'm leaving. I don't feel like telling stories any more.*'

The house is full of cats, and Monika is chasing after them. Then Granny says: '*I brought a kitty home, but there turned out to be two of them...*'

And I can see them romping about on the rug, one bigger, the other smaller.

'*... and I'm just going to wait for a fine day in spring. I'll go outside at dawn, into the sunlight, and keel over. Or else in the evening, one fine evening.*'

I woke up feeling extremely scared – not because the dream was about death, but because I'd dreamed of Granny the way you dream of the dead: distant, illuminated, behind an intangible curtain. As if the spirit world were made of muslin.

And a few pages further on:

Next day, as soon as I got up, I rushed over to see her. I found her outside the house, because she'd come back from the allotment with Monika and then stayed out in the fresh air a while longer.

The whole garden has been ploughed up by wild boar,

here and there, poking through the soil, through the hogs' hand-iwork, are some crocuses, some snowdrops, and something else too. And amid it all Granny, looking rather lost, just like in a dream – I'm writing this a week later, and if not for the memory of the facts I'd have been sure it was just an illusion; or maybe it was one – in the two p.m. light, she seemed to be floating away on the ridges of earth. Holding some wilting flowers, some sprigs of forsythia, picked out of old habit to bloom indoors, looking at the world with the gaze of a five-year-old, as if it were all new.

I went up and hugged her, and as I led her along the furrows to the house, in a sudden wind we walked down the path past the little cherry tree.

Once indoors, I took off her shoes, settled her in her armchair, made the tea, and heated up some food. When I left, she was nodding off in her chair. Shamefully, as if removing something from a church, I took a piece of paper that was lying on the basket in the hall: 'I'm at the allotment. Granny.'

And as I took it, I knew I wasn't doing it out of joy but out of despair. That one day I'd find it in a book, in the desk, in her papers, and be reminded not just of her, but of that day, and my sense of shame, and – as I already feel now – this tremendous, raging sorrow.

For some time her personality became unsteady; depending what the weather was like or who came to see her, Granny assumed various masks: Little Miss Smarty-Pants, the terrified old lady or the listless hulk.

'Why are you closing the window?' asks Mum.

'Someone might get in.'

'Through the window? Upstairs?'

'Yes, of course. I came in here myself a few days ago. Along the cable.'

And she refused to be persuaded that it wasn't possible. For Little Miss Smarty-Pants went hand in glove with the Wise Old Owl. What we feared most was that she'd do herself an injury, if she really did decide to go out through the window. Like the time in autumn when the neighbours had found her lying under the cherry tree.

'Mrs Karpińska, what's wrong?'

'I fell.'

'Please get up, oh yes, just a little more, that's it. What's this chair doing here?'

'I was trying to climb the tree to pick some cherries.'

XXVII

I'd arrive, sit down in an armchair and do my best to remind myself of her golden background of old; I knew she would never return from the place she was in now, and her star quality would be less shiny from now on... Meanwhile my mother ran about the house, putting on the washing machine, doing a lot of shouting and playing the role of 'Inspector Clouseau investigates', meaning that she kept asking her a series of questions, what year is it, what's your name, and so on; and when Granny tried to shine by telling a story, Mum made her drag out the words at such length that finally she'd lose her way in her statement and, like a sort of home-grown Socrates, Mum would crow: 'There you are, you see – all because you refuse to exercise your brain! Just a bit more and you'll be a decerebrate moron!'

'How on earth can you speak to me like that?'

'Because that's how you address a woman who doesn't read books and won't put her teeth in!'

❧

'Mum,' I say, 'you mustn't shout like that. You mustn't. It doesn't help at all.'

'But I can't cope. I can't stop myself. I think I'll have to go to an exorcist, because I keep telling myself "don't shout", but then I see Granny, I smell that stink of urine, I see Granny and I want to scream... it's like being two different people...'

'Being possessed,' I venture to say, 'is rather a rare condition. What you need is a psychiatrist, not an exorcist.'

'But I'm not going to the same moron as last time, who'll only prescribe me more pills. That's no use.'

'And I can only agree. But try using kindness. As I do. Take the night before last – we were going up the stairs, when Granny proudly said: "When I look at these works of art of mine…" and I wondered which ones she meant. "These ones, right here," she said, and pointed at the murals I painted above the door a year ago. "Granny, I painted that." "No, I did!" said Granny, with the smile of someone who knows better.'

'Oooh, yes, that smile is a classic.'

'Well, so I asked: "Did you? Or maybe not?" Then she echoed the question: "Maybe not?" "Maybe not." And then what did I hear? "Oh well, probably not." And that was it, game over. I won without a fight. But you come in, and at once you're on the war path.'

'No. You'll see what it's like when you try living alone with her. Once you've lived at that pace for a while.'

❧

And I moved in there again. I arrived kitted out as if I weren't going to a fully stocked – or rather overstocked house at all: I took a cardboard box containing my favourite English tea set, my favourite Secession cutlery made by Fraget, my favourite goblet made of honey-coloured glass, though there really was more than enough glassware here already. I settled in and made myself at home. Clothes in the wardrobe, CD stack on the chest of drawers, clock in front of it, the same mirror on the desk that I put here a year ago, the one I dug out of the dustbin two years ago, next to an inkwell, a wooden letter rack from Wiktor, and a pen holder marked 'Souvenir de Varsovie', dating back to Siedlce, possibly Bila Tserkva too. On the shelves I set out the photographs I always take with me – 'Madame', in other words a Belgian lady from Namours, in a varnished frame with openwork decorations and a purple moiré mount; 'Mr Herski', whom I once invented and wrote about, but who then turned out to exist in reality – but that's another story; a photograph of Granny with Romusia and their parents in the garden in Kielce, or maybe at Lisów, which I'd been given as a gift, because by some miracle there are two prints of it, and finally a photograph of me that Basia took here a year ago, in the gutted sheds, which were demolished that summer – I'm reflected in an old mirror, covered in spots and blemishes of light, half in the shade, half in the sun; if only I could stay like that for ever.

There was nothing left of the sheds now – they'd been razed to their foundations; from the kitchen window you could see the street and a fence on the other side. The view was ugly with them and ugly without them, but at least they were a hundred years old. Things were no better at the front of the house. The earth, ploughed up in the winter by wild boar, was a very sorry sight. The flowerbeds were choked with weeds. The walnut tree, stripped of its bark in January by the neighbour for shading his windows, had in fact put out leaves, but was slowly withering, dropping undersized, empty shells. This was probably its final year. Anyway, the State Forests would probably want to sell off the land for building lots. The garden was at an end. Along with Granny, everything of beauty here would be gone for ever, as if rolling up in her wake, just as the angels in Gothic paintings roll up the cardboard firmament.

❧

Over the next few days I got used to the way of life in Oliwa; I learnt how to take advantage of the lulls in Granny's mobility which allowed me to deal with the household chores (doing t laundry, hanging it out to dry, cleaning, cooking and laying the table), and I had some free time as well. Nevertheless, these petty daily activities managed to prolong themselves to incredible proportions.

The morning rituals took at least three hours. It started with dragging her out of bed. And then escorting her to the bathroom ('No, Granny, not into the kitchen... you can eat once you've had a wash... no, not now, first you have to take off your wet pyjamas and nappy, have a wash and get dressed'), sitting her on the toilet, stopping her from scratching (she had developed an obsessive way of mindlessly scratching herself, and neither by asking nor threatening could we stop her from carving holes in her own knees, shins and elbows with her fingernails), getting her off the toilet ('Granny, this isn't a lord's palace. Granny, Granny, get up. Don't scratch. Get up, don't scratch, don't scratch, don't SCRATCH. Good. Now get up'), sitting her in the bath ('Granny, you undress in front of me every day of the week, don't make such a fuss'), washing her, getting her out again (before that, she had her five minutes for pouring hot water on her back, which she liked the best, while I took the sheets off her bed and stuck them in the washing machine), towelling her dry, rubbing cream onto her nappy rash, doing up the nappy, dressing her, brushing her hair, making breakfast, getting her to take her medicine, and later on, emptying the bladder again. But that was just the start of the day – we had to remember that Granny had to drink water, or she would get dehydrated, go to the toilet once an hour, do some mental exercise, but not overheat her brain, and so on; probably only a Tamagotchi would have been more trouble, and not even that, because at least it wouldn't have kept arguing about everything.

Granny was also full of traps and cunning plans. At first I let myself be taken in by her. She knew she wasn't allowed to go out in the sun during the hottest weather, so she promised me she was only going outside for a moment, to sit in the shade, but after five minutes she broke loose and headed off to the allotment. I went in pursuit, but only in a chaotic sort of way, because I didn't know where she had gone, whether to the city, or the corner shop, or into the woods perhaps… All this caused me an asthma attack, but finally I caught up with her on the road; it was as hot as blazes, but what did she care? I was furious. I took her to the allotment (because it was nearby, and I was afraid to go straight back in such heat without a rest). And we were very angry with each other. All the more since she turned out to have told me a barefaced lie, because she had taken the summerhouse keys from home. I didn't know she could be so cunning, though my mother reckoned she took the keys with her out of habit.

The next day she said: 'I want to go out…'

'You can't in this heat.'

'But I want to.'

'Do you solemnly promise me you'll sit in the shade and protect your head from the sun?'

'Well, I can't promise you that.'

'Then I can't let you go.'

If I had to leave the house, I locked her in. When I got back, she'd be standing by the door, with her beret pulled over her left ear at a jaunty angle (she refused to accept that she didn't have to wear anything on her head when there was a thirty-degree heatwave), and she'd cry in an accusatory tone: 'Yes! Yes! You imprisoned me. It's like being in prison here.'

'Granny, you're not allowed out in this heat. Do you remember how you fainted a year ago? Do you want to end up in hospital again?'

'Nonsense.'

If she wasn't standing by the door, she'd have grown tired waiting and fallen asleep in an armchair. When she woke up, she wouldn't remember a thing, and I would quietly remove from the hall the screwdrivers, hammers and other tools with which she had been trying to open the lock. ('I have very strong hands, you know…')

❧

Wiktor has arrived. This has animated Granny a bit, but not for long. I feel sorry for him and often find myself thinking he's very patient. He waits for me to haul Granny from her lair, and hears me shouting through the closed door: 'Don't scratch,' 'Get up,' 'Wash your bum,' 'Don't scratch'; he helps me with the breakfast, peels a tomato, persuades Granny to swallow her pills, makes sure she doesn't devour anything harmful (she has done, more than once; she'll sneak into the kitchen and drink the marinade from a jar of olives or eat the rind trimmed off some yellow cheese; luckily she hasn't got into the tallow candles yet). He helps me a great deal, but even so from time to time I say to him: 'I'm finding it a bit hard to take. I'm going to call Basia.'

'Aha.'

'Hi, Basia. I've had enough.'

'Of Granny?'

'Your skills of perception amaze me, Dr Watson. The worst thing is the peeing. Every morning I have to drag her out of bed by force. And I say: "Granny, get up, please." "I can't right now," she says, "I'm having a pee." Or I come and say: "Get up, Granny, come on, get up." "In a minute, I'm so sleepy…" Well, I think, it won't make any difference, let her sleep another ten minutes. So I sit in an armchair, and take a look at the newspaper, and from off stage, from Granny's nook, comes the following announcement: "Am I wetting myself or not?" and then a joyful cry: "I've wet myself!" '

Basia laughs, says sorry, and laughs again.

'No need to apologise, the comical side of it is the only thing that makes it bearable. Wiktor's here. He was terribly surprised I take such good care of Granny, and that I'm so loving and patient with her. He just walks about saying: "Well I never, Jacek, who'd have thought you were such a good boy…" or: "So you just pretend to be an awful swine, but deep down…" He didn't finish the sentence, because he heard himself and felt stupid.'

'Well, sure,' says Basia, 'no one will kick you as sincerely as a close friend…'

'Exactly. Or a brother, he's good at that too. He looked after her recently, as usual, when I have time off during the day. But the way he did it, when I came home for a while before six, I found a note saying: "Feed Granny when you get back because I didn't have time and she's hungry." And that's all. You can't leave him in charge of a stick insect, let alone a granny.'

'Listen, you're calling from Gdańsk, it'll cost you a fortune…'

'What the hell, I need consoling. And the worst thing is the bickering. About everything. "Granny, go to the bathroom." "No." "Go on then." "No. I don't want to pee." "That's the whole point – you should go when you don't want to." And so on for hours. "Granny, don't scratch." Or: "Get up from the toilet," and she's staring at me, she keeps staring, and finally she says in a lordly way: "All right then. But I'll only do it because I love you very much." '

'That's lovely.'

'Well, sort of. It's disarming. But you know, it's like that with everything. I start screaming, like my mother. I ask her to take her pills. She won't even open her eyes, she just sticks out her tongue. So I ask her again, she gets in a huff and shows her tongue again. Finally she puts it all in her mouth, but just takes tiny little sips of water. "Granny, swallow it," I say for the hundredth time. "No, because it's such nasty medicine." What on earth can you do?'

'What can I suggest? Nothing. And can't your brother...? He can't. Well, quite.'

'Such is fate.'

'Such is fate.'

I go back into the other room. Wiktor is reading something. 'Well?'

'Well what?'

'What do you mean, what? Is Granny OK?'

'She's fine. I called Basia, I had a good moan and now I feel better. But I'm worn out; I'm going to sleep. Go on reading, if you like.'

'Won't the light bother you?'

'No.'

'Goodnight, then.'

'Night night.'

And I go to sleep with a heavy heart, because there's another battle on the cards for tomorrow. Now here's a surprise. At nine thirty Granny comes in at a brisk pace (well, a brisk toddle) and stands in the doorway, blinking.

'Granny,' I ask, 'what are you doing here?'

'I'm up. It's half-past nine already.'

'But yesterday you were still asleep at ten and I had to drag you out of bed almost by force.'

'That was yesterday, but now it's today. Today there's the attack.'

'What?' asks Wiktor from under his duvet at the other end of the room.

'The military attack. The Polish army. Mrs Kowalska is talking to an officer.'

I'm lost for words. She has caught me off guard, got me out of my sleep. I wrap myself in the duvet and dash into the front room. I look through the window, and there's the neighbour, Mrs Kowalska, talking to Mrs Sławińska. Back I go, and meanwhile Granny's explaining to Wiktor: 'I couldn't sleep all night; there were some sort of regroupings and manoeuvres; all night I could hear them giving orders.'

🌸

Each night I sit at the computer and write down these dialogues, for all their comedy, tenderness and crazy metaphors; what I love best are the heroic passages, such as: *My holidays with Judith, the warlike widow from Bethulia, under one roof.*

We're on our way to the allotment, when suddenly Granny extracts an old umbrella handle from her pocket and shows it to me proudly. 'Look what I've got!'

'What's it for?' I ask, though I know the answer.

'To defend myself against thugs.'

She went to bed at nine, but got up again for a while.

'Go and fetch a stick,' she says to me in a sound-advice-giving tone. 'Go and fetch a stout stick.'

'What on earth for?'

'In case someone creeps in through the window.'

'But Granny, no one has ever climbed in the window here.'

'Oh yes they have, when you were little. He threw a sort of grappling hook and got in.'

'And then what?'

'I bashed him, because I saw him climbing in. I hit him over the head.'

Well I never.

'*This spray of flowers has collapsed,*' I say, '*the silver and pink ones. The sticks supporting them have snapped. We'll have to tie them up or they'll fall over.*'

'*I need tying up too. I've collapsed too.*'

'*Oh, that's a bit harder to fix.*'

'*Ah, if only those young ladies from Ravensbrück would tie me up...*'

'*Well, I don't know if that would do you much good...*'

'*Ah, now that's quite another matter.*'

And so I tap away at the keyboard, giggling to myself from time to time, but affectionately, thoughtfully, without any crude sneering. I'm writing away, but I can hear someone shuffling about in the hall, and I know there's some more nocturnal wandering. It's a quarter past eleven, and Granny is pulling a stunt called '*defending the castle,*' in other words she gets out of bed, arms herself with a wooden rod for drawing back the curtains, and sets off on her round of the flat. It's Rembrandt's *Night Watch* as performed by Hals's *Regentesses of the Old Men's Home*. She even opens the front door, so if anyone really did want to hit her over the head, it would be easy – just make a bit of noise and wait on the threshold with a piece of lead piping.

'Granny, what are you doing?'

'I thought there was someone out here.'

It's hard to rule out: there are sometimes people coming home, laughing, chatting and arguing, or cats ripping each other apart in the bushes.

'Granny, go to bed,' I say, partly cross and partly amused, 'you've got a senile obsession, that's the medical term for it.'

'Which means I'm an old lady?'

'No. It means you're an old lady with a senile obsession.'

'Aha. So will you defend me if I make a racket in the middle of the night?'

'Yes, I will.'

And she goes to bed, gripping the rod.

I don't know if anyone will ever trust me as fully as she did. 'Will you defend me?' 'Yes I will.' But not against everything.

The speakers pour out eternal Brahms, and I go back to my writing.

She comes into the room and says she wants to go out.

'Then first go to the bathroom for a pee.'

'I've had a pee already. In my knickers.'

I look, and her trousers are all wet down to the ankles.

'Oh Christ, weren't you wearing a nappy?'

'Yes, I was.'

She wasn't.

'Is the armchair wet too?'

And at this point – here comes a verbal tour de force:

'Pre-su-mab-ly.'

What a fine word, 'presumably'. I noticed it one day over breakfast. So refined and unimposing; young people speak in harsh terms: 'never', 'always', 'everywhere'. I myself often write 'everything', and 'final'. But Granny says 'presumably'. No one talks like that nowadays; it's a word from the cool, measured vocabulary of Counsellor Karnaukhov.

Next morning at breakfast:

'This bread's not very good. Somehow I never have the energy to go to Maciejczak's in the morning.'

'To Maciejczak's? Where's is this Maciejczak's bakery?'

'In Kielce,' says Granny as if it's obvious.

'And where are we?'

She laughs. As if nothing were wrong. But before now she has sometimes said we're at Lisów. 'Oh what a pity,' she once informed Mum, 'we didn't get some milk for our coffee from Lisów, it's far better there.'

'So where are we?'

'In Kielce.'

'And what year is it?'

'1943.'

She lives in a curious zone outside of time; she isn't aware of her debilities. When asked, she'll reply that every few days she goes to the market, does the cooking herself, and the cleaning, reads a lot, and this year she made some preserves. Somehow she hasn't the energy to go to Maciejczak's for bread, but otherwise everything's fine. Now and then she asks: 'Where's the father?' which could mean either my great-grandfather, or my grandfather, or my dad. Mostly she asks about dead people. I wonder if she can see them.

Today was idyllic. Not as hot, so we went outside, and I climbed the cherry tree.

'Just don't go too high,' says Granny, who on this particular occasion remembers that she hasn't coped too well with climbing trees.

But I'm already high up, and as I lean out to reach the more distant branches, grab the stumps of snapped-off boughs and feel the touch of the strange cherry bark, alternately rough and smooth, I toss the sweet, sun-baked cherries into a plastic bag.

'For once there were no scrumpers this year,' I call from above. 'It's a pity I didn't come earlier, we could have made some compote, but as it is the nicest ones have either fallen off already, or the birds have pecked them. Oh well, I hope they

enjoyed them.' I move a little higher. 'Shall I toss some down for you?'

'No, no, there are still some here,' and I can see Granny bending over to spot the cherries lying in the grass: wide shoulders in an old coat and white hair topped by a little beret, because she won't go out without her beret, nothing will stop her from wearing it, not even in the greatest heat.

'Eeee, just rotten ones. Oh, these are nice, here we are.' But she doesn't even straighten up to see where they fell. 'I was at Lisów,' I say. 'My friends and I were on our way to Szczawnica, so we stopped off to visit Lisów.'

'Hmm? And?'

'Nothing much, someone's building on the site of the manor,' I say, as calmly as I can; no one could have guessed from my tone of voice that when I saw the concrete foundations in the spot where a few years earlier I had seen the stubs of stone walls, coated here and there in plaster with vestiges of paint in pastel colours, I let drop one of those words that Basia invariably provides with the comment: 'Oops, I would never say that word, not for a hundred zlotys.'

'A local?'

'No, from Kielce. I ran into Iwański.'

'The old one?'

'No, the son. The old man's been dead for ages, and Gienia died two or three years ago. I found the manor-house door in the ruins of the stable. The front door was filled in with panels below and had panes of glass above, didn't it?'

'Yes. Oh dear, don't go so high.'

'I'm just about to come down. Are you feeling all right?'

'Yes, if I get tired I'll sit on a tree stump.'

And so we chat through the leaves on a vertical axis, and on a quite different one through time. Across the fence the ladies *from next door go by, so there's an exchange of courtesies and comments, how big I am. Ha, what can you do? I won't see sixteen again, but this isn't the last time I'll climb the cherry tree. And so on, and so on.*

Indoors we'll wash the cherries in a red colander and make a pot of tea, as ever since the world began.

❧

Wiktor left, Basia came and went, and I went on sitting in Oliwa, endlessly repeating the same refrains: 'Get up,' 'Go to the bathroom,' 'Don't scratch,' 'Have a pee.' The standard diary entries said:

Not very quiet on the Granny front today. First of all, at break-fast there was soaking the feet for an hour and cutting the toenails, which since the last operation have managed to grow half a centimetre. Thickness – in some places normal, in others two millimetres; but somehow I dealt with it and set about putting on a dressing, because Granny has scratched away at her forearm so badly that it's inflamed. 'Don't scratch!' I shout, and then either she goes on scratching, or she moves her hand and scratches a bit higher up or a bit lower down, or on her knee. And so on, every few minutes – in the lavatory, in the bath, in the armchair, at the allotment, endlessly. I'd made a poultice, but it turned out you have to dilute the arnica and not just slap it on neat, so I removed it, and asked Granny to wash her arm. A little later I go into the bathroom, and she's on the lavatory seat in a strange pose, half-lying, half-sitting. She'd fainted. She doesn't drink enough, she's dehydrated. I brought her round, Mum told me to pump a large mug of Isostar into her, and that'll do the trick. Afterwards she was in better shape, she even went to the allotment with my parents. But she talks

Lala departs. Oliwa, c. 1995.

*about death more and more often and, worse yet, I can sense it
too. Like today when she said: 'Well, it's time for me to say my
goodbyes.'*

*It made my heart turn to lead. Of course, we all started
joking about it, making light of it and so on. Mum shouted in
her standard way: 'What? Right now? Don't be silly, we haven't
bought this flat off yet, if you pop your clogs what are we going
to do with all this stuff?' Because Mum's like that. In winter she
says flowers are too pricy, and in summer she says we'll have no
use for the piano. People have various ways of showing each
other love.*

And it would have gone on like that to the end of the summer,
if Granny hadn't fallen sick. We thought it was dehydration, as
a year ago. I left for Warsaw to look for a new flat, but when I
called home Mum said: 'Granny's in hospital. She has to have
her gall bladder removed.'

By the time I got back, Granny had had the operation, and a
streak of my mother's hair had gone white above the ear, just
like Grandpapa Leonard's.

We went to the hospital. Granny was in a reasonably good
mood, but admittedly she wasn't entirely aware that she'd had
an operation.

'I've got some sort of pain in my stomach.'

'Mama, they took out your gall bladder.'

Granny starts to peep and poke about under the duvet.

'Mama, don't touch it, you've got a dressing there.'

'Hm,' she says in surprise. 'So I have.'

Another time she suddenly casts into the void: 'I must ask Dr
Orłowski if I can get away with not smoking.'

'Who's Dr Orłowski?'

'You know, from Oliwa.'

'We don't know a Dr Orłowski. Only Ela Orłowska.'

'But she has a husband.'

'But he's not a doctor.'

'But I'm in love with him.'

'But you were already a much older retired lady when you met him.'

'But to my mind I was young and beautiful.'

A short silence.

'I must ask Dr Orłowski if I can really get away with not smoking...'

'But Mama, you've never smoked.'

'What? I've always smoked a lot.'

'Maybe at nursery school...'

Offended, she shrugs and says: 'Maybe.'

Yet another time, at the sight of my father she whispers to the nurse conspiratorially: 'That's not a burglar. That's my son-in-law.'

❧

And yet she did come home, she did, though by now we'd all made up our minds where to put the piano and the glassware collection. She's indestructible. And once again I sat beside her, like the setting sun.

Then came the end of September. And so the summer in Oliwa ended, just like that. I gathered up my cutlery and plates, the yellow glass goblet, inkwells and photographs, packed them in cases and cardboard boxes and headed off to Warsaw. So now I'm sort of here, far away from those problems, and just go home once a month, but occasionally my mother or father calls and asks: 'How's the novel?'

'I'm working on it.'

'I've got something new for you.'

Just as if it were a bit of drawing-room gossip.

'Well?'

'We borrowed an exercise bike from Zosia to see if your granny would at least move a bit. "Mama," we say, "come and sit on it, give it a try, do some pedalling." "No." "Why not?" "Because I tried it at Lisów, and it wasn't a success." "But Mama, this bike is just for exercise, it hasn't got any wheels, it won't go anywhere." "Aha," she says incredulously, "they said there were no wheels that time too, they said it wouldn't go, but it did."'

Or: 'I arrived the other morning, and the bedclothes were sopping. I groaned, and Mama said reproachfully: "Why are you shouting? When you want to pee in the night you get up, do you?" And she's surprised by such an idea.'

Or: 'Jacek, I can't stand it any more. I ask "What was your father's first name?" She doesn't know, she can't remember, her mind's a blank. "What about your first husband?" Silence. Your father? "Bieniecki." Finally she comes up with Karnaukhov, she remembers him, both of them, Karnaukhov and Bieniecki, but Julek and my father never existed, I don't exist, you don't exist, she never had children. And I'm her sister.'

'Romusia?'

'No, her younger sister.'

But perhaps it's not entirely without sense. The house at Morawica that was once converted into an isolation ward gradually falls into ruin and no one remembers the door frames hacked out by the Austrians or the melons that Mościcki didn't like. In place of the Lisów ice house, from which on a fine day Chęciny was visible, a new house is arising. The Oliwa garden is overgrown, and the bunches of dried flowers are crumbling under the burden of dust and damp. Time has negated everything that once was, even Jadzia Kontrymówna, so why stop at minor truths such as 'you are my daughter', 'God exists' or 'Macondo'?

Tomorrow I'm going home. I've finished the book. I shall read Granny the typescript, but she won't be listening. And when I stop, if she says anything at all, she'll ask: 'And what happened after that?'

'After that,' I'll reply, 'everyone got older and older, my mother finally found the right man, who would one day be my father; it's true that for a time she painted sad pictures of silent, stone telephones and empty wardrobes, but that's another story. Either way, in the end they were married; it was just at the start of October, and two days before the ceremony my future father climbed the tree to shake down the walnuts, and then gathered them with his bare hands. And went to the wedding with hands half-brown and half-red from being scraped with pumice.'

And after that, as Julek, who died a few months later, would have said, one word led to another, and Jacek was born. Meaning me.

XXVIII

And so the circle is complete. This is where I am born. And I'm at the end of my book. In fact, if I'm honest about it, it's all happening at the same time anyway – even now, as you start to close the cover of this volume, the coachman in Ukraine turns away from the large greengages that are virtually feeding themselves to him and says: 'I didn't plant them, so I'm not going to eat them.'

And the sun rises in the east, while setting in the west.

Gdańsk and Warsaw, IX 2000–XI 2002

TRANSLATOR'S ENDNOTES

Chapter I

Oliwa – a suburb of Gdańsk.

Lisów – a small village in south-central Poland, twenty kilometres south of the city of Kielce.

Kiev – capital of Ukraine, but before the First World War it belonged to the Russian Empire, as did a large part of modern Poland.

just two, sepia shots – fortunately, more photographs came to light after the Polish original of this book was first published.

Wandeczka – a diminutive of the name Wanda. Polish first names may have more than one diminutive form, by degree of intimacy. I have left these as they appear in the original Polish text. Thus Roma also appears as Romusia, Lala as Lalunia or Laleczka, Jacek as Jacuś, Juliusz as Julek, Zygmunt as Zygmuś, Paweł as Pawełek, and so on.

January Uprising of 1863 – one of several uprisings by Polish patriots fighting for national independence from the three empires that partitioned Poland in the period from 1772 until the First World War.

Mnin, Morawica – villages in the Kielce area; the village of Mnin is some thirty kilometres west of Kielce, and Morawica is about ten kilometres south of it.

peasants – there are numerous references in this book to the 'peasants', in Polish '*chłopi*', which describes the post-feudal class of people who before the Second World War lived in the countryside and worked the land, as opposed to the 'nobles' ('*szlachta*'), or the 'landowning gentry' ('*ziemianie*').

Chapter II

Pelplin – a town sixty kilometres south of Gdańsk.

the Hutsul region – an area in the Carpathian mountains, straddling the Ukrainian and Romanian borders. The Hutsul people have their own distinct culture and ethnicity.

King Jan Sobieski – John III Sobieski (1629–96) was the Polish king who defeated the Turks at the Battle of Vienna in 1683.

Grand Duke Konstantin Pavlovich – (1779–1831) second son of Russian emperor Pavel I, was governor of the Kingdom of Poland.

Bolesław Leśmian – (1877–1937), one of the most influential Polish poets of the early twentieth century.

Szymiczek, Szymiczkowa – many Polish surnames change according to gender. The feminine form of Szymiczek is Szymiczkowa; similarly, Mr Brokl's wife is Mrs Broklowa. Male surnames ending -ki change to -ka in the feminine form, hence Dr Bieniecki's wife is Mrs Bieniecka.

Hofmann – Józef Hofmann (1876–1957), composer, inventor and pianist.

Chapter III

Vistula Land – the name of the Russian partition of Poland after 1864.

the Black Hundreds – members of an extreme nationalist movement in the early twentieth century who supported the Romanovs and the tsar's autocracy. They were known for their strong Russocentric beliefs, for anti-Semitism and for inciting pogroms against non-Russians.

Dr Yevgeny Botkin – (1865–1918) court physician to the Russian imperial family, assassinated with them.

Felix Edmundovich – Dzerzhinsky (1877–1926), head of the Cheka, the Soviet secret police, notorious for mass executions during the Red Terror and the Russian Civil War.

Chapter IV

President Mościcki – Ignacy Mościcki (1867–1946) was a chemist and politician, president of Poland from 1926 to 1939.

Bouchers, Potters – by the French painter François Boucher (1703–70) and the Dutch painter Paulus Potter (1625?–54).

the battles of Grunwald and Berezina, paintings by Matejko and Brandt, the Winged Hussars – Grunwald and Berezina were epic battles featured in classic Polish paintings by painters such as Jan Matejko (1838–93) and Józef Brandt (1841–1915). The Winged Hussars were the crack cavalry force of the Polish–Lithuanian Commonwealth in the sixteenth to eighteenth centuries.

Chapter V

Siedlce to Białystok – Siedlce is a city ninety kilometres east of Warsaw, and Białystok is two hundred kilometres north-east of Warsaw.

High Priest in *Forefather's Eve* – the epic drama by Poland's greatest poet, Adam Mickiewicz (1798–1855) features a character called the 'Guślarz', a religious figure similar to a druid or a shaman.

Berma – a famous actress who features in Marcel Proust's *In Search of Lost Time*, based mainly on Sarah Bernhardt and Gabrielle Réjane.

Chapter VIII

'porcelain troubled us most' – a quote from Czesław Miłosz's poem 'Song on Porcelain'.

Kujawiak **by Wieniawski** – Henryk Wieniawski (1835–80) composed many works based on Polish folk dances, including the kujawiak and the mazurka.

Mechówna – in certain forms, the Polish surnames of

unmarried daughters end in -ówna, hence the daughter of
Mr Mech and Mrs Mechowa is Miss Mechówna.

Chapter IX

Marshal Piłsudski – Józef Piłsudski (1867–1935), Poland's leading statesman for most of the inter-war period from 1918
when the country regained independence as the Second
Polish Republic.

Chmielewska's crime novels – Joanna Chmielewska (1932–
2013) was a prolific novelist, author of dozens of (humorous)
crime novels.

Gombrowicz – Witold Gombrowicz (1904–69) was a novelist,
diarist and dramatist, famous for his psychologically disturb-
ing novels that take an ironic look at Polish society and
attitudes.

Pawełek Hertz – Paweł Hertz (1918–2001) was a writer, poet,
translator and publisher.

Iwaszkiewicz – Jarosław Iwaszkiewicz (1894–1980) was a poet,
novelist, playwright and short-story writer, one of the major
figures of twentieth-century Polish literature.

Chapter X

National Democrats, National Radical Camp – National
Democracy (known as the Endecja) was a right-wing nationalist political movement. The National Radical Camp was an
extreme-right party formed by radical members of its youth
wing, and inspired by Italian fascism.

King Stanisław – Stanisław August Poniatowski (1732–98) was
the last king of Poland before it was partitioned by the
Russian, Prussian and Austro–Hungarian empires.

Witkacy – Stanisław Ignacy Witkiewicz (1885–1939), known
as Witkacy, was a writer, painter, philosopher, playwright,
novelist and photographer who belonged to the absurdist

school, and whose reputation only took off after the Second World War; he died at his own hand at the start of the war, when, days after the Germans, the Russians also invaded Poland.

Boy-Żeleński – Tadeusz Żeleński (1874–1941), nicknamed Boy, was a stage writer, poet, critic and translator of French literature. The *enfant terrible* of the Polish literary scene at the start of the twentieth century, during the inter-war period he was regarded as a classic author. In July 1941 he was murdered by the Nazis, along with twenty-four other leading academics in the occupied Polish city of Lwów.

Mrs Żeromska – Anna Żeromska, widow of Stefan Żeromski (1864–1925), who was a novelist and dramatist four times nominated for the Nobel prize. She and her daughter, Monika, saved a number of Jewish lives during the Second World War.

Słowacki or Mickiewicz – Juliusz Słowacki (1809–49) and Adam Mickiewicz (see notes for Chapter V above) are Poland's greatest Romantic poets.

Chapter XI
Barynia – the Russian word for 'lady of the manor', a pre-revolutionary term of address.

Chapter XII
Anatole France – (1844–1924), French poet and novelist, who won the Nobel prize for literature in 1921. Julek hid with his books, of course, some of which he translated into Polish.

Sigismund's column – originally erected in 1644, Sigismund's column stands outside Warsaw's Royal Castle and is one of the city's most famous landmarks. It commemorates King Sigismund III, who moved the capital from Kraków to Warsaw in 1596.

Tadeusz Kościuszko, Emilia Plater – national heroes; Tadeusz Kościuszko (1746–1817) was the military leader who led the Kościuszko Uprising of 1794, and went on to fight in the American War of Independence. Countess Emilia Plater (1806–31) was a noblewoman and revolutionary who fought as a captain in the November 1830 Uprising.

Chapter XIII

Summer in Nohant – a play about Chopin's life with George Sand, by Jarosław Iwaszkiewicz.

Nina Andrycz – (1912–2014) an actress who was married to the communist prime minister Józef Cyrankiewicz.

as the poet puts it – a reference to a poem by Zbigniew Herbert (1924–98), 'Breviary (1)', where in fact they are Roman nymphs.

the Liegenschaft – in Nazi-occupied Poland, an agricultural property administered by a German official.

Maciejowa – among the Polish peasantry, women were often addressed by a feminine form of their husband's first name, thus the wife of a man whose first name is Maciej (the Polish equivalent of Matthew) is called Maciejowa.

Chapter XVII

Home Army – the Home Army (AK or Armia Krajowa) was the Polish resistance army, taking its orders from the Polish Government in Exile, which was based in London.

Miron Białoszewski – (1922–83), poet, novelist, playwright and actor, wrote the classic *Memoir of the Warsaw Uprising*.

People's Army – the Polish People's Army, formed during the Second World War, was largely under Soviet command.

Andrzej Munk for his film *Eroica* – Andrzej Munk (1921–61) was a film director and screenwriter whose classic *Eroica* is about the Polish concept of heroism.

Chapter XIX

'**this is what Poland is**' – a quote from *The Wedding*, the definitive play by Stanisław Wyspiański (1869–1907), which describes the perils of the national drive towards self-determination following the two unsuccessful uprisings of November 1830 and January 1863.

Buczacz tapestry – Buczacz was the site of a nineteenth-century textiles factory where Armenian weaving masters were employed to produce distinctive wall hangings.

Wyczółkowski – Leon Wyczółkowski (1852–1936), a leading artist of the Young Poland movement.

Mniszkówna, Courths-Mahler – Helena Mniszkówna (1878–1943) was a Polish romantic novelist, Hedwig Courths-Mahler (1867–1950) was a German one.

Gerard Labuda – (1916–2010) was a historian of the Middle Ages.

Jolly Fellows – a 1934 Soviet musical film, directed by Grigori Aleksandrov.

Nalewki Street – is in a part of Warsaw that was once a Jewish district.

Queen Jadwiga, Emilia Plater, or a heroine out of Żeromski – Polish heroines; Żeromski's neo-romantic novels often feature characters who have dedicated their lives to the battle for Polish independence.

Recovered Territories – the parts of pre-war Germany that were given to Poland after the Second World War, when Poland lost its eastern borderlands to the Soviet Union.

Mariacka Street, Upland Gate – both are in central Gdańsk.

Kielce pogrom – in July 1946, forty-two Jews were killed and more than forty others were wounded by Polish soldiers, police officers and civilians in an outbreak of violence against Jewish refugees in Kielce.

Chapter XX

the Memling painting – Hans Memling (c. 1430–94) was a German painter who moved to Flanders and worked under Roger van der Weyden. The painting at the National Museum in Gdańsk is his famous triptych, *The Last Judgement*.

Słupsk – a city near the Baltic coast, one hundred and twenty-five kilometres west of Gdańsk.

Gałczyński – Konstanty Ildefons Gałczyński (1905–53) was a major poet and satirist, with a reputation as a hell-raiser.

Silver Natalia, Kira – Gałczyński's wife Natalia was a children's writer. Her husband famously called her 'Silver Natalia' in a poem dedicated to her, and that is also the title of their daughter Kira's biography of her mother.

Chapter XXI

The Unknown Masterpiece – a novella by Balzac.

Bila Tserkva – is a city in central Ukraine, ninety kilometres south of Kiev.

Virtuti Militari medal – Poland's highest military decoration for heroism and courage in the face of the enemy at war.

Bandera's nationalists – Stepan Bandera (1909–59) was a Ukrainian political activist and nationalist and independence movement leader, whose name is associated with violence against the Poles in Poland's pre-war eastern provinces.

impoverished gentry, gentry villages – in the eighteenth century, towards the end of the First Polish Republic, the poorest nobility (or *szlachta*) were no better off than the peasantry (or *chłopi*), and formed villages (known as *zaścianki*), where they farmed plots of land that had once belonged to a mutual ancestor. Despite being impoverished, they still regarded themselves as nobility.

Morena – a district of Gdańsk where there is a communist-era housing estate.

Benya Krik – the fictional Jewish mob boss who appears in Isaac Babel's *Odessa Tales*.

qahal – a Jewish community council with jurisdiction over charitable and religious affairs.

Chapter XXII

Semiramis – the Hanging Gardens of Babylon are also known as the Gardens of Semiramis, after the legendary Assyrian queen who ruled c. 810 BC.

Lochner, Witz – Stefan Lochner and Konrad Witz were both German painters active in the first half of the fifteenth century, who produced notable altarpieces.

Chapter XXIII

the old poet... his translation of the gnostic *Hymn of the Pearl* – the *Hymn of the Pearl* is a passage from the apocryphal *Acts of Thomas*, and the poet is Czesław Miłosz, who translated it from ancient Greek into Polish.

Witkacy's *Farewell to Autumn* – this novel by Stanisław Witkiewicz (see above) describes the rise and fall of a young decadent whose narcotic, sexual and psychological experiments drive his wife to suicide, while he becomes infatuated with Hela Bertz.

Czajka, Czajnik – 'Czajka' means 'Lapwing', while 'Czajnik' means 'Kettle'.

The Golden Legend – is a collection of hagiographies, likely compiled around the year 1260, and widely read in late medieval Europe.

the one hundred and forty-four thousand sealed – Revelation, chapter 7, verses 1–8.

Chapter XXIV

Małcużyński – Witold Małcużyński (1914–77) was a distinguished pianist who specialised in the work of Chopin and

won the third International Chopin Piano Competition in
1937.

dark stain on the... carpet – a reference to 'Old Age', a poem
by Maria Pawlikowska-Jasnorzewska (1891–1945).

a new Tokarczuk – Olga Tokarczuk (born 1962) is a leading
contemporary Polish novelist.

Furtwängler – Wilhelm Furtwängler (1886–1954) was a
German conductor and composer, regarded as one of the
greatest symphonic and operatic conductors of the twentieth century.

Argerich and Kremer – the Argentine classical pianist Martha
Argerich (born 1941) and the Latvian classical violinist
Gideon Kremer (born 1947).

Oriflamme – the battle standard of the King of France in the
Middle Ages.

stronghold Notre Dame – a reference to 'Notre Dame', a
poem by Osip Mandelstam (1891–1938).